THE SO

JASON— He was everything bad about Hollywood, from the gold chains around his neck to the slimey deals, to the blackmails threats when he didn't get his way. And he wanted his way. He wanted his mother's successful agency for himself . . . even if he had to sacrifice the only good thing he had, his wife, Nicole.

MICHAEL— He hated everything about Hollywood, but he was going to have to love it or leave it. Young, naive, idealistic, it would take a complete reversal to adjust to the deal-making, the behind-the-scenes intrigue, the power-plays. But his job was to keep Ada Stone's agency away from Jason, and he was beginning to dislike Jason, even more than Hollywood. And then there was Nicole.

NICOLE— Once a wounded sparrow, now a beautiful bird of paradise, she had been rescued from her past by Jason, and now she wanted a future. She was one of the Beverly Hills beautiful people . . . in search of a soul and someone to love.

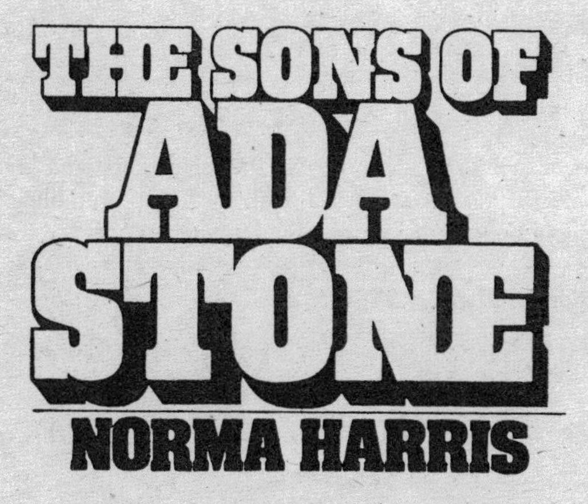

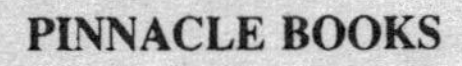

NEW YORK

This is a work of fiction. All the characters and events portrayed in this book are fictional, and any resemblance to real people or incidents is purely coincidental.

THE SONS OF ADA STONE

An original Pinnacle Books edition, published for the first time anywhere.

First printing, November 1983

ISBN: 0-523-41597-4

Can. ISBN: 0-523-43048-5

Cover illustration by Dan Gonzalez

Printed in the United States of America

PINNACLE BOOKS, INC.
1430 Broadway
New York, New York 10018

9 8 7 6 5 4 3 2

To my loving husband Leonard, without whose help and support this book could never have been written.

THE SONS OF ADA STONE

Book I

LIMITED PARTNERS

Chapter 1

EVERY MUSCLE IN HIS TALL lanky body was naturally taut and visibly defined. But Ada's eyes kept migrating back to the bulge in his trousers. She knew damn well it was not an erection but the work of some clever skin-tight white jeans doing their thing to his thing.

"Take off your shirt," she told him, "and turn around." Her keen gray eyes slithered across high pectorals, tan, silky skin and the kind of broad shoulders young women love to lean on.

He kept rotating his body like a radar screen and the signals he sent were raising her blood pressure. She hated to admit that. Certainly not at her age, an age that had hovered around fifty for the last eight years.

She buzzed her secretary. "Elaine? Get in here!" The door swung open and Elaine Shagan entered. If she was startled at the sight of Paul Kiley's naked chest, she didn't show it.

"What do you think?" Ada asked. "Does he have it?" Elaine studied the man for a minute. "C'mon, c'mon," Ada snapped, "give me the first words that come to mind."

"Quiet, cool, vulnerable," she paused. "Robert Redford."

"Exactly," Ada said, "Robert Redford." The phone rang suddenly and Elaine answered it.

"Just a moment, I'll tell her." She clicked the hold

button to a flashing signal and turned to Ada. "It's the network, Mrs. Stone. On Del Gado's deal? Mark says they absolutely won't pay a hundred thousand an episode."

Ada Stone threw her head back and roared with laughter. "Who the hell does that dipshit think he's playing with? He's got no choice. Del Gado's show is a season short of syndication. Tell him the deal's off and hang up."

Elaine did as she was told, then quickly left the room. When the door closed behind Elaine, Ada turned her attention back to Paul whose skin was developing goosebumps. "Put your shirt on, Paul, and have a seat." She paced for a moment then turned to face him. "You know I'd really like to help you, but . . ."

"But, but, there you go with the goddamn *buts,*" he interrupted. His voice, now drenched in frustration, rose to a crescendo.

"Hey, take it easy," Ada said. "I haven't even finished. You need experience my friend; you need film I can use. What the hell do I show casting agents and producers, my pulse rate?" She smiled but the joke was lost on him.

"You can set up a screen test," he shouted at her. "You can do that." Of course she could but that wasn't the point.

She glared at him. "Are you gonna tell me how to run my business?"

"Jesus, Mrs. Stone." He suddenly jumped up and began swinging his arms like a wild man. "I've been getting the damn Hollywood runaround for months now and I'm up to here with it." His hand cut across his throat. "I'm so damn sick of it I want to punch someone." He pointed a steady finger at her. "There's a 'Catch 22' here and you bloody well know it." He banged a fist on her desk and her papers flew up. "Shit! Nobody will see me at the studios cause I have no agent, and the Screen Actor's Guild won't let me join cause I have no job. Christ! It's a no-win situation." Spinning, he turned his back on her.

"Go ahead, Paul. Act like a schmuck and for sure nobody will help you," she said, nevertheless empathizing with his position. "Why the hell don't you listen a minute instead of talking so damn much."

Paul turned to say something when an odd expression

suddenly covered his face. In an instant he was doubled over, clutching at his stomach, then his body began to reel. Ada grabbed him by the shoulders and led him quickly toward the couch. "When did you eat last for God's sake," she asked, but he couldn't seem to answer. He just lay there quietly with his eyes closed, one arm drawn over his sweaty brow. Ada caressed his clammy hand for a moment, then called loudly for Elaine.

"Have Duggan help him up to the house," she told her. "And tell Cranston to fix him something to eat." She looked at Paul and threw up her hands, not knowing whether he could hear her or not. "Okay, okay. I'm convinced. Maybe I'm nuts but I'm going to help you. I'm going to give you a chance."

When Duggan arrived to help, Paul tried to thank her. "Save it for the big guys," Ada said. "You're only an investment to me."

When the door finally closed she sat down in a chair letting her head fall between her legs. She felt dizzy and pressed her fingers deep into her scalp. When she raised her head, her face was flushed pink and a throbbing pain began in her left arm. She rubbed it, then reached across her desk for the intercom and buzzed Elaine.

"Make an appointment for me at La Costa. One week . . . for the end of this month."

"Mr. Stone going with you?"

"No. I need to rest."

"Anything else?" Elaine asked.

She was silent for a moment. "Yes, call Inez. I want something sexy and sensational for Bobbi Sands. She's doing a big benefit . . . there'll be lots of foreign press around. Also call David Price. Tell him to give her a terrific hairdo, something weird and out of the ordinary." She closed her eyes. "I think that's all." The phone rang suddenly and Ada jumped. "Jesus, I almost forgot," she said. "Set up a screen test for Paul Kiley and give the kid some cash for living expenses." She pressed the button on a remote control device and watched a T.V. screen light up. "No more calls," she said, listening as the phones rang off the wall. "I have to watch Bobbi's soap, then dress for Hugh Parker's birthday party at Orloff's Cafe."

* * *

Exhausted, wondering what in the hell she was doing at Orloff's in Sidney Gross' company, Ada sat in the cream leather booth trying to listen to Hank Mason's high-pitched voice croon "Happy Birthday." His large fingers strummed an acoustical guitar, while his lap lay open to suggestions. Sidney Gross slyly reached across and made a few with his fat little fingers, then brought his hands joyously together to applaud the end of the song and, of course, Hank's prick.

Hugh Parker, slowly shook his head, a slight smile breaking his stoney features. "If it's not against the law for a solicitor to sue his own clientele, you're all in trouble for throwing this party."

"You love it and you know it," Ada said and began to cut the birthday cake. "Besides, if you sued us, you'd not only be shit poor, you'd have to go back to the mob."

Hank Mason's ears perked up. Mob? Not his attorney. Not Hugh Parker, esteemed and venerable graduate of Harvard Law School. No sirree! His voice sang out, filled with Mid Western honesty. "Ada? You're one hell of a woman. Yessirree. One of these days, I'm gonna write me a book about you."

Armando Del Gado had been trying to get Ada's attention all evening, but it had proved futile. He wanted desperately to know whether or not she had read the script he'd given her. He wanted very much to have her consent; it was his chance to show the public and his critics that he could handle the heavy dramatic roles as well as he handled the mundane, stupid show he was currently starring in. Del Gado wanted her to say he could do it. But he knew her well enough to remain quiet, and so he changed the subject. "How about that volcano," he said. His dazzling white teeth gleamed as he smiled and his blue-black hair threw off light like an oil slick. "It's Armageddon, as sure as we're sitting here."

Sidney Gross burped and countered, "Armando?" His chubby cheeks puffed up while his fingers pushed back another gas bubble. "Pass the fucking cake will you?"

Armando reached across, and handed Sidney a slice of the rich chocolate cake. Ada wondered if he'd crumble it onto Hank Mason's lap and finish it later, but he merely stuffed it all into his mouth, the icing sticking to his fingers. *How typical,* she thought.

Sarcastically, she queried, "When's the new movie opening, Sid?" She didn't really give a damn about it. It was just one way to get a few zingers in.

"Soon, Ada. Roxanne should get terrific reviews. I'll send you all tickets to the opening."

"I hear that Elvira St. James has dubbed the sound track for her," Ada said.

Sidney's eyes narrowed. Score one for Ada. "Who told you that?" he said, spitting a few crumbs out. "Who the fuck told you that damn lie?"

"God, Sidney; you know how people talk," Ada said.

Sidney smiled. "That might have been true when you handled her, Ada, but not now. She sings it herself. Amazing what new management can do." He smiled again and shoveled more cake into his fat little mouth. Score one for Sidney.

It made Parker uncomfortable to sit between Sidney and Ada. He enjoyed the birthday party and the thought that these two enemies would bury grievances long enough to join him in celebration—but now they had said too much. He changed the subject. "So, Armando. You think it's Armageddon?"

"I do. Word for word, it's all in the Bible. I hope you're all saved, cause the next stop is Hell." His expression was serious and Ada almost burst out laughing, but Parker's fierce glance steadied her. Sidney remained quiet. Then, a familiar look overcame Sidney's face.

Ada studied him. She had seen that look before. It was the kind of expression he'd always worn when some new idea or project was incubating. *What could it be this time,* she thought?

The more Del Gado went on about Mount St. Helens, the more Sidney's face said tilt, and Ada finally knew. She watched the wheels or whatever Gross had in that sneaky little fag head of his, go round and round. She knew that without a doubt, he was trying to figure out how to beat Vincent Piper to the punch and sign Robert Redford, Paul

Newman and O.J. Simpson to make the *Mount St. Helens Story*.

When Ada saw him smile and relax way back into the booth, she knew that he had finally figured out how to once more exploit American stars, using European money to make the movie. European money meant he didn't have to bother with American unions. If he used America's bankables, star names as collateral, then half a dozen countries would shell out bread faster then the United States of America could print it. None of the trade unions knew how to stop him and the American public never really knew, perhaps didn't care, that they were lining up to see films whose enormous profits left the country while also lining Gross' pockets.

When the saliva bubbling on Gross' fat lips dribbled down to his chin, Ada swallowed whole, the last morsel of velvet cake on her plate, kissed Parker on the cheek and said goodnight.

At three in the morning Ada was forced from a sound sleep into a sitting position. Sweating and trembling, her eyes desperately searched the darkness to see if she was in Hell. She wasn't. The familiar sight of her large French provincial bedroom should have calmed her, but it didn't. She clutched at her pink-flowered sheets, watched the pale, pink chintz curtains billowing against the open balcony window and switched on the lamp beside her.

Her legs dangled over the side of the bed like a puppet's, and when she took one deep breath, something grabbed at her innards in a place she had no name for.

She placed a red scarf around her neck, rubbed at her breasts, her back, her arms and thought she should summon the housekeeper, Mrs. Cranston, perhaps wake Max. No, she decided. It was nothing. It would soon pass.

Her manicured toes resolutely pointed their way into black satin slippers and she covered her black satin nightgown with her favorite black satin peignoir. Very slowly she stood, walked to the door of the bedroom and carefully made her way down the long mahogany staircase to the living room.

She breathed a little easier and moved to the large stone

fireplace. She took a foot-long match, struck it and touched the flame to paper. In a few minutes, a crackling fire bathed the white wash walls in brilliant shades of orange with quivering purple shadows. Log sap spit and hissed into the flames and Ada adjusted the flue.

In the next half hour, she tried desperately to relax, but the heavy drumbeat of her heart and an impending sense of doom kept her pacing up and down, then back and forth, criss-crossing the huge mansion corridors.

Down the hall, she could hear her husband Max softly snoring. Sweet Max. How much did you lose at the track today?

God! She was feeling so lousy—feeling so—oh Hell! She'd been here before. Many times. Indigestion most likely. Nothing more than all that rich food she'd wolfed down at the party.

Her wandering eyes strayed to the mantle. They lighted on a photograph of herself and Max, taken ten years before. Ada lifted the picture and studied it. Max. Snow-white hair and smiling. A perfect balance to her own dark seriousness.

At fifty-eight, she looked ten years younger. Everyone said so. She'd had the good fortune to inherit her mother's thick, tar-black shiny hair, including the gray streak near her left temple. And her father's clear and penetrating gray eyes. Pure luck. Even her weight held at one hundred and thirty; good for her five-foot-six-inch frame.

The pain persisted. It traveled and throbbed deeply into her ear. *Forget it,* she thought. Perhaps she should look at that new script Del Gado gave her. His highly publicized multi-million-dollar network deal would include a two-hour special among other things, and she would have to find just the right script. She picked the script up from off the coffee table and rolled it around her hands into a tube.

Armando Del Gado. The ladies' choice. Number one in their hearts, their pants and more importantly, the Nielsens. If they only knew. Four times he'd called her today to inquire about that script and four times she'd refused his calls. He was by far one of the best-looking men on screen today and very persuasive, but she'd fought too damn hard, too damn long to get the upper hand in this business.

She was not about to relinquish it to some egotistical, spoiled Latin lover who sported a perpetual hard-on, and who had a knack for trouble.

In the last ten years, she had grown to be a shrewd, crusty lady. It was necessary. She had to protect her interests. All of her clients were "bankables." Their name on any television show, movie or theater marquee meant business, meant attendance, meant profit. They were the supreme hallmark of her ability and her power. They knew it and she knew it and the people who paid the bills and bought product knew it.

She placed the rumpled script back onto the coffee table and checked through some of her mail. There was a memo from Parker confirming his receipt of the newly signed will she'd instructed him to draw up just last week. Thank heavens! She perused the note, then tossed it into the fire and watched the paper curl up and flash-flame. That made her feel good. This was one time she wished she believed in God and the immortality of her soul. This was one time she wished she could see her son Jason's face . . . when he discovered upon her death that she had changed *everything* in her will.

She found next a cable from Paris. Merely a formality. The pouch had already arrived via courier and she had locked away its highly explosive contents in a secret safe. She tucked the confirmation cable into her bosom.

Slowly, she lowered her body into the rose-colored tapestry wing chair and caught an uneasy reflection of herself in the smoke mirror on the nearby wall. She appeared distorted, disconnected, as though someone had trained a fisheye lens on her in a camera closeup.

Even with the roaring fire in June, she was cold. She shivered, drawing her legs up close to her firm body, but it was useless. The cold was inside her bones, not outside.

Thoughts of the courier pouch warmed her, made her relax. All these years of waiting, waiting for something to turn up and now she had more than she'd dreamed of. She couldn't possibly get sick, or heaven forbid, die. She had to be there. She had to see Sidney's expression, Roxanne's reaction. She had to see them both squirm when she revealed the contents of that pouch.

She jumped. Had she locked the office safe securely? She had. Remembered every detail and relaxed again. What a field day Jason or anyone for that matter would have if they got hands on the contents of that safe. Not even Parker knew. Not even her secretary, Elaine.

In this business she knew, learned the hard way that today's best friend was tomorrow's enemy for the right deal. It was not unusual for lawyers to sleep with other lawyers in the legal as well as the literal sense, or secretaries for that matter. She trusted no one and she was never disappointed.

Ah! The pain stopped. Thank you. She looked at Del Gado's script and wondered how he had gotten it. And why hadn't he learned? Why wasn't he satisfied being the personality he was instead of the great actor he imagined himself as? She could just see the producer flattering Del Gado, telling him he would be great in this lousy film. They would collect their huge fees for writing, producing, directing, casting, put their relatives on the payroll, and when the film came out Del Gado's ratings would plummet along with the career Ada had helped him build.

Ada Stone selected his properties, only she. If choices were to be made for Del Gado, only Ada would make them. It was her function as his manager.

Suddenly, she felt as though some unknown sharp and steely object had hurled itself into her back, driving home clear through to her breast. She lurched back deeper into the chair tightly gripping the arms, snapping several long red fingernails instantly.

Her entire body lunged forward and she fell, landing on her knees hitting both her kneecaps. Her lips parted, but she couldn't cry out. Her dry mouth sucked at the air but her lungs drew in nothing. Along the floor, she crawled like a dog, pulling at random anything on either side of her, cloying at her heart, her head, the furniture, as if she were slipping away to some unreal place, and needing to grasp onto the only reality she had ever trusted.

Things fell, cracked, as she groveled by. From a table, she pulled at the tassels of a Turkish Kulah prayer shawl and like dominos, one object passing its energy onto the other, her collection of porcelain figurines fell to the floor smashing, trailing after her like obedient disfigured servants. A music box tumbled, delivering a jangled, grating discordant melody.

When she passed the parson's table, she made an heroic gesture toward the English tapestry and pulled down a vase she had that morning filled with tall blue and lavender stock. It smashed into a thousand pieces. The flowers fell and trailed, clinging to her black satin gown.

Her head felt as though it had burst and she knew that blood must be oozing from her mouth, her nose, her ears, perhaps even her eyes.

Her eyes. She saw them now, up close as she reached the mirror. It hadn't been the fault of the mirror at all. She could see it. The ugly reflection was real. It was the documentation, the culmination of so many years of bitterness, of paying "dues", of anger inside finally emerging, showing itself at last in the bulging eyes, the stiff, open jaw which revealed a thick and coated tongue.

Is this how they would find her, she thought? *Is this how she would look? Oh Max! Who would take care of him?*

Suddenly a scream, one long and chilling, terror-striking scream, which had been welling up inside, escaped in a continuous breath from her gaping mouth, filling the entire house. It would be useless of course. The servants were in private cottages and her husband, Max Stone, was totally deaf.

At six, A.M. the telephone rang. Nicole's sleepy eyes, watched her husband's hand reach out for it. "Hello," he said, his brown eyes still half-closed, his husky voice almost an octave lower than normal.

Abruptly, he sat up, brushed back his thick salt-and-pepper hair, then cleared his throat. "Yeah, uh-huh. When?" His attitude made her extremely anxious. She reached out lightly and touched his hairy arm.

"What's wrong?" she whispered. He pushed at her and grimaced, covering his ear against her voice. She moved closer to him. "Jason," she said softly, "what is it?"

"Shh!" he hissed, spraying her with saliva, continuing into the telephone. "Yeah. I'll be there in about twenty minutes. No, don't wake him yet." He hung up the phone and stared straight ahead, his face without expression.

Nicole pleaded. "Oh Jason, please. What is it?"

"My mother. She's at St. John's. She's in a coma. They don't know if she'll live." He said it like that, straight out, no minced words, no hesitation, then he stood up and walked to the bathroom.

Stunned, Nicole pulled the brown satin quilt closer to her body, shivering. She listened to the endless stream of urine hitting the toilet bowl, then the flush. Her first thoughts were of Max. Someone had to be there. Someone had to. And Ada. She was sorry for Ada, disgusted with herself for not being sorrier, but that was Ada's doing, not hers. She'd tried harder than anyone to please her, but it only made Ada more demanding. From the very beginning it had been like that.

Jason turned the shower on and Nicole could hear him hum. Why wasn't he at least respectful, she thought? But she knew perfectly well how he felt about Ada and vice versa. His attitude, or what seemed to be his attitude, didn't surprise her. He ambled back in, wrapped in a brown terry towel, a tiny tuft of tissue clinging to his broad chin. "Jason? Is there anything I can do?" she asked.

He thought for a moment as he buttoned his shirt. "Call Viva. Tell her to meet me at the hospital."

"But, she's your sister. You should talk to her."

"Yeah, well, you call her for me anyway, okay? Tell her to find Michael, too. I think he's in Cambodia or something. She'll know."

"What about Max?" she asked.

"What about him?"

"Somebody's got to be there. Nobody will know how to talk to him, to tell him."

Jason smiled. "You and Mike," he said. "You think you're the only one's in the whole world that can handle him. Well, maybe." He finished combing his hair, deliberately forcing a style that it wasn't in the mood for. "Then, you go to him. Take care of Max for me." He turned and spotted his wristwatch. "Hand me the Rollex, will you, babe? I've got to get to the hospital." Suddenly he stood perfectly still. Nicole was startled.

"What is it? What's the matter?"

His silence was followed by short, sharp breaths of air and she rushed to help him. His eyes darted back and forth glazed with fear and his sticky, cold palms kept grabbing at her.

"Take it easy," she repeated. Slowly he recovered and began to breathe more evenly.

Jason looked at her, terror still in his eyes. "Nicole. You have to go. You gotta meet Viva. You have to do it. I can't. I just can't. You understand?" He was shaking all over, his face the color of pale white egg-shells.

Oh God. She had forgotten. She took his broad, handsome head into her arms and held him close. "Yes, of course, I'll go."

"That's my girl," he said. "Thanks." The color returned to his cheeks and he moved away from her with new energy. "I'll call Dr. Morgenstern and tell him to meet you at the house, okay?"

She watched him walk to the bedroom door, then turn and wave to her. "Take care. I'll see you later," he said, and raced down the staircase.

She needed a shower to wake up. The water was warm, and refreshing and she slipped her slender tan body in and out of the fine spray. She bent over and separated the cheeks of her behind, soaping herself, rinsing the matted hairs from Jason's semen which clung stubbornly to her body like some form of sealing wax.

When she finished, she toweled briskly, slipped on tight blue jeans, a beige silk jersey top and rolled her honey-colored hair into a high French nub.

From her window she could see the gardener bending over. He reminded her of Michael, Jason's younger brother. Rich, shiny black hair, strong hands and a soft brushy mustache lightly grazing his pouty bottom lip. Michael. He'd have to come home now. God, how she'd missed him. The man even moved like Michael. He was strong and quick, compassionately tending a rose bush that needed pruning. She watched him using deft, delicate and protective strokes to destroy a side sucker from the main stem.

She telephoned Viva, agreed to meet her at the hospital and left for Casa Piedra.

Jason sped down Sunset Boulevard toward Santa Monica. The traffic was light from his Holmby Hills home and he was glad. He looked neither left or right, just propelled the red Ferrari straight ahead at thirty miles an hour. Around U.C.L.A., the traffic grew thicker and as he creeped along the boulevard he made a decision.

He opened the leather box to his right and removed the telephone. In a few seconds the mobile operator asked for the number of the call he wished to make. He listened to the telephone ring. Finally, a sleepy voice answered. "Mimi?" Jason asked. "Get a pad and pencil." He listened to her scream, keeping his eyes on the traffic. "I don't give a fuck what time it is, okay? Ada's in a coma at St. John's. Yeah, yeah, save it for the press. Just get a damn paper and pencil."

A pretty girl passing in a Triumph honked at him. He smiled, winked at her, and continued on the telephone.

"First, call Hugh Parker. I want copies of Ada's important papers in my office today, all of them, and immediately. Then you get your own ass over there and write some kind of release from Jason Stone and messenger it over to *Variety* and the *Reporter*."

He paused at a red light and began screaming at the top of his lungs. "You write it you dumb jackass. I don't give a rat's ass what the hell you say, that's what I pay you for." He slammed the receiver down and dug out at the light change. God he was excited.

The thought, the actuality of getting his hands on Ada's properties, her business, her everything—it was insane. He could taste the respect he craved, the prestige he coveted, the people he'd like to get even with for treating him like shit. And the idea of never again having to put his Holmby Hills house up as collateral for some second-rate movie he wanted to produce, or a gambling debt he'd incurred. God, the power made him feel crazy.

Now came the difficult part.

Who the hell was this Parker? And how much influence did he exert over Ada? He'd ask Mario in Vegas to do a quick background on him, then put Meyer Wolfson on his tail in Los Angeles. When it came time to dealing with Hugh Parker, Jason would make sure he held all the aces and maybe a few jokers.

He squirmed in his seat and rubbed his hands between

his legs. A lascivious thought entered his consciousness and then another. He picked up the telephone again.

Max Stone lay blissfully sleeping. His pale, unlined face was perfectly round and his widely set baggy eyes were slanted and lashless. With his thick, short arms outstretched on either side of his body, he appeared to be a smiling great Buddha.

His dreams, vivid, alive and poetic, were fantasies of wild and silent ponies floating effortlessly through the far and free regions of his mind. Here he would command the golden reins of Pegasus, Citation, Alborak, Seabiscuit, skillfully scaling clouds of crystal.

Awake, he was the great god Moloch and the closest he ever came to that vision was at Hollywood Park, Del Mar or Santa Anita where the only reins he held were purchased at the Exacta or Daily Double windows.

Nicole was filled with apprehension as she swung the Mercedes onto Bristol Circle. When she finally reached Casa Piedra she parked on the opposite side of the street, and waited. Sticky drops of sweat slid down her armpits and small black dots floated before her eyes.

Dr. Morgenstern's car was nowhere in sight and she wondered if Jason had forgotten to call him. She would wait five more minutes, then go in.

Her eyes roamed Ada's great mansion. It was a magnificent Spanish-style hacienda painted a deep umber with an orange clay tile roof and matching window trim. The entire estate was almost six acres, ringed by a continuous eight-foot-high fence of umber wrought iron, towered over by coconut palms and California pepper trees. Walls of vine-covered, bright orange bougainville complimented the dark stucco and shone like Day-glo paint in the sunlight.

She could wait no longer. It was almost 7:30 A.M. and Max would be getting up. She started the motor, approached the electronic gates and poked at the buzzer.

"Ja?" Mrs. Cranston's teutonic voice squeaked through.

"It's me, Nicole."

"Ach! Thanks Gott you're here." As she spoke the gates slowly parted.

Nicole drove the circular driveway and parked. Mrs.

Cranston stood at the doorway in a wrinkled pinafore wringing her hands, her face crimson.

She took Mrs. Cranston in her arms and held her. "Has the doctor called?"

"No. But Jason did. He said the doctor vould be here soon." Nicole was glad he hadn't forgotten. Sometimes he was careless about details.

Inside the house, Mrs. Cranston led her into the living room. She looked at the cracked glass, the dead flowers and the shattered crystal. Her whole body trembled and shook. "Max?"

"Still sleeping, thanks Gott." Suddenly Mrs. Cranston's body went limp and she began to sob. She needed to tell Nicole how she found Ada, how she looked, where she had fallen, how she thought for sure Ada was dead and how guilty she felt. "Ach! She vas a hard voman to vork for, but she vas alvays fair. If she only let me stay in the house instead of a cottage, I could have helped her."

Max sneezed. Nicole's heart skipped a beat and Cranston's hand flew to her mouth. "Call the doctor again," Nicole said and headed for Max's bedroom.

When she reached his room, he was sitting on the side of the bed, his eyes just beginning to open. She studied his wrinkle-free face, his white hair glinting of silver in the sunlight. She bumped against a wall and the vibration startled him. He stood, squinted and finally recognized her. "Ah! Nicole." He started then stopped a smile. "What time is it? Why are you here so early?"

She approached him, rubbed his back and kissed a cheek. He was not so easily fooled and pushed her away. "Where's Jason?" His voice had always sounded strange to her. The unaccented, monotone voice of the deaf. It was intelligible but unlike any other human voice.

Nicole patted his bed and Max sat down. She looked directly into his eyes and spoke slowly. "Listen," she said pointing to her ear. "Mom is sick." She drew a hand across her throat in a cutting gesture. A stubborn man, he had refused to learn sign language. Whatever he did understand came from signals Mike had devised or hastily scribbled messages on note pads.

"Jason is sick?" he said. He had misunderstood her.

She shook her head and pointed to his wedding ring. He knew instantly. Max ran toward the door screaming for Ada, but Nicole grabbed his shoulders and swung him around.

"No," she said and shook her head.

He stared incredulously at her. "She's not here?" Nicole grabbed a pad and pencil and scribbled "Sick . . . St. John's Hospital." Max read it aloud slowly, beads of sweat popping from his brow.

"No! Can't be," he said, and ripped the paper into a thousand pieces. Suddenly, without warning, he flew into a wild rage. "Nobody woke me. My wife is in a hospital and nobody woke me." He stormed around the room, throwing things, spilling, ripping, banging whatever got in his way, trying to find something to wear.

The doorbell rang. "I want to see her right now," Max bellowed. There were drawers on the floor and shoes all over the room when Dr. Morgenstern and Mrs. Cranston appeared in the doorway.

"He needs a sedative," the doctor said. "Give me a hand, both of you."

"I'm going to the hospital," Max shouted, noting, then ignoring the doctor's presence, banging a closet door shut. "Call Duggan," he ordered. From the corner of his eye he saw Dr. Morgenstern draw open his black bag and he bolted for the door. Nicole and Mrs. Cranston grabbed him, pulling him across the floor, wrestling him onto the bed. Cranston held his arms while Nicole pinned his body.

"Don't touch me you son of a bitch," Max screamed. "I'll kill you."

He thrashed about, body jerking, legs flying, all the time screaming. He caught Mrs. Cranston's face with his left hand and blood fell from her lips.

"Keep him still for God's sake," the doctor yelled. Max jerked one knee behind Nicole and caught her in the small of her back. She winced. Dr. Morgenstern tested the contents of the needle with one hand and held onto Max with the other. "Now keep him perfectly still," he commanded.

They finally had him. The needle cracked through his dry, thin skin and the contents flowed. When the needle was withdrawn Max tossed his arm in the air. The empty syringe flew across the room toward the mirror, chipping the beveled edge.

And, then he sobbed. "Oh, God, oh my God . . . Ada . . . Ada . . . Where's my Jason . . . Ja . . . son."

Jason knocked softly.

"In the tub, cherie. It's open."

He entered, closed the doors and headed for a white chenille easy chair. Pushing aside the ottoman, he lowered his body into the soft pile and kicked off his shoes.

The bathroom door opened slowly and he watched her emerge from a dense white cloud of steam like some fairy-princess-whore. She wore only a short blue terry cloth towel and her body glistened. Small droplets of water clung to her thick dark hair sparkling like tiny diamonds in the soft light behind her. She was without makeup and her classic Roman features and swanlike neck would have driven Modigliani to a canvas.

Jason wondered just what it was that most excited him about her. Was it the color of her eyes? Blue-gray, gray-blue. Indescribably bluish? Or her full and juicy lips, the color of purple plums? Perhaps it was only because she was a whore.

She stood there, defiantly, her legs planted slightly apart and let the towel fall. He looked at firm, mammoth breasts with plum-colored nipples, gently curving hips and a full hairy mound.

He felt it first in his stomach. Hot lead, heavy lead dripped down inside his abdomen and burrowed deeply inside his bowels.

She helped him slide off his trousers and kneeled down before him. He watched her reach for his penis and sucked in air when she grasped it. She kissed it, caressed it and teased it with the tip of her tongue and wet lips.

She lifted both his legs from the floor with her shoulders and suddenly jammed them hard, up against his body. He went limp and dreamy against the chenille, sliding down exposing his rectum.

She sat on the floor and flicked her soft, wet tongue over and around his anus. When he was slippery, she separated the anal folds and slowly slid her middle finger deep inside him. He moaned and grabbed at it with his sphincter muscle pulling it high inside. She sucked his scrotum and blew hot and cool air between the sacs.

The lead reached his cock and he became crazy. He grabbed at her hair, her ears, his own penis, a table, his belly; sticking his fingers into her mouth. With her other hand, she guided his hard, thick cock into her mouth. Slowly, she sucked along the shaft then fluttered her tongue across the tip.

"Now," he screamed.

Inch by inch she pulled him deeply into her mouth, her large baby doll eyes fixed shut. He grabbed her hair, twisting it, crying out in ecstasy. She closed her lips on the last of him and relaxed her throat and tongue. He could feel her sucking him, her movements urging him on.

He thrust his body up and around her face, down, up, up, down, under, over, around, short even strokes, fucking her face, her beautiful face. She pinched his buttocks tightly, waiting for his screams. "Suck me, suck me, su . . . ck . . . it . . . Mama . . . suck . . . it . . . ma . . . Mama!"

She pursed her mouth and pulled in her cheeks until the boiling lead left his anus, his balls, his cock, finally sliding down her throat in quick bursts.

He fell back groaning, his body jerking, mind drifting, occasionally studying her features, amazed at how much she resembled Ada.

Chapter 2

MICHAEL JAY STONE sat resting comfortably in the midsection of a Pan Am 747. He had received the call from Viva, courtesy of the Red Cross, and he was now cruising over the Pacific Ocean crossing the International Dateline. Bone-tired, contemplative, apprehensive at what lay ahead of him, he stared out of the window into the endless pitch.

For seven years he'd been running . . . eager to extinguish the pain, hoping to obliterate the loneliness, the terrible, unending desire she had unknowingly created in him. All this time, going to school in the East, working abroad, taking soul-wracking, self-appointed assignments such as the last in Asia. All this time . . . and still, the pain persisted. He had extinguished nothing, obliterated absolutely nothing and desired her more than ever. Returning home now, was a terrifying prospect.

He shut his eyes and listened to the simultaneous sounds of the powerful jet engines and the gentle hiss of a fresh air vent softly blowing onto his face. Shadows, forms, voices, all from other times and other places drifted in and out of focus across the fertile dimensions of his mind. He leaned back, pressing his long body deeply into the contours of his seat, and watched the montage assemble itself.

The faces of a thousand hungry Asian children with protruding bloated bellies and bulging black eyes set in oversize boney heads, screamed silently to him, extending empty expectant arms. He imagined himself back in the refugee camps on the Cambodian borders trying to feed, trying to comfort, trying to keep some terrified human being from dying alone.

He wondered if Ada had been alone in her dark hour. She must have been. Everyone was. After three months in that God-forsaken refugee camp, he was sure of it.

To comfort himself, he thought of Nicole. He needed to see her. His tired eyes slowly fluttered open and he removed an old, worn photograph from inside his breast pocket. It was warm from the heat of his body and frayed from the many times his perspiring fingers had caressed it.

She was laughing, clowning on a sunny Malibu beach, in a funny ballet pose and he was instantly transported to that day and that place. They were barely twenty-one and in January of that same year, Jason had brought her home, his new bride. . . .

Noon. June, 1976. The sun cast no shadows and the towering cliffs that encircled the cove gave Michael a sense of Eden and Adam and Eve and timelessness. Ocean breezes carried cool salty air and the only sounds were those of the waves lightly basting the shoreline and a lone seagull calling from above.

Lying on a towel, Nicole sunned on her back while Michael, his head growing from his elbow, sand-planted-palm, watched her. Her long thick lashes swept across her high cheekbones and her delicate jelly breasts fell from the sides of her thin white bikini curving under her armpit where some sparkling sand grains clung to her body.

She suddenly shifted and he self-consciously turned his head, directing his gaze toward the sky. The lone seagull had gained a companion.

"Look! Lovebirds. Up there to the right at two o'clock."

Nicole shaded her eyes to see. "They're birds alright. But what makes you so sure they're in love?"

"It's obvious," he said. "Anyone with half a soul could see that. Look again. He's kissing her."

Nicole sat up to watch. "He's stealing her food, dummy." She was right. The bigger gull wrestled a fresh catch from the smaller's beak and flew off. She threw her head back laughing, then saw a look of disillusionment cross his face. "Mike? You really believed that, didn't you?"

He rolled onto his side and burrowed his face into the crook of his arm. "Of course not," he mumbled.

"Yes you did," she insisted. "You're a wonderful dreamer Michael, but a terrible liar."

Some silent time passed between them. Michael just lay there, his eyes shaded from the sun by his arm; Nicole, folding back the towel corners from the wind. She spoke finally. "You're not angry with me are you?"

He looked surprised. "Angry with you? No, of course not."

"Can I have an eenie, weenie smile then?" she asked and reached for his lips to force it. "What's this?" she said, parting the silky hairs of his moustache.

His mouth held firmly against her touch. "It's just some old scar."

"I can see that, Michael. But how did it happen?"

"It's . . . a ridiculous story. . . ."

Her amber eyes grew wide. "I'm listening."

"All right, all right," he said, "I took one dumb punch in the second round of a Golden Gloves match, that's all."

"Boxing? I don't believe it. I can't imagine you hitting somebody."

He smiled. "Boxing's not exactly hitting. It's an art. Haven't you ever watched a good match?"

"No. Never." She shuddered a bit. "I don't like it. I don't like it when people yell at one another. Why would I want to watch them smack each other around?"

There was an expression which crossed her face and from time to time, it made him wonder. It was an impossible expression, one he had never before seen on a person, but witnessed many times in the face and eyes of a frightened puppy. She wore that look now. Eyes huge and watery, curious, perhaps even frightened, anticipating something.

He fingered the scar, spoke the words quickly. "I've been considering some plastic surgery for it. What do you think about that?"

She studied his features. Handsome, dark-brown waves slipping lightly over his ears, curling along the nape of his broad, long neck. The head and jaw drawn from an old

Roman coin. His captivating, deeply set velvet brown eyes, which always seemed to sparkle and flirt. "Nope," she said, "absolutely not. Actually, I think it's kind of sexy. Like Stacy Keach or Jason Robards and I don't think you should touch it."

Now he was lost in her face, drawn hypnotically to her sun-glowing amber eyes, her honey-colored hair dripping onto her shoulders.

"Michael? Did you hear me?"

"Yes, I did," he said.

"Well, then. Promise you won't change it." He nodded, affirming, and watched the dimples flutter back onto her cheeks. "Good," she said and leaned over to kiss the scar.

He felt as though someone had plugged jumper cables onto his heart, his soul, maybe both. He rolled over quickly, onto his stomach, embarrassed, afraid she would see what was happening to him. Afraid his heart would fly from his chest into his mouth and words he'd regret, could never take back, would come tumbling out in some kind of fit, and she'd know.

He swallowed hard, trying to think of something to say . . . and noticed her books.

"What's that you're reading?"

"Modern American Literature."

"Interesting?"

"Some of it is," she grimaced. "Actually Jason insisted I read it. It's all part of his attempt to play George Bernard Shaw."

"Sounds like Jason," he laughed.

She jumped up and grabbed his leg. "Let's take a swim."

"You go," he said. He was still dizzy from her kiss.

He watched her slender body gracefully sail the sands, the cheeks of her buttocks, jumping beneath her swimsuit like plump quartermoons.

When she reached the water, she turned. "Hey Michael. It's wonderful. Come on and play."

He waved and watched her splash about, then trained his camera on her. That moment in time became the picture he held now in his hands, the one he had taken that day seven years ago.

Looking at it now, in the 747 he was utterly amazed. So concentrated upon her form, her wonderful playfulness, all these years he'd never noticed, high in the corner of the photo, the lone seagull still circling.

That summer he had to leave. He had to go as far away from her as he possibly could. He could no longer tolerate her gentle, purely affectionate touches. He could no longer look his own brother in the eye, or himself in the mirror for that matter.

He wanted to defend her each time Ada or even Jason chided her and that puppy dog look crossed her face. He had to constantly guard his words, afraid he'd say "I love you, I need you," knowing if he said it he would mean it. All the time wondering what she would do if he did. And when he went to Viva, to discuss his "sudden desire," as he put it, to go to New York and continue school, perhaps work at the United Nations or join the Peace Corps, she asked no questions. She just wrote him a blank check, then pulled a few strings so he could live in a beautiful apartment overlooking Central Park and sent him off to Europe in the summer of 1977 when he refused to come home.

He wasn't sure if Viva knew what was wrong, why he had gone. But if anyone did or even had a right to know, it would have been her.

* * *

Viva Stone Candelli glanced at the clock in her bedroom. She had one hour and fifteen minutes to get to the airport.

"Hand me that journal, will you, darling?"

The young blue-eyed man lying next to her reached for the leather-bound book which rested on the nightstand near a splendid cigarette case. He passed it to her halfway, then quickly tucked it under the sheet. He smiled, brushed a yellow-colored finger curl from off his wide forehead and lay back down.

"There it is," he said. "Get it." She could see the outline of the book lying on top of his groin, excitement painted on his face.

She sighed, "Not now darling. Mike's plane is due."

He frowned. "No time even for a quickie?"

"Darling, if you don't know by now that I loathe

quickies—'' She stopped in mid-sentence and watched the book rise magically beneath the covers. ''But it needs you,'' he begged. ''It may die if you go.''

Her cinder-gray eyes took aim. ''If you don't hand over my journal right now, darling, I'll probably kill it myself.'' She waited for him to laugh with her, but he didn't. Obediently, he handed her the book.

''Thank you,'' she said, and blew him a kiss.

She put the book on her lap and opened it to where a leather marker had been placed, then with a tiny pink jade pen, she made one small note on a page, and put it away.

''Now darling, I'm going into the large bathroom and take a shower. You know where the towels are and I expect you'll be gone when I come out.'' She slid out of bed and covered her body with a sheer blouse. He watched her walk arrogantly away, detached from him and their previous intimacy.

The door closed behind her and she let the blouse slip to the floor. Every mirror in the huge pink room validated what she already knew. She had been graciously blessed with a magnificent body.

She ran the shower and wrapped her thick, wild, mahogany mane into a nub and covered it with a plastic cap of wildflowers. Inside the shower the hot water falling on her back and buttocks, soothed her aching, tired muscles. She let the spray cover her and spread her legs to the warm, stinging pressure. Suddenly, she winced. The spray had fallen on a tender spot inside her thigh. She looked down, her fingers and eyes probing flesh and found it; some tiny love-bite inside her right thigh where he had bitten a little too hard, a little too long.

She massaged it, thinking how handsome and strong he was. How rich and sweet the flesh tasted on his long neck when they had been in bed a few hours ago.

They had shared a tai-stick and the effects were stunning. Unlike even her best Columbian grass, the stick hit more quickly, made her body hotter and every physical sensation seemed exquisite.

Music swirled around the room and each time the

piano rippled, she felt as though the keys were a part of her. The scent of her rose oil turned her into a rose, delicate, velvety, glowing a neon red.

She was lying on pink satin sheets, her bountiful breasts pointing upwards in two high, soft mounds. He kneeled across her, his stiff penis jutting out, poised directly over her vagina. With large strong hands, he rubbed her breasts in time to the music, then bent and ran his tongue across her nipples.

She arched upwards, her legs lightly spread-eagled and she began swaying under him, twisting, turning with the rhythm. Her fingers circled the shaft of his penis and she slowly rolled the tip across her moist vagina. It slid so easily and the sensation was thrilling.

Smiling at her, he brushed his fingertips over her soft belly. A burning current ran through her center and she closed her eyes.

He caressed her breasts, throat and face, moving his fingers down past her naval, plunging them high up into her creamy slit. His fingers played there for a while, feeding the fire, stirring and provoking, his mouth watering as her belly rose and fell with each deep thrust.

His penis grew thicker, heavier and he slid it back and forth across the outer folds and soft hairs of her opening. Halfway he entered her, rocking back and forth, straining his neck, his mouth drawn back in a grimace, holding the tide, quickly pulling out before he burst.

She reached for him, pulling him down to her moist mouth and running her tongue over his lips. He pressed down hard over her and their lips fastened together in a passionate kiss. She pulled and twisted handfuls of yellow curls, biting his cheeks, sucking his chin, slipping her tongue in and out of his syrupy mouth.

When she released his hair, he moved down to her thighs and with his head he pushed apart her legs. He explored her with his lips and she murmured and sighed and sucked on her own fingers. He kneaded her buttocks with strong hands, pinching, licking her with his tongue, deliberately drawing his breath in and out over her glistening clitoris, making her shiver and shake at the heat and cold.

She screamed out loud, "God, my God, right there. Yes," and pushed his head deeper into her. His upper teeth and lower lip drew in her clitoris, and he devoured her, sucking, until she screamed again. Then, he bit down hard inside her thigh, leaving the mark she was now massaging in the shower.

She turned off the water and rubbed her body dry. With the cap removed, her hair fell free and she shook her mahogany mane into a large halo. When she opened the bathroom door, he was gone. All that remained was the scent of roses and sex, a disheveled room and his gold cigarette case lying on the carpet.

Davey Sullivan sat in the navy blue Bentley, and watched Viva shut and lock the door to her Santa Monica beachhouse. He thought she looked lovely in her pale-blue silk shirtwaist, and hand-hammered gold jewelry. Yet, the most arresting thing about her, besides her fabulous breasts and curves, was her hair. It swirled and whirled wildly around her head, framing her face.

She opened the back door, entered the shiny auto and comfortably relaxed. Davey waited for instructions. He knew damn well they were heading out to meet Michael at the airport, but he had to wait until she said it.

"You forgot your cigarette case again, Davey," she said, and balanced it on the top of his seat tipping it over with her long red fingernail. "Don't you like it?"

He started the motor, adjusted his chauffeur's cap and waited.

"International, Davey. Pan American," she said, and leaned back into her seat.

Away from her bedroom they were no longer equals. In the beginning, he believed that he could easily live out this arrangement. That it would eventually change and it would change to suit him. But, after six months, he felt like a fool.

In the beginning he believed he had found a golden goose that would lay him some golden eggs. Through her, he would be close to the jobs he desired, the people he believed could help him, and the money he craved and itched to get his hands on. Davey Sullivan wanted to be a star and she could help him. At least that's what he thought.

But it somehow got turned around. It was he who had become the golden goose, laying anything but golden eggs. Yet, he didn't mind screwing her. He just didn't like getting screwed.

The telephone rang.

"This is Sullivan," he said. "Just a moment." he pushed down on the hold button. "It's your brother Jason."

Viva banged her fist down on the car seat. "Damn! Tell him I'm not here. No . . . Oh, damn! Give it to me." She picked up the carved ebony telephone and waited. Her face screwed up instantly.

"Jason darling, how are you?"

"I'm very unhappy dear sister. Very unhappy with what's been going on."

"Tell me about it, darling. I haven't any idea what you're talking about."

"Don't shit me, with that 'darling' shit," he said, mocking her. "You know very well what I'm talking about. I'm talking about this son of a bitch Parker. Who the hell does he think he is? I called him a few days ago, and he still hasn't given me the courtesy of a callback. Somebody should attend to Ada's business and I can't get near a damn thing."

A bright, energetic smile covered Viva's face. "Jason darling, there's nothing for you to attend. Honestly, I've talked with Parker and as soon as Mike's here—"

"Mike! What the fuck does Mike have to do with anything?" His voice was shattering her eardrums and she held the receiver away from her.

"Darling, I thought you knew. Mike's a corporate officer," she said. She knew very well no one had told him that.

"What the fuck are you talking about? Don't hand me that horseshit. I'm no goddamned asshole. I don't like the games you or your friend Parker are playing. I don't like them at all. Don't push me into a corner, Viva. I'm a part of this family too."

"Jason, darling, of course you are! And no one's playing any games, or trying to push you anywhere. Mike signed some papers two years ago after Maurice's death. The board had to replace an officer after he died, and we all agreed. It's a matter of record. Very legal and proper."

"I don't fucking believe what I'm hearing. Mike hates this business. What's more, he doesn't know one thing about it. Christ Viva, you've diapered that kid's ass ever since Ada brought him home from the hospital. What the hell are you trying to do for him now?"

"Nothing, darling. Believe it or not, Mike's signing on was as much Ada's decision, and Max's I might add, as it was mine." There was dead silence on the other end.

"I really appreciate how concerned you are, and, Jason, it's nice to know I can count on you if I need to." She screwed up her face again and Davey caught sight of it. "I have to run now. We're almost at the airport."

She cut him off and called Parker's private number. Her long red fingernails drummed along the ebony waiting for him to answer.

"Parker? I'm glad I caught you. Yes, it's me. I have only one thing to tell you, one thing darling, and I won't repeat it again. If Jason Stone gets one finger on this corporation, regardless of what happens to Ada, I'll personally skin you alive and boil you in oil. I promise you, Parker, I mean it! I won't bother going to the bar association, I'll hire some very professional people to do it. You understand?"

Parker laughed. "Viva, what is it about your family that makes you all so warm and loving and trusting?"

"Lovely sentiments. I saw them on a Hallmark greeting card. But, you know what I mean so I won't beat a dead horse or a potentially dead lawyer. Just keep your eye on him, Parker—at all times. . . ."

She hung up and felt just a little better. She'd feel a whole lot better when Mike was on terra firma taking care of business and keeping Stone Management from falling apart. Nothing in her life could ever fall apart again, no matter what. It was one of the promises she had made to herself when her beloved husband, Maurice, died in 1981. He had been in New York City tying up the loose ends on a major packaging deal for S.M.A.

When she received word of his heart attack, Viva had flown to his side immediately. For one week there was hope as he held on, the doctors held on and she held on. Then another attack weakened him and he quietly and suddenly departed on the eighth night. While the tubes clicked and the respirators blew up his lungs like two dead balloons, she had not noticed that her mother-in-law, Martine Candelli, had stopped sobbing.

For Martine Candelli, her only son was home at last; away from the athiest Ada; the Jew Max and their mongrel daughter Viva who had separated them all these years. Unknown to Viva, prior to his expiration, Martine Candelli quietly provided a priest to deliver the Rite of Christian Farewell, then, from under Viva's dazed, temporarily insane and stupified nose, snatched away his body to a mortuary to prepare Maurice for a Catholic burial. With his soul restored and his remains safely under holy Christan ground, she, Martine, could once again expect to be reunited with him in Heaven.

When Viva finally awoke from this hideous nightmare, she visited Maurice's grave to say goodbye. She had refused to stage a fight for his casket and body. As for Martine, Viva believed that she could steal Maurice's body, God would decide upon his soul, but she could never steal the happy years that Maurice and she had shared. Not one thing could ever make her fall apart like that again. Not one thing and no one.

At Los Angeles International, Mike's trek to retrieve his baggage was fast becoming the most trying portion of the entire journey. He'd caught a flight at Manilla International Airport on June 17th, 11:40 A.M., touched down later in Guam at Agana Field and arrived in Honolulu precisely on schedule.

On and off, for fifteen and one-half hours, he'd been in the air, literally and emotionally, and now, here in Los Angeles, they'd had difficulty locating his suitcase. He was tired and drained.

He adjusted his watch and thought how odd it was, that by crossing the International Dateline, some imaginary line drawn by men on the earth's surface, and traveling eastward, he'd gained a day. He wondered if it was possible to take a boat, a raft, something and just float timelessly inside that space. . . .

The main terminal teamed with people, noise booming from loudspeakers announcing arrivals and departures, constant and continuing movement. Everyone was in a hurry and he hated all of it. The crowds, the searching eyes, the baggage racks rolling around and around endlessly clanking and shifting. The intense and impersonal way people bumped into him hardly ever saying excuse me, as though he were a pole or a wall.

Outside and through the glass doors, he caught sight of Viva. His chest took a stitch and he grasped his well-worn burgundy leather suitcase, moving through the opening doors.

For a moment, they just stared at one another. Then he threw his case to the ground and pulled her into his arms; the smell of her expensive, familiar perfume reminded him of home.

"Michael," she said softly into his neck. "Michael." She pulled back a bit, her hands resting on his shoulders, "You . . . you . . . need a shave."

"I know," he said kissing her on the forehead.

"My God," she gasped. "What on earth have they done to you?" Michael smiled and waited for the lecture he knew would follow.

She pushed him farther away for a better perspective. "You're nothing but skin and bones." It wasn't exactly true, but it satisfied what he knew were her maternal instincts, protecting him and asserting themselves.

"You're not so bad yourself kid," he said then picked up his case and linked arms with her. "Where's the car?" She pointed to the Bentley parked nearby and his eyebrows raised up. A low whistle trilled from inside his throat.

Inside the car, she leaned to Davey. "Ada's house," she said, and pressed the window partition closed. They were finally on their way.

"Well," he said, "tell me all about it. How's Ada?"

She settled back, curled her legs up under her and held onto his hand. "She's in intensive care naturally and the doctors are using words like, cerebral and stroke and a million other things I don't understand. Dr. Morgenstern gave it some fancy name, I can't remember what, and a fifty-fifty chance for her recovery. She's still in a coma, feels absolutely nothing. If she does recover, he can't even tell whether or not she'll be able to speak . . . or walk . . . or God knows what.

"Anyway, I'm glad you missed it. It was awful. Every damn Hollywood phony sent flowers. Including the s.o.b.s that screwed her: Roxanne and Sidney. Some of the damn designs even looked like funeral wreaths, especially the one from Sid."

She continued on like a bottled up fountain that had finally found release.

"Sidney Gross had the goddamn nerve to take out ads in the trades, even rimmed them lightly in black, saying how wonderful it had been working with her all those years and for her to hang in there. My God! Broomsticks would have grown in all the horseshit he slung."

Mike watched her face. Totally alive, animated, those piercing gray eyes framed by her wild mahogany hair. "I know," she said. "I know exactly what Sid's after and what he's waiting for, and he'll get that over my dead body. I won't lie, Mike. I won't sit here and tell you I'll miss her if she goes. At least I don't think I will. But I won't let him or anyone else make garbage out of her while she's down and defenseless."

She stopped suddenly the pressure released, as though the fountain had pushed out all it had to and could simply flow easily. The traffic sounds surrounded them and the freeway lamps blinked on. Michael waited a moment, then gently, stroked her fingers.

"Tell me about Max. How's he taking it all?"

She took back her hand and removed a flask of Corvoisier from her purse. "Oh, I think Max is going to be all right. I would have taken him with me to the fights this weekend in Montreal, but he won't go. He's taken up some kind of vigil at the hospital, with Nicole driving him back and forth. Of course, the first day was a mess. He had one hell of a fit. He fought like a tiger and poor Nicole had the bruises to prove it. Morgenstern had to put him out for a while until he calmed down."

She bent her head back, took a tiny swig, then offered the half-pint flask to him. He shook his head, refusing it, clearing his throat. "Wasn't Jason there?"

"You're joking of course. Jason can't even handle anyone with a headache. He certainly wasn't going to be anywhere near Ada or Max."

Michael removed a lambskin pouch from his pocket and sprinkled, tobacco into his pipe. He pressed his thumb down into the rich brown of the bowl then placed the stem into his mouth and lit it.

"Do you mind?" he asked her, his palm caressing the shiny bowl, smoke curling out from his lips.

"Of course not, darling." She sniffed at the aroma. "It smells like vanilla; like you." She touched his cheek, then looked out the window to see where they were.

The Bentley turned right off the San Diego Freeway at the Wilshire Boulevard Exit. The crowds, traffic and new buildings astounded him. "Everything's changed," he said, his face a Kaleidoscope of surprise, awe and dismay.

"It's all new darling. Restaurants, banks, high-rise buildings, condos. Awfully crowded. But I suppose like everyone else, you'll get used to it."

He'd never get used to it. He hated crowds, loved and required space, sought it every chance he got. He had lived by the rhythms of another, slower culture for too long.

"How's Jason?" he asked finally.

"How's the devil?"

"Nicole?" He didn't look at Viva. He sounded nonchalant.

"I haven't seen much of her lately except for those few days at the hospital. She looks fine. No, gorgeous, but rather delicate and pensive. The best thing for her would be to have a baby. Even better, she should leave Jason."

He tried not to appear too concerned. "What makes you say that? She seemed happy when I left."

"I can't tell if she's happy or unhappy. I just know something's wrong. Something I can't quite put my finger on. Anyway, she's alone alot from what I hear and I think being alone makes her very unhappy. She's never really had a family of her own and Jason's being away so much has to have an effect on her.

"Mike." She became quiet and spoke seriously. "There's something we have to talk about. Something very important. With Ada sick, Jason is going to do everything he can to take control of the business. I know you're tired now but there's a great deal we must discuss after you have a chance to rest."

He pulled the pipe from his mouth. They were at Bristol Circle and Davey turned the Bentley north.

"What are you trying to tell me, Viva?"

"You're not going to like this, Mike, but here goes. When I came back to New York, after Maurice died, you signed some papers for me. Do you remember?" He nodded. "Most of them were corporate papers."

His eyes and brows began to knit together and a sudden uneasy feeling hit him in the pit of his stomach.

"It was only a formality then, Michael, but now, well now . . . under the corporate charter, you're not only a vice-president, but the acting president of Stone Management Associates. You must run things until Ada gets well—or if it comes down to selling, make that decision."

His jaw hung open, the pipe sitting almost cool in his palm. "You're joking, Viva."

She stared at him. "No, darling. I'm not."

"Jesus Viva. I don't know anything about career management, much less show business. No. Wait! I take that back. I know all I need to know. I hate the industry. I despise the people crawling around in it. I can't do it—I won't do it. Let Jason handle it."

She grabbed him by the shoulders. "Michael, listen to me! Right now, you have no choice. No matter how we both feel about her or this business, Ada's worked too damn hard for us to hand it over to Jason so he can piss it away. And that's what he'll do if he gets his hands on it. At this point, you, me, Pop, we hold the stock and the power. But if Pop has any legal rights to Ada's stock, that, along with his own, could be a majority. We both know how Max favors Jason. Just the right words to him from Jason and it's all in the toilet. And Michael, everything I have is tied up in S.M.A. so I go into the toilet, too. I'll stick with you, if you decide we should sell. But there's the chance that Ada will recover and there would be nothing for her to come home to."

The car stopped and she looked at the front of the house. "Please, Mike, there's too much to talk about. I'll call you on Monday when I get back from Montreal. Rest, darling, please. And don't be too angry with me."

He watched the Bentley drive off down the driveway and felt the birth of a silent whirlwind beginning to build within himself. His throat ached from the smoke, the air conditioning, the long flight and now an intense primal need to cry out to her. He heard no sounds; not a single sparrow, a rustling palm, the car or the iron gates closing shut. Not even Cranston who stood behind him now, calling out his name.

* * *

Sidney Gross ripped June 17 from his desk calendar. He was filled with rage and with righteous indignation. Roxanne Calder had just telephoned. He stared at her enormous photograph which hung on a large teak wall, his blood beginning to boil.

She was truly one of the most beautiful actresses in the industry, today or any other day for that matter, and she was beginning to screw up her career. *Why in hell had she done it?* he thought. She had it *all*. Fame, two beautiful kids, twins that were her spitting image, money to burn and today, at thirty-five, she looked more beautiful than ever.

Now he'd have to deal with her new husband's youth, ego, frustrations, plus once again face the terrifying possibility that everything about her would be found out. He was sorry he had taken the call.

Her voice had sparkled.

"Sid? Hi, sweetie. It's Roxanne. I'm in Hawaii and I have wonderful news." He had already heard it over the radio and the phones were ringing off the wall. "Luis and I were married!" There was silence and Roxanne began to press the phone button. "Hello? Hello? Sidney? Are you there?"

He was sitting in a white leather chair and snapped the pencil he was holding, in two. "I'm here Roxanne. I'm here," he said, and plugged her into the speaker phone.

Her voice echoed throughout the room. "Well, sweetie, congratulate me then."

His silence continued and the anger welling up inside him was beginning to activate his ulcer, his blood pressure and his hemorrhoids.

"Oh shit, Sid. Stop worrying will you. I'll be all right. I know why you're worried, but I'm not an idiot."

He swung his chair around placing his back contemptuously to the telephone, and stared at the dark, early evening vista of Los Angeles.

"Well for God's sake, say something, Sid. Anything."

He muttered, "Congratulations, Roxanne. Let me know what happens when you get fucked."

"I can't hear you sweetie, say again?"

He swung around and snarled loudly, "I said congratulations Roxanne and good luck."

"Be happy for me please, Sid," she begged. "I can never be without you. You know that. Look, I have to go now. I'll see you on the fourth. I'm really looking forward to it. Kisses to you and Tony." She hung up the phone and he had not been able to take his eyes off that photograph since then.

That face. The round, exquisitely chiseled Indian cheekbones covered with rich, carmel-colored, womanly flesh and dark nutmeg hair. She oozed sex: healthy, exotic, robust sex. Her famous, beautiful, cantaloupe-succulent breasts; her wicked smile of even, pure white teeth framed by full and naturally tinted cherry lips; the exotic cinnamon-dipped eyes buried above her cheekbones like a carnelian treasure in mother-of-pearl. The total look of her face and of her body promised endless and secret pleasures.

And now, she'd gone and married some asshole. She also stood a chance of shattering not only her career, but jeopardizing her life and the lives of her children.

He thought about how much he depended upon the income she generated for him. If she blew it, he'd have to have new blood. Trouble was, the only bloodtype that appealed to him went for seven or more figures. That's when it hit him.

Sidney buzzed for his secretary, Tony Meredith, and flipped his desk calendar to July the Fourth. This time, he'd use one of his famous parties to his own advantage.

Chapter 3

MICHAEL OPENED HIS EYES to a sea of green grass and an opaline sky. A lilting breeze carried the fragrance of Ada's roses, and his nostrils, like a bellows, extracted the drifting bouquet. He stood, shifted the position of the chaise longue and lay back down on his belly.

Three hours before he had visited Ada, or what appeared to be Ada, and he had been unable to remove that image from his memory.

This once robust and absolute woman lay meek and humbled like a stuck pig, on sterile white sheets, her face and hands the color of chalk. He had never seen his mother lie so still or look so pale or feel so cold. He had never even seen her with her hair down.

He closed his eyes again and tried to remember her the way she was; the way she used to look; the way he had seen her seven years ago, before he left. Then, she was the essence of movement, a blue streak. "Get to the point, Michael," she would say. "Get to the point!"

"The point is there is no point," he'd answer. All at once, she'd whip her body around, chilling his bones with a look she'd spent years perfecting.

"Don't mind-fuck with me, Michael."

"Hey listen. I'm not," he'd answer. And of course he wasn't. He mostly didn't know what the point was, and even when he did, she'd scare him so he'd forget it.

She'd slap her palm down on a nearby table and like

thunder following lightning, she'd bellow, "Okay, Mike, okay. What's the bottom line? Just give me the bottom line!"

For Ada there was always a bottom line. Everything was negotiable and everything had a bottom line.

Michael felt hot and he wanted to swim. He walked to the pool's edge, hugged the rim with his toes and dove in. The water was clear, and refreshingly cool. Back and forth across the length of it he swam ceaselessly, until his arms ached and his breath gave way. Then he pulled himself out, and walked back to the chaise.

Dark wavy hair clung to the sides of his beautifully formed head and a few singular curls spun down across his forehead and temples. Nut-brown from the Cambodian sun, lean and muscular from heavy labor, he looked healthy, wholesome and strong.

He wiped his forehead and chest then stopped as the sound of excited voices bounded forth from inside the house. Motionless, he strained to hear, and then he saw her. Nicole. She was a flash of flying hair, a glowing lean figure . . . arms and legs moving like windswept willows, a mile-wide smile flashing a thousand Christmastree lights . . . rushing toward him, covering him with hugs and kisses and misty eyes. Growing suddenly petulant, she punched at his bare chest.

"You rat," she squeaked, "you crummy rat. You left without saying one word to me. You never even sent me one postcard." He tried to hug her again, but she arched away.

"Hey, what kind of a welcome home is this?" he said, and kissed the tip of her nose. Her dimples almost made up their mind to appear.

"Oh, Michael. How could you go away without saying good-bye?"

He hugged her. She had a right to feel betrayed, he thought. Betrayal had been the essence of her life, but he hadn't thought about it then. His own pain was all he could handle. Had he gone to her to say good-bye, she would have pressed him for the truth. He took her hand. "C'mon, let's walk," he said, starting a ramble toward Ada's office.

"That was a long time ago. I had to get away from L.A.," he explained. "Away from the family, from this whole crazy scene."

That's all it took. In a matter of minutes, whatever hurt or anger she was experiencing, he had diffused and they were holding each other, her head resting lightly against his muscular arm.

"You look terrific," he said.

"No I don't. I'm almost twenty-eight, practically an old lady. Look!" She angled her head up to his face and the scent of fresh lemon soap hovered under his nose. "Look at the wrinkles near my eyes and the gray hairs on my head."

He politely searched her face. "I don't see anything. If it's possible, I'd say you're prettier."

Nicole just smiled.

They resumed walking, heading back to the patio talking, laughing as though they had seen each other yesterday.

"OhmyGod," she said, then grabbed his wrist. "I'm shooting a commercial in half an hour and I'm late." She started to run away but turned to kiss his cheek. "There's so much to talk about. So much I want to ask you. You look positively wonderful and I'll call you later."

She ran, returning quickly to give him an envelope that was stashed inside her purse, swiftly running off again.

"What's this?" he called after her.

"Don't know," she shouted, turning and running backward. "They found it on Ada when they took her to the Emergency Room." Nicole reached the top of a knoll and stopped. "I'm really glad you're home, Michael," she yelled. "I've missed you."

Michael watched the last of Nicole trail off into the distance, then he started back toward the patio. This meeting, this first encounter with her, was what he had feared the most. Now, it was the past and he was proud of himself. Not once had he betrayed the depth of his real emotions, his strong passion for her. It hadn't been easy. She still made his skin tingle and she still aroused him with that certain look, her casual touch. But this time . . . this time he was in control.

His training at control had come out of his first weeks in

Cambodia. When the night screams came and tiny babies would waste away in front of his eyes and there was nothing he could do. He had spent the first four days retching, finally stopping by the fifth, only because there was nothing more left inside him to vomit. By the seventh day, he, like all the others, could sleep through the night screams and speak of the mortality rate as improved when the number of dead babies did not exceed the prior day's count.

He became aware of what Nicole had given him. It was an envelope with a French postmark. Inside was a cable and he slowly read the English wording.

June 12, 1983

MADAME STONE.
I HAVE SENT ALL DOCUMENTS IN A SEALED POUCH VIA COURIER. ANY OTHER MODE OF TRANSPORT WAS OUT OF THE QUESTION. I CONSIDER MY PERSONAL DEBT TO YOU SETTLED AND OUR BUSINESS CONCLUDED. PER OUR AGREEMENT, I TRUST YOU WILL DESTROY THIS CABLE.

Michael looked for a signature but there was none. Just one large, illegible letter at the bottom of the page.

What an odd message. And more, what was *he* supposed to do with it. If he could locate that pouch, perhaps he'd know.

But, now, it was time to get ready for that board meeting.

*　　*　　*

Elaine Shagan was crazy like a fox. As Ada's private secretary she was envied by most of the Hollywood ladies who played the typewriter and wrote in Morse code on steno pads.

Daily, she would speak to Names. Names and Voices of Names, whose faces and mythical legends were celebrated around the world. But that wasn't what turned Elaine on. She was amazed in fact at how little it mattered. What did exhilarate and stimulate her, what did warm and stir her blood was the power that position gave her.

Because of that power, she was treated with uncommon respect by not only her peers, but by anyone who wanted to get to Ada. Elaine was the one, the only one, who could "open sesame" for them.

Six years before she had worked in the typing pool at a studio. Often, she would look around, contemplate the women banging away at the keys and visualize her own face growing older and grayer and more tired. It was a mental image that terrified her. She knew she had to make changes in her life and she tried. But everytime some new and important position opened up, one that she was fully qualified for, it would be filled by someone whose credentials were not as good as her own, but who had the right inside connections. It made her bitter.

"*Be in the right place at the right time,*" her ambitious mother's words came echoing back to her. "*The early bird catches the worm.*"

Well, Elaine had made up her mind. She'd be in the right place at the right time from now on, by God. All she needed to find was the right "worm".

Like everyone else in Hollywood trying to get ahead, Elaine read the trades, *Variety, The Hollywood Reporter* mostly, and one day for some reason an obituary caught her eye. It noted the untimely death of Caroline Robbins, Ada Stone's devoted secretary who had been only twenty-nine-years-old.

She pondered Caroline's death first because they were exactly the same age. But then, she had the most brilliant idea. Elaine dressed herself in black and made preparations to attend the funeral services.

"*Be in the right place at the right time,*" came those shrill sounding words again from her mother, and she was certainly doing just that. Moreover, she couldn't have been an earlier bird.

The door to Ada's home office had opened and Elaine was startled.

"Hi," he said, extending a hand. "I'm Mike Stone."

She felt the rhythm of a singular firm handshake.

"Elaine Shagan. I'm glad to meet you."

"I thought I'd stop in, say hello," Michael said. "Hello."

"We're all yours, Mr. Stone."

Michael looked embarrassed and his voice carried a note of shyness. "Why don't you just call me 'Mike,' " he said.

"Okay, Mike, fine." Elaine's large blue eyes scanned the room. "This is my office. As you can see it's very simple, very utilitarian except for my blood-red typewriter."

Michael ran his fingers over the typewriter and smiled. It did look out of place with the rest of the room.

"I needed it immediately," Elaine continued, "and it was all they had. Anyway, I've grown accustomed to its typeface." She walked ahead, toward a doorway. "This way."

Michael's starched shirt collar began to itch and he rubbed his neck for some relief.

"This, is Ada's main office," Elaine said. "There's another one located in Beverly Hills. That's where Viva handles all the new talent. Here, Ada walks a few hundred feet and falls into bed when she's tired. She also provides a homey atmosphere for her "bankables" and they love it. Some come here to relax; swim, play tennis, eat Cranston's cooking. She's like a mother to her clients." Michael listened as she went on.

"Personally, I think that's a great part of Ada's appeal. Not to mention how good she is at bargaining." She looked at Michael. "But I guess that's no news to you." The telephone rang. "Saved by the bell," Elaine said and excused herself.

Michael surveyed the large *L*-shaped room for the first time. Recessed windows diffused the sun's rays so that the room was bright but without glare.

A beige velvet couch with full, soft foam pillows hugged the whitewashed walls, cradling half a dozen Indian-handcrafted, brightly colored pillows.

Tables made of free-form glass, balanced themselves neatly on chunks of natural driftwood. Large ferns billowed at every stir and English ivy cascaded from window corners. One large fig tree wept bits of leaves down onto the floor.

To the right was Ada's massive desk. Stained the color of driftwood, it was as neat as a pin. Behind it stood a matching assemblage of three etageres surrounded by photographs of stars and dignitaries hugging and kissing Ada. In front of it, TV monitors and a magnificent pale oak liquor cabinet.

Elaine returned. "That was Viva," she said. "She wanted me to remind you about the meeting at Parker's office."

"Thanks," he said. "I haven't forgotten."

He walked behind the desk and looked at his watch. "What's Parker's address again?" he asked, pulling at the top drawer to look for a pencil and a pad.

"Don't bother," Elaine answered. "I'll write it down for you before you leave."

Intrigued by its weight, Michael continued pulling at the drawer. When it was finally open he stared at Elaine then immediately turned around.

Elaine spoke quickly. "It's for new clients," she said to the back of his head. "It gives Ada a chance to see how they react in cold readings or under pressure."

Michael ran his fingers across the bookcase, then the wall, finally finding what he was looking for. "Where does she keep the tapes?" he asked, inspecting the carefully hidden lens of a noiseless video camera, the guts of which he had discovered in the top drawer.

"Locked up," Elaine answered. She pointed to a door that had a security system's sticker on it.

"I'm afraid I don't have a key," Elaine said apologetically.

Michael sighed, then checked his watch again. "I've got to go," he said, and escorted her to the outer office. "I suppose we'll start working sometime tomorrow. Line up anything you think needs immediate attention and we'll check it out." When they reached her desk she stopped and wrote the address of Parker's office on a piece of paper and handed it to him.

"Thanks," he said slipping the page into his pocket. "I'll be depending on you an awful lot these next few weeks, Elaine. I have a feeling we're going to get along just fine."

"Yes," she said, "just fine."

* * *

Back and forth Jason paced. He clutched, scrutinized, shuffled and shook a small sheaf of papers until the fingers on his left hand closed into a tight fist and suddenly hit the nearest wall. He had been doing that now for half an hour, long enough for Meyer Wolfson to drink a full quart of extra-rich milk.

Every so often, Jason would look at Meyer's beady black eyes, which led inevitably to Meyer's sharply pointed nose, then back to the papers again. He finally slammed the papers down onto his desk. Meyer jumped.

"The only thing here is that Parker's humping my sister. Who the hell isn't?" Jason pulled a handkerchief from his back pocket, blew his nose and opened the wrinkled square to inspect the contents.

"You ain't usin' your head, Jake," Meyer said, his thin legs crossing over one another.

"Don't shit me, Meyer. I've looked at it. There's not a damn thing I can use on Parker."

Meyer grinned. "You got larceny in your heart, Jake, but shit for imagination. Take a look on Page Four."

Jason put the handkerchief back and rifled through the pages. "So? He's fond of his kid."

"But his kid's not ordinary. Christopher Parker's a junkee."

"Ex-junkee, according to this."

"Once a junkee, always a junkee," Meyer said.

"So, what do I do? And where do I find him?"

Meyer's thin flat lips bound themselves into a straight-line grin. "One of his best friends, one of the few friends his father allows him to see is your sister's kid."

"Shauna?" Jason asked.

Meyer nodded. "They're in love." He chuckled. "I told you, Jake. There ain't a man alive what ain't got an Achilles heel."

Jason sat there smiling, reflecting on the possibilities before him, then spoke. "Mario say anything? I mean about doing business with me?"

"Look, Jake," Meyer told him. "I'll give you the skinny. You got the I.R.S. and a half a dozen state agencies up your ass. It don't do Mario no good to wash clothes with you. Understand?" Jason nodded.

''It don't mean the boys won't help you out if you need it. Fix up your problems, then he'll talk to you.''

Meyer stood, straightened out his trousers and embraced Jason. ''Keep outta trouble, Jake,'' he said, and left.

Jason sat by the window, a sunbeam boring through his back like a bullet. His left hand throbbed and he rubbed it. But he felt so damn good again. He thought about Parker and knew that now he had a chance to get what he wanted, the way he wanted. With some clever planning, a little pressure in the right places, all the plumbing would start to hum.

Now, how to deal with Michael. He'd either have to gain the kid's confidence or just out and out intimidate him like the old days.

In half an hour they'd be sharing a cocktail and a late lunch. He could decide then.

* * *

''For the time being,'' Parker said, lighting up another cigarette, ''you'll be dealing more with Ada's clients than anything else. The cigarette smoke curled up and floated abstractly toward a sunbeam.

With the board meeting over, Michael and Viva listened thoughtfully, as Parker referred to his notes.

''Divert all contractual questions to me, unless they come from one of your bankables. Then, find out what they want and we'll discuss it. That way I can guide you and you'll still keep everything on as personal a basis as Ada. The point is not to upset the clients.

''You and Viva can settle on any new properties and I'll negotiate the deals. Forward all mail you can't handle to me.'' He looked up for a moment. ''This is usually the time of year when one of Ada's big names will try to buy a Rolls or some fancy mansion and we have to sit firmly but carefully on them. Never, ever solicit business for a client. A manager is strictly prohibited from doing that. If you find a project, there are ways to play the game without breaking any laws or codes. Never put the agency in jeopardy.''

Parker glanced back at his notes. ''Refuse all personal interviews. I've already issued a statement on your behalf and Elaine has a copy. Read it. It was necessary to counter a statement issued by Jason." Viva made a face. Parker inhaled and blew out smoke as he spoke.

"Call each of your bankables and introduce yourself. Take them out individually for a very expensive lunch or dinner and . . . charm the hell out of them. We're counting on the publicity you'll be getting in the trades, etc. We want you established as S.M.A.'s president in the minds of everyone."

Parker took a last drag and stubbed the butt out in an ashtray. "Now, are there any questions?"

"Yeah," Michael said. "Go over this takeover business again."

"Okay. Stone Management Associates is a closed family corporation. Ada controls 60 percent of the stock and the rest is held by you, Viva and Max. If, as Viva fears, Jason decides to pull a fast one, he'll try to convince Max to either sell or transfer his shares to him."

"That gives him Max's 20 percent," Michael mulled. "As much as Viva and I hold together."

"Right," Parker said. "It also gives Jason a foot in the door." He paused. "There's another problem. Ada's 60 percent." Viva's eyes grew wide. "Technically, Max shares half of that by virtue of community property."

"God," Viva shouted. "I knew it."

"Take it easy," Michael said to her. "Don't forget that Max loves Ada."

"He also loves Jason," Viva reminded him.

"Can Jason do all this easily?" Michael asked.

"Nothing's done easily Michael, but all things are possible. You've also got a potential problem with your bankables. They're the backbone of Ada's income. Need I remind you of the old story about rats and sinking ships."

"Can they leave just like that? Contracts and all?" Michael inquired.

"Hell yes. A contract's nothing more than a treaty. And treaties are made to be broken."

"Any recourse?"

"Lawsuits. Expensive lawsuits."

"Where's loyalty when you really need it?" Michael asked.

"Only in the boy scouts, darling," Viva said. "You're in the army now."

Viva stood up. She straightened her white open-necked silk blouse, and a dozen gold and silver bracelets jingled halfway up her arm. "Anyone care to join me?" she asked, walking to the bar.

Parker passed with a nod of his head, but Michael held up two fingers. She poured their drinks and returned to her chair.

"Here, darling," she said. "Here's to an interesting adventure—you, me, Jason, Max—just like old times."

Inside Ada's white Jaguar, Michael waved good-bye to Viva, then followed a fast-moving Porche Turbo 930 through the underground parking lot. When he hit the blinding California sun, he pulled down the visor, checked the traffic and swung onto Constitution Avenue.

Early for his appointment with Jason, he drove leisurely through the Beverly Hills streets, his mind alternately sifting through thoughts of Jason, and the commitment he had just made. All that talk about takeovers concerned and confused him. He wanted to work, to do a good job for Viva, for Ada, for himself. He didn't want to be some kind of company watchdog and combination babysitter, but it went with the turf. And, the thought of behaving as though Jason was his enemy didn't appeal to him either. He'd have to seriously consider everything Parker told him, but wait and see for himself.

There were twelve years between Michael and Jason, not to mention Jason's personality which Michael had found hard to deal with when they were growing up. Jason had been aggressive and pushy, developing qualities that Michael fought hard against cultivating in himself . . . qualities that were prized and nurtured by Ada and also Max.

He could clearly recall how awful Jason had always treated Max. Walking behind miming him, inventing a million and one pranks like salting his food and swiping things from his plate. Max would think he'd already eaten it. How Ada had laughed. "Just boyish fun," she'd say. How she loved and worshipped Jason then.

Michael remembered when he was seven or eight, standing in the doorway to Ada's bedroom watching Jason rifle through Max's trousers and Ada's purse, pocketing cash. Jason was oblivious to his presence until Michael asked what he was doing.

"None of your damn business, squirt. Get the hell out of here."

"I'm gonna tell Mom—"

Before Michael had finished the sentence, Jason had grabbed him by the throat, his thumbs pressed lightly against Michael's Adam's apple.

"You do that, squirt, and I'll beat the shit out of you. You understand.?"

Michael's face turned red, then blue and his body hung limp with terror.

"I'll break every bone in your body, squirt. Just you go and run to Ada. I swear I'll kill you."

A loud horn blasted behind the white Jaguar and Michael's heart skipped a beat. His blood raced from a shot of adrenalin prompted by the awful memory of Jason standing over him.

He drove east on Sunset Boulevard following the winding, wide road. There, ahead of him, rising like some pink confection nestled in camellias, stood the Beverly Hills Hotel. He drove by slowly, remembering how much Nicole had loved going there.

Jason. What kind of man was he now? Things change. People change. The only thing that doesn't change is the notion of change. Even in death, things change, decompose, decay and rot.

He thought about himself. What would he do if he caught Jason with his hand in Ada's purse again? Would he react like he did twenty-one years ago? This time, would he be able to make Jason put the money back?

He reached the restaurant, parked his car and crossed the busy intersection. Inside, a sudden smell of beer enveloped him and the darkness of the room distorted his eyesight. He waited patiently until he could see, then searched the room. Jason was there, sitting at the farthest end, in a wide red leather booth.

As Michael approached, he could see the whites of Jason's eyes glow in the dark and a single candle reflected the sparks of silver scattered throughout Jason's thick hair.

Jason stood, grasped Michael's cool strong hand, a welcoming grin upholstering his face.

"Hey, Mike," he said. "Good to see you. Here, have a seat." Jason called the waiter and ordered drinks for the both of them. Before Michael could refuse, he'd sent the waiter away. "Hey," Jason screamed after, "get us some menus."

With the menu firmly in his hand, Jason looked up.

"How about a steak, squirt?"

The muscles in the back of Michael's neck grew taut.

"No. No thanks," he said. "I'll try a sandwich maybe." Before Michael could reach for his menu, there was a drink in front of him and Jason was ordering for them both.

"A steak for me, rare, baked potato. And give my kid brother here a grilled cheese sandwich with well-done bacon."

The waiter hurried away again. Everything was happening so fast, Michael hardly had time to think.

Jason pushed Michael's glass toward him. "Here—drink up."

Michael sipped his Scotch, then lit his pipe, trying to regain his composure.

"Well, Mr. S.M.A. President," Jason said, "how the hell are you? You look great."

"I'm fine, Jason. How's yourself?"

"Great, kid, great. Couldn't be better. Got a new house in Holmby. Two classy cars. Got a Ferrari you've got to feel to believe. I'm makin' a new movie in about a month. Things are pretty terrific."

Jason took a slug of his Scotch, his eyes riveted on Michael's distorted face, through the bottom of the glass. "So, what's new?" he asked.

Michael leaned back. "Not much really."

"C'mon. You can tell me. Christ, you've been halfway around the world. What are those chinky broads like?"

Michael didn't speak. He smiled weakly just dismissing the words as if he'd never heard them.

Jason went on. "So, how'd the big meeting go?"

"Fine."

"That's good, that's good." The liquid from Jason's drink glistened on his lips. "That's real good. So, what do you think of this Parker guy?"

"So far? Pretty good, I guess," Michael replied. "I'm not one for snap judgments. He seems fair."

"Oh yeah? Well I hear he's a real fuck-up."

Michael studied him carefully. "Where'd you hear that?"

"Hey it's all over the street, Mike. Beverly Hills is a small town. People are close and these things travel fast. If I were you, I'd keep an eye on him. With Ada holed up, he'll be robbing her blind."

"Makes no sense to me, Jason," Michael said. "He's been with Ada for a long time. I'll trust her judgment."

"You've been away a long time, squirt. Ada's a broad; an old broad. She thinks like a broad. They used to make it together until he started humping Viva."

He was going too far and Michael wanted to stop him right there. He wanted to tell him to shut up. To quit speaking about the family like that. But instead, he only listened, stirring the ice cubes in his drink with a finger and quelling the growing anger within.

The waiter set down Jason's steak, then Michael's sandwich and hurried away again. Jason cut hungrily into the blood-red meat and kissed his fingertips to the ceiling relishing the first bite.

Michael took a bite of his sandwich, chewed for a minute, then inspected the food on his plate.

"What's wrong, kid?" Jason asked.

"Bacon's a little raw."

"Gimme that," Jason said reaching for Michael's plate. Before Michael could say "skip it, I'm not very hungry," Jason was standing up. Michael's plate was in his hand and he screamed for the waiter.

The waiter rushed to Jason's side. "What're you deaf, or something?" Jason shoved the plate into the waiter's ribs. "I said well-done bacon, for Christ's sake." The waiter took the plate without uttering a sound and started for the kitchen. Jason screamed after him. "Get it right this time."

He sat down. "You can't let those bastards push you around, squirt. It never pays. People only respect you when you scare holy hell out of them. Then you'll get what you ask for. Always remember that kid; always remember that."

Jason cut into his rare steak again, the bloody juices curling around his plate, Michael's eyes studying their path.

* * *

Nicole inspected the living room from stem to stern and was pleased. It all looked so beautiful. Fires lightly crackled in all three living room fireplaces and the dim outdoor lighting faintly outlined the huge terrace with its tall square marble colums. It was almost eight.

She walked outside and listened as a soft breeze caressed delicate, hand-blown Venetian wind chimes. She inhaled the intoxicating aroma of night-blooming jasmine, then switched on the pool lights.

Thirty feet below her, a perfect transparent aquamarine jewel came electric and an over-sized redwood jacuzzi bubbled a warm, enticing welcome. She walked back inside.

Her maid, Tiu Phong, carefully moved from table to table, arranging floating gardenias and birds-of-paradise in radiantly glinting crystal vases and bowls.

"Thank you, Tiu," Nicole said, and returned the young woman's graceful bow.

In the main room, plump red and beige pillows sat puffed up invitingly on randomly arranged red and beige crib sections. At each grouping, stood a thick glass table with a sculpted glass pedestal that permitted the colors of the antique Feraghan Oriental rugs to show through.

All there was left to do was to turn on some soft music, switch on the light that illuminated a mammoth Odalisque painting, and check the bar.

She heard the sound of the Ferrari booming its way up the driveway and walked to the front door. Hoping his mood was pleasant, she smiled, opened the door and waited.

"Hi," she said to him, peering out. "How'd it go today?"

Jason quickly brushed by her into the house. She followed after him hoping he might notice the new eye-shadow and lipstick she was wearing.

He walked the length and breadth of the living room inspecting cigarette boxes, lighters and finally the bar. He glanced around the room again.

"Who put those damn flowers there?" he shouted.

"I did," Nicole said quickly. "I thought they would look pretty."

"Tell her to get rid of them," Jason ordered, then turned to face her. "Don't think so much Nicole," he told her. "It's bad for your little brain." He patted the top of her head.

Nicole stood there watching Jason move around the room, searching for things to criticize. She understood. He needed to criticize. He had to get angry because it made his hustle so much better.

"I saw Mike today," he said brushing by her again. This time he stopped and stared at her face. "Jesus Christ, Nicole," he exploded. "You look like a whore. What the hell did you do to yourself?" He gripped her arm and pulled her into the light. "Some goddamned fag put makeup all over you?"

She started to stammer. "I . . . I . . . tried something new, that's all," she said. "If you don't like it, I'll wash it off." He let go of her arm.

Tiu Phong appeared from the dining room. "Madame and sir have dinner," she whispered, her head bowed. Nicole told her to remove the flowers and hurriedly followed Jason's long strides to the breakfast nook.

Small tureens of steaming hot onion soup smothered in Gruyère cheese sat waiting on the table near a tray of hot garlic and cheese toast. Jason dug in, slurping and swallowing, his eyes constantly checking his wristwatch.

"What did Mike have to say?" she asked.

Jason laughed contemptuously. "He didn't say one damn thing. He's never said anything important in all his life. He's got this dumb idea of doing a documentary on these miserable camps in Cambodia." Jason bit heartily into his toast, crumbs splattering everywhere as he talked. "Who the hell wants to see a bunch of chinks and gooks starve to death in some damn refugee camp?"

Nicole looked over at Tiu Phong and prayed she hadn't heard that. Members of her family were still lost over there, still caught in the political webs woven by despots, overthrown governments and the displacement of war.

Jason continued. "I told him, tits and ass. That's what it's all about . . . tits and ass. Nobody makes money from message pictures, much less documentaries. People want to relax, enjoy good-looking broads for Christ's sake. That kid's a real asshole."

The service doorbell rang.

Jason raised his bowl to suck up the last tasty onion bits. He pointed his finger at Nicole. "You get your face washed and make yourself scarce. I don't want you down here anymore cause you talk too much."

Nicole rose from the table. She made her way up the back staircase to the bedroom, her ears tuned to the sound of Jason's heavy foot steps.

Inside her bedroom, she walked to the mirror and gazed at her face. The usual moist glow of her skin seemed oily and streaked, somehow. She didn't look at all the way she thought she had this afternoon when the makeup artist at Nieman Marcus painted her lips and softly brushed her eyelids with colors from the rainbow. Then, she thought she looked pretty. Now she just wasn't so sure.

In the living room, Jason surveyed the crowd. Seated comfortably around the main room were approximately thirty people of varying ages and backgrounds.

Their individual successes lay in diverse areas, fields of endeavor that had nothing whatever to do with the film industry. Engineers, realtors, plumbers, executive secretaries, all of them looking for a tax shelter or a long shot. It was important that no one be connected with the industry. Jason could not afford for anyone to ask the right questions.

Each of them possessed an ego that Jason understood, knew how to successfully cultivate and exploit. And all were carefully chosen by Jason for their maverick successes and their greed.

Jason called them to order by clinking a spoon against the side of a glass, then told a joke. Everyone laughed.

"Most of you know me or know about me," he said. "I'm part of a long tradition here in Hollywood; by that I mean, I belong to a family that's been a successful and highly visible part of filmmaking and star building, for at least fifty years." His eyes scoured the room.

"Anyone here who's never heard of Ada Stone, president of Stone Management Associates, has been either dead or in a coma." Several ladies tittered. "Before my mother, Ada, my Uncle Julie Stone helped to build some of the biggest talent agencies in this country. Agencies whose offices extend all over the world. Right now, he's a happy old billionaire living in Hollywood, Florida.

"Stone Management Associates is as good as money in the bank. Check it out. We represent names like Armando Del Gado . . ." Several women swooned. "I know just what you mean girls," Jason said and laughed lasciviously. "You and about twenty million others. To continue," he said, "there's Hank Mason, Bobbi Sands—you soap opera fans know who she is—and the list is endless." He walked to and fro, as he spoke, his hands alternately invading his pockets or brushing his hair.

"My mother and I built those stars and others like the one and only Roxanne Calder." He paused, smirking, as several men licked their lips.

"To begin with, all my films are budgeted below two million bucks—which is considered very low-budget in this business. You're all smart enough to know that, or you wouldn't be here. An example of what I mean is *Rocky*. I don't have to tell any of you what that film and its sequels went on to make in terms of hard cash. If I do, you don't belong here. Take your money and buy something safe like municiple bonds or try the money markets. Don't forget IRA." Jason drank some water, as people chuckled.

"The reason I can make a good and profitable low-budget movie has to do with the fact that I refuse to deal with unions." The crowd applauded their approval. They understood union demands. "There's no waste," he went on. "I also utilize a system of product trade-off and I maintain a crackerjack staff. There is, however, one union I must deal with and that's the Screen Actors Guild. There's no way out of that. What's up front does count. But, because of my connection to S.M.A., I can get my stable of stars to work for scale and sometimes have them defer their high salaries. Nobody—I mean *nobody*—holds me up for a three-million-dollar salary." There was resounding applause again and Jason grinned. The lump of clay he had started with was beginning to take a lovely shape in his clever hands.

"Frankly," Jason said, "there's practically no way to lose money with this kind of a budget and I'll show you why. In the first place, the major networks always need product. ABC, CBS and NBC will pay somewhere in the neighborhood of $600,000 for most films shown in prime-time. Right there, we recoup a major portion of our investment. Then, there's cable T.V., video cassettes—and by carefully selecting the right music, we can get a sound track, a hit song and a big record deal with some major record company.

"I can guarantee you, except for Murphy's Law, which I'm sure everyone of you in business for yourselves will understand, at the end of a three-year run in foreign and domestic markets, anybody who invests ten thousand dollars should realize a profit of around eighty grand."

The rich and famous hold a special lure most people long to be a part of. Jason knew this, and it was this motivation he always used as bait. His negative approach, the use of his mother's credibility, the promise of meeting some stars, becoming a part of the fabulous Hollywood scene, enticed and betwitched them all.

And when he was all through, when he had their checks in hand, he could make his overdue mortgage payments, his overdue car payments and still have something left over for a cheap little film.

Chapter 4

HE WAS A MAN WHO had his finger on the Hollywood heartbeat from the beginning. One year after he arrived, he could lie down with dogs, get up with fleas and turn them into a profitable act. And he was famous for his parties. To him they were grand epic films to be plotted, cast, produced and directed with great care and bravado. For everyone else they were a place to deal; to get some coveted assignment, to get close to that bankable star or studio executive; to converge, merge and emerge.

For Sidney Gross it was a place to get his rocks off.

Sidney Gross stood on the balcony of his Beverly Hills mansion. He was loosely wrapped in a green velour robe, watching hungry hills devour a blazing orange sun. Below him, a hive of uniformed servants buzzed about, lighting lanterns, decorating champagne fountains, setting buffet tables around a mammoth pool. He was supremely satisfied. At this moment, he was a long, long way from the poor, fat, miserable Brooklyn teenager who almost died at sixteen.

From the age of eleven, Sidney Gross had known he was different. But the difference had confounded him. All of his friends were obsessed with sports, girls and their own sex organs. They spoke incessantly of Suzie's jugs, dry-humping Jean and the "All-American" touchdown. But none of that interested him. Some of it made him ill. And, he was forever wrestling with his weight.

"Baby fat," his mother would say. "Baby fat." Then she'd shove just one more bagel into his mouth, "for Mama."

Kids at school teased him mercilessly about his tattered clothes, his "dinky" height and his corpulence. They called him fatty and midget and he spent his time in tears. By the time he was fourteen, he had developed defensive asthma and was granted permission to stay at home. A tutor was found for his schoolwork and when he wasn't studying, he was hopelessly engrossed in the T.V. set or some romantic novel. At sixteen he knew exactly what he would do with his life. If he couldn't live life's great dramas he would produce and direct them.

"I'm going to be a movie producer," he told his parents.

"Bum," replied his mother. "You'll be a bum."

"In the movies are only bums," his father agreed. "Bums and whores. You'll get a job in civil service like cousin Abe."

But his tutor, Robert, encouraged him. "You can be whatever you want to, Sidney, if you want to badly enough." He gave him books to read: Napoleon, Machiavelli and Camus, and they spoke endlessly of his future.

Robert showed him affection, taught him to believe in himself; enveloped him in laughter. One night the difference that had always puzzled him became clear.

When they were discovered, their arms wrapped about each other, there were words about hauling Robert into court on a morals charge, but Sidney swore he'd never cooperate. Shamed and tormented by his parents, burdened by so much loneliness, so much guilt, he slashed his wrists.

Near death when his mother found him, she called the doctor but spent the waiting time cleansing his blood from her carpet. He hovered near death accepting three transfusions and slowly his body healed. He searched unsuccessfully for Robert and at seventeen left home to make his way, knowing if he ever again saw blood, it would be someone else's. . . .

The lanterns below were glowing in the darkness and Sidney could see Tony Meredith rushing about issuing orders. In the ballroom, guitars were tuning, a drummer snared and the amplifiers shrieked. It was time for him to dress.

*   *   *

"Take that damn thing off," Jason shouted. "You look ridiculous."

"But Jason," Nicole pleaded. "You bought it for me yourself. Don't you remember? Last year, at Christmas."

He studied her dress. A simple black crepe with black satin piping. "Yeah, I remember. But something's wrong. You look awful in it now."

Twelve outfits lay on her bed. Each one had been carefully chosen, laboriously placed on then taken off her body. She had been unable to decide. The choice she finally made was the black crepe.

"I just don't know what to wear Jason," she said, her voice transmitting a sense of despair. "Help me, please."

Jason pushed abruptly past her, then flung open the mirrored doors. One by one he scrutinized her evening clothes, choosing finally a wine-colored two-piece silk jersey, with shoulder pads.

"Here. Wear this," he said, flinging it at her. "And get those pins out of your hair. Let it down for a change."

He began to walk away, then turned to her pointing an ominous finger. "One more thing, Nicole." She stood still. "Don't hang on me all night, for God's sake. Okay?" She nodded her head and began to dress.

Michael smiled at the mirror; one of those phoney smile to check his teeth and the shape of his moustache. He decided he should have gotten a haircut, then straightened his white safari suit and adjusted his brown silk shirt for the tenth time.

When the invitations first came, Viva and Michael enjoyed a good laugh. "If I want to see sharks, I'll go to Marineland," he said. Why would he want to go to Gross's party? But in the last few days, Michael had dined with most of Ada's clients, discovering they all had invitations. Now it was necessary to go. They would have to let Mason, Del Gado and all the others know they could play the game along with Sidney.

They were seated in the Jaguar, on their way to Gross's house. Viva adjusted her diamond necklace and rebuckled a gold lame sandal, occasionally checking for the right street.

"Tell me about Gross," Michael said.

"Let me put it this way, darling. He's as clever as Ada and as ruthless as Jason."

"Maybe you're exaggerating about Jason," Michael said. "His bark's probably worse than his bite."

She laughed derisively. "If you think that, I suggest you get a tetanus shot."

"That bad?" Michael said chuckling, stopping at a light.

"Worse," she insisted. Viva brushed lint from her gold lame jumpsuit and fluffed her magnificent hair with both hands.

"What I don't get is why Gross even invited us," Michael said. "He's better off without us being there."

"Ah, but this way he gets to see us squirm, or so he thinks. It turns him on. But I plan to have one hell of a good time in spite of him." She sighed and checked her manicure. "He learned that from Ada you know. Divide and conquer. It gets interesting results."

The light changed and Michael accelerated. "Another thing I don't understand about Jason . . . he seems to be doing fine."

"Bullshit, darling. He's in hock up to his hairy asshole. And even if he were doing fine, he'd still go for it. Like everyone in Hollywood, he runs on hi-octane greed."

She spotted the street sign. "There it is. Just pull it up. The valet will park it for you."

Michael stopped the Jaquar on Sunset, below the long hill up to Gross's house. A handsome blond pony-boy slapped at the hood, took Michael's keys and jockeyed the Jaguar away. Viva removed her gold lamé butterfly jacket and draped it across her bare shoulders. A white Rolls Royce pulled over and they entered.

"Mink," Viva said annoyed, running her hands across the upholstery. "It isn't enough for him to destroy human beings. He has to kill defenseless animals for pleasure too."

The chauffeur clicked open the bar displaying a variety of liquors. Viva chose some brandy. "Join me?" she asked. Michael declined and punched the video board. A game of electronic football appeared and the car began its journey.

At the top of the hill the Rolls turned to the right. Wrought-iron gates parted and they drove through.

Suddenly from the darkness, a towering castle materialized. It was covered with ivy, dramatically lit, with a drawbridge, turrets, even a moat.

"I'm going to pee," Viva said emerging from the Rolls, seeing a coat-of-arms a few feet away. Michael couldn't believe his eyes. He had seen castles like these on the Normandy Coast. This was definitely the real thing.

Raucous laughter, shouts of glee and loud rock music vaulted from the open doors as Viva drank the last of her brandy.

"You realize I hate all this bullshit," Michael said.

"I know. It's a sacrifice. But think of all those good marks you can show to God." She took his arm and walked across the drawbridge into an elegant ancient time. People were everywhere and Viva searched the pale-green rococo rooms for Sidney Gross. Instantly, she heard his shrill voice. Her eyes held to his direction and through smiling clenched teeth, she spoke to Michael.

"There he is darling, right near Hank." Michael followed the direction of her gaze. "Look at his face. Just like a praying mantis. You know, those little green things with big bug eyes and mouths made for piercing and sucking."

Michael stiffled a guffaw. She waved at Sidney and he gestured back. "And there's the cunt herself," she said as they entered another room.

Queen Roxanne was holding court sitting on a throne knee-deep in admiring princes and jesters, one of whom was her husband, Luis. She was stunning, a show-stopper, dressed in a navy tank dress embroidered with bugle beads, a Russian silver fox cape draped across her back. Viva looked at her in disgust.

"Imagine," she told Michael. "All those poor little foxes died for her sins."

"She is gorgeous," Michael said watching her.

"Silicone," Viva whispered. "All of it silicone. Ass, tits, armpits. Her toes, for all I know. You name the surgery, she's had it."

They walked a bit farther. "There's Hugh," Viva shouted. "I'll see you later. Do try to have a good time." She kissed his cheek and sailed away.

He watched her dissolve into the throng and felt intensely proud of her. She had really pulled her life together after Maurice's death, he thought. Seemingly, none of his fears for her had materialized.

Michael entered the huge dim ballroom and was overcome by the enormous crowd. For just an instant he felt like running. He knew what this business had done to Ada, Viva, to Maurice, to Jason. All of these people were a part of that.

He stood there contemplating them. A galaxy of luminaries, stars dressed in stone-washed jeans, diamonds, satins, and furs, draped across silk-print chaises and green velvet side chairs sipping expensive champagne. Some stood against pale-green woven silk walls near silver rococo candlestands lighting cigarettes. Those not chatting, drinking, laughing were huddled on the dance floor under candlelit crystal chandeliers dancing to soft pop music. The room was bathed in shimmering shadows and when a candle flame brushed a crystal drop, fireflies ignited.

Del Gado was there, in tight black pants, an open black silk shirt, a large gold crucifix around his neck. Beautiful women stood on either side of him and above the din, Michael could hear Hank Mason's wild cowboy *whoop*. Elaine Shagan lounged in a dark corner, much to his surprise, with Viva's chauffeur. He remembered Viva's words about dividing and conquering.

Across the room, alone near the French doors, he spotted Nicole. He stood there just gazing at her. She looked lovely and delicate in some kind of silk jersey that flowed down her body like fine wine. Her thick honey hair was curled, brushed to one side and a huge butterfly made of white silk and seed pearls nestled behind her ear.

She waved to him and he weaved his way through the crowd. The music grew suddenly loud and Nicole covered her ears.

"C'mon outside," she said. "There's a great gourmet buffet and a fantastic garden." He followed her through the open doors into the jasmine night.

Champagne flowed from flower fountains and giant ice sculptures filled with caviar, crab and lobster ringed the pool. Caterers flipped omelettes, prepared tempura and offered exotic curry dishes. A beautiful girl in a string bikini lay in the pool floating on a pair of red rubber lips. Her eyes were shut and she was high on something.

Michael held two hollow-stemmed crystals goblets under the champagne, then offered one to Nicole.

"Here's to you," he said touching her glass.

"Back at you," she answered and they drank. "Isn't this exciting?" she said. "I've never been to a party like this before."

Michael looked puzzled. "I thought you worked for Sidney at one time."

I did. For about four months. That was a long time ago. That's where I met Jason. Sidney just wasn't that big then. He's known for these parties, you know," she said. "He gave one on the grounds of some mortuary once. He's had them on trains, blimps, submarines. Last year, he flew fifty people to Paris for breakfast."

Michael listened, watching her amber eyes glow with excitement.

"You'll see," she went on, "at the end of the evening, there'll be a surprise of some kind."

The music began and Nicole closed her eyes, swaying to the rhythm.

"C'mon, kid," Michael said, smiling. "I get the message." He took her hand, ignoring her snicker and led her into the ballroom. His arm circled her waist, his hand caressing the curve of her buttock and began to dance her through the crowd. Her breasts pressed against his chest and he felt intoxicated. She pressed even closer to him, resting her head against his chin and he was bombarded with sensations he couldn't identify.

"Where's Jason?" he asked defensively.

"Business," she replied and snuggled her head back to the warmth of his neck.

* * *

Sidney sat at his library desk watching Jason pace. He fingered a brass plaque which bore the inscription, "You Are Who You Eat." Tony Meredith watched them both.

"Calm down, Stone, before you blast off."

"This is big, Sid," Jason said turning swiftly. "A merger between Stone and Gross—"

Sidney choked.

"Excuse me, 'Gross and Stone,' would be phenomenal. Can you imagine all those bankables combined into one talent pool? Shit! The industry'd be on their fuckin' knees to us. We'd own the keys to every bank in the world."

"It's a wonderful idea, Jason. But then you always have wonderful ideas." Gross rose. "I'll tell you what. When you figure out how to get rid of your kid brother, Hugh Parker, your sister, Viva, Max . . . and, of course, Ada—" He took Jason's hand and escorted him to the door, "—then we have a deal."

Jason stood there peering into Sidney's eyes looking for the loophole. "You mean that?"

"Sure I mean it," Sidney said opening the door. "Keep in touch."

"I will," Jason said walking out. "I will."

Sidney slammed the door. "Like mother, like motherfucker," he told Tony and sat down. "That guy makes me laugh. Right now, he's at a two-dollar window in a million-dollar horserace. Tony," he sighed, "take a note. Next week we contact Mike Stone regarding a merger."

Tony looked up, his pen still scribbling on the note pad and smiled.

Jason made his way up a labyrinth of stairs and hallways back to the ballroom. He wondered if Gross really meant what he said. Of course he had. If he could pull this off, the way that he wanted to, that would be a coup. If not, there was always Max.

Michael caught Jason's circuitous route through the melee. Instantly, he was aware of how closely he was holding Nicole and drew apart from her.

"Hey, squirt," Jason said approaching them on the dance floor. "Do me a favor, will you? Take Nicole home. I've got some things to take care of.'' He didn't wait for an answer. He just patted Michael's shoulder, pinched Nicole's cheek and headed for the door.

Shauna Candelli and Sally Quinn had just removed their wraps. They were standing at a foyer mirror repairing their makeup. Upon seeing his reflection, Shauna screamed.

''Uncle Jason.'' She turned and ran to him perching her delicate fingers upon his shoulders. Jason grinned and hoisted her up.

''Hey, you're getting beautiful,'' he said placing her down. ''I'll have to make you a star I guess.''

She whirled, her silky brown hair flying about her face, setting off brown fawnlike eyes.

''Not bad,'' he said. ''Not bad at all.''

All at once, warm, velvet fingers with curved fuscia nails curled around his palm.

''Hello,'' a sexy voice crooned. ''I'm Sally Quinn. You must be Jason.'' Irridescent blue eyes collected the room's light and flashed it back at him.

Jason was startled. ''Now where have I seen you before?'' he asked. Shauna looked at Jason as if he were crazy.

''Don't you watch T.V.? The Olympics? Sally's a gold medal winner,'' Shauna said.

''Ah yes,'' Jason said remembering. ''You do all those makeup commercials now.''

''Right,'' Sally said sliding very close to him. ''Why are you leaving Uncle Jason? It's far too early.''

Jason couldn't take his eyes off her. Her shiny blonde hair cascaded down her shoulders and her healthy complexion was flawless.

''I have some things to do,'' he said, ''but why can't the three of us have lunch next week?''

Shauna turned to Sally Quinn. Sally lowered her head and her silky blonde hair swept over her face. She peered up at Jason, a wicked smile on her lips. ''We'd love to Uncle Jason,'' she said, letting her fingernails click along the buttons of his vest. ''Next week then,'' Sally whispered. She took Shauna's arm, those blue, blue eyes still focused on Jason and glided toward the staircase.

Her body was typical of an athlete's, he thought as she

walked away: healthy, hardy and restless. How fortunate to have run into them both. He was orchestrating another part of his plan and if Shauna refused to help him, he was sure Sally Quinn would oblige.

"Are you sure you want to do this Sidney?" Tony Meredith asked. He couldn't believe his ears. "Stealing that casket from the cemetery and torching it at the lake was one thing."

Sidney chuckled. "Yeah! That was real fun. Bastard sold more damn records dead than alive. Besides, he wanted to be cremated. I did him a goddamn favor."

They were speaking of the late Dusty Hammer and the publicity stunt Sidney had engineered after his death last year.

"But this is going too far," Tony insisted.

Sidney rose, his fingers caressing the plaque on his desk. "You just make that phone call and I'll worry about the rest. No one's going to get hurt. You get squeamish on me and you can look for another job. I know what's best for Roxanne."

Down below in Sidney's game room, a different party was taking place. Hot music, loud pulsating punk rock blared on a quad-sound system. A single light traveling through a color wheel turned the dancers different shades of the rainbow. At five-minute intervals a strobe flashed and the room full of dancers appeared jerky and uncoordinated. People played pinball, video games and fondled each other. The smell of grass and hash mingled with perfume, sweat, musk and the "food" in crystal bowls included top-grade coke, China white, amphetamines, barbiturates, Quaaludes, anything a chic doper could wish for.

Along a raised walkway, Sally Quinn stripped her clothes to the beat of hypnotic music. Everyone cheered, egging her on. Shauna sat on a couch in the rear, her head rolling back and forth while somebody sucked on her toes. The music stopped and Sally removed the last of her garments arrogantly celebrating her body. She sniffed coke, drank wine and when the music started again she began rocking her hips. Her breasts bounced with each jerky movement and as she sank to her knees someone pushed cocaine into her vagina. It seared her moist, tender flesh and as the light came red, a pair of powerful arms lifted her into the air.

She was high, she was laughing and her vagina was on fire. The man with powerful arms threw her down roughly onto a daybed. "You're too much baby," he said, then grabbed her hand, grinding it into his crotch. "Feel this," he said holding onto her wrist. She pressed his hard huge growth, then pulled him down to her.

"Fuck her, fuck her," the crowd chanted.

She gripped his belt and clawed at his zipper until his pants came off, then his shirt. Exposed, in a golden light, he was a rippling Greek God, a hunter poised for the kill.

He teased her with his cock, rubbing it all over her, until she begged for it and the crowd grew frenzied.

"Go, go, go, go, go," they yelled and began to rhythmically clap.

She lay there writhing on the daybed, her legs bent at the knees exposing her fiery, glistening parts.

"Go, go, go, go, go," they screamed until he mounted her. She arched her buttocks up to receive him then threw her legs around his broad shoulders.

The sight of his moving buttocks, the sound of flesh slapping flesh, drove the crowd wild. "Come, come, come," people screamed until the man and Sally Quinn came, howling like two wild animals in a lonely night. Then they fell apart and passed out.

Michael heard a familiar voice. "Hey Stone! How are you, buddy?" It was Armando Del Gado. He was marching toward them, flanked by a feminine honor guard. Armando was grinning. There were introductions and Nicole extended her hand to him. Armando grasped it tightly, brushing his lips across her fingertips, his eyes lewdly examining her.

Del Gado told Michael he had enjoyed their lunch and was looking forward to their upcoming trip. There was some self-conscious chatter about the terrific party, then, the blonde in black satin whispered in Del Gado's ear. He cackled obscenely. "C'mon *mujer*. We go downstairs and boogie." He bowed gallantly, winking at Nicole. "Adios, *muchachos*," he said. "See you later."

Then Hank Mason ambled by, a short cute redhead on his arm. "Howdy, Mr. Stone," he said, tipping the brim of his white felt Stetson. The facets of a ten-karat diamond ring ricocheted off the light and strafed the walls. Hank was slightly drunk but still elegant and country charming.

"Hello, Hank," Michael said. "This is Nicole."

"Real nice to meet yaw'l," Hank drawled. "This here's my wife, Alma. Say howdy to the people, Alma," Hank said. Alma launched a few daggers at him then walked away.

"She's purty," Mason apologized, "but she's yankee hot." He looked uncomfortable and embarrassed. They all did. " 'Scuse me please," he added touching his brim and followed after her.

In a few seconds, loud angry words passed between Mason and his wife. Then Mason grabbed her arm, ripping her filmy dress. A crowd encircled them, and the words grew more harsh and ugly.

Michael hated to interfere but somebody had to do something. The columnists would have a field day. Before he could reach him, Hank Mason stormed out, a bottle of Russian Vodka under his arm, his bodyguard Big Al after him.

Sidney heard the altercation from the hallway. He ran in and grabbed the microphone. "Attention, everyone," he shouted. "Attention please." Nicole took Michael's arm.

"Out front," Sidney announced, "are busses. Get your coats and have a seat. The champagne's on ice. We're going on an excursion."

The night was dazzling, clear and they boarded huge luxury buses drinking icey champagne. They sat on mink-lined seats laughing, causing a ruckus at red lights, offering goblets of bubbly through open windows to passersby.

Some smoked grass, snorted coke or dipped cigarettes in China white. Nobody worried about police. Two off-duty cops were being paid to escort them by motorcade through the streets. If the cops saw anything illegal, they made no allusions.

The buses arrived at Marina del Rey and at the sight of the brigantine everyone grew more rowdy and applauded. The *American Lady* looked as though she had been lifted out of the pages of history. A one-hundred-eighty-foot, three-masted schooner rig, carrying over 5,000 feet of sail; she looked like a pirate's treasure.

They boarded quickly, squealing with delight, jostling one another, gaping at the sheer size. Nicole clung to Michael waiting anxiously for the brigantine to sail.

"End tie," someone shouted. There was an echo, a series of orders issued from the bridge, then they were on their way.

Below deck, six cooks were at work arranging a melange of fruits, confections, cheeses and imported wines. All about the midnight blue harbor, ships' masts and their bridges were ablaze with flashing lights and clanging bells, wishing a happy Fourth of July.

"This must be heaven," Nicole whispered to Michael. He sniffed the salty fresh air, and smiled. He couldn't have agreed with her more.

"Are you cold?" he asked her.

"No. I feel so alive. I feel marvelous."

He watched the moon sweeping the waters, silver-tipping the waves, complimenting scattered stars, finally glowing in Nicole's bright eyes.

A combo began to play and Michael didn't ask. He just swept Nicole into his arms and they swayed to the music. All at once, there was no band, no crowd, no ship or harbor; it was just the two of them silently skimming the ocean's mist.

The brigantine slowed and the noisy throng covered the top deck, laughing, cavorting, climbing up and down the intricate rigging, to the dismay of the earnest crew.

Suddenly thunder rumbled nearby and the dark velvet sky ignited and crackled. Everyone stared as a shower of sparks, red, white and blue, glowed, then rained down on them. All around them, colorful explosions, pinwheels curling, rockets screeching, bursting forth from the ocean floor, exploding and glowing, dissolving into the night.

"Fireworks," Nicole shouted, her voice filled with excitement and wonder.

Fireworks, he thought. For him, they had gone off half an hour ago.

They were half-way to Catalina Island when a sudden gust of wind swept across the ship and swung her completely around. Some of the passengers screamed, were thrown to the deck while others steadied themselves against the rigging. The sails slapped violently, the deck vibrated and the timbers squealed.

Then, all at once, the wind died and it grew deathly quiet. From out of nowhere an eerie pink fog bank drifted towards the *American Lady* and the malodorous smell of mildew permeated the air.

''We're having some problems everyone,'' Sidney Gross yelled out. ''Don't anyone panic. We'll have it fixed in a jiffy.'' Then he just disappeared. The ship buzzed with tension and speculation.

Michael had fallen away from Nicole and was caught in some ropes while she sat huddled, against the ship's bowside observing the strange pink fog as it drifted closer still. She heard a sound and turned her head in its direction. A large, wet hand slid across her mouth, another around her waist and her heart almost stopped.

''Don't say one word,'' a man's voice whispered ominously in her ear. ''Don't call out or I'll kill you.'' She felt the unmistakable sensation of a knife point at her throat and her blood curdled.

Suddenly the sails of the *Lady* took the wind again and the pink fog floated across the deck of the ship. There was a loud rumble like the sound of thunder, then columns of red and blue smoke surrounded them. Nicole knew then that was happening.

Through the fog and smoke, men came flying through the air dressed in black tights and gaudy shirts, sporting eye patches, brandishing swords. The *American Lady* had been boarded and seized by Hollywood pirates on the high seas.

Framed by the rigging, a grand Spanish galleon finally emerged from the fog bank and drifted toward them. A pirate captain sailed on board and paraded the deck. He was lecherous, wore an earring and sported a beard. ''I am a free prince of the open seas,'' he declared dramatically. ''I claim this ship as my prize.'' His accent was pure Brooklyn.

A one-eyed pirate captured Nicole and was about to strip her. "Aye, me proud beauty," he cried. "I'll show you the meaning of love." But she had already been claimed and a sword fight ensued. As Michael watched, the two pirates parried and thrust, thrashing their way across the deck and up into the rigging. Their steel sharp swords clinked together and Max Factor's blood spilled all around them. Everyone cheered.

"Shall we throw them overboard, mates?" the captain yelled when the fight had ended.

"Yes!" screamed a group near Michael, and they promptly did.

Nicole finally slipped away from her captor and ran towards Michael.

"Seize him," a pirate yelled out. They grabbed Michael and put him in irons. One man came to his rescue and they quickly hung him; another was made to walk the plank.

"Standby to starboard," the captain yelled and everyone cheered. From out of nowhere, Wagnerian music blared out across the ocean and into the dark night.

"How goes the wind," the captain shouted, lifting a bottle of wine to his lips.

"Nor'westerly and steady, sir," came the reply.

"Take the wheel, Mr. Stewart," the captain commanded.

"Aye, aye, Captain. Make the way," he called above.

"Sail-ho," yelled the lookout. "Sail on the lee-quarter."

There was a rumble of drums, the firing of cannons and the *American Lady* began to move.

"Ho, all you rumheads," the captain yelled. "You are all my prisoners and tonight we set sail for Tortuga."

Chapter 5

VIVA WAS DROWNING, her body spinning wildly in a murky whirlpool, her flesh devoured by hordes of tiny fishes.

"Eat! you bastards, eat!" she screamed.

One by one they sank sharp teeth into her flesh, ripping, chewing, rapidly swallowing. She felt no pain; just an interminable spinning and the hopelessness of it all.

The telephone rang, jarring her from the nightmare and she was grateful. Her heart still pounding, her fingers shaking, she cradled the phone between her ear and shoulder.

"Yes?" she said breathlessly, lying back down on her bed. She listened attentively to the caller, her eyes growing wide and alert, a bulbous knot growing in her stomach.

By the time the call was concluded she had examined all the graceless humps and crevices on the acoustical ceiling and was unconsciously holding her breath.

"Thanks," she said finally. "You deserve one hell of a bonus for this. I'll see that Parker sends it to you."

She hung up and searched the nightstand for a cigarette. Finding one, she lit it and leaned back onto the satin pillow, smoke curling leisurely from her lips. She glanced quickly at Davey's sleeping figure. His closed eyes and forehead were almost obscured by a shock of long yellow curls, his breathing, deep and even.

It was almost noon and she would have to call Michael. But first she would have to find the right words.

* * *

Michael was seated in Ada's office, his thoughts involuntarily drifting. No matter how hard he tried concentrating, images of last night and Nicole barged in. He rose, ran his sweaty palms along his jeans and poured himself a cold drink at the bar.

Lingering, he admired the natural oak wood panels that graced the sturdy bar cabinet with its matching paneled wall and ran his fingers lightly across the tiny herringbone patterns. It had been recently oiled and his fingertips left unsightly smear prints.

Determined to take care of business this time, he reached for the itinerary Elaine had prepared for him.

Del Gado's Lear jet would leave tonight precisely at ten. For the next two or three days they'd be in San Francisco shooting pickups near the Golden Gate Bridge. Several suites had been reserved at the Mark Hopkins Hotel on Nob Hill and two Cadillac limousines would be at their disposal.

Elaine had sent the press release Michael had prepared and an interview had been scheduled with a reporter from the San Francisco *Chronicle* for Sunday afternoon. By granting the interview, not only would Del Gado's ego be stroked but there'd be an opportunity for Michael to make a statement on his own. All the wire services had picked up on conflicting releases and the hint of a split within S.M.A.'s ranks had been suggested by the media.

There were also credit cards, an envelope with cash and a proposed shooting schedule. Elaine had even suggested a wardrobe he should pack, taking into account the weather and possible invitations. Very efficient, he thought. Very efficient indeed.

The telephone rang and Michael answered.

"Hiya beautiful. I'm glad you called." He fingered a film cassette which lay on top of an 8 X 10 glossy photo. "I've got this screen test Ada ordered the day she got sick." He picked up the photo. "It's some guy named Paul Kiley. Any ideas?"

He waited a moment for Viva's reply, then placed the photo back down. "Fine, I'll have Elaine send it by messenger on Monday. What's up?"

He picked up a pencil and started doodling absentmindedly on a pad. As Viva spoke he could feel his heart begin to throb and his mouth go dry. The continuing heavy pressure he was exerting on the pad caused his pencil point to finally snap.

He reached for his cold drink and pressed it against his hot, drumming forehead.

"You're joking," he said when she was finally though.

"No. I'm not," she answered. "My God, I wish I were."

"Where the hell is he now?"

"At the investigator's, sleeping it off. Ada employs a couple of P.I.s to take care of things like this." She recited the address.

"Very efficient," Michael said writing it down on a slip of paper. "And you want *me* to get him?" His voice reflected the disgust he was feeling. "Is that it?"

"Yes. Of course. And do go easy on him, darling. He was bombed out of his head. Probably doesn't even remember a thing."

"How convenient. Should I remind him or spare his delicate home-grown sensibilities?"

"Don't be cute, Michael."

"Cute? Is that what you think I'm being? I'm surprised at you. In my opinion he should be turned over to the authorities, not protected like this."

"For God's sake, Michael. Stop it. He's a human being who made a mistake."

"Some mistake. And you want me to look the other way, right?" She didn't answer. "Is that what Ada would have done?"

"Yes," Viva answered. "Hank's morals are really his own damn business." He sensed her growing anger but he felt justified continuing.

"Not when you ask me to wipe his ass they're not. If you're so hot to save Hank Mason, save him yourself."

"Listen to me, Mike Stone," Viva said. Her voice was seething now and he was stunned. He couldn't recall a time in his life when his sister sounded like this. "It's time you clearly understood that what we are saving is this business—Ada's business—and not Hank Mason. Stop being so goddamn self-righteous. Where the hell do you think the money for your fine Ivy League education came from, not to mention all those expensive trips to Europe and the South Pacific? Don't you dare set your lofty standards up as examples for the rest of us to follow. Everybody makes mistakes; don't you forget that. As far as Hank Mason is concerned, he *is* your responsibility. You're the president, like it or not, and protecting him is part of your job."

Viva loudly clicked off and the sudden snap popped his eardrum.

"Goddamnit!" he shouted, standing, kicking at the chair. He slammed the phone onto its cradle and swept his arm across the desktop. Pads and pencils sailed, the telephone flew apart and thumped its way down to the floor. All of Elaine's neatly placed papers rustled up then settled softly like snow flurries.

He paced angrily between the desk and the bar, one fist smashing into the other palm. He was furious at Mason, upset about Viva and disappointed in himself.

Once again he had allowed someone to con him. Hank Mason, passing himself off as a decent, simple, down-home kind of guy when all he really was was a fraud—a human dirty trick. And so much more than the imposter, he hated the fool. The trusting little pigeon sitting neatly on some fence waiting for some breadcrumbs, eating a bullet.

His fury was fierce and he drove his boot recklessly against the bar and its delicate paneled wall. Again and again the tip of his heavy boot kicked swiftly, violently until one of the panels splintered and bounced off. Then he just stood there, silent and still, utterly surprised at what he was seeing.

Hidden neatly inside, behind the panel was a perfect gem of a safe and he bent to examine it.

It was wired into the security system and there was no way to open it without summoning the police. He thought first of that elusive pouch he'd been searching for all over the place then automatically of his old buddy Van Tilden.

He repaired and replaced the splintered panel as best he could, then covered it with the fig tree. It looked fine. He checked a number in his personal phonebook, dialed and left a message on Van Tilden's machine.

They drove in utter silence, Hank nudging his rumpled body against the Jaguar door, Michael staring straight ahead at the darkness ceremoniously attending the road. The crowded freeway was bursting with holiday travel and the drive home was filled with endless stops and starts.

Hank began to fidget. "Mind if I play the radio?" he asked. The words almost hid inside his throat.

"No. Go ahead," Michael answered in a monotone.

Hank switched on the radio tuning in a country-and-western station. He pushed back, leaning against the door again, pretending to listen to the music. He tried smiling at Michael. "I sure do appreciate your coming to get me," Hank said. "I never could learn to drive."

Michael was silent.

Hank stared at the multitude of cars ahead. All those damn red lights, blinking and glaring, flashing and flaring made him remember something he had forgotten.

He was somewhere in Mexico at a private nightclub and the flashing red lights all around were making him dizzy. Heavy acrid smoke clung to the ceiling and one loudly beating conga drum reverberated in his brain.

On stage, he watched the slavemaster—a dark-skinned naked boy, tightly close a leather cockring around the huge genitalia of a naked blond captive. The captive's wrists were tied securely with chains while a dog collar kept his neck rigid.

To sensuous, heavy drumbeats the slavemaster slowly curled and twisted his body spreading glistening oil on his captive's muscular frame. Then, with one loud drumbeat, he stopped, produced and displayed a leather whip to the spectators, flailing and snapping it high in the air.

"Ole!" The crowd screamed rising to their feet.

Suddenly Hank felt heat throbbing at his insides and it frightened him.

Thwack! The first hard blow struck the slave's leg. He wailed to the audience but his cock grew huge and stiff.

"Ole!" The crowd cried again.

Thwack! The slavemaster struck the slave's thighs and the audience gasped. He was only an inch away from hitting the slave's genitalia. Against the red backlight, his engorged, choking prick jutted out perpendicular to his struggling torso and his testicles stood stretched and swollen from the ring.

Thwack! Hank could feel the last angry blow as it struck the slave's glistening red penis and the fear it generated inside him made him run from the club. He searched frantically for Big Al then remembered losing him an hour ago at a cockfight. Loaded out of his mind, confused and terrified, he needed someone to keep it from happening again. . . .

Michael hit the brakes, thrusting his arm across Hank's chest. Hank missed cracking his skull on the dashboard by inches.

"You okay?" Michael asked.

"Yeah, sure," Hank said shivering. He pushed his way back into the safety of his corner.

A yellow cab pulled alongside the Jaguar and the driver recognized Hank, waved hello. Hank weakly returned the enthusiastic gesture then watched the yellow streak ahead. He remembered that other taxi in Mexico.

He'd been with the Mexican cab driver for two hours, ever since he had left the nightclub and they'd been in and out of several low-down bars. Hank was growing angry and suspicious. The driver had made several promises he wasn't keeping and Hank decided he would end the game. He guzzled the last of his tequila.

"Hey cocksucker. Put up or shut up. I can always get it in America you know, land of opportunity."

He demanded that the driver get him what he wanted, cursing him, profaning his country, defaming his family. The cabbie spit on him. Who the hell does this Hank gringo think he is anyway? He tossed him out on his ass, near a bus depot, screamed his own choice expletives and left Hank lying in a trail of chicken dust.

"Christ!" Michael suddenly shouted. A van pushed

across three lanes of traffic cutting him off. He braked and swerved muttering to himself.

"There's one of them reasons I don't drive," Hank said. "My reflexes just ain't quick enough to handle that."

Michael adjusted the rear-view mirror and kicked over the glare panel. Hank began shaking again. He took a deep breath and placed his hands between his thighs. "Shit! Ain't you gonna say anything?" Hank cried out.

"There's nothing to say," Michael said. His voice was without expression.

"Now that's a crock of hot shit. You're saving it up, Mike. Jesus, I can feel it. At least tell me you hate the sight of me."

Loud static noises brought Hank's fingers quickly to the radio selector button. It was then his finger began to throb and he noticed the lightly burned flesh on his finger tip. A Greyhound bus squealed by and Hank covered his nose and eyes against the fumes trying to blot out the memory.

The fumes inside the old Tijuana bus depot were sickening. Monoxide mixed with urine and sour wine. Hank held his breath and weaved his way over to the counter. In halting Spanish he asked his questions. Yes, there would be a bus back to the U.S. border in a few hours and no, he did not want to use the telephone. At this precise moment he hated everyone, and everything. And especially he hated Mexico.

He sat on a bench watching some rickety old bus unload its passengers. Around him, a few winos lay sleeping huddled across wooden benches, clutching paper sacks with empty wine bottles. There were some ludes in his pocket and he slipped one into his mouth swallowing until the large white tablet eased far down into his throat. When the bus had finally emptied the last of its human cargo the driver blasted his horn and drove off.

Michael waited as an impatient horn sounded, then another. All the lanes had stalled and frustration was mounting. Up ahead, there was an accident and Michael strained to see. Two policemen on motorcycles whizzed by Hank's side of the car and his body grew instantly rigid reflecting his panic. The Jaguar idled waiting for traffic to begin when Hank noticed a pretty, young boy in another car. His dark eyes were glowing under a fringe of thick bangs the color of a raven's wing and he smiled. Hank quickly covered his face with his arm tossing his head against the bucket seat. His blackened finger was on fire again as he recalled the beginning of the incident.

Inside the bus depot, he saw the boy's dark eyes and instantly felt heat, between his thighs. There was something about the black iris sitting like bits of glowing anthracite on fresh snow that excited him. And then, there were those lips. Young, full-blown tea roses, ready to burst into a dark and juicy red. The boy's gaze rested on Hank, then he smiled, approached and asked Hank for a light. When Hank held the match to the boy's face, he deliberately gripped Hank's wrist until the flame died on Hank's fingertips. Neither said a word.

"Mind if I smoke?" Michael said, slipping his pipe into his mouth. Hank was startled, examining Mike's expression.

"Shit, no. You're welcome to it." He watched Michael's unsuccessful search for a pipe lighter, then reached into his jacket to look for a match. It was then that Hank remembered everything.

Now they were in the depot toilet together, alone. The boy urinated watching Hank's face, a tantalizing smile on his lips. His pointed, syrupy tongue traced the line of his full dark lower lip and Hank knew he had to fuck him. He was wracked with so much desire he thought he would burst into flames.

Oh God! How young is he? Thirteen, fourteen? No. Don't think about it.

Hank unzipped his trousers and stood at the urinal. He knew the boy wanted him, but he also wanted money. How much? Not enough. More? The boy grew restless. Hank was afraid he would leave. Oh God, no! Don't leave. Take it. Take it all.

Hank removed his last hundred dollar bill from a money clip and flapped it high in the air. The boy nodded and the deal had been struck. Hank folded the bill the long way into a strip.

"If you want it dark eyes, you'll have to suck for it," he said and slowly removed his belt. He wrapped the thinly folded bill under his balls and around the shaft of his penis pulling it all up tightly. The young boy laughed and fell to his knees. Hank yanked the bill tighter about him as though it were a cockring and struck the boy with the belt.

Oh God, it was working. The erection he could not sustain with Alma or anyone for that matter was firm and hot and the explosions it set off in his stomach, his balls, his asshole and his brain were what he had been dreaming of and suppressing for the last five years.

Thwack! The boy worked harder sucking on his penis, his pursed lips eating their way to the money. Mother of God, take it, take it, take that! He couldn't remember anything after that, just a door slamming, the boy's bloody face and pandemonium.

"Oh God, no!" Hank yelled. He lost control sobbing, thrashing about, wailing and screaming outloud. Michael was stunned. He lost his voice and sat there paralyzed as Hank ripped his own flesh and punched the sides of his skull.

"Stop it!" Michael heard himself repeating. "Stop it."

They were traveling at ten miles an hour creeping past the Santa Monica Freeway turnoff when Hank opened the door and bolted from the moving car, and rolled about on an island. Around him, brakes screeched, lights blinded his eyes, horns blasted loudly away. He stood and screamed for somebody to hit him. One driver called him a "fuckin' maniac," another gave him the finger. A VW screeched to a halt and barely hit Hank as he ran across two lanes to the dark ivy hillside. He finally made it onto the ivy, staggering, then falling down the steep hill, crushing the foliage with his body. And then he lay there, sobbing, howling, ripping the thick ivy vines up by their gnarled roots.

When Michael finally reached him he was twitching and bloody. He looked pathetic and beaten. And Michael could feel his pain.

He grabbed Hank's shoulders and raised his torso halfway up. "It's okay Hank. It's okay now." He searched Hank's wild and rolling eyes, insisting they focus on him.

"God! Help me, Mike, please," Hank wailed. "That boy was only twelve. I . . . I could have killed him. Oh God, Jesus."

Michael wanted to vomit, but he fought it back, holding Hank's head in his palms, wiping away some blood from the sides of his lips.

"I'll do everything I can," Michael said. "I promise you that. I'm leaving for Frisco in a few hours and when I get back we'll find help for you. Trust me."

Hank opened his heavy-lidded eyes and the tears spilled down his cheeks. His head nodded and his arms hung onto Michael's shoulders.

"Let's go home now," Michael said. "You need to rest."

Michael held him, patting his back, realizing a kind of compassion he never thought he could feel, knowing again how beautiful Viva really was and how much further he had still, to go in this life. Pain was pain, whether it ate at a person's guts or his psyche.

The small crowd gathering to see the human spectacle did not recognize the singing millionaire whose voice was Number One all over America. Yet, there he was, Hank Mason, country singing cowboy, Everyman's buddy, Everygirl's sweetheart, Everymother's son, reduced to groveling in a pile of thick and filthy ivy, home to all things that slither and crawl.

Michael dropped Hank at his Beverly Hills home in the care of Dr. Morgenstern, whom he trusted and Big Al who was there, waiting. They would carefully watch him until Michael returned from San Francisco when Hank could be given the support and assistance he desperately needed.

Michael parked the Jaguar in the garage where Duggan stood slowly polishing Ada's green Rolls Royce. His crinkly blue eyes were steady on the fender as Michael secured the Jag's alarm, placing the keys in his pocket.

"How be your mother, Michael me boy?" he asked, his lilting voice edged in Irish.

"She's the same Duggan. No change. In fact I saw her this morning."

"You'd best be getting on if you're wanting to be making your plane," Duggan said tossing away the rag he was using. "I'll be outside in front when you're needing me."

"Thanks," Michael said smiling. "I'll be ready."

Inside Ada's office, he poured himself a stiff drink and checked the service for messages. Van Tilden had returned his call an hour ago. He swallowed his drink in one gulp and rubbed the back of his stiff neck. Then, he dialed the number he'd scribbled on some piece of paper and waited till Van answered.

"Hey good buddy," Van shouted, laughing uproariously. "What the hell kind of trouble you into this time?"

"You got the wrong guy Van. I just miss you."

"The hell you do," Van told him. "You ever call me when you ain't in some kind of shit?"

Michael couldn't wait. "You won't believe this Van, but there's this safe I need to get into." He cringed, holding the phone away from his ear.

"A safe? Shitfire, boy, are you nuts?"

"If I remember correctly, you still owe me one," Michael said bringing the phone back to his ear. The silence that followed was loud and Michael knew he had him.

"I don't know what the hell you're talking about," Van insisted.

"If I can refresh your memory, I seem to recall picking your face up from the floor of some sleazy bar in Honolulu, then paying a physical debt you owed a sailor."

"Oh shiftfire, boy. Not that old thing again." Van thought for a moment. "Whose safe is it?"

"My mother's, but it's legit. She sick and . . ."

Van interrupted. "Shitfire, boy," he said. "Save it for the police. Just tell me what it looks like."

"There's a number combination; it's set into the wall with magnetic switches and some heat sensors. I just hope it's not burglarproof."

"No such animal," Van said confidently, laughing at him. "My thermal lance can burn through six inches of tempered steel in fifteen seconds. Did you see any smoke detectors?''

''Didn't notice. Do you think you can do it?''

''Trust me good buddy. The damn thing won't know what hit it. I'll be in Los Angeles in a few days and I'll buzz you then. Line up some broads like old times, will ya?''

Michael laughed. ''How many can an old geezer like you handle these days?''

Van Tilden shouted ''shitfire, boy'' one more time and clicked off the line.

Michael glanced at his watch. He had just enough time to throw a few things in a bag and catch Duggan out front. He'd call Viva from the Rolls and tell her all was well. Then he'd meet Del Gado at the airport and sleep on the plane.

Chapter 6

JASON WATCHED the last pair of lazy smoke rings rise toward the canopy, then he ground out his cigarette stub. Sally Quinn raked her long red fingernails across his broad hairy chest. They were sated, lying on a plump brass bed in Sally's rustic Malibu apartment and it was long past midnight.

Outside, wild ocean waves rhythmically rolled up the shallow beach crashing violently below while moonlight glanced through the bay window licking their naked bodies.

Jason twisted the ends of Sally's long blonde hair, brushing them lightly across her nipples.

"What is it you want from life, Sally?" Jason asked

"Everything I can get my hands on," Sally said without pause.

Jason smiled, watching as she reached for a champagne glass. She had a long smooth back, creamy skin and well-developed legs.

"We're a lot alike Sally," he said. "You like excitement, money, power, the good life. I wish Shauna wanted all that. But, I suppose that's her mother's fault. Shauna's always lived in Viva's shadow." He waited for some feedback, but she remained quiet, sipping champagne, watching him. "How long have you two been friends?" he added.

"About six months," Sally said placing her empty glass down. "We're pretty tight though. Do everything together."

"Then you must know all of her close friends."

"Hah!" Sally exclaimed. "What friends? She only has eyes for Chris Parker and he's a born loser. He might even be a goddamn fag for all I know."

Jason was taken by surprise at the extent of Sally's resentment toward Chris but utterly delighted with the information she was providing him.

"Now what makes you say all that?" Jason asked, his deep brown eyes glowing with false alarm, his husky voice padded with concern.

"Oh, I don't know. I guess I just don't like him too much. He's got nothing to offer, he can't go anywhere, do anything. She could do a hell of alot better."

Jason studied her for a moment then turned his gaze toward the window. "You know something? You're right, Sally. In fact, I've been doing alot of thinking about her. If Chris is as bad as you say, then I'll have to discourage her from seeing him anymore."

Sally bellowed with laughter. "Are you crazy? You and what goddamn army? You'll never get her away from Chris. There isn't a thing in the world you could do or say that would tear her away from him."

Jason smiled and poured champagne into their empty glasses. "Well then," he said, raising his glass to hers in a toast. "If we can't tear her away from him, we'll just have to tear him . . . away from her."

* * *

Nicole ran frantically through the house endlessly climbing the stairs, peering under beds, scouring closets, fully expecting some faceless and terrifying demon to leap out and carry her off into the bowels of Hell.

She was alone in the house, it was 2:00 A.M. and for the last fourteen years she had been terrified under those circumstances.

Nights like this were filled with grizzly images, unnamed horrors, unspeakable memories, all ugly reminders of another time. She could feel the terror couched deeply inside her tensed muscles, in itself an act of comfort, perhaps a way of holding her own body tightly.

And, no matter what she did or how hard she tried to fight it, under these conditions this fearsome drama with its bag of dirty tricks would return, inflicting its torment until the first light rays.

She rummaged once more through the downstairs rooms, crying, wringing her hands together, wiping tears and perspiration from her face and body, checking and rechecking the windows, locks and alarms. Once, she picked up the telephone to call the police, felt stupid and changed her mind.

She took another tranquilizer, sat down in a large armchair and clicked on the television set. There was news, an old movie, and more news but the sound of T.V. voices calmed her and for a while those awful noises ceased and most of her demons lay silent. Perhaps, she finally dozed.

She was a child whose nose seemed forever pressed against cold and dirty windows. Always wanting, always needing, always hungry for approval and affection, she was driven by an intense desire to belong to someone, somewhere.

There were her parents who thought she'd be a cure for their ailing autumn marriage, a tough assignment for a child and at two years old Nicole experienced the first of many failures.

When that marriage finally ended, the lines of parental responsibility could not be easily drawn and Nicole was sent to a temporary foster home.

By the time she was five, she had seen the inside of four institutions and she sadly remembered them all. A child's memory some say is fragile, like the wind passing through, ruffling things a bit, then dissipating. Others call it indelible, capable of recording and storing each and every experience, even to conception. Nicole's survival depended upon her ability to remember everything accurately. Perhaps then, she could choose what to forget.

By the age of twelve she had abandoned hopes of her parents ever claiming her. Daddy had been married three times, ripe and ready for wedding number four. And her weak, sniveling mother fell prey to an insane man of letters who loathed children in favor of prize Angel fish. Any inquiry by Nicole to her mother regarding her future was handled with clean, swift backhands across the girl's tender mouth, rendering her face black and bloody.

At thirteen, two things of significance occurred. Nicole became a woman showing every sign she would grow into a great beauty and she found her first real home.

Barbara and Joe Billings, childless, middle-aged, fighting time and tragedies of their own, took her to their hearts.

For the first time in her short unhappy life, Nicole felt wanted and cherished, came flying home from school to Malomars and rich milk, hugs and kisses, her own room, a mirrored dressing table. For the first time in her life she began to trust somebody.

"Isn't she pretty?" Barbara Billings would lisp, her fat stubby fingers stroking Nicole's thick honey-colored hair. Joe Billings sitting in his wheelchair would nod appreciatively, his withered legs encased in cold steel, his powerful arms embracing and curling barbells.

Nicole's days and nights were heavenly, unlike anything she'd ever known and she treasured them. Even though Barbara Billings was the breadwinner, there were warm family dinners to look forward to, constant doting and affection, new dresses, silk underwear and clean sweet-smelling sheets.

Then came Barbara's trip to Phoenix, a long visit to her desperately ill sister and the awful days and nights that followed.

"Take care of Uncle Joe," Barbara said to Nicole, when she left. And of course, she was pleased to do it.

The first day passed easily. The second night, Nicole dressed for bed, kissed Uncle Joe goodnight and went peacefully to sleep. Wakened later by mysterious noises, she ran to Joe's room but found it empty. It was past midnight and she was alone in the house. An awful terror chilled her body and she felt sure her heart would just stop beating. Suddenly, the noises came again; metal noises, creaking noises, grunts and groans. She ran panic-stricken for the front door, then to the safety of her own room. Awe-struck, she stood there. Her closet door was flung open, her things chaotically strewn about the room, one nightgown shredded into bits. Then, from inside Joe's bedroom, she heard Joe call her name. Her heart started beating more rapidly, her legs grew paralyzed. Just a few moments ago she'd searched Joe's room. No one was there. Maybe he'd fallen. Perhaps he was buried under the bed, hurt or in pain.

"Help me, Nicky," Joe called again and she ran to him. Inside his darkened room, the odor of urine seized at her nostrils and for a moment she thought she would choke. But, she went to him, smiling, arms outstretched, trusting, grateful he was there to protect her from whatever stirred her darkest fantasies.

The covers lay at the foot of his bed and she wondered how he had managed to get into such a sitting position without any help. The moonlight streamed through the windows and its light upon him was sharp. She started quickly pulling the covers to him, then suddenly stood there gaping, her body frozen once more.

"What's wrong, Nicky?" he asked sheepishly.

"Nothing," she answered trying hard not to stare at his awful, grotesque nakedness.

"I'm cold, Nicky," he said. "Help me get the covers back on." Joe sat there grinning, his back resting against a portion of the headboard, his shriveled ugly thighs spread, one dead withered leg dangling off the edge. He watched her frightened cautious moves as she began again to pull the covers toward him, her eyes carefully avoiding the lower half of his body.

"That's a good girl," Joe said and held his arms to receive the cover's edge. Suddenly his powerful arms gripped her wrists tightly and her heart leaped into her mouth. She began to whimper.

"Don't be afraid, little Nicky," he said pulling her close to him. "Sit here with Uncle Joe for awhile. You have no idea how pretty you are. Soon, you'll have a lot of boyfriends and Uncle Joe won't get to see you anymore."

He let go of one wrist and flung away the bedcovers she had carefully placed on him.

"Ever see one of these before?" he asked her, his mouth sucking up close to her tender face and neck.

She shook her head averting her eyes.

"It won't bite you," he said waiting. "Go on. Look at it!" he commanded.

Nicole looked at his face, her sad amber eyes pleading to be let go but it was useless. He dug his fingers deeper into her flesh. Slowly she moved her focus down to his ugly red penis. She began to gag but the terror she felt kept her from vomiting all over him.

"See?" he whispered, "That's not so bad." His powerful thumb pressed above her wristbone rendering her hand and fingers limp, then he pushed her down onto him.

He sighed. Spittle collected in the corners of his mouth, rolling down his square, thick chin. His breathing grew loud and heavy.

Suddenly, without warning, he ripped her delicate nightgown from her shivering body with his powerful hands and she stood there; little lamb, naked and ashamed, powerless, helpless, the color of smut, wishing she would die.

Animal noises rattled inside his throat as he stared at her. She was soft and slender, tiny hard buds sprouting on her chest, hair softly curling between her legs. He spread her limbs and jammed his fingers inside her. She made no noise. No sound at all. He pulled her closer to him, one arm pinned behind her back and masturbated himself. Afterwards, he jerked and twitched awhile, making her swear to Almighty God she'd never tell Aunt Barbara.

That would be easy, she'd never tell anyone. Who'd believe her anyway?

In the days that followed, until Barbara Billings returned, Nicole lived in a constant state of fear. She'd return from school, think the house empty then find Joe naked, hiding in her dark closet behind her things staring at her, masturbating, ruining and sullying all of her beautiful clothes. He was inventive, first hiding his braces then dragging his bulk to different places; sitting in the shower, propped up behind a door, skulking under her bed, always catching her in a state of undress, unaware he was still in the house.

She spent the next days in the library or roaming the streets. When it was late she'd return home, run to her room and lock the door, waiting all night for him to rip the hinges off, hearing his steel braces grate and grind outside her door.

Later, when Barbara Billings returned, she accused Nicole of being a tramp, of using the Billings' good nature and kind heartedness. Of shamelessly having sex with all the neighborhood boys, her stinking and foul-smelling clothes the proof of it. Nicole remained docile, unable to defend herself, not knowing how, watching Uncle Joe sit silently in his wheelchair looking so helpless and pitiful.

At sixteen she found the courage to run away and after more terrifying lonely years, years of searching for Uncle Joe in every closet, under every bed, she married the first man who asked. Jason Stone became her husband and for the last eight years of her life she had come to depend upon him for just about everything. Plugging into his identity, unable to thrive in such a shadow, she was as before, half of something, an extension, unable to function without nourishment from some main source, afraid of poverty, afraid of life, filled with the knowledge that there was no love—there was no love. And, there never would be.

The creaking sounds started again and Nicole's heart pounded like a jackhammer; a silent scream escaped from her lips. Her body bolted up and out of her seat and she ran to the back door.

"Oh God! Please! No!" she sobbed. "Make it stop!" She ran nervously checking the locks, inspecting the windows, testing the alarm system. She wrung her hands, caressed her body and thought of calling someone. But who? Who could she call? There was no one. No friend, no family, no one.

Something flashed through her mind. An image. An image of Michael. Yes. There was Michael now. She could always call Michael. He'd understand.

She dialed his number and Cranston's sleepy voice came on the line. Michael was in San Francisco at the Mark Hopkins Hotel. He'd be home in a few days. Was there anything she could do?

Forlorn, trembling, Nicole thanked her for the generous gesture, then placed the telephone down. She raised up the volume on the television, tears streaming down her face and let go of all the howling fear buried inside her. The ring of the telephone startled then stilled her and she reached for it.

"Hello," she said quickly, trying to hide the nervousness in her voice.

"Nicole? It's Michael. Cranston just called me. Are you all right?"

Her face brightened and she wiped at the corners of her eyes with her hand.

"Oh Michael, I'm fine," she said. "Cranston shouldn't have bothered you. It's so late."

"You sound upset. Like you're crying," he said. "What's wrong?"

"Oh God. It's so stupid, Michael. When I'm alone in the house I get frightened. I guess maybe I should see a shrink or something." She tried to laugh but a sob emerged.

"Where's your maid?"

"On vacation."

"Jason?"

"Business, I guess," she said.

"At 3:00 A.M.?" Michael asked.

The tears started flowing again and a tiny shrill sound crept into her voice. "Michael. It's so crazy. I know no one's here but I still get scared. Oh, I'm so sorry. Cranston really shouldn't have bothered you."

"Listen," Michael said. "Why don't I have Duggan pick you up, take you to Casa Piedra for the night, then drive you to the airport in the morning. You can catch the first flight out here and we'll spend the next few days together. I could use a little help with some interviews and things. What do you say?"

She was silent, tears gently flowing, holding her breath.

"There's a big, beautiful suite next to mine, you won't be alone and we can talk all about it."

She wanted more than anything to say yes. She wanted to shout it a dozen times, at the top her lungs. She was overwhelmed with dear and tender feelings at how gentle and kind he was. Not once had he suggested she imagined things or that she was being silly. Not once. A key was slowly turning in the latch and she could hear Jason's voice above the television din.

"Michael. It's Jason," she said. "Jason's home."

"The offer still stands."

"That's sweet," she said wiping her eyes, her reddened nose, "but there's no need now. Thanks, Mike."

She hung up the telephone and watched Jason close the front door. He stood there dumbfounded, staring at everything around him. All the house lights were blazing and the television was tuned to a deafening volume. He stormed into the living room glaring at her in disgust and clicked off the television.

"I didn't hear your car, Jason," she said quietly.

"Are you crazy or something!" he said coming close to her chair. She crouched deeper into her seat.

"You seeing little green men under the beds again? How could you hear anything with that fucking set blaring like that?" He started clicking off all the lamps.

"You're a very sick girl, Nicole," he said. "Maybe you need some kind of a pill or a dose of electric shock."

"Stop it, Jason," she heard herself almost shouting. "You know very well why I'm afraid. You don't have to rub it in."

"Yeah, well," he shouted back, "it's still nuts. I mean Uncle Joe's probably dead by now." He chuckled at his clever little remark.

She choked back some tears and bit her bottom lip. Jason poured himself a drink. She realized she should never have shared those painful memories with him. Jason was the last person she should have trusted with secrets like that.

He began to circle around her, twirling his drink, finally settling down near her. "Shit! You must have been hot stuff then," he said sarcastically. "You barely have enough tits now, for Christ's sake. What the hell did old Uncle Joe see in you anyway? Maybe you wanted it? Huh? Did you ever think of that?"

She jumped up, sobbing, running wildly for the bathroom, each of those words painfully cutting into her like sharp knife thrusts.

He was after her instantly, grabbing at her hair then her

wrists, spinning her around. All those horrible memories came flooding back. She pulled away, struggling to get free of him but it was useless. He was as strong as an ox.

"Oh God, Jason please. Please don't hold my wrists like that," she begged.

He led her back into the living room, deaf to her pleading, and set her down onto the couch still clutching one of her wrists.

"Don't tell me what to do," he shouted. "I put this big fancy roof over your stupid head, and those expensive clothes on your back and all that fancy food in the refrigerator. I own you. I own you lock, stock and barrel and don't you ever forget it. Don't you ever run away from me like that again."

He was breathing rapidly, glaring at her, his eyes burning with anger. He released her wrist and she sat there motionless, horrified, waiting for his next aggressive move.

"Now," he said adjusting his cuffs, picking up his drink again, "who was that on the telephone?"

She hesitated, evaluating him. "It was Michael."

"Michael! What the hell did he want?"

"Nothing. I called him."

Jason's eyes flashed. "You called him? What the hell for?"

"I called everyone I could think of. I tried to find you. I was frightened," she explained.

"What'd he have to say?"

He invited me to San Francisco for a few days. They're shooting pickups there."

"San Francisco?" he repeated, wheels turning quickly inside his head again. Suddenly his countenance changed and he sat down next to her, gently taking her arm, careful to avoid her wrists.

"I think maybe you should go," he said. His voice was oozing honey.

Nicole was nonplussed. "Are you serious?" she asked.

"Sure, I'm serious. Why not? I think it'll do you some good. Besides," he added, lighting a cigarette, "it wouldn't hurt for you to be nice to Michael."

She caught his drift and it maddened her. She remembered that other time. A time he wanted her to cozy up to some union official so he could make a huge loan. "Like last year?" she said, "when you wanted me to screw some union official?"

"Sure why not? Lots of wives do it for their husbands. You ain't the Queen of England you know."

"I'm not a hooker, either."

"You, baby, are nothing. You are what I say you are. And what I say, is that you go to San Francisco and be nice to Mike. You don't have to fuck him if you don't want to. Just turn him on a little. You know how to do that. Just think of . . . Uncle Joe."

Her hand flew swiftly to his face but he grabbed it, twisting it back, causing her to cry out in pain. He held the lit cigarette close to her eye and she could feel the ash heat.

"You'll go there," he said. "You'll go to San Francisco because I say so. You'll go because I won't be home for a few days and you'll be all alone with Uncle Joe again."

He reached for the telephone and handed it to her.

She took it.

Jason dropped Nicole at the airport, then headed for Casa Piedra. It was early and the northbound traffic on the San Diego Freeway was light. That was nice, he thought. He could push the Ferrari at top speed and still be able to think. He shifted up, accelerated and reached the far inside lane riding the wall divider.

For the last few days he'd tried to find out why the California Board of Corporations was holding up his money. Almost half a million bucks, hard-earned money, was sitting in escrow waiting for the damn board's okay.

He had bills to pay for Christ's sake. He couldn't wait much longer. And, lately, they were holding up his money every time he filed, citing little nit-picking ordinances he'd never even heard of before, ordinances they said he might be in violation of. Might be! That was the joke. They were stalling for time, going over everything carefully, deliberately. Everyone knew what he was doing. They just couldn't catch him at it.

His thoughts turned to Stone Management Associates.

Next week, he'd try for Hugh Parker's cooperation. Ask him, outright, nicelike. Suggest some bonuses, some perks. Maybe a percentage. Then, if Parker refused, he'd have to put some pressure on him. That meant Sally Quinn.

And now, with Michael away, he could start working on Max without interference. Fly him to Vegas for the day where Max'd be knee-deep in tits and poker chips, in comfortable red velvet roulette surroundings. There amongst the ponies and poker tables whatever resistance he might have could be softened.

Meyer could arrange a special poker game, high stakes, where Max would be sure to win big, then lose even bigger. And, Jason, beloved first-born son would bail him out.

He'd place a bug in Max's ear about Parker and Viva. Show him Meyer's report. Tell him that Parker's accounting appears questionable. Max would be angry. He'd believe Jason. Jason would never lie to Max. That's when he'd hit him with Michael. Incompetent Michael, fooling around with Nicole. All four of them dragging down Ada's business, making a fool of her, milking her dry while she lies dying.

By the time Jason was through, Max would be furious, ready to sign over his 20 percent of the business so Jason could protect and defend everything Ada worked for all of her life. With that and Parker's cooperation, he'd be in business.

He was near the turnoff. Jason skipped across four lanes, shifted down to third and took the Wilshire Exit West. He drove past the V.A. grounds and hung a right onto San Vicente. The morning was cool for July and the green velvet strip that divided San Vincente Boulevard in half was alive with breathless joggers and barking, playful dogs.

Jason lit a cigarette and thought about contingencies. If for some reason Max refused to sign his shares over, there were two other ways to handle matters. One was legal and costly, a longshot, but he'd go for it if he had to. The other, almost unthinkable.

And Michael couldn't do one fucking thing to stop him.

He just didn't have the balls. When it came down to it, Michael would find that out.

He reached Bristol Circle, turned right and headed up the street smiling, wondering whether or not sweet Michael would have the nerve to really fuck his wife. He actually thought about that; saw them together in his imagination delicately humping each other. Diogenes and the Madonna. Cute. He wouldn't have the nerve. Then, suddenly, Jason frowned. "Son of a bitch," he said out loud. "Goddamn son of a bitch!"

Chapter 7

AT 6:35 A.M. NICOLE BOARDED a San Francisco bound 727. At 6:45 the jetways were unhitched, a pretty stewardess mumbled something into an oxygen mask and an eager Hollywood pilot exercised his adenoids by way of a microphone. At 6:50 they had taxied into runway position, engines clamoring, plane vibrating, beginning a quick and noisy ascent.

They flew as the crow in a clear and cloudless sky, the sun's brilliant rays and rainbows glinting off the plane's silver wing tips.

Lying back in her seat, Jason's grinning image hovered over her like some dark and sinister tower. She shuddered. She felt confused, frightened and filled with a thousand terrifying questions. Did she love him? Of course. And of course not. There was no such thing as love. She was born with that knowledge: nothing had occurred to alter her perception of it. And, if Jason continued tormenting her, as he did last night, threatening her, making her life unbearable, she'd have to leave. But where? Where could she go this time? How could she ever live alone again? At sixteen there were hopes and dreams; at twenty-eight only a vivid reality and those nightmares.

At 7:45 she could feel the easy weightless descent. When the plane passed through a dark cloud carpet, there was turbulence with no visability.

At two hundred feet she saw the wing once again, its

red light blinking a faint signal and soon, below, she could almost touch the murky bay waters. At 7:55 A.M. she was safe in San Francisco, anxious to forget the last days and eager to see Michael.

She looked stunning in a white Halston suit, a luxurious white Texas mohair cape clinging to her shoulders. Her thick honey hair was plaited from the nape of her neck out to her forehead and she moved through the busy terminal with the grace of a swan.

She located the Cadillac limousine Michael had sent and when the chauffeur opened the door there was a rushing fragrance of roses. One dozen long-stemmed yellow buds adorned with maidenhair ferns lay neatly wrapped in soft green velvet, a note beside them. She sat back for a moment watching the airport recede, then read it.

Nicole,
I think that I shall never nose a poem, lovely as a rose.
The chauffeur knows where we are if you're up to it.
Otherwise rest. Dinner's at 7.

Mike

She smiled, removed one velvet bud and touched it to her lips.

She felt safe and protected, wrapped in this Cadillac cocoon. She ignored the harsh city sounds, turned on classical music and closed her eyes. Within fifteen minutes they'd hit the San Francisco County line, then Market Street and were soon negotiating the steep San Francisco hills.

At the top of Nob Hill, she faced the gleaming white facade of the elegant Mark Hopkins Hotel and within ten minutes she was in a luxurious suite slipping her body between cool, sweet sheets oddly remembering the pleasant touch of Michael's fingers upon her flesh.

It was a gray, foggy morning and Armando Del Gado had been storming about the set like a madman. He'd complained about the dialogue, the location of his motorhome, the makeup artist and his co-star. Now, he was driving the lighting director insane pushing the best boy to the brink of distraction by demanding they change the position of his key light once more.

"I can tell when it's right, goddamnit. A good actor knows that."

Only the director really knew what Del Gado was up to and if he expected that matching footage to be safely in the can before the fog drifted off he'd have to give in. He'd already checked with the studio and they'd acquiesced, but he just wasn't ready to submit. He'd give it fifteen more minutes and see.

They were located near Fort Point on some old military garrison under a landward arch of the Golden Gate Bridge. It was chilly.

A bank of arc lights ringed the hillside, interspersed with spots and nine-lights. And miles of cable snaked their way across the grass. Off-duty, uniformed police maintained an eager, fascinated crowd behind wooden barriers and teenaged girls cried silently at the sight of Del Gado.

Some crew members drank steaming hot coffee, munching doughnuts and chatting about the next shot. Others moved in and out of trucks with heavy equipment, placing sandbags over lightstands to keep them from toppling in the wind. Two helicopters were poised on a nearby hillside like overgrown ceiling fans waiting for their flight signals.

The tall lanky director, wearing faded jeans and an Irish wool cable sweater, sat high up on a Titan crane peering through the lens of a Mitchell camera. Beside him the camera operator and his assistant.

Seated on a canvas chair just inches from the tossing bay waters, Michael watched the spectacle. Much to his surprise he was fascinated.

When they were ready for the shot, the assistant director bellowed into his bullhorn. "Okay. Hold it down. Let's get this before we lose the fog." There was another call for quiet, then they began.

"Sound!"

"Rolling."

"Lights!"

The bank of arcs lit up the ghostly hillside.

"Camera!"
"Rolling."
"Mark it!"

A young man slid a black-and-white slate in front of Del Gado's face. "Scene 67, take 11," he shouted into the boom, then loudly snapped a flap at the top.

"Action!"

The scene began and the helicopters started to lift.

They shot over Del Gado's adversary's head, the adversary's gun shoved in Del Gado's ribs, the camera filming Del Gado's reaction to the threat. He spoke his pleading words with ease, then somewhere in the middle of the scene he kicked at the dirt calling "Cut." Shocked crew faces strained up toward the director. The camera was still rolling.

"Cut it," the director shouted, signaling the crane operator to let him down. "What's wrong, Armando?" he said stepping off the crane. "That scene was going great, just great. Why'd you stop it like that?"

Del Gado's face was red and he was cursing in Spanish. "My key light's off again, *Chingado*! Either that or my makeup's kicking. I told that *baboso* to be sure it doesn't hit my neck. I can feel that it's off. *Mierda*!"

The best boy threw his gloves to the ground and some of the grips groaned. The lighting director joined them. There was a quick discussion and Del Gado's light was shifted an inch. He looked smug and satisfied but the crew was disgusted. Before shooting had begun again, Del Gado insulted the soundman, demanding an immediate playback of his dialogue. The director finally threw up his hands and ordered a short coffee break for everyone.

Michael rose from his seat and rushed to Del Gado's side. "What's wrong? Why are you stalling?"

"Hey, *amigo*," Del Gado said. "who's side are you on anyway?" He grinned, first at Michael then at his screaming fans, waving thumbs up to them.

"I wasn't aware of sides," Michael said. "I can't imagine why you don't just take the shot and get it the hell over with, that's all!"

"Wrong," he answered. "And, what's more, your old lady would have known better. She'd have backed me up.

Stick around, *amigo*,'' Del Gado said. ''You've got alot to learn. Watch me very closely. In the next five minutes, I'll earn me a hundred grand.'' He slapped Michael's back and sauntered back to the director.

Puzzled, Michael returned to his seat wondering about Del Gado and what Ada would have done in his place. A pretty young woman weaved her way through the enormous crowd and settled beside him. She had glistening green eyes, black curly hair and a chin cleft deep enough to hide a penny. After adjusting her emerald green turtleneck sweater she leaned toward him.

''It must be the fog making him blow his horn like that,'' she said laughing, referring to Del Gado. ''Isn't he a pile of shit? Can you imagine the size of his ego?'' She extended a hand to Michael. ''Hi, Diana Sharpe, *San Francisco Mantle*. I'm doing a story on him.''

Michael maintained a serious face, swallowing the smoke from his pipe, trying to keep from choking. ''Hi, Mike Stone.''

Diana's eyes opened wide. ''Armando's manager?'' she said, her voice climbing in register. ''Oh Jesus.'' Her tape recorder fell to the ground as her hand flew across her mouth. ''Pardon me. I seem to have swallowed my entire foot.''

''Just a toe,'' Michael said. ''But it's okay. I won't cancel the interview as long as it's favorably biased.''

''Sir, I could do nothing less . . . considering.''

The director shouted, ''Let's take this shot.''

The lighting director checked his meter against Del Gado's face and the filming process started once more. In a few minutes Del Gado began to swear and the director swiftly removed him from the set. Once more they shut down and waited.

''Listen,'' the director told Del Gado, his eyes focused on the ground. ''I know how difficult the last few months have been for you, all that pressure about the network and Ada. I also know you're doing us a hell of a favor with these pickups.'' Del Gado smiled at him, then winked at Michael. ''So,'' the director continued, ''I'd like you to keep that new motorhome you're using. It suits you. Enjoy it. Some small token of appreciation from the studio for your . . . cooperation."

Del Gado shook his hand. There it was. Some fucking compensation for the work he was doing for practically nothing now. Some respect and acknowledgement for who he was. "Hey man, thanks. That's real nice of you guys. I'm sorry if I upset anyone. I only want to do my job right. Tell the gang I'm sorry and we'll try it again."

In half an hour, just before the last fog clouds drifted across the far end of the Golden Gate Bridge, the director had his footage and Armando Del Gado had his new motorhome.

"That's a wrap," the assistant director called. "Let's pack it up."

Del Gado signed some autographs, kissed a few of the swooning young ladies, then swaggered over to Michael with a grin smeared all over his face.

He noticed Diana immediately and extended his hand, delivering the "A" version of his scintillating smile. "Armando Del Gado."

"Diana Sharpe."

"I'll bet you are," Del Gado said holding onto her fingers.

"Careful," Michael warned smiling. "She's a member of the press."

Michael sat there watching them fence, playing word games . . . the lady needing a story, the star wanting a piece of ass. In a few minutes, they were like bacon and eggs; one crispy-hot the other soft and buttery, cooking in the same smelly pan.

Michael glanced at his watch. Nicole would be in her suite now probably resting and he was looking forward to seeing her. Now it was time for lunch and Del Gado's interview. He would have lunch and they would have each other, under his watchful eye.

* * *

She bathed leisurely, extravagantly in piping hot water and mink oil, bubbles bursting up and over the tub's rim. When the water was no longer warm and comfortable, she rinsed and let the shower spray run icy cold.

She dressed in pearl gray satin trousers, a shimmering

gray wrap-around top that plunged a path to her waist. She had fallen asleep with her hair still plaited and when undone, the thick strands flowed from the crown of her head in diminutive waves. She brushed it lightly for sheen, letting it fall where it would.

There were huge pearls and dark burgundy garnets in Florentined white gold for her ears, a matching bracelet for her wrist. With burgundy gloss on her lips and pearl gray shadow for her eyes, she was radiant.

At seven precisely there was a knock at the door. It was Michael. He stood there simply admiring her. Then he took her outstretched hand and spun her.

"You're beautiful," he said sounding as though he were seeing her for the first time.

She tingled inside at his words, her heart rapidly beating and she knew she was blushing.

"And so are you," she answered admiring his elegant black suit, pale blue shirt and mulberry tie. "Come in for heaven's sake."

"Thanks for the roses," she said, nodding towards the bouquet in a crystal vase.

For a moment they stood there, eyes intimately engaged, the only audible room sounds, a loudly ticking clock. Embarrassed, she gathered up her full white cape. He placed it across her shoulders and escorted her to the elevator, smiling.

It was 7:45 P.M. when they met Armando Del Gado at the popular Fleur de Lis restaurant. He looked outrageously handsome in a dark navy suit and a red silk shirt moving like some proud toreador, skillfully tossing the bull.

The beautiful dining room was lit by candle lamps, their table richly laden with flowers, silver and golden goblets: All of it sitting uniquely under a fabric canopy of autumn leaves and fruit. They dined leisurely, on pâté de champagne, coq au vin rouge and for dessert, crème caramel. Del Gado was charming, ebullient, the quintessential star, as they drank the Givrey-Chambertin, 1973, Michael had ordered.

"I hope you learned something today, Mike," Del Gado said, raising his wine glass to his lips.

Michael appeared puzzled, glancing first at Nicole then at Del Gado.

"I'm talking about my new motorhome," he expanded.

"Oh that," Michael said. "Neatest shakedown I've ever witnessed. He raised his glass in a toast. "You should get an Academy Award for that fine performance."

"For heaven's sake," Nicole said. "What are you two talking about?"

"They actually had to bribe this man to finish his movie. He had them by the golden gonads."

"Bribe?" Del Gado said. His dark eyes narrowed for a second but then he smiled. "Yeah! I suppose you could call that a bribe . . . if you want to. I like to think of it as using my influence."

"Will somebody please tell me what you two are talking about," Nicole said, sounding exasperated.

Del Gado told her how he was doing the producers a favor working for scale, finishing some old shitty movie they had dragged out of the mothballs after he hit it big; a movie nobody would touch with a ten-foot pole. But now, because of his name, they stood to make a bundle distributing it. Screw that. He was entitled to something and he settled on the expensive newly decorated motorhome.

Nicole had a smile on her face. "Mike," she said turning to him, "He's absolutely right. They will make a bundle exploiting his name and he should rightfully share in that."

"See?" Del Gado said. "She understands." He placed his large hand over Nicole's and stroked her soft slender fingers, toying with the bracelet on her wrist.

"That's star power, Mike," he said making a bold symbolic gesture with his clenched fist. I didn't just get an expensive motorhome. I got satisfaction. I made a statement. All those years crawling around at the bottom, hauling ass, kissing ass, ready to sell my soul for a chance. All the rejection and humiliation, the phonies who promised me the sky, then rubbed my face in dirt. Now," he sat back, "now it's my turn. So, I hang what they want just above their heads. I make them beg like I did. I let them know how it feels to want, to need something . . . like a narcotic."

He chuckled. "Now that's really funny. I'm somebody's fix."

He drew a long breath then patted Michael's shoulder. "Don't worry, Mike. You'll catch on. It takes time to understand it all. And even if you never do, you've got nothing to worry about. With your connections you can always be a producer." For a moment, the gleaming smile on Del Gado's face turned into a hideous scar and Michael looked away.

Del Gado glanced at his watch, then asked the waiter for the bill. "This one's on me kids," he said, "or should I say the 'suits' as Robert Blake calls them." He stood and placed his crumpled napkin on the table. His lips curled devilishly at the sides and his powerful fingers grasped Nicole's hand. She smiled nervously as his lips grazed the soft inside of her palm, his eyes massaging the plunge of her neckline.

'I'll see you in the morning, *amigo*. We'll leave as soon as my pilot radios that the fog's lifted. And don't bother looking for me tonight," he snickered. "I'll be all wrapped up."

Michael caught his drift. "Have a good time," he said. "Who's the lucky lady?"

"Oh," he hedged, "a little green-eyed monster."

"Do you think Ada would approve?"

"Ada would say, 'the newspaperwoman's using you Armando' and I would say 'everybody uses everybody.' So she'd figure out a way to get Diana to promote me. And then she'd say 'good night, have a good time, check for a tape recorder and watch what you say.' "

"Goodnight, Armando," Michael said, "have a good time, check for a tape recorder and watch what you say."

They laughed and Del Gado swaggered off.

Michael lifted his brandy snifter and rolled the liquid around to warm it. "Do you feel the same way he does, about the industry I mean?"

"I'm a realist," Nicole said. "I suppose so. And he's not that different from the rest, you know. It does get to you after a while, being treated like garbage. But I don't know if I'd ever grow strong enough to do what he did. But I'll tell you this. I do envy him taking control of his life like that. I envy anyone that can do that. But why are you so shocked at his behavior? Surely none of it comes as a great surprise. You've been around this business all your life."

"I'm surprised at myself to tell you the truth." He tamped fresh tobacco down into his pipe and held it in his palm. "Yet every time I come across the rage, the bitterness, it makes me wonder. Why do they stay in the business? Why don't they change it once they're in? Make it better for the one's on the way up?"

"It's not that simple. By the time you make it you're so damn tired. There's so much pain and disappointment. All you can do is cover up the scar tissue and try like hell to enjoy the limelight and the money. And it doesn't stop there. He's got to fight to stay on top. There's no time to worry about anyone else. You're only as good as your last job."

Michael lit his pipe, listening to her words watching the waves in her hair ripple as her head swayed.

"Are you enjoying the work?" Nicole asked.

"I'm not sure yet. I've never been all that crazy about the people in it, but I have to admit, there's an odd fascination about the business."

She covered her mouth to hide her smile. "You're getting hooked Michael," she said. "I'm not surprised. Everyone does, sooner or later."

They walked in dark and whistling winds, high above the city on the rim of Twin Peaks. Below them as far as the eye could see, San Francisco glittered like a vast set of florescent dominos, silhouetted against midnight, engaged in neon conversations.

Breathing the chilly night air, he searched for the courage to ask her. "You want to talk about it?" he said with difficulty.

She hesitated, looking down at the shimmering panorama. "It sounds stupid when I try. Maybe Jason's right. Maybe I am crazy."

His strong arm warmed her shoulder. "No, I don't think so," he assured her. "It's personal and you're probably afraid I won't understand. Maybe you're even a little ashamed."

She turned to face him. Her fingers went to his face and she touched his cheek. "For all those reasons, Mike, and so much more." A sudden gust of wind *whooshed* by, tossing her hair about, sticking it to her lips. He pulled the strands from her face, brushing them back over the crown of her head, then lightly kissed her cheek.

"It's okay," he said resuming their walk. "You don't have to talk about it if you don't want to. But when you're ready, I'm here. Now," he said opening the door to the limousine, "let's go back to the hotel."

As they stood in the glow of soft pink light near the door to her room, he was filled with restraint, tenderly touching her fingertips, while she nervously knotted the ends of his tie.

"Oh Michael. I do feel better," she told him. "I'm so glad I came."

"Me too." He felt the drumming of his heart rise to his throat. After all these years, after all he'd done to prevent it, he couldn't stop wanting her.

Her delicate, warm hand circled the nape of his neck and she raised up to hug him. He took the room key from her, unlatched the lock, then watched as the door closed between them.

He stood in the hallway, dazed and dizzy, still holding onto her key. His fist raised to knock at her door, to return it, but some indescribable fear overwhelmed him. He knew without question if she opened that door this very minute, he'd take her in his arms, make love to her and that was unthinkable.

And so, he chuckled, flipping the key once into the air, walking away. Most men spent their lives searching for some key to their happiness and here he stood holding it in the palm of his hand.

Inside the dimly lit room she threw her cape to the chair sitting quietly for a moment, resting her head against her arm. There was the faint scent of him still clinging to her hand where it had rested against his neck and she deeply breathed it. She could smell his presence, almost taste him . . . and it aroused her. A hot sensation inside her scalded its way down through the center of her thighs, melting her ankles and curling the ends of her toes.

Nonsense, she thought quickly, defensively, then rose and kicked her shoes to the floor. Utter nonsense!

She tuned the radio to soft music, undressing slowly, seductively, listening as Michael moved about in the next room. She leaned her body against the wall that separated them. Naked and bold, she conjured the forbidden.

She dismissed it and slipped on a short filmy nightgown the color of ripe apricots then brushed her thick shiny hair. A large mirror sketched her movements and she watched herself. Long neck . . . delicate arms and legs . . . firm high breasts . . . the face of a cameo.

She stretched her body, exercising her legs then pirouetted on one foot stumbling hard against the wall. She sat there on the carpet, laughing, waving at herself in the mirror, then jumped when the phone rang.

"You okay in there?" Michael asked. "I heard funny noises."

"They were funny, all right," she giggled. "I tried a fast double pirouette on the carpet. It doesn't work."

"Dancing? At this hour?"

She giggled again. "I told you I was crazy."

"This time I won't argue. Get some sleep. I'll see you in the morning."

"Sweet dreams, Mike," she whispered into the phone. He was silent, then hung up.

She placed the receiver on the cradle, sighed then slipped into bed. Her fingers traced the warm soft curves of her body—she felt drunk and dreamy—her images of Michael utterly provoking. His perfect smile, his tan muscular body, those brown velvet eyes, his lips, his. . . . This is ridiculous, she thought, shifting her position, trying to avoid confronting or recognizing the sensations swarming over her.

She closed her eyes, took deep breaths to relax and slowly drifted off to sleep. But her dreams were unpleasant and she tossed and turned fighting some unknown and terrifying invader. And then she awakened.

A knock at the door roused her and with eyes half-closed, sleepily, she stumbled across the room to open it.

The force of a whirlwind pushed from the other side of the door and she was powerless. Del Gado's arms and legs, like some great octopus, curved first around the door frame as he thrust his way in.

He was drunk and disheveled leaning against the now-closed door to her room looking victorious, his breathing the rattle of a snake. There were screams inside her but none emerged. Instead they lay fruitless, stillborn, buried far beneath her paralyzing fear.

With his eyes fastened on her, he crept, stumbling through the darkened room, hitting the sides of the furniture cursing each piece.

She was terrified and began to retreat inching her way backward on some unknown journey. Oh God, she thought, don't let him touch my wrists. Let me die here and now instead.

Three feet away and groping for her, she saw his thick powerful hands, saw his glazed crazy eyes, heard his harsh heavy breath sounds.

"C'mon, baby," he spit, "I know you dig me. I know it," he tripped suddenly falling over her shoes. "*Mierda*," he bellowed rising and kicking them out into the air. Suddenly she reached the wall and he lunged, pinning her body against it. She held her breath. Her buried sobs became hot streaming tears burning pathways down her cheeks spilling into her mouth delivering hot salt.

Del Gado pushed his hard strong body up against hers, his arms circling her, his lips hurling quiet obscenities into her ears. He squeezed her shoulders then began moving his hands down the length of her arms. But when they drew close to her wrists something crazy went off in her head and she began to fight him, screaming, exploding with the fury of a thousand haunted nights.

Del Gado's hand flew savagely to her mouth crushing her lips against her teeth. His other arm closed tightly around her waist. He lifted her, carrying her kicking thrashing body across the room and threw her forcefully onto the bed. He became a human prison leaning over her grinning, his arms heavy upon her shoulders.

She kicked him and he grabbed her foot, twisting it. He bent his knee and pushed it deeply into her groin. But when his powerful arm raised to slap her frightened face, the force of another's hand stopped him.

Michael gripped Del Gado's wrist, pulling and bending it back, causing him to drop to the floor. He grabbed Del Gado's shirt collar, choking and lifting him by it, angrily thrusting him up against the wall, one fist poised to strike his face. Nicole leaped between them straining at Michael's arm and naked chest, trying to keep him from crushing Del Gado's face.

"Oh God, Mike don't. He's drunk. Stop it!" she cried. Those words only increased the strength of his hold on Del Gado. She pushed harder against his arm, pleading and begging for him to stop, while Del Gado unafraid, stood there, his arms hanging limply at his sides. He was laughing at them both.

"Hey man, I'm sorry," he tried to say. "I didn't know she was your chick. Why didn't you say so. Shit, she came on to me. She opened the door and let me in. Didn't you? Tell him I didn't hurt you. Go on. Tell him."

"Please, Michael, let him go. I'm okay, please." She began to cry and slowly he relaxed his grip, each finger slowly peeling away one by one from the folds of Del Gado's shirt.

When he was free, Del Gado's drunken laughter filled the room. He straightened his shirt, tucking it into his trousers then brushed at the sides of his hair. Michael shouted, "Get out of here, Armando. Get out and stay out! If I ever catch you like this again I'll kill you."

Halfway out the door, Del Gado laughed outloud. "The hell you will, *amigo*. This beautiful face pays your mother's doctor bills and don't you ever forget it." Michael lunged for him again, but the door clipped at his face missing his nose.

Nicole ran to his arms and he held her tightly. Then he lifted her and carried her to the bed.

"Did he hurt you?" he asked, stroking the back of her head.

"No," she answered.

"I . . . he . . . he was trying to . . . to. . . ." She couldn't finish the sentence. "Oh Michael, I'm so ashamed. Please don't leave me alone. I don't want to be alone."

She buried herself against the warm nakedness of his chest, tears of relief spilling onto his skin.

"Sh . . . sh . . . it's all right now . . . don't try to talk . . . you don't have to tell me. Just get some rest."

He kissed her cheeks and placed her in the center of the bed, settling her between the sheets. She let her head drop to the pillow and from exhaustion she fell right to sleep.

She slept fitfully, dreaming of darkened hallways and large black closets with strange noises and steel arms and legs reaching for her, gripping her, smothering her to death. At 7:00 A.M., she screamed and bolted upright from sleep. Michael was there sitting on the blanket next to her, calming her, his bloodshot eyes wide open.

She looked around the room remembering everything and a rush of nausea stoked at her stomach.

"Take it easy," he said patting her hand. "How are you feeling?"

"I don't know," she mumbled. "I'm so confused. These last few days have been hell." She paused, looked at the clock and realized it was noon. "Have you talked to Armando?" she asked.

"No," he said. "He checked out last night right after he left here."

"But his plane."

"His plane took off at 3:40 A.M., an hour before the airport closed down."

She looked at the window. A ghostly shroud covered the city.

"How will we get back?"

"We'll get a flight out as soon as the fog lifts. In the meantime, you relax and have some breakfast."

Chapter 8

DAVEY SULLIVAN SLAMMED the heavy beachhouse door. Outside, the blazing sun blinded him and he blinked his watery eyes. Where were his sunglasses? His heavy boots struck an even cadence on the brick pathway and his clenched body was primed to strike—or be struck.

He slammed the door to his blue '70 Mustang, sitting, listening as the windows rattled, holding a broken sun visor in his lap. God, he was sick of the poverty, tired of hanging by a thread, sick and tired of her.

He kicked over the motor, an uneven idle tossing him about. Pulling quickly onto the coast highway, he headed south for the Santa Monica hill. He picked up the broken sun visor and tossed it onto the seat beside him, an angry expression on his face.

The sound of her voice still echoed, pounding away at his ears and he pressed down on the gas pedal. Behind him, a trail of dirty gray smoke.

That cunt! That damn, mean, selfish, arrogant, cunt! She came ten times. He'd massaged her, kissed her, made her laugh, licked her ass. All he wanted in return was a small favor. One lousy fucking favor. She could do that. She could help him if she wanted to. She had all those friends in high places. All she had to do was make one lousy, miserable phone call. Why? What did she have to lose? Him! That's what! Now, somebody else would have to take his place. He'd fuck her again all right, he thought, glancing in the rearview mirror, but it wouldn't be with his prick.

He changed lanes nervously, slowing as a Santa Monica police car appeared suddenly behind. He brushed his fingers through his blond curls and felt the stinging pain of her words ripping away at his ears.

"It doesn't mix, Davey, my business and my pleasure," Viva told him. Her hair leapt from her scalp like a flaming halo against her satin pillow. "It never does."

Davey rose to his knees eager to convince her, his fingers caressing her naked thighs. "All I'm asking is for you to make one phone call to a casting agent or a producer; one lousy phone call, please!" he begged. "Why can't you do that? You have that power."

She sat up tugging at the satin covers drawing her knees under her chin. "I can't do it because that's how I make my living. I won't do it because I never have and I never will. It has nothing to do with you. I don't ever want anyone in this business to question my integrity."

"Integrity," he laughed. "Don't hand me that shit. What the hell do you know about integrity?"

"Why darling," she said purring, "as much as you know about acting."

That's when he gave her the ultimatum and she laughed in his face.

"Make that call, Viva, or so help me God I'll take what I know to the newspapers. They'll have a field day with that shit about Hank Mason, not to mention a few other things I could tell them. Then we'll talk integrity."

She looked at him, her stare digging away at his tanned face, then she spoke in low, articulate tones. "Do that, Davey. I can't stop you and what's more I won't. It isn't me you'll hurt. You can never hurt me. But, if you hurt any of my clients or my business I promise you this. I'll treat you to a taste of real power. You'll not only *not* make it in Hollywood. I'll see to it that you'll never even begin."

"You can't do that," he screamed trembling, his blood stampeding to his brain. "I'll go to Sid Gross. He'll help me."

"You've already been there, darling. I know that and like all the others, you'll conquer only after you stoop for him. Real low. I don't believe you have the stomach for it—or the ass—I might add."

That's when he almost hit her. Instead, he jumped from the bed, dressed and stormed from the house.

Screw her, he thought pulling off the highway, climbing the hill into Santa Monica. One way or another, he'd make it to the top. Sooner or later, he'd be somebody and he'd make her remember.

He checked the rearview mirror and was instantly reminded of something. He smiled, pulled into a supermarket parking lot on Wilshire Boulevard and made two phone calls. In less than one hour he was standing in Sidney Gross's living room, wearing the tightest pair of jeans he owned.

* * *

Hugh Parker and Jason Stone sat eyeball to eyeball in Parker's office. Keeping them from flying at each other's throat was a huge wooden desk and some self-imposed restraint. Parker studied the papers Jason had thrust across his desk. With great care he scrutinized each individual document, a studied, worrisome expression flickering in his icy blue eyes.

"These aren't properly executed," Parker said. "There's no date here and the signature's barely legible." He thrust them back at Jason. "Look at Max's signature. He must have been drunk when he signed this, *if* he signed it at all."

Jason snickered. "You can do better than that, counselor. We both know that's Max's signature and we both know it's legal. I threw you a good curve. Catch it. Run with it like a sport."

Parker glared at him. "No," he said. "I don't see it that way at all. I caught it, if that's how you want to phrase it, but from my point of view it's nothing but a strike. These documents can be contested and that's what I'll advise Mike and Viva to do."

"I don't think you want to do that," Jason said, his words crisp and confident. "What's there to gain? All that adverse publicity, exposing the agency to negative speculation from every corner of the industry. You don't want that. Mike and Viva don't want that. Then we all lose. Nobody wins that way."

Parker was silent, his arms folded against his neat Brooks Brothers button-down shirt, ostensibly warding off any aggressive posture Jason might assume. Inside, he fumed.

"Look at it this way," Jason added. "Viva, Mike, me, we split it nice like; nobody loses. Ada's gonna kick sooner or later, and either way I get to share."

"No! You don't!" Parker shouted, his hand slapping the desk, fluttering the papers about. "Ada cut you out a month ago. There's a brand-new signed will—and you're out!" He had just breached an ethic and it made him feel sick.

Jason sprang to his feet, his eyes blazing with anger, his hands and fingers digging into the top of Parker's desk. "You listen to me you two-bit son of a bitch," he snarled, "you don't give me trouble and I won't hurt you. That's the deal. Take it or leave it. We don't go to court and I don't have you investigated by the bar association for impropriety. For instance, all those conflicts of interest you seem to have going on. Between the clients you hold in common with Stone Management and fucking my sister, you and S.M.A. together won't be worth shit."

Parker stood, trying to keep his cool, perspiration beading on his forehead. "You're a pile of worthless junk, Stone. You've always been junk and you'll always be junk. Get the hell out of my office and take your phony stock certificates with you."

"Junk, huh," Jason said smiling, standing and gathering up his papers. "Well, you oughta know man. You should be an expert on the subject. First your wife and now your son."

Parker lunged across the desk for Jason's throat, some horrible sound emerging from the pit of his bowels. Jason stumbled back from the impact, startled—his arms searching blindly behind him for something to grip.

Parker leaped on top of him. He was crazed and frenzied, his fists pounding Jason's face and chest.

Jason's knee pelted Parker's back, his arms wrestling the fury of Parker's fists. Suddenly, Jason yanked at Parker's tie. Parker's chin rushed downwards and Jason's fist cut across his chin, snapping his neck.

Jason had broken Parker's stronghold. He shoved Parker off, then rolled over standing, his hands snatching at a huge bookcase for support.

Parker sprang at him again, but Jason's foot shot out hitting him in the stomach. Parker bent to hold his gut and Jason's uppercut clipped him under the point of his chin. Parker lurched backward stumbling toward his desk, his body slumping down against it.

Jason stood over him, tall, menacing, blood trickling down the side of his lip, shirttails hanging, chest heaving, one eye swelling and turning blue. "Listen to me, fucker," he heaved. "Don't you ever mess with me . . . again. You hear me? I'll make you . . . the sorriest son of a bitch . . . that ever walked the face of this earth." He staggered backward toward the door slowly opening it, his gaze stamped on Parker. "And that's the bottom line," he shouted slamming the door.

"The bottom line maybe," Parker mumbled, "but not the last word."

Parker agonized to his knees wincing, flinching, pains shooting up piercing his limbs, chest and neck. He staggered to the bar and poured himself a stiff drink. Quickly he let his head drop back, the liquor burning its way down into his stomach, a taste of blood lingering after. He had to get to a phone immediately.

He sprawled his body across his leather chair, his lungs still gasping for air and dialed a number.

"This is Steele," a voice on the other end said. Parker tried to catch his breath. "Hello, this is Sam Steele," the voice repeated.

"It's Hugh," he panted. "How's Chris?"

"Mr. Parker? Anything wrong?"

"No. No. I drank some water . . . wrong pipe. How's Chris?"

"He's just fine Mr. Parker. Sitting right here with Shauna and," he hesitated, "they're playing Monopoly."

"Good. Good." He paused. "Steele?"

"Yes sir."

"Take care . . . Chris . . . okay?"

"Sure, Mr. Parker. That's my job. Say, are you sure you're okay? You sound awful funny to me."

"I'm fine," Parker said, wiping a trickle of blood from the side of his mouth. "I just want you to be sure and watch Chris . . . carefully."

After he hung up, he felt foolish. He'd probably scared the hell out of Steele and for no good reason. Now he was sorry he'd called.

Sam Steele rubbed the top of his wide bald pate. His slitted fat eyes kept wandering back to the telephone and why he hadn't mentioned Sally Quinn to Hugh Parker. It was her first visit here to see Chris and he saw no harm in the female company. Besides she had great legs.

"Who was that?" Christopher Parker yelled straining his dark, handsome boyish face over Sally's blonde hair.

"Your dad," Steele said, chewing on some Vitamin C tabs.

"What'd he want?"

"Just said hello."

"That it?" Chris asked.

"Yeah," Steele answered wandering into the living room. He moved his massive bulk over to where the game was being played and stared down at Sally's shapely legs. They were all lying on the floor around a Monopoly board and Shauna was moving her man.

"Park Place," Shauna shouted. "I'll take it."

"Just remember, I have Boardwalk," Sally said handing her the blue bordered card, collecting money for the bank.

"I know," Shauna told her. "When I'm ready I'll trade you for Marvin Gardens."

"Maybe yes and maybe no," Sally said glancing at Steele, rearranging her limbs. "It's warm in here, isn't it?"

Chris reached behind for a box of tissues and wiped his nose. "Anymore tea?" he asked Steele, sniffling.

Steele stared at him, his bald head shaking from side to side. "Your memory ain't worth a damn, Chris. I said we had none this morning. I got to go to the store later."

"Now," Chris answered tossing the dice. "I need it now. I think I'm catching a cold."

"Okay, okay," Steele said. "Chew on these." He tossed him some vitamin C tabs. "I'll be back in a few minutes." Steele rattled the keys on his chain and glanced over at his locked bedroom. He hesitated, running some kind of checklist over in his mind of ways Chris might smuggle dope inside. Every room was bolted except for the bathroom and there was nothing in there. Both girls had handed over their purses and shoes on entering. Neither one wore a bra and he could tell from their tight shorts they had nothing hidden under their pants. No one could open the front door after he locked it and all the windows were wired to alarms. Besides, Shauna loved Chris. She'd never hurt him. Jesus! Hugh Parker had given him the willies.

Steele checked his wallet, reset the air conditioner to 70 degrees then opened the front door. "I'll be back in five minutes," he said closing it.

They heard the bolt click shut then Sally wiped the perspiration from the back of her neck and went to the bathroom. In one minute she was back, a small leather pouch in the palm of her hand.

"Where the hell did you have it?" Chris asked, his hands grabbing for the pouch.

"The only place Steele couldn't reach when he searched," Sally said laughing.

Chris roared. "Is this gonna smell like codfish or shit?"

"Does it matter?" Sally asked. "You'd snort it anyway." She opened the leather pouch and carefully arranged the contents. She poured white chunky powder from a tiny glass vial onto a small square mirror. With a 14-karat gold single-edged razor blade the size of her fingernail, she cut the powder into fine particles. "This stuff's the best Bolivian flake there is," she said drawing three straight rows of the now-fine powder across the mirror.

She handed Chris a six-inch, 14-karat gold straw. "Here," she said, "toot some."

Chris placed the straw up one nostril, then closed off the other with his finger. He sniffed powder until one of the white lines disappeared. He rubbed his nostrils hard, then sneezed. Shauna followed after, then Sally. Their high was immediate. Soon they were giggling, euphoric, falling all over each other, their eyes wide and alert, their omnipotence showing.

"Now," Sally said, lying back down on the floor, "let's talk about the rest of Plan B."

* * *

Sidney Gross slipped a long green challis robe over his small rotund body and settled comfortably back in his favorite chair. It was large, accommodating his bulk and covered in the skins of unborn calves.

He was more than a little pleased. Things were going very well. His plans for the movie *Explosion!*, based on the Mount St. Helens story, were materializing and all the Hollywood gossip columns were buzzing about an apparent rift within the ranks of Stone Management. His Fourth of July party had been the talk of both coasts, plus he had let Armando Del Gado and Hank Mason know he'd be there if they needed him. And now, this afternoon, the sweet blond with the blue eyes and very tight buns had paid him a visit. Unlike that selfish cunt Viva, he could help the sweet boy. It was all up to Davey.

He watched Tony Meredith running to and fro setting the tapes on the video board so he could watch replays of all the late news as Tony had earlier recorded them.

"Almost ready," Tony said disappearing again from the room.

Sidney placed his fat little feet on a soft cassock and picked at a large, hard callous under his right foot. He was growing impatient.

"Okay," Tony said reentering the dimly lit room. "Let 'er rip."

Sidney punched up the master switch on the video board and seven identical T.V. screens lit up simultaneously. He punched the sound up on only one. Smirking, he watched as each channel's lead story concerned the gala opening for the movie he had just produced. A television announcer spoke.

> Good evening ladies and gentlemen. A horrified crowd looked on helplessly tonight as Luis Marano, husband of movie star Roxanne Caulder, was knifed in the back by an unknown attacker, at the opening night gala for the movie, *Baby Grand*. Mr. Marano was attending the festivities with his wife, the star of the movie, and her manager, Sidney Gross.

Sidney's fingernails gouged away at the hard flesh on the bottom of his foot.

> Hundreds of photographers and world-wide television crews on hand for the big event caught the bizarre incident exactly as it occurred in front of the International Theatre. Miss Caulder was signing autographs as . . .

Sidney switched the sound off, then watched in silence obsessed, fascinated, as a smiling Luis suddenly gasped and stiffened, his eyes wide as silver dollars, then slumped gracelessly to the floor. A screaming, horrified Roxanne covered his bleeding body, her white fox furs spotted with blood. Sidney watched himself on the screen flying to her side, clutching her arm, calling soundlessly for an ambulance.

Seven channels, seven glorious angles; front-page news all over the world and it was only the beginning.

Sidney glanced quickly at Tony. "Somebody goofed," he said. "It wasn't supposed to happen that way. I hope you realize that. I hope you believe I never meant for that to happen."

Tony said nothing. He just sat there in the darkness, his cigarette tip glowing bright orange, a drink in his hand.

"Did you call the hospital?" Sidney asked.

"Yeah," Tony said. "He'll be all right in a few weeks. He won't be able to go with her on the tour to promote the movie though, if she'll still go, after this."

"She'll go," Sidney said confidently. "She'll do exactly as I say. Don't you worry about that. What about Elaine Shagan? Did you talk to her?"

Tony plunged a hissing cigarette into the remnants of his drink. "I talked to her today. She'll let you know sometime after Mike Stone gets back.'' He rose and left the room.

Sidney was smiling. He'd lied to Tony. It had all happened exactly as he'd planned it and he was tingling with excitement. He switched off the screens, calculating in his mind the millions of dollars he'd saved, against the worldwide publicity he'd garnered for nothing. Now he'd accompany Roxanne on the tour himself, the both of them gaining sympathy, creating enormous interest in the movie, traveling with an entourage of bodyguards, answering questions about the terrible ''accident'' and the awful rise in crime. Box office will be fantastic and his name would be on the lips of everyone. They'd do Carson, Griffin, Donahue, all the talk shows.

He felt like patting himself on the back but instead caressed the unborn calves' skin and thought of Davey Sullivan's buns as he looked standing in the doorway, a hundred dollar bill tucked inside his trousers.

It was 2 A.M. and Davey Sullivan dialed that number again. He had to. He had to try it one more time before taking Sid Gross's offer. At least Viva had screwed him only in the vernacular: Sid Gross would do it up his ass. He had to give that more thought. Five rings and someone picked up the phone.

''Hello!'' The voice was sleepy and hoarse.

''Mr. Stone?''

''Who the hell is this?'' Jason asked.

''I work for your sister, Viva, and I have some information I think you might be interested in.''

Jason was silent, his breathing heavy. ''What's it about?'' he asked finally.

''Hank Mason,'' Davey said then paused. ''There will be a small price, but I think you'll find it worth your while.''

''Be at my house in half an hour,'' Jason said and gave him the address.

Chapter 9

THE SAN FRANCISCO FOG hung over the city like some dingy gauze shroud. Each call to the airport was an exercise in futility.

Michael checked on Ada. No change. Then he called Hank. Big Al was concerned. Hank was depressed and threatening to leave. That's when he made the decision to rent a car and drive back. On an inland route, they'd avoid the fog and with shared driving they could make Los Angeles in less than ten hours. Waiting for a flight out left too much to chance.

Someplace south of Salinas on Highway 101 a gentle unseasonable rain began to fall. The windshield wipers beat a steady rhythm, smudging and shaping a pair of spotted fans on the window pane.

It was growing dark and Michael, exhausted from his previous nightwatch, had twice drifted across into other lanes. He was forced now to find a place for them to stay the night.

East of the Carmel Valley he had located a cabin group, its vacancy sign winking welcome in the rain. He parked, glanced at Nicole's sleeping face, then headed through the rain for the registration office.

"Welcome to Monterey County," the proprietor said, peering first at his guest roster, then out at Michael's automobile.

"I need something for tonight," Michael said, wiping his hands on his jacket.

"Got some good news and some bad news," the proprietor told him turning the register around. "The good news is there's one cabin left."

"The bad news?" Michael asked signing their names.

"It's expensive as hell."

Michael reached inside his pocket and handed him a credit card.

The proprietor swung the register around then squinting through his glasses he read their names. "Michael and Nicole Stone." He looked up at Michael. "Hope you and the Mrs. have a nice stay," he said handing him a key.

Before Michael could correct him, the proprietor had taken the credit card, recorded the entry and called his staff to freshen up their quarters.

"You've missed dinner," the proprietor said, but I'll see you get something." He handed Michael the credit card, then gave specific directions to a hilltop cabin situated behind the office.

Michael turned up his collar and ran for the car. The rain, falling hard now, drenched his thick dark hair and streamed down his face. He wiped the drops from his eyes and drove the narrow winding road up a steep hill until he located a rustic A-frame cabin. There were small lights strung along a pathway leading to the cabin, all of it towered over by huge oak trees.

Nicole was still asleep when he parked the car and for a moment, he stayed there listening to the rain and watching her, thinking of the proprietor's mistake. Then he nudged her and she opened her eyes.

"Where are we?" she mumbled, her knuckles lightly rubbing at her eyelids.

"Somewhere east of Eden I think," he answered, "around Steinbeck country. And, I don't think this driving idea was a very good one. I drifted into someone else's lane twice so I thought we should camp for the night."

"Yes, of course," she said agreeing, looking out the window appearing surprised at the darkness and the rain.

"You ready to run for it?" he asked her.

"As ready as I'll ever be."

Michael opened his door, slammed it shut then grabbed their suitcases from the trunk. He opened Nicole's door and she followed, clinging onto the back of his jacket. Along the pathway they navigated long and irregularly spaced redwood rounds which led to the cabin. A heavy rain fell around them; their shoes splashed through deep occasional puddles of muddy water.

Inside the warm cabin they stood speechless, staring at the vastness of the A-frame redwood ceiling, tall stained glass windows and hand-carved Victorian furniture. Flames crackled in an old-fashioned fireplace, the firelight reflecting upon a huge white alpaca hearth rug.

"This is lovely," Nicole said shedding her wet shoes and outer garments heading straight for the fireplace. She crouched down low, her arms thrust forward toward the heat, and her palms and fingers rubbing together. Michael removed his shoes and followed.

"You'd better change your wet things," he said, then laughed with her at the sight of his own.

In the bathroom Nicole squealed with delight at an antique copper tub with gold claw feet. It sat poised on a dark red carpet, lush green ferns hanging from every corner. The scent of magnolias drifted here and there from bars of home made soap and sachet.

In the bedroom, standing antique mirrors reflected the many angles of a huge, rosewood, canopied four-poster bed with its matching pink satin comforter and six pillows. The room was softly lit by tiny Tiffany lamps and there were fresh bouquets of wildflowers everywhere.

They were silent, staring at each other. Than Michael dropped her luggage and left the bedroom.

He headed for the bathroom, showering quickly, changing into pale-blue pajama bottoms and a short navy velour robe. Nicole followed after, bathing, emerging wrapped in a long chiffon robe and gown the color of pale milk trimmed in delicate cream lace at the neckline and sleeves. She carried two terrycloth towels.

Michael sat on the soft rug close to the fire, a glass of Chenin Blanc in his hand, hot fresh baked bread and home-made cheese on a china plate nearby.

She poured a glass of wine and joined him on the rug.

"I tried to get two cabins," he said staring into the leaping flames. "This was all they had."

"This is lovely," she said sipping her wine. "All of it's lovely. Besides," she reminded him. "If I were alone I would have spent the whole night lying awake waiting for the bogeyman."

"Who knows," he said smiling. "The bogeyman might be right here with you."

"I don't think so," she said. "I'm a pretty good judge of bogeymen. You don't stand a chance."

She wrapped her long thick hair in a terry towel, then moved to Michael. He felt the towel cover his still damp hair, felt her gently tossing it about. The fragrance of the magnolia soap was intensified by the heat and he inhaled its subtle scent.

"There," she said running her fingers through his hair strands, "that's much better."

"Needs another log," he said raising up on his knees placing a thick log in the center of the blaze. He raked the fire for a minute letting the small glowing embers fall to the bottom then sat back and sipped his wine.

"Have something to eat," he said gesturing toward the bread and cheese. "There's some fresh fruit on that table, if you like."

She rose and from a large pewter bowl which rested on an antique cart, he chose a ripe sweet orange. She took a small sharp paring knife and began to cut through the crinkly thick shell. Suddenly she screamed and Michael sprang to her side.

Her index finger was bleeding and he pressed it to his lips, sucking the blood from the small wound. Her other hand lightly touched the side of his head and for just one crazy moment he thought he would crush her to his body.

"It's not deep," he said standing up looking for a clean white handkerchief he had stashed in his suitcase. "Wash it and wrap it with this," he told her, "then get some sleep. We'll make it an early start in the morning." He turned and walked away. "I'll camp out here," he told her taking off his robe. His voice had a cool edge to it.

She headed silently toward the bedroom, wrapping her finger, her eyes sweeping the grainy floorboards.

''Better leave the door open a bit,'' he called. ''It might get cold in there.'' She nodded and shut it half-way. He stoked the fire once then rested his weary body on a red floral sofa sliding a knitted afghan across his legs.

Her door slowly opened and sheepishly she approached him, a goosedown pillow in her arms. ''You'll need this,'' she said avoiding contact with his eyes. He took the pillow, thanking her, rolling and tucking it under his head and then gazed after as her slender silhouette glided back across the room.

Alone staring at the flickering shadows, he experienced all the painful hunger he'd been submerging for so many years. He swung one arm across his eyes to shut out the faint firelight. He'd have given anything to shut out the gnawing pain in his gut.

Sometime, somehow, he fell asleep twisting and turning, tormented by an endless stream of forfeited, relinquished dreams. Asleep, he thought he heard her cry out and he jumped awake. He listened but there was no sound. Was he dreaming, perhaps too vividly? He settled back then for sure heard her again. He ran to her room and pushed open the door. She was sobbing in her sleep, lying at the edge of the bed, her fists pummeling the pillow, that satin comforter lying in a heap on the floor.

He walked quickly to her bed, grasped her bare shoulders.

''Nicole, wake up. You're having a nightmare.''

Her eyes blinked open and she stared blankly at him. There was a curious, frightened look on her face but then, she softened.

''Sh, sh,'' he repeated, comforting her, then realized his fingers were tightening about her warm flesh. He drew his hands away quickly and reached below for the quilt to cover her.

''Goodnight again,'' he whispered, walking toward the door, ''sweet dreams this time.''

In the living room he started the fire noticing that some of the blackened embers he poked were still red-hot inside. So like his love for her, he thought. Lying there still and quiet, seemingly innocent and cool, but inside, glowing hot ready to burst into flames.

He moved the red couch closer to the fire and settled

back drifting off again to sleep. He dreamed he was swimming in a cool clear lake surrounded by lily pads. He was alone, floating on his back watching sun-drenched dragonflies flit across lily blossoms. Then something beneath the water tugged at his arm, then his leg pulling him below and he came awake.

She was lying on the hearth rug, her back to the fire, her arms cradling her neck and head.

"I was afraid," she said. "I keep dreaming things and I don't want to be alone."

He sat, his bare feet touching the damp wooden floor, his fingers wiping the sleep from his eyes. "It's all right," he said rising, taking her hand. "I'll stay with you."

He helped her to her feet then trailed after as she went into the bedroom. Her gown could have been woven by spiders, he thought watching her as the light drifted in from the bedroom and floated through her pale sheer garments.

She climbed in under the soft satin comforter, her long honey-hair falling over the pink pillow like a silk fringe. He followed, his firm body next to her on top of the quilt, careful not to touch her with his arms.

"You'll be cold," she said, her eyes skimming over his naked chest.

"Just close your eyes."

She lowered her lids and in a matter of seconds tears collected in the corners of her eye then glistened down her cheeks. He touched them lightly with his finger wiping them away. "What's wrong, Nicole?" he said softly. "Tell me, please."

"Just hold me, Michael," she cried. "Just hold me." Her eyes were shut tightly as she spoke and he could feel her body shiver.

He slid beneath the smooth covers then guided his muscled arm carefully under her silky back. He drew her close to his naked chest and those damned magnolias enveloped him.

Lying there, he tried to think of anything but her. He recalled the last time he had been with a woman. It was in Honolulu; his crazy days with Van Tilden. He was roaring drunk making love to a slim and beautiful wahine with hip-length hair and copper-colored skin. All he thought about then was Nicole. Now he was desperately trying to remember Leila.

He felt Nicole's sweet breath blow cool and warm upon his skin, her damp lashes fluttering lightly on his chest. His nostrils inhaled the scent of her hair, sweet and clean like the rainwater that had passed through it. He thought then, of Hank. He wanted to tell him that he understood the lure of the forbidden and the pain of denial and he promised himself he would do that when he returned to Los Angeles.

He listened to her breathing. She was still and soundly sleeping now, her lips slightly parted. Her arm lazily extended, curving its way around his back and he turned further on his side to see her. On an impulse, his fingers caressed her long silky hair, then marked the shape of her bottom lip. She didn't move.

He could kiss her and she'd never know. He could just move his head closer and brush his lips across hers . . . just to see how it feels.

She pushed herself closer and he felt her strong even heartbeat, the contours of her soft breasts cushioned against him, rising and falling with each breath. Suddenly she stirred and her body grew rigid. Some nightmare was stealing its way through her subconscious. He held her close, comforting her, and the feelings inside him were unbearable.

She began to cry out, pushing him away. "Oh God, no. Joe. Please don't touch me." Her amber eyes clicked open and she tried to focus on him. "Oh, Michael," she said whispering. "Oh, Michael, it's you." Her arms wrapped around him.

They were locked in an embrace, merging and floating, then suddenly spinning wildly. Some strange and strong ocean tide had rolled in over them, pulling them out to sea into deep, sweet, mysterious whirling waters. His mouth swept across the length and breadth of her face and eyes, covering her full lips. Her body grew soft and pliant. He felt her fingers tighten about his neck weaving through, pulling his hair. He tasted the honey from her mouth and that terrible, terrible longing for her slowly slipped away. He wanted to cry.

"I love you, Nicole," he whispered in her ear. "I've loved you from the moment I first saw you."

She didn't answer, but he knew from the look in her eyes she was content. Her limbs pushed up against his, her pelvis arching its way toward him and it happened.

They were moth and flame, wind and weathervane, lock and key. There was nothing for him to fight any longer.

She wakened floating, lost in some reverie, bathed in the sunshine that streamed through the stained glass windows, as if the room were a French cathedral. She was in the middle of a love story, her own. All night long he'd kissed her, made love to her, touched her hands and her heart. For the first time in her life, her body had unfolded like some dormant flower after a long winter's sleep. It was spring at last.

She watched him sleep. His sensuous hair was tousled, drawn over his tanned forehead in waves. His lashes, thick and shiny. The look on his face in repose, soft and satisfied. She wanted to kiss him, to taste the flavor of his mouth and feel the soft hairs of his lips brush across her eyes and cheeks.

He had been strong and tender last night; a perfect lover. Passionate and shy, gentle but assertive, giving and receiving, tuned to her in ways that seemed strange and mystical. And that feeling. Like floating on some soft and silky cloud, each of her senses heightened, alive and reaching. Now, feeling his arms about her, his head resting over her heart, breathing in his masculinity, she was invincible.

All those years building layers of protection, selecting and discarding bits and pieces of her life just to survive. All those years now receded, shattered, finally fading away as though they had never happened . . . all because of him.

And who was she now? What was she? No. No questions. At least not now, she thought and closed her eyes just listening to the sounds of him, afraid she was dreaming—afraid she was not.

After breakfast they drove south heading home, fingers

curling into fingers, meaningful and awkward silences. She talked of Joe and Jason, her career or what there was of it. He spoke of his long-felt heartbreaking love for her and how he'd endured it all by running away. They spoke of the future.

"What will we do?" she asked.

"I want to be with you," he told her. "Not just for now and certainly not like this."

"It's all so crazy, Mike. Your mother and father. Jason. My God. He could even kill you." She started to panic thinking of all the things that could happen. "Why can't we run away somewhere?"

"No," he replied. "I won't do it like that."

"But you ran before. It worked for you then, didn't it?"

"No. It didn't," he replied. "What's more I ran away because I knew things would never change. I tried for a new life. But it's different now. For you and for me. We have a chance."

She sat, staring out an open window, the wind fanning her hair, her eyes searching the vast stretches of fertile farmland, her stomach churning. "Jason scares me," she said. "Sometimes I think he's capable of anything, even murder. He'll be very angry."

He laughed nervously. "I know what you mean," he told her. "There was a girl once, *my* girl. Her name was Lee. I was about sixteen and she was a little older, I think. Jason had been away in New York for about six months on some deal. I thought I was really in love with her until Jason came home. In three days I found him sleeping with her in his bedroom. I went crazy. I couldn't believe it. We fought. I'm pretty good with my fists, but he pulled a gun. Aimed it square up, right against my temple. Jesus, it made me sweat. Then he pulled the trigger real slow. All the chambers were empty; his idea of a practical joke. Man, I was relieved. I didn't care two bits about that girl any more.

"Later, Jason had me convinced, he'd taken her because he loved me. He wanted to show me she was nothing more than a tramp. I believed him and I suppose in some way it was true. He is weird that way. He's always had this thing about women too. 'Only two kinds

Michael,' he'd say, 'whores and angels, that's it.' So typical of him."

"I wonder what he thought of me back then?" she said.

"Definitely an angel."

"No more," she said, her voice cracking, her eyes starting to glisten. "Not after last night."

He pulled the car quickly to the side of the road and took her into his arms. "Do you love me, Nicole?" he said.

"Yes, yes, but . . ."

"No. No buts. Do you love me, yes or no?"

"Yes," she whispered.

He pushed her gently away, his eyes searching hers for meaningful truths. "Are you sure?"

"I . . . I've never felt this way . . . before," she managed to say. "Not ever."

"Then tell me this." He was focused, demanding her attention. "Are you happy?" She shut her eyes. "Are you willing to spend the rest of your life living it the way you've been living it?" She was silent. "Answer me! Answer me now. Because what you say will affect us both—forever!"

"No!" she finally shouted, her hand leaping to her lips. "Oh God, no!" She burst into tears, her body a quivering mass.

He pulled her tightly to him, his lips resting on her cheek. "There. Then it doesn't matter what Jason thinks. It simply doesn't matter. Just remember that. We'll find some way to work this out. You and me together."

He kissed her eyes, then her lips, cupping her chin. His hunger and energy flowed through her and soon they were one breath, one spirit, one heartbeat, one. She felt her body grow weightless, passing through his, and she was thrilled and terrified at the power they shared.

She grew stronger every minute, her mind clearer. She listened as the cars whizzed by, believing what he said, knowing this as an infinite moment in time, immortal and impenetrable, eternally theirs and theirs alone.

Chapter 10

"WHAT HAVE YOU GOT FOR ME KID," Jason asked, tying the braided cord on his gray satin robe. They were standing in Jason's living room and it was almost six A.M.

Davey, carefully noting Jason's swollen jaw and black eye, nervously presented his case. "I . . . I have information," he said. "And I don't want money for it . . . I . . . I want a job."

Jason studied him, bewildered. "I don't get you, kid. You want to mow my lawns or something?" He gestured for Davey to be seated then lit a cigarette.

Davey obliged tugging first at his jeans, then opening the zipper on his short blue jacket. He rested an elbow on the chair's arm, his thumb and forefinger sliding across his sweaty forehead. "I'm an actor," he said. "A damn good one too. I read *Variety* last week and I want a leading role in that new film you're starting . . . with commitments for your next three features."

"Don't make me laugh kid," Jason said. "It hurts my jaw too much." Then Jason's gaze grew cold and brittle and his arms waved about his head like semiphore flags on a warship. "Don't you play games with me kid. Don't you jerk me off at six in the morning handing me wild ultimatums. You fucking better tell me what you came here for."

"I told you," Davey repeated trembling, his dime-store confidence starting to disintegrate. "I have information

. . . in exchange . . . I want a job. I've listened to the way Viva talks to you. Just like she talks to me. Like you're garbage or something. I'm only trying to protect myself."

Jason listened, slowly inhaling and exhaling smoke, then seated himself beside Davey. "Okay," he said extending his hand. "You got it. Now, let's hear this vital information."

Davey stared at Jason's hand but didn't move. "I want it in writing," he said boldly, amazed at his own impudence.

Jason sprang to his feet. "Fuck off, kid. I don't have time for all this bullshit. You either take my word or take off."

Davey stood quickly, his heart pounding wildly. He walked swiftly to the front door, then hesitated. He turned to Jason and all at once, as though he were fearful of losing his nerve, recanted the story about Hank Mason and the conversation he had overheard Viva have with Michael. "I don't want my name to come up," he said. "Viva's got it in for me. She could really screw me up if she found out about this visit."

Jason smiled reassuring him, the flat of his palm gently patting the space between Davey's shoulder blades. "I understand, kid," he said taking Davey's arm, escorting him to the front door. "I really do. Don't worry. Your secret's safe with me."

"What about our deal?" Davey reminded him as he stood precariously perched on the front doorstep. "I want a contract of some kind."

"Sure, kid, sure. Later. At my office. It's six in the morning," Jason said. "Give me a break. Besides, I gave you my word, didn't I? Trust me."

Jason's spirits were uplifted by Davey's visit and he suppressed a deep-rooted urge to laugh outloud when he'd closed the door. He sauntered back through the living-room opening the glass doors onto the quiet patio. Outside, he stood between the huge marble columns listening to the new morning begin, feeling like some great distinguished general contemplating his weapons and troops before a grand winning battle. And, it felt good to be on the winning side for a change.

And poor Davey. What a joke! He'd give him a break

all right, just below the kneecaps, if he was lucky. He'd entered the big leagues after his fight with Parker. The last thing he needed was a Davey Sullivan hanging around.

The big leagues, he thought smiling. Screw the Board of Corporations and Ada's new will, for that matter. He didn't need any of it now. No more scrounging around, no more unpaid markers in Las Vegas, no more frantic, threatening phone calls from the local money lenders. Instead they'd be calling him now, wanting to invest in *his* stable of bankable stars, wanting a piece of *his* action.

He walked inside and checked the time. It was seven and he was as hungry as a bear. He'd shower, have breakfast and give Hank Mason a call.

It was almost ten when Jason finally called Hank. He made him an offer he couldn't refuse. If Hank would support Jason's efforts as the official head of Stone Management, absolutely refuse to work in any medium unless Michael stepped down, then he, Jason, wouldn't release any news to the press about Hank's escapade in Mexico. That particular secret would be safe with him.

"What happened to you was Mike's fault," Jason told Hank. "He should have taken better care of you. Now, me? I'd have gotten you exactly what you wanted right here in town. When I run things you'll never have to go to Tijuana or anywhere else for what you want or need."

Hank was silent, then said he'd call Jason later.

They dined in Santa Barbara at the lovely old Spanish Inn high above the Pacific. The sun-dappled dining room was bursting with greenery and the wainscotted cream walls contrasted elegantly with dark, carved wood ceiling beams and cranberry leather booths. One wall of tinted windows provided visual access to an endless and changing seascape while a flamenco guitarist wailed softly across the room.

They drank salty margaritas, as Michael watched a lazy sunbeam stalk Nicole's face, while she, squinting, tried to avoid it. He remembered the taste of her mouth and the feel of her firm, silky thighs against his. There was power in her body, the kind that comes from discipline and training; from years of willing her body to leap and bend unnaturally, dancing inside the heart of space, exploring and capturing its reality.

She seemed relaxed, engaging, dressed in a lemon yellow dirndl skirt and antique peasant blouse.

"What are you thinking about?" Michael finally asked.

"Us," she replied. "What will happen when we get back?"

"I'm not sure. We'll just have to take it a step at a time. Play it by ear, I guess."

She toyed with her coffee, lightly stirring the creamy liquid. "I keep coming back to your family and what they'll think."

"There you go again," he said. "Why, is what they think so important to you?"

She mulled that for a moment. "I suppose because I've never had a family of my own and I value one," she said.

Nor I, he wanted to say and wondered if that was precisely why that same thought had not preoccupied him. He removed a hand-carved Dunhill pipe from the pocket of his jacket. He poured fresh aromatic tobacco into the briar bowl, tamping it deftly then lighting it. The smoke drifted lazily upward fading, dissipating. "Tell me about your career," he said at last.

"What career? I've done one commercial in three years and that was for some renegade English company." She smiled. "I was a plump raisin," she said with mock pride.

"They're not only renegade, they're blind."

She giggled. "Honestly, if I didn't know better I'd think there's a conpiracy against me. I just can't seem to make any connections."

"That's crazy," Michael said. "Right now, here in this room you're dining with the very pinnacle of power. You have influence now," he said blowing on his fingertips and brushing the nails back and forth acrcss his shirt, a devilish grin on his lips.

"Seriously, Mike. When I go on interviews, all anyone wants to know is whether or not I'm related to Ada."

"And?"

"Nothing. I've always said no."

"Why?" Michael asked.

"I was always afraid they'd call Ada and she'd be angry."

"Next time," he said pointing the pipe stem at her, "you tell them yes. You tell them to call my office. We'll see how fast your career options open up. Your face belongs on magazine covers, television screens. I can make you a star," he said with playful enthusiasm.

"You're bad, Michael Stone. Bordering on awful," she told him, "and I believe Hollywood has gone to your head."

"When it reaches my heart, I'll kill myself. Until then, you listen to what I say. Besides," he added, "maybe you have two left feet. I'd like to know how really lousy you are."

She tossed a sugar cube at him. "Okay, Mike. You're on. We'll see which one of us is lousy."

Outside, a strong gust of wind caught the folds of her skirt blowing it up around her thighs. She thrust her arms down, laughing, trying to keep the soft yellow cotton from billowing up over her waist.

He stooped to help but the wind suddenly diminished leaving his arms wrapped around her buttocks. He lifted her roguishly high into the air, clasping her tightly, suddenly aware of the heat from her body, the contours of her throat and naked shoulders.

"Everything will be okay," he said feeling a tightness in the pit of his stomach. "I promise."

She gazed down at him threading her hands through his dark wavey hair, slowly drawing him to her. His mouth opened to speak but she clasped his head tightly. He closed his eyes, listening to the sound of her heartbeat, his face buried deep between the soft curves of her breasts.

* * *

On any given day, Stone Management's Beverly Hills office bristled with activity. Phones jangled off the walls, agents laughed, wheeling and dealing, shifting their clients about like pawns on a chessboard, staking out their territories and shaping their individual futures: A dozen typewriters clicked interminably, sheets of paper rustled, flying in or out of anybody's hands. There were scripts to read, that special movie or television show to package, a conversation with the head of a major network or perhaps Robert Redford.

Spread across rows of desks, glossy photographs, 8X10 black-and-white smiling faces of beautiful children, their heads filled with Cinderella dreams, their futures hovering in the fragile space between stardom and the wastebasket. And Viva loved it all. All of it excited her.

Now, she sat poised on a brown velour chair in the dim wood-paneled viewing room, two Joan Miro lithographs observing her. She rose, her mind thoroughly engaged, examining, analyzing, cultivating the elation she was feeling.

Jesus! That kid had something. Ada was right on the money. She chose a brown Sherman cigarette from a Waterford crystal dish and lit it, inhaling deeply, wondering how to proceed. She brushed lint from her white handkerchief linen shirt dress and clicked her long orange fingernails across her pale coral beads. It was warm in the windowless room.

She buzzed her secretary and waited impatiently for the door to open. A young, slim California blonde with long blue-jeaned legs entered carrying a steno pad.

"Close the door and have a seat," Viva said. "I want you to watch something, then give me your gut reaction."

Viva stationed herself behind the blonde to observe her response, then switched on the viewing machine. Paul Kiley's screen test began again. It was the third time she'd seen it and the goosebumps rose to the surface of her skin immediately. Jesus, she thought, few people have that kind of presence. Monty Clift, Diana Ross, Marilyn, Liza, James Dean. Something about them, their special vulnerable beauty that hypnotized; made you stare only at them, even in a crowd scene. Every angle was interesting, special. Every movement filled with some tense, raw power; their personna, elusive and spiritual, vibrating over the finite line dividing life from the valley of the shadows: death's own and brightest angel. And that special quality, it could never be bought or taught. You either had it or you didn't.

Viva observed the blonde. Her face had that look of amazement.

"What do you think?" Viva asked.

"God," she sighed. "He's unmercifully beautiful. I don't know if I want to screw him or mother him."

"That's precisely it," Viva said, clicking off the machine. "That's it, exactly!" Her mind took off at ninety miles an hour. "Call him," Viva said thrusting Paul's photo and telephone number at the girl. "Tell him I want him here first thing tomorrow morning. And, don't disturb me unless it's about that damn Del Gado."

Now, she thought, listening to the door close, how to handle him, how to bring him along. It had to be done right or it could backfire.

Kiley'd need a drama coach, maybe singing lessons and dancing lessons. She wanted the best in the business. The right publicity, his name and photograph would appear in the Hollywood columns and fan magazines. He'd need new photos. Also photo sessions with Bobbi Sands, Hank Mason, and that shit Del Gado if he'd give a newcomer a break.

Paul Kiley's resume wasn't bad. New York. Some leading roles, off Broadway. Good solid New York theatre training and some summer stock. Classy. Could be another quick eruption like Brando.

He'd need an allowance, an apartment in the canyons or Beverly Hills; some very good clothes, a tux and a car. She'd consider a name change, invent some things in his bland biography. Make him the son of a coal miner, perhaps. The little people like that. One of their own makes good. Always pleases the public.

She'd escort him to Chasens, Ma Maison, the Polo Lounge. Get him a publicist and let the columns buzz for a while. Follow with a full-page photo in *Variety*, opposite Army Archerd's column. Classy spot. Introduce him to the industry. Need some mystery. Then, with a few well-placed feature parts and the right fan-mail. . . .

New blood. She loved it almost as much as Ada did. She rang her secretary. "Have Parker draw up a contract on Kiley. Commercials, film, T.V. full representation. Lease a new Jag for him at Southwest and call the realtor. Tell them I need a terrific apartment in Laurel Canyon. Ask Josef to take Paul to Rodeo Drive—Gucci's Bijàn." She paused to breathe. "That's it for now," she said and hung up.

Now all she had to do was calm down and hope that Paul Kiley really would be worth all the time, trouble and money.

* * *

Driving down the coast toward home, Michael's head swarmed with a thousand questions. Each one complex. Each one playing itself over and over, like a series of broken records. He wondered if Ada would ever get well. If she'd ever leave that hospital alive. How would that affect him and his plans? *His plans.* What plans? To steal Jason's wife? Ride off into the fabulous sunset?

He thought of Nicole and the powerful desire she aroused. It was wonderful and it was awful, similar to the way Hank described his own crazy compulsion.

Then there was Del Gado and the fight they'd almost had. He'd gone to San Francisco to perform a manager's duty. To be sure the interview went well, the film proceeded smoothly. To be sure no one took advantage of Ada's star. To protect him. Hah! From who? Himself?

He recalled the smug look on Armando's face as he left Nicole's room after the fight. As if his stardom alone granted him the privilege to be drunk, to attempt rape, reminding Michael as he left that there was nothing he could do to prevent the star's lawless and tyrannical behavior. Michael would have a talk with him. He would have to meet Armando half-way for Ada's sake, regardless of his own feelings.

He traced the wild, unpredictable beauty of the California coastline. Tall eucalyptus trees were shedding their sandy barkshells. They stood like fine old soldiers crossing their lances forming archways along the road.

The sky was cloudless and pale blue setting off acres of green and rolling hills or towering rock cliffs, drunk and heady, overgrown with California poppies, shrubs and daisies.

All the way to Ventura, the blue restless Pacific, its white foaming waves breaking on the shore, swallowed and regurgitated rocks, creating infinite, living tidepools and fishing grounds for screeching skybirds.

At Malibu, he suggested a course of action and Nicole agreed. There'd be no meetings between them until Michael and Jason had spoken. Then and only then could they contemplate any kind of life together.

This love they shared, this magic between them was

some kind of miracle. It was far too valuable, too beautiful to sully with clandestine meetings or secret rendezvous. They were determined to do it right.

He turned on the radio. "Do you mind?" he asked, country music drifting from the speakers.

"Nope," she said. "I love it."

She sang along with the music encouraging Michael to join her. Suddenly the music stopped. A news bulletin. Nicole turned up the volume.

> "Sad news today, ladies and gentlemen. One of America's brightest lights lies near death at this hour in St. John's Hospital. Hank Mason, winner of two grammys. . . ."

Michael gasped. Nicole bit her bottom lip.

> ". . . tried to take his own life this afternoon and was found by his companion and bodyguard, Big Al Thomas. We'll have more on this story in a few minutes."

Michael's foot jammed down hard on the accelerator, his fingers gripping the steering wheel. If he hadn't known better, he'd have sworn it was raining.

There was bedlam in the hallways of St. John's Hospital. Newsmen and women, photographers, television crews clustered in the corridors like vultures over carion, their cameras and mini-cams poised, waiting for the real story. Uniformed nurses and weary physicians rushed in and out of the intensive care unit, carefully, intentionally avoiding the constant, the persistant and sometimes tasteless questions put to them regarding Hank Mason's condition.

And Hank Mason was definitely news. There was no doubt about that. *Why?* people would ask. Why would America's son, the young and randy cowboy who had overnight captured the hearts and souls of his country, the one whose ballads and songs rejoiced and celebrated the purple mountains, verdant hills and blue rivers of America;

whose songs of love, of life, of hope beamed like bright beacons across the nation—*why would he kill himself*?

He lived the American dream. He was the American dream. A dream can die perhaps, but not commit suicide. The public would have to know.

Michael rode the slow-moving hospital elevator, his fingers impatiently drumming against the walls, an overwhelming sense of guilt gnawing away at him. Why? Why did he do it? Jesus. God. What if he dies? It would be his own fault, Michael thought. Clearly his own responsibility for leaving him. God. He should never have gone to San Francisco. This would never have happened. Then he glanced at Nicole, huddling in the elevator corner. A lot of things would never have happened.

Michael charged through the opening elevator doors. He stopped at the nurses' station to identify himself and receive an escort through the news-hungry mob.

"Who's that?" one newsman asked another.

"Hank's brother, I think."

"He has no brother, asshole," another said.

"Then who the hell is he?"

"I'll get it from the nurse when she comes back out."

Michael burst through the swinging clattering doors, Nicole trailing behind. Viva was leaning awkwardly against a wall near Big Al, their faces set and grim. Viva ran to Michael's arms. Her sobs wracked her body, some unintelligible account of the day's events burst forth from her lips.

"How is he?" Michael asked when she was calm.

Viva wiped her eyes and nose, her shoulders shrugging the only answer she had.

He pursued it. "Where's the doctor?"

"Still in there," she managed to say. "Oh God," she broke again. "What if he doesn't make it?"

Michael grasped her shoulders. "Don't say that. He has to make it. He has to."

Michael turned to Big Al. His six-foot-four-inch frame was hunched over, his eyes swimming in pink pain. "I let him down, man. I ain't worth shit."

"What happened?" Michael asked.

Through gasps and an heroic attempt at composure he explained. "I don't know. He was depressed like I said when you called. Then he got this call sometime in the morning and when he hung up his face was white . . . like a sheet or something. I asked him who it was, what it was about, but he wouldn't tell me. He skipped lunch ... walked the grounds for a while, then went back to his room. He said for me not to bother him . . . that he needed to sleep . . . and I believed him. Shit!'' Al kicked the wall and turned away. ''Christ Mike, I'm the one who did it! I let him go in there without checking on him or anything. The only reason I found him was because of his wife, Alma. She called and wanted to speak to him. I wasn't going to let her but she insisted. And that's when I found him and called an ambulance.''

Michael tried to console him, but Big Al pushed him away.

Suddenly the door to Hank's room opened and Dr. Morgenstern emerged. The expression on his face was haunted and desolate.

''How is he?'' Michael asked.

''Can't say, Mike,'' Morgenstern said. He slid his stethoscope into his pockets and just shook his head. ''He swallowed a large quantity of mixed pills. We're doing everything we can to help him but I just don't know, frankly.'' The hospital intercom interrupted, announcing a call for Dr. Morgenstern. ''I'll see you later, Mike, when I know more.''

Michael felt helpless and sick at heart, all the time wondering why Hank had done it.

He peered into Hank's room on an impulse. Two nurses were busy charting logs, checking a myriad of clicking, sucking machines, engrossed in and observing Hank. Hank. He looked so damn pitiful, bottles dripping their life-sustaining liquids into his blood stream. Michael felt the taste of sour bile oozing its way onto his tongue and he quickly closed the door.

''I have to talk to you, Michael,'' Viva said, leading him off to the side. ''It's as good a time as any to tell you,'' she said puffing on her cigarette. ''We've got other problems. Del Gado's threatening to talk to the Labor Commission. Since he got back from San Francisco, he claims we're stealing money from him. And there's Max. . . . He's done it. He's signed his stock shares over to Jason."

Michael's face turned white, his eyes staring at her in disbelief.

"Parker says we should fight it," she continued, "try to stall things for a while at least. But it looks legal and will more than likely stand up in court if it comes down to it. We have to make a decision. We either sell, fight Jason or try to make it work the way it is."

"Damn!" Michael shouted, "I just don't believe this." He whirled and suddenly his mind went blank. There were no intercom sounds, no hospital smells, no images. Nothing but an eerie, blinding rage that overcame him. He didn't know why and he cared little to understand the reason, but some other voice inside kept repeating Ada's name. When he finally spoke, his voice was disembodied and filled with a frantic despair. "I've got to get out of here for a while. I've got to think, to clear my head."

No one tried to stop him. He ran blindly through the swinging doors, past the hordes of news people away from the jockeying, posturing crowd.

He headed straight for Ada's room. He stopped outside her door, to collect his random thoughts, to compose what there was of his senses.

She's grown thinner, he thought, as he opened the door, her pale white face lost in a tangle of long black hair, her neck and arms boney and frail against the sheets and covers. He placed a hardback chair by her bedside, sitting down, folding his hands. He reached out to touch her, then changed his mind.

"I screwed up, Ada," he said, his hands clenching. "Hank's sick," he stumbled, "half-dead, and I had a fight with Del Gado." He leaned an elbow on the bed and rested his forehead. . . .

"And that's not all," he muttered clearing his throat, "Max has given Jason that 20 percent you let him own. That was always your fault about Max; not wanting to make him look like some damn fool. Well, it backfired—on you, Ada.

"Christ!" His head fell heavily into his hands. He felt stupid and childlike, without a defense. "Jason finally owns a piece of you. Honest to God. If that doesn't make your pulse jump I don't know what the hell will." He felt his insides ripping.

"I guess I went a bit Hollywood, too," he said raising his head and staring at her seemingly lifeless form. "This business has a quiet way of sucking you in." He bit his lip. "I never thought it would happen to me. But, I was wrong." His gentle laughter was touched with irony. "You should have seen me with the wines and the credit cards." He stared out the window. "We're at that notorious bottom line you always spoke so much about Ada, and I'll tell you the truth. I'm just a little bit scared. I mean, I hope I can really keep it all together. How the hell you did, I'll never know."

He leaned in close and whispered into her ear. "You have to get well—you hear me?" There was desperation and panic in the sound of his voice. "You have to get your act together."

He began absent-mindedly to adjust her pillows.

"And, I want you to know this, for sure. I'll be here. Nobody's getting rid of me. But I can't do it without you. And, Oh God, Ma . . . I need you." He was surprised at the ease with which the tears rolled down his cheeks. "I mean, Jesus, I . . . really need you." He wiped his eyes with his arm. "I'll give it all I have, I swear. They'll have to bury me before I give another inch. But please, Ada, please—"

His head collapsed on the side of the bed near Ada's hand. He placed his hand on the inside of her palm. And then he lay there, desolate, feeling his mother's touch for the first time in almost sixteen years and it was cold and limp and very still and he shook, sobbing for all that had never been.

Book II

RETAKES

Chapter 11

THEY WERE HUMAN CARGO. A vast migration from Eastern Europe carrying their rag-bundled dreams aboard old and rusting ships telling tales of a promised new land. Some never saw the land they yearned for. Instead, they died in the arms of hope, their dead eyes spellbound, still searching the dark horizons for the Liberty Statue.

The spring of 1922 was cruel and harsh to those who dared cross the awesome angry Atlantic. Somewhere near the New York City Harbor a young woman, her breath heaving with the waves, died in childbirth. Her legacy, a healthy baby girl she wished to call Ada.

In the New World the child's father, Sergei Raschenkov, grew increasingly bitter. He found it all too difficult; the loneliness, the new language, no hope of finding a decent job, the care of this hungry, churlish child who had caused the death of his beloved wife. He despaired ceaselessly, and at the outset of the Great Depression he left, placing Ada in care of waterfront missionaries.

"I return," he told her in halting English.

"*Kogda* Papa?" she asked in Russian.

"*Ne znayoo,*" he answered averting his eyes. Then he gave her a frayed brown envelope and left.

On a tiny cot inside the bleak mission, Ada cried herself to sleep. Before morning she wakened and in the dark stillness opened the envelope to study the contents. There were certificates of health, birth, immigration and one tattered photograph of her beautiful mother, Vibiana. She searched the features, her baby fingers tracing her mother's long shiny black hair with its odd streak of white near the left temple. She drew the photograph to her lips, closing her tear streaked eyes, then tucked it inside her dirty bib. Alone, at the tender age of seven, she resigned herself to surviving.

Ada Raschenkov adjusted. She worked, went to school, scrubbed toilets and floors thriving on all of life's adversities. Where others seemed weak and unable, Ada was strong and willing. Where others had given up, Ada was only beginning. When her colleagues worked fourteen hours, six days a week, Ada worked eighteen and seven. It would not be for the Lord she would rest. She could not abide this mystical vengeful God who had taken her young mother and cast her desperate father to the four winds.

She weathered the Great Depression years along with the rest; begging, sometimes stealing, standing on bread lines using her street-sharpened wits to survive. She was tough, tenacious and highly adaptive.

At sixteen she boarded with a poor imigrant family and worked the crowded sweatshops of the garment district. Day after day she would take her seat among the rows of the weary and shopworn, her agile fingers and legs working the old noisy sewing machines. In the evenings she would wash and iron her frayed skirts and middies, dreaming, watching from the small cracked-glass window of her room as young lovers strolled along the avenue.

In the mornings she rode the same streetcar to work sitting near the polite conductor, listening as he greeted the other passengers. One of them spoke Russian. He was a handsome youth with dark brown eyes and wavy black hair who had daily difficulties with the rate of exchange. Ada mediated.

He took to sitting near her, conversing fluently in his native Russian. She would encourage his English. Maximilian Stone courted Ada Raschenkov for six months; first on the noisy streetcar, then the summer-filled streets and parks of New York City. He eventually asked for her hand in marriage.

"You are not Jewish?" his mother asked Ada.

"I don't know," Ada replied truthfully.

"You know nothing of the faith?"

"Nothing," Ada said.

"Then you must learn," the mother insisted.

"Never!" the girl replied.

Max was astonished. Forbidden to see her again, he was forced to choose.

The Stone family sat *shiva* mourning Max's dead soul on the day of his wedding. They covered the mirrors with rags and turned the calendars to face the walls. They removed their shoes and prayed. His brother Julie tried to intervene on Max's behalf but it was useless. His brother Barney sat on the ritual wooden box and wept. To his family, Max Stone, age 26, was dead and buried.

"We have only each other," Ada told Max. "We must always remember that."

They took rooms on Mott Street and set up house. Side by side they worked the garment district of New York City; Max blocking hats on the hissing steam machines, Ada spinning wheels and bobbins working her sewing treadle until the birth of their first son, Jason. Then Ada's attention turned to what she had always longed for, a home and family.

She dickered eagerly with Fulton Street fish peddlers and haggled with the iceman. She was fierce in her bartering, knowing what it meant to labor, knowing the value of a single penny.

In 1942 Ada gave birth to their second child; her name would be Vivian Diane after her mother. For this immigrant family, life was sweet and fulfilling. Spring weekends were spent in Central Park and the zoo; summertime meant trips to Coney Island and Nathan's hot dogs. They listened with pride to President Roosevelt's fireside chats on the radio, thankful they were in the safety and bosom of America. Patriotic, Ada saved cans of cooking grease and bits of scrap metal for the war effort; Max manned the night streets during practice air raids.

In the winter of 1943, Max contracted a violent grippe with high fever and was put to bed. It was fast and filled with fury lingering for weeks, tracking its treachery deep into his fragile inner ear canals.

For weeks he suffered pain and some hearing loss.

When the fever had gone he ran frantically from doctor to doctor cursing them, calling them frauds and quacks when nothing they did relieved the swelling or the horrible pain.

"You stand too close to the open window at your job," one doctor theorized. "There are drafts."

"It's not the drafts," said another. "It's the steam from the blocking machines. You must quit your job before your hearing is completely gone."

"The nerves in your ears were affected," the last one told him. "There's nothing I can do."

Max wouldn't believe them. They were liars and cheats and he refused to pay their bills. Ada poured soothing warm oils into his ears, tucking in clean absorbent cotton to keep out the dirt and the cold air. But by 1946 his hearing had diminished more than 50 percent. Ada was told he would soon lose his job.

In the spring of that year Max's brother Julie finally located him. It was the first time they had seen each other since 1938.

"We buried Pa three months ago," Julie said.

Max was silent.

"We buried Ma one week later."

Max placed both his hands across his eyes and let the quiet tears slide down his cheeks.

When Max had composed himself Julie continued. "I'm going to California. Come with me. You, me, Barney, we're all that's left. I have a job at a movie studio. Maybe I can find something for you there."

Ada listened.

"The warm sun will be good for you and your family," Julie told him. "They have good doctors there. Who knows, maybe they'll be able to help you."

"We have nothing to lose," Ada said and they went.

In sunny California they rented an apartment in Inglewood. Ada chose it because it was bright and cheerful with a large backyard for the two children. But mostly because it was near the Hollywood Park Racetrack. There, she theorized, Max could spend time indulging in the one thing that made him come alive, enjoying the roar of the crowd for as long as his hearing permitted. Resigned to his worsening condition, she hired a babysitter and quietly prepared for a lifetime of work.

At Metro Goldwyn Mayer, Julie Stone secured a job for Ada as a file clerk and she flourished in the hectic star-studded atmosphere, dining frequently near the commissary, sneaking onto the sound stages where her spirit feasted on the beauty and opulence that were trademarks of the M.G.M. Productions.

Then in the fall of 1951 Max's condition worsened still further. A raving lunatic, he was incensed, unable to adjust, jealous of those whose silent laughter surrounded him, bitter with his lot. He fought daily with Ada, his brothers, the neighbors, finding solace only in his son Jason and the ponies. Everything and everyone else had no meaning. Within six months Max Stone would never hear another sound.

At M.G.M. Ada was promised a promotion and she eagerly awaited the passing of the Thanksgiving holidays. She couldn't know it then, but she was pregnant.

Had she known, she would have had an immediate and illegal abortion. Michael Jay Stone would have been one more fetal roe flushed from this earth into one more raging indifferent river. But Ada had been so absorbed in the act of survival that she completely ignored the calendar she so carefully monitored and her own reliable body signals.

Her physician's diagnosis was entirely clear. "You have either a tumor, or you are pregnant." At the end of the month it was conclusive. When she spoke to him of termination, he became stern and angry not only because of the medical difficulties he believed she would encounter, but, as he stated, "Even if it were permitted, which it is not, it is against my religion." *Shit!* she thought. She would have preferred the tumor, or at the very least an atheistic practitioner. The last thing she needed at this time in her life was a baby.

The delivery was hard and Ada was terrified for the first time in her life. She thought of her dead mother and wondered what would happen to her family if she died? Who would take care of her children and Max? It was an awesome and frightening experience.

"Bear down," the doctor's voice instructed.

Ada was awake. A blinding light penetrated her eyes and her eyelids. Her legs were bent at the knees, tied into stirrups, her body and arms strapped onto a cold hard table.

"She has to push harder," a male voice said.

A thousand hands were pressing onto her belly and a fierce pain made her scream like an animal. She howled and bayed and yelped and pushed onto her bowels.

"I have the baby's head," the doctor's voice said. "Give her some gas."

Someone placed a gauze covering over her face then a mask and a sickening cool odor invaded her nostrils and lungs.

She tried to breathe. Her hands jerked at the leather straps. The more she struggled the more it grew dark and she breathed ice. Then she howled and it was over.

When she wakened, young Jason was at her bedside.

"Talk to me, Momma," he cried. "How do you feel?" He had spent the night in a hallway.

"I'm dying," she screamed. "Help me. I'm dying."

Her body convulsed heaving itself over the side of the bed. Jason grabbed her before her head hit the nightstand. He yelled for a nurse, but nobody came. He watched helplessly as his mother began to shake. Then her body grew rigid and she bit down on her tongue. Bits of flesh and blood ran down her lips and chin. Jason ran away falling and vomiting on the staircase.

When she brought the baby home, Jason eyed it with dark suspicion. Who was this intruder? This enfant terrible, who almost killed his angel-mother? Max buried his head further into the racing forms ignoring the child. But young, impressionable, hopelessly neglected Vivian came to life. The wild and beautiful child-woman suddenly found meaning to her insignificant, lonely life and responded to the helpless infant with tenderness and compassion. She had something of her own, someone who needed her.

For Ada, any and all of her responsibilities toward the child were concluded. Michael Jay would have to fend for himself. Ada had a job to do, to take care of a whole family, to provide food and clothing and shelter for them all, to pay all of Max's medical bills.

At M.G.M. Ada rose through the ranks. From file clerk to typist, then on to secretary. Through Julie Stone, she managed to secure a plum position as an executive secretary to an important producer and began to think of herself as something more than just a taker-of-other-peoples-notes and follower-of-other-peoples-orders. She knew she was as capable as the men she worked with. For a woman in a male-dominated industry, that kind of reasoning was unthinkable.

The mid-fifties brought forth radical changes in the movie industry. Television had invaded Hollywood's formative, sunshine years and powerful corporate agencies began absorbing old and new talent like sponges absorb blood. There were great opportunities on the horizon and Ada foresaw the occasion. She quit her job and sought a position with General Talent Management, one of the most powerful world talent agencies. Starting as a secretary she insinuated her way up the crowded ladder becoming a talent agent.

From G.T.M. she made the agency rounds, each time gleaning and learning, picking the best brains she could find and eventually, she moved out on her own. She was ready.

She met Maurice Candelli, head of Artists Unlimited who would later become her son-in-law. They spoke often of an eventual merger, which made Jason Stone jealous.

"What's wrong with you?" Ada asked the twenty year old Jason. "You have so much talent and potential. Why do you use it destructively?"

"I don't know what you're talking about," Jason replied.

"The hell you don't. Your friends are mobsters, your women, hookers. You seem to have no desire to accomplish anything worthwhile."

"I will if you'd give me a decent chance," Jason told her.

"Not the way you want it. You have to earn things on your own, dammit. Not barter off my name and reputation."

"This town is built on nepotism," Jason shouted. "Why the hell do you have to be so different?"

"Because I am," Ada replied and left the room. There

was something he could have said to hurt her—something about Uncle Julie—but he held his tongue.

By the mid-sixties Ada Stone had single-handedly established a small but reputable talent agency. A smart businesswoman, she was well thought of by members of the industry and her peers. But to build further, to begin packaging, which was where the big money lay, she needed clout. She needed stars.

Roxanne Caulder was young and beautiful, starring in several European-made spaghetti westerns. Convinced she could turn her into a major star, Ada signed her in 1969. She devoted all her attention to Roxanne's career, guiding her, coaching her, bringing her carefully along. Two years later when Roxanne was beginning to show signs the investment would pay off, Ada hired a young man teaching him what she herself had had to learn the hard way. His name was Sidney Gross.

He was bold and confident and his timing was excellent. Ada had devoted so much of her time to Roxanne's career all of her other clients were complaining of neglect. She needed help.

"I need a job," he told Ada.

"What can you do Sidney?"

"Anything."

"I could use some help," Ada said. "But what I need is an agent."

"Just point me in the right direction," Sidney said.

"What's your background?"

"Sales, public relations and the school of hard knocks."

"Who do you know in the business?" Ada asked smiling.

"You," Sidney replied. "Isn't that enough?"

Ada laughed. Sidney Gross was funny.

"You remind me of my mother," Sidney told her.

"Thanks," Ada said accepting his remark as flattery. She couldn't have known what a diabolical compliment it was—that years later, he would try and settle unfinished scores through her.

She saw Sidney as the kind of son Jason would never be. Someone she could share the business with. Someone who was willing to start at the bottom, to do things the right way.

She took him first to parties introducing him to important studio and network people. "Parties are important," she taught him. "Remember that. Here, it's not what you know, although that's important, it's who you know." She interpreted the industry language for him. 'Hello, how are you?' means 'hello, who are you and what can you do for me? Should I waste my time talking to you or move onto the next guy?' When someone says your name sounds familiar, that means he's not sure of who you are and is asking for your list of credits. Run a good list for him Sidney. That way he'll stick around."

They'd lunch at the finest restaurants where she'd casually introduce him to other important people. "Who you're seen with at lunch or dinner is important. Check out where a potential buyer is eating some evening then invite his biggest competitor to dine with you at the next table. You'll get a phone call in the morning with interesting questions."

They'd discuss the rules, the protocol for Hollywood behavior as she saw it. "The one rule is there are no rules. Don't make friends, make contacts," she'd say. "Fight fire with fire. Don't waste time thinking about water. Ask any fireman. He'll tell you the first thing they build around a big blaze is a wall of fire. Make friends with the secretaries. They're the ones on the front lines. They can make you or break you when it comes to putting through your phone calls or making appointments with their bosses. And respect them Sidney. Don't ever take them for granted. They're after your job."

On weekends she'd instruct him to play tennis and swim. "More deals are made poolside or on tennis courts than in any conference room in this city."

She loaned him money for a new car and expensive clothes. At a political rally she took him aside. "Influence is important," she said. "And political influence is the most important of all. Politicians have power and connections everywhere in the world. One day when a politician needs the Spanish vote or the black vote, you'll be there to deliver your Spanish star or your black star whose appearance at a rally could deliver the election to him on a platter. Then sit back and wait until you need him and you'll need him, eventually."

When Sidney needed to hire a secretary, Ada told him. "There are people in this world happy being number two. They love to look at the limelight, but can't stand the direct glare. When you choose a secretary find someone embarrassed by center stage but who loves to stand in the wings. And," she added, "most of all, don't trust anyone, Sidney, not ever."

Two years later Sidney Gross, the man who had fed at Ada Stone's table until he developed "legs," left to open his own talent agency. His first client was the fabulous now-famous Roxanne Caulder. He was in business one week and already in the black.

Ada was seething, furious, as angry as she'd ever been. How could she have been so stupid? Why didn't she see it coming? She should have taken her own advice. She wanted to file a lawsuit but wisely decided against it. She couldn't permit anything, even this horrendous setback to interfere with her plans for upward mobility. She sadly counted her losses and moved on knowing that one day, no matter how long it would take, she'd get back at them both. And then she swore that no one would ever again make a fool of her like he did.

In 1976, after she had spent years fighting with him about his cheap porno movies, his lies, his deceit, his casual use of her respected name to raise money for his work, Jason Stone married Nicole Warner, Sidney Gross's first secretary. Jason had, with full knowledge, hurled the last of his insults in her face. From that day on, they would never again speak.

In that same year Ada met attorney Hugh Parker, finished her grand plans to build Casa Piedra and merged her management service with that of Maurice Candelli's talent agency. Stone Management Associates took off like rockets on fire locking in the talents of Hank Mason, Armando Del Gado, then Bobbi Sands. By the late seventies, Ada Stone was a power to be reckoned with. She was among the top in her field and there was nothing to stop her.

*   *   *

The first thing she felt was the movement of soft butterflies on her eyelids. Then a tunnel voice called her name.

"Ada? Ada? Wake up. Can you hear me?"

There was a blinding light deep inside her brain which gradually diminished, clicking off again leaving her in total darkness. She lay balanced somewhere between night and day, a place that was neither dawn nor dusk.

"I think she's waking up. Call Dr. Morgenstern."

Ada opened her eyes. Ten nurses and four doctors were clustered at her bedside like some out-of-focus collage. When her field of vision grew clear, the multitude converged and she could see Dr. Morgenstern, an intern and two nurses.

"Welcome back, Ada," Dr. Morgenstern said smiling, patting her hand. "How do you feel?"

Ada tried to speak but her tongue stayed glued to her palate. Her wide eyes quivered with terror.

"Can you feel this?" the doctor asked touching her arm. She tried to respond, to move, but her body felt drugged and heavy.

"Can you hear me, Ada?" Dr. Morgenstern shouted and lifted her right leg. She fluttered her eyes in response. "Do you feel this?" He ran a pencil down the center of her foot but there was no reflex. He tried the other. Still nothing. His smile was weak and forced. "You'll be all right, Ada," he told her. "Don't worry. You've had a stroke but you're going to be all right."

Chapter 12

MICHAEL WALKED TOWARD the elevator. He removed his blue-tinted sunglasses, then scanned the names on the lobby roster finally locating Hugh Parker's suite number. Throughout all the excitement of the past few weeks, he had somehow forgotten it. He heard the brisk clatter of hurried high heels behind him and turned. It was Viva.

"Darling," she said frowning, "you look tired." She kissed his cheek then linked her arm to his. Her hair was piled high upon her head in Victorian splendor and her raspberry, cotton lisle sundress complimented her deep suntan and gold jewelry.

Michael opened the button on his beige jacket and jerked free the knot of his striped, white knit tie.

"You look beautiful and just a little bit tired yourself," he said leading her into the elevator. "Anything new?"

She became excited, displaying a devilish grin on her full, pink lips. "Remember that screen test you sent over?" she said hitting the elevator button. "A Paul Kiley?" Michael nodded. "Well, I've decided to sign him. Then you and I can plan a wonderful campaign to promote him into a major star. He has magic, Michael. A wonderful and rare kind of magic."

The elevator stopped abruptly and the doors jerked open. "You're not biting off more than you can chew right now. Are you?" Michael asked.

She smiled. "No, darling. But if I do, I'll just suck on it for a while, until it's soft. Then swallow as usual."

He grinned. "What I mean, smart mouth, is, do you think it's wise to take on such a generous project at this particular time? I mean with things going the way they've been going."

"I not only think it's wise, I *know* it's vital. New blood is a symbol of any agency's health and vitality; the whole point being appearances. We're in a big power game and if you're suddenly short on power, you should at least try to keep up appearances. Besides," she added, "I refuse to let Jason Stone rob me of a glorious future."

"It isn't only Jason I'm referring to," Michael said opening the door to Parker's outer office. "It's everything."

Inside Parker's office, a slender black secretary with corn-rowed tresses and pale green eyes smiled. "Hi," she said. "He's expecting you both. Go right on in."

They crossed the navy shag carpeting to Parker's huge office and opened the door.

"Hello," Hugh Parker said rising from his blue leather chair, shaking Michael's hand. "Make yourselves comfortable. There's fresh coffee on the serving cart, over there." Parker removed his gray tweed jacket and draped it behind his chair. Viva poured herself a steaming mug of freshly brewed coffee while Michael, now seated near the balcony window, observed the silent, dramatic passage of a low-flying helicopter.

"Let's get to it," Parker said immediately. "We've got problems with Jason and also Del Gado. For some reason, Armando's been threatening a trip to the Labor Commission."

Michael's face had the look of a scattered jigsaw puzzle. "On what grounds?"

"The usual stuff. Some fiduciary breach, co-mingling of funds, a little fraud, deceit. None of which would stand up under any scrutiny, of course. So I figure it's a message he's sending. He either wants to scare you or cut himself loose from S.M.A. altogether." Parker rotated his head for a moment, working out a kink, then lit a cigarette and exhaled. "If he files a claim, however, I'd be forced to step out between you. He's my client also."

"Can't you talk him out of such a measure?" Viva

asked sounding annoyed. "Obviously, he'll be impugning your integrity along with ours. You do handle all the money."

"I wouldn't even try, Viva," Parker said. "There's no point to that and it's certainly not my place."

Michael rose and headed for the serving cart. "I'm just not ready to cut the son of a bitch loose. So if he wants a real fight, tell him he's got one." He poured himself some hot coffee and sat back down.

Viva leaned over and fiddled with a tight shoe. "What on earth happened between the two of you in San Francisco?" she asked Michael.

"Whatever it was," Michael said sipping the steamy liquid carefully, "it had nothing to do with fiduciary breaches." He smiled and his eyes held a mischievous light. "Maybe a little co-mingling, if I can use your phrase, Hugh, but of a purely personal nature." The sudden silence in the room made him uncomfortable and he quickly changed the subject. "About those documents Max signed. Suppose I had a talk with Jason. A kind of business talk. Maybe there's a way to settle the issue with a simple money offer. A buy out."

Hugh Parker thoughtfully rubbed the point of his chin. "Don't waste your time talking to him. I tried. If his answers match the ones he gave me, you'll need a team of paramedics on standby."

"My God! He hit you." Viva cried out. She placed her empty coffee mug on the desk and leaned across for a better look at his face.

"Let's just say we had a 'close encounter' the day he brought over the signed transfers," Parker said. "But I'm fine now. Go on, Michael."

"Tell me about the transfers. What does it actually mean, Hugh?" Michael said.

"That all of Max's corporate privileges will transfer legally to Jason."

Viva's eyes narrowed and her bare arms fluttered to her hips. "And what the hell does *that* mean?"

Parker dragged deeply on his cigarette. "If it holds up in court," he said expelling a mouthful of smoke, "Jason will share in the equity; year-end profits. That amounts to 20 percent according to the shares."

"I don't believe it. That's Max's track money," Viva said. "He must have been highly motivated to sign it over to Jason like that."

"Yes. I agree," Parker said.

"Anything else?" Viva asked.

Parker leaned far back into his seat, crossing his long tweed legs on top of the huge antique desk. "He can also use S.M.A.'s name in certain business dealings and he has voting rights, plus the right to inspect the corporate ledgers. . . ."

"What the hell's left?" Viva suddenly cried in despair.

Michael gently tapped her arm. "What course of action are you proposing?" Michael asked Parker. "I don't plan to hit the canvas and take a count."

"I agree with Viva that Max was highly motivated all right; and we can talk with him about it and see. The way it looks, I believe he signed those papers without fully comprehending the significance of his actions. To my mind, he was either drunk or somehow illegally influenced into signing. That's the position we'll take in court."

"In other words, duress," Michael said.

"Exactly," Parker said sitting up, grinding out his cigarette stub in an ashtray. "In the meantime, I'll have a restraining order placed on Jason's using S.M.A.'s name or functioning in any way as an S.M.A. officer until we have a shot at the courtroom. We stand a fair chance of beating him on this. At the very least we can stall him long enough and hope he'll run out of money for legal fees or just tire of the long fight and give up."

"Don't anyone hold their breath," Viva said opening and rebuckling the strap on her tight shoe. "It looks like a fait accompli."

"I don't think so," Michael said, turning to Viva. "Hugh has a point. You said it yourself. Jason isn't financially solvent. He also has a notoriously low threshold for frustration if I remember correctly. It might just work."

Parker's outburst of sardonic laughter surprised them both.

"And what's so goddamn funny?" Viva asked.

"Nothing . . . only there's been an epidemic of low and frustrated thresholds on the West Coast," he said rubbing his knuckles. "From the most diplomatic corners." He suddenly appeared embarrassed by his remarks and encouraged Michael to continue.

"Okay on the 'duress' thing," Michael said lighting his Dunhill. "But just suppose we lose in court. What then?"

"Then," Parker said, "we possibly reduce Jason's participation in the business by 10 percent. Technically, we can argue that Max's 20 percent is still community property and since the transfer was made without Ada's consent, all Max could legally transfer to anyone is half of that. The other half still belongs to Ada. That way, you'll be able to outvote Jason on all policy decisions."

"Good," Michael said feeling some sense of genuine relief. "At least there's. . . ." A phone call interrupted Michael's last words and Parker picked it up.

"Put him on," Parker told his secretary, glancing at Michael, then Viva with concerned apprehension. "It's Dr. Morgenstern," Parker whispered switching on the speaker-phone.

"Hugh?" the voice fairly shouted across the room. "It's Morgenstern. I'm trying to find Mike and Viva. Any ideas?"

Parker gripped the arms on his chair. "They're right here with me," he announced. "You're on the speaker-phone, so go ahead."

"Good news. Ada's out of the coma. We're evaluating the effects of the stroke right now."

Viva breathed a sigh of relief. Michael cleared a lump in his throat.

"This is Mike. That's great news. What's the prognosis?"

"I really don't care to speculate at this point, Mike. At the moment we have no speech and some reflex problems, but as I said before, we'll know much more after the tests are in."

"Will you be at the hospital for a while?" Michael inquired.

"Yes." Morgenstern paused. "Until about 1:30 this afternoon."

Michael glanced at his watch. "Fine. Viva and I will see you there when this meeting's over."

As soon as Dr. Morgenstern clicked off, Hugh Parker's secretary burst into the room. "I'm awfully sorry," she said looking nonplussed, apologizing. "But there's a Miss Sheldon for Mrs. Candelli on the telephone. She insists it's an emergency."

Viva's body tensed. "That's my secretary," she said apprehensively and reached for the telephone receiver. Michael watched her features strain from bewilderment to anger then exasperation. She finally held her palm over the mouthpiece and looked at Michael. "It's Jason. He's at the Beverly Hills office throwing his weight around."

"Ask her to get him on the telephone if she can," Michael said immediately, reaching for the speaker-phone and flipping on the switch. He'd been anticipating Jason's first move all night and now he was ready. In a few seconds Jason was on the line.

"This is Mike, Jason. Get your damn ass out of that office before I have you thrown out." He felt his heart beating rapidly and his dry tongue sticking to his palate.

"Hey, squirt," Jason said pleasantly. "Didn't the counselor tell you? It seems we're partners now."

"We're not partners yet, Jason. And I'm not sure we'll be brothers when this is all over. Just do as I tell you or I'll call the cops and have you thrown out."

"Hey, squirt. . . ."

"Don't 'squirt,' me, Jason. Get yourself a good lawyer. I'll see you in court."

There was a pause, then Jason spoke in a clear strong voice. "No, you listen to me. I already have a good lawyer. The best in the business. You and Viva have really fucked things up and I'm stepping in. Like it or not, we're gonna cook in the same pot. And I'll tell you something else, squirt. I'm filing for conservatorship of Ada's estate. Before this is over, I'll control everything. So if you want any more fancy schools or extravagant vacations, I'd watch what I was saying if I were you."

"Then you haven't heard the news yet," he said to Jason, smiling.

"What news?" Jason asked.

Michael sang the next line with great relish. "Ada's out of danger now. She's awake; out of the coma. So save your money and your breath. It's her you'll have to fight, not me."

There was a shrill silence on Jason's end of the line, then the sound of a sharp click.

"Round one, darling," Viva said laughing. "And it's all yours."

The hot, July sun beat down on Beverly Hills as Jason's red Ferrari sailed across Sunset Boulevard toward Holmby Hills. He was furious, angry as a hornet. That lousy kid brother of his. That miserable fucking bastard. And that damn bitch, Ada. Who was she anyway? Just another whore. He lifted the telephone and dialed his office. His secretary, Mimi, was getting ready to leave for lunch and quickly recited his messages for him. One from Armando Del Gado wanting assurances that the planned meeting between them would be held in private and in the strictest confidence. It would. Jason preferred it that way. Especially now, now that he'd had that phone conversation with Michael. No one would disturb them.

The gook maid was still with sick relatives and Nicole would be sweating her ass off at some dance class. But he had already told Del Gado all that. There was nothing for him to worry about.

And, there was another call from Davey Sullivan. Mimi just didn't have the heart to tell him to fuck off like Jason had instructed her to. God! He was stupid. Jason was fighting for his own life. There was no time to hold somebody else's hand. Davey would have to make his own luck like everyone else.

And Max. Jesus! He'd been to the office a half hour ago asking about the stock transfers. Shit! He probably wanted them back now that Ada was out of the coma. Probably wanted to renege on the whole deal . . . take it all back . . . yield to Ada once again. But Jason couldn't permit that: Not like before, not like the old days when she always got her way.

* * *

"Bring me the racing forms like a good little boy," Max said.

Jason assembled the newspapers on the table, opening the kitchen curtains so the light would be clear and strong on the newsprint.

"Let me help you, Papa," Jason said, his sharpened pencil poised on a blank sheet of paper.

Max smiled and began the numbered litany. The eager child moved his fingers to the tune, as the needs of the father visited the son. At last. Here was something. Something Jason could share with Max. Something that satisfied his terrible need to be wanted, to feel close to someone, to feel important.

Each day, they'd assemble the racing form, assess the horses, and calculate their winning chances. On days when Max didn't visit the track, Jason would meet the bookie on some designated street corner carrying Max's paper slips clutched in the palm of his small hand. His importance to Max was increasing daily and he was proud.

And how he loved the bookies; especially Meyer Wolfson. He loved Meyer's shiny, black Buick, his frequent and beautiful women companions, the Palm Beach silk suits and diamond rings he wore, even the Havana cigars he smoked.

And Meyer liked him, too. He nicknamed him Jake, taking him for casual rides in the Buick when the blonde of the month would permit. Occasionally, Meyer would peel a dollar bill from his thick green bankroll and hand it to Jason with no instructions to save it for a rainy day. That was magnificent.

And Jason was happier than ever. Even Ada said so. His schoolwork improved, his sense of belonging came into focus. He didn't spend his time glaring at Michael's crib anymore. He could even envision some kind of romantic future for himself. He treasured Meyer's friendship and actually believed that Max needed him. It was a special time in his life.

And when it all ended, he was crushed, reduced to tears and pleading. In one wild gesture, Ada, home sick from work, shattered the only link that connected him to his father and his special friends. Max was forbidden to ask for his help and Jason was forbidden to meet Meyer Wolfson on the streetcorner.

He begged. He pleaded. But she was adamant. No child of hers would wallow in the filth of bookies and blondes and horseracing. It was one thing for him to help his father. It was quite another that he become involved with all the trappings of vice. He could have nailed her then and there about Uncle Julie but he didn't.

Ashamed, he watched Max surrender to her, easily abandoning him according to her wishes. He tried to explain, but it was no use. From then on, Max quietly engaged in his favorite pastime, while the boy watched from a safe and vanquished corner feeling isolated, lonely and bitter. Something triumphed here, but it wasn't Ada.

Now, here he was some thirty years later, fighting her all over again. Ada. Coming back from the dead. Insinuating herself between him and Max and his future. Only this time she was too late. This time he wasn't a helpless child as before. This time, more importantly, he hadn't invested a child's heart so there was nothing she could break. He had a sense of his own power now. The kind of power he'd witnessed her wield and had always jealously coveted.

He slowed down when he hit a large pothole near Beverly Glen Boulevard, then hung a left toward his Holmby Hills home.

"Nice place you have here," Armando Del Gado said entering Jason's home office.

Jason pressed a button and the drapes leisurely hummed along the ceiling rod, opening and revealing Nicole's sunny garden plus a portion of the swimming pool below.

"Have a seat," Jason told him opening the mirrored bar. "What'll you have?"

Del Gado thought for a moment, his eyes watching the hundred faces of his reflection in the bar. "A small vodka tonic," he said, cocking his head to the right, "with ice and a lemon twist." He straightened the collar on his Yves St. Laurent jacket and caressed the sides of his hair.

Jason poured their drinks while Del Gado roamed about the outer room for a moment. "That's a great staircase out there," he said walking back in, sipping his cool drink.

"It came with the joint. Italian marble or something." Jason pointed to a chair and waited for Del Gado to sit down. "Okay. What's on your mind?"

"I hear things," Del Gado said slowly. "I hear you may be running things at S.M.A. Is that true?"

Jason's eyes smouldered. "Who told you that?" he asked in a flat even tone.

"A bird."

Jason snickered. "You mean a vulture, don't you? Like Sidney Gross?"

"Okay. I'll be straight with you." Del Gado placed his half-empty glass on Jason's lucite desk. "I've been thinking of making certain changes. I don't like the way things are going at the agency since Ada checked out and I want to know if it's true."

Obviously, Jason thought, he hadn't heard the news of Ada's recovery yet. He leaned back into the leather chair and patted the documents inside his breast pocket. "It's possible," he said. "What kind of changes are you talking about?"

"Well," Del Gado hesitated. "Sidney's kinda offered me a good deal. . . ."

"Sidney can't offer you jack shit," Jason interrupted. "He knows better than that. He'll find himself saddled with a fifty million dollar lawsuit if he's not careful."

Del Gado sat upright, stabbing the air with his forefinger. "Look, man. Save that crap for the legal people. It doesn't scare me at all. What I want is assurances. I have to know that your *puto* brother isn't going to flush me down some rat hole. He knows *mierda* about this business and I've worked too damn hard and," he paused, swallowing, "and sacrificed too fucking much for that to happen."

"I see you've met my brother," Jason said smirking.

"Yeah. I ran into him over the weekend."

Jason peeked nervously at his wristwatch and waited for Del Gado to continue.

"Hey, *amigo*. Am I boring you? I mean are you in some kind of hurry?"

"I'm expecting a call if you must know," Jason said. "Some big people in Vegas are interested in the agency and I expect to spend a few days with them. Is that all right with you?"

Del Gado's serious countenance brightened. "Now, there you go. That's what I'm talking about. I've got ideas. Plans for myself to make top money. I want to sing, man. To do other things beside situation comedy. That's what Ada and I talked about before she got sick. Me, getting a shot at some big Vegas hotel—headlining."

Now, he thought, *you're on my turf, sucker.* Jason smiled. "Yeah. Well, I'll tell my people all about it when I talk to them. Anything else?"

"Yeah. Here's a friendly tip. Watch out for your brother, man. He spent a lot of time making your pretty wife happy in San Francisco. If she was my *mujer*, I'd kick shit out of her, then kill him."

Jason's chin jutted forward and his eyes narrowed to tiny slits.

Del Gado rose and moved toward the door. He turned and grinned. "And don't forget to tell them about me in Vegas," he said. "I want to know about your plans when you get back."

Jason angrily snatched the ringing telephone as Del Gado slammed the front door.

"It's Davey," the frightened voice said on the other end. "Davey Sullivan. We had a deal, remember?"

"Yeah. I remember," Jason said sourly. "Fuck off!"

* * *

News of Ada's recovery had elated Michael, then depressed him. He was glad she was coming out of the coma but ashamed of the mess he'd made of everything. He was anxious to keep it all from her, for now. He could hold out for as long as necessary, not disturbing her as the doctor had instructed, but what about the others, the well-meaning friends and gossip mongers. Somebody would slip about Hank or Armando sooner or later and that could set her condition off again. He just didn't want that to happen.

And she looked pretty good, he thought. Even though she couldn't speak yet, or move too well. He thought she smiled once when Max tickled her feet and sang, "By the beautiful sea." That Max. He was impossible. Why had he signed over those shares like that? What had Jason told him? And did he know about the conservatorship threat Jason was making? His mind reeled with all the right questions. And at last, his feet were beginning to make tracks.

At 2:00 P.M. Michael excused Elaine Shagan for the day and waited for Van Tilden to arrive. It had been a year since the two of them touched base and Michael recalled with fondness the many hours they'd spent drinking and carousing together.

Van was a macho Texan whose common sense and southern-fried way of expressing himself kept Michael first in stitches then in serious contemplation. Van loved hard drinking and soft women, in that order and it had been Michael's experience that anyone within Van's earshot, who knocked America or country music, would pay a dear sweet price.

They'd met seven years before on Oahu in Makakilo City. Then again at Schofield Barracks a week later. Michael found Van honest, sincere and fearless, able to laugh at problems, to drink away the blues.

He was like some wild, romantic figure from a seedy novel: A real live cowboy, a C.I.A. career man, someone like the Greek, Zorba, who welcomed life and every lousy thing in it. Michael adored him.

At three Duggan rang the office telephone. "There's a Mister Van Tilden here, Michael," he said. "He's insistin' on drivin' to the back shed near your office."

"Fine, Duggan. I've been expecting him," Michael said. "Just point the way." Michael moved to the patio window and watched as Van's rented Oldsmobile wound its way past the trees and green shrubbery toward the back shed.

"Shitfire boy," Van shouted as he jumped from the car. "Ain't this one hell of a spread!"

Michael snatched a large floor fan and a black suitcase from Van's cluttered arms and led him toward Ada's office. Inside, the pot-bellied Texan with the pitch-black eyebrows removed his beige Stetson and scratched the top of his pure white crew-cut.

"Just hold your mud, boy," Van shouted. "First, pour me some crazy water." He grinned, slapped Michael's shoulder, then vigorously tossed the dark hair on Michael's head.

"Let me look at you, you old geezer," Michael said standing back.

"Shitfire! Ain't nothing to look at. My git up and go done got up and went. I got gold in my teeth, silver in my hair and lead in my britches. But I can still keep it hard, son. I just think snow."

Michael laughed heartily. "C'mon. I'll get you something to drink." He moved to the pale oak bar and poured two bourbons with ice, handing one to Van. "Have a seat," Michael said pointing to a soft chair near Ada's desk. "I want to know where you've been and what you've been doing."

Van wiped his sweaty brow with a clean white handkerchief, raised his glass to Michael and chugalugged his drink. "Hot damn, that's good!" he said slapping his knee. "Well, let's see now, where should I begin?" He thought hard for a moment as though his own life were some strange distant blur, then smiled. "I got hitched again. Number five, I think. Just opened my wallet one night and there she was. A lush blonde or a blonde lush, take your pick. But it didn't work too good," he drawled shaking his head, extending his empty glass for a refill. "Shoot! You know me, boy. I can take 'em or leave 'em . . . so I left."

Michael's face hurt from grinning. He reached for Van's glass, filled it with fresh ice, then grasped the whiskey bottle, setting it on the desk where Van could reach it.

"You should have seen her, boy." He slapped his thigh. "Red hair, peaches and cream complexion, wall-to-wall titties. A real live popsicle . . . sex on a stick." Van opened the bottle and poured another drink offering one to Michael who declined. "Now," he said raising his glass to Michael, "tell the old mick-Injun everything."

Michael began with the phonecall from Viva, Ada's illness, the job he had reluctantly accepted and was mucking up, then finally how he came to know about the safe and that damn pouch he had been looking for, ever since the first day he arrived.

"Okay boy," Van said spitting on his palms and rubbing them together. "That's what I'm here for. Let's open her up."

Van glanced about the room, then inspected the safe. "You're mighty lucky, boy. No smoke detectors on the safe and no sprinklers on the ceiling. It's a piece of cake." Van slid his gear across the room, slipped off his brown western-styled jacket and rolled up his sleeves.

While Michael watched, Van fit together sections of a one and one-half-inch diameter pipe-pieces, which were malleable and stuffed with aluminum, steel, and magnesium alloy wire. Then, he set a small oxygen tank and an oxyacetylene torch on the floor near the safe door. When the pipe fittings measured about six feet in length, he slipped into a heat resistant jumpsuit.

"Set that big fan over there," Van said pointing to the patio window. "Open the doors real wide then get on the horn and call your butler or whomever the hell he was and tell him not to call the damn fire department—no matter what the hell he sees!"

Michael followed Van's instructions, then helped him remove the batteries from two ceiling smoke alarms. "All this for one safe?" Michael asked placing the batteries on the desk top.

"It'll be over in less than thirty seconds, boy. Stop complaining. My burning bar is fast and efficient, but it's a little tricky."

Van found a pair of asbestos-lined gloves on the bottom of the black suitcase, then carried what looked like a small version of an astronaut's clear headpiece over to the safe.

Michael chuckled nervously. "Why do I have this funny feeling you're not telling me about the worst thing that could happen here?" Michael said.

"Worst thing?" Van repeated, polishing the clear headpiece. "Let's see. Well, we could find some copper sheeting buried inside the safe lining. That always sets off a heat sensing alarm. Or if the safe interior is too narrow, we could easily burn up everything inside."

"Great!" Michael shouted rolling his eyes to the back of his head.

"Shoot! What the hell you complaining about?" Van shouted. "I'll be the one rotting in jail. The only place they'll send you is the Jewish Home for the Terminally Weird." He pushed Michael away. "Now stand back, boy. This'll get hotter than a fresh-fucked fox in a forest fire."

Michael couldn't believe his eyes as the pipe, ignited by the torch and fed by the oxygen, began to disappear into thin air. Dense smoke filled the room as Van deactivated the relocking bolt then the locking bolt. Within thirty seconds the six-foot pipe measured two feet and the safe was open. The floor fan had effectively disseminated most of the smoke out the patio door and by the time Van had removed his headgear and asbestos gloves, the smoke had cleared.

"Shoot! I still got the touch," he whooped. He slipped off his sweaty jumpsuit while Michael searched the open safe.

"Jesus," Michael shouted throwing up his hands. "All that for nothing." The safe was empty.

Van turned off the noisy floor fan, wiped his forehead with a handkerchief then moved to the safe. He looked inside and roared. "Hell boy," he said. "You're a lousy land rat. There's a false back inside, you know, sorta like a false bottom." He gripped the ring on a second steel door easily opening it. "There's your shit."

There in front of him was the pouch, along with some assorted video tapes.

"Thanks," he said locking the patio door and covering the safe again. He wouldn't be able to inspect the contents until he was alone. "Now let's get you cleaned up and out for a thick steak."

"Take me to the Palomino," Van insisted. "I like my steak country-fried and my music Willie Nelson." He paused. "And don't you forget the broads," he scolded, putting on his jacket. "I may be old, but I'm still in there pitchin'."

It was midnight when Michael finally returned to Ada's office. Van was on his way back to Houston, a bottle of good bourbon and a steak in his belly, with a rented blonde at his side.

Besides the pouch, there were two video tapes inside the

safe, one marked "Hank Mason," the other, "Armando Del Gado." He sat there, curious, then casually pushed Armando's into the video machine. Del Gado's dark and handsome face appeared instantly on the screen. He was seated in this office facing Ada, delivering a highly emotional monologue. Michael listened as Del Gado suddenly broke down sobbing, lowering his head into his arms.

Michael lit his pipe and studied Del Gado's performance. He recalled Elaine Shagan's words the first day he found the hidden video camera behind Ada's desk. "She uses it for new clients and cold readings," she had said. But the date on this tape indicated it had been taped months after Del Gado had signed the management contract with her. Was this some new play he was planning to do? or was Ada just coaching him? No, he thought, it couldn't be. Why then would she hide the tape like that? She could easily have locked it in the file room with the others like it.

Michael studied Del Gado's performance a little while longer. It was so honest, so very real. Too real in fact. And that was just it! Suddenly, Michael sprang to his feet. Those were no lines made up by some Hollywood writer and that sure as hell wasn't acting. Del Gado was confessing . . . spilling his bloody guts out to Ada. Those were his own words, and what he was telling her was all so horrid he couldn't bear to listen any longer. He snapped off the machine.

If he was right about Del Gado's tape then Hank's tape would prove it. He pushed it into the video machine then sat back and waited.

There it was. Hank was begging Ada for help. Revealing bits and pieces of his life as though Ada were some hundred-dollar-an-hour psychiatrist and could give him the treatment he needed.

So that was it. That was how she kept her superstars in line. Threats of exposure. A kind of blackmail-in-waiting. Waiting for Hank or Armando to make a false move so she could checkmate them at the right moment and keep them from leaving her.

Deep furrows lined his forehead as he pondered questions and searched for more answers. How did she get them to confess to her? What did she do? Lure them with promises of friendship and motherly love as Elaine Shagan had suggested? "Actors are children," he remembered hearing Ada say. "They are wonderful children, who need strict supervision, guidance and discipline."

That was it. That's how she did it. She would make them feel at home, at ease, with swimming and tennis games and Cranston's good cooking. She would wait until their spirits were low, then feed them her own brand of chicken soup, encouraging them to tell her all about "it."

A strong, sour sensation churned deeply inside his stomach tracking a slow burn into his chest. He dropped his pipe into the crystal ashtray and slowly fingered the pouch.

God only knew what she had stashed inside that.

He tossed the contents of the pouch onto the desk. What he found inside was astonishing. It concerned Roxanne Caulder. Over and over he perused the documents. What kind of sick joke was this? But it was no joke. These were authentic, all right.

In the wrong hands, they could wreck Roxanne's life and the life of her children. He was tempted to burn them, but he knew he wouldn't. They didn't belong to him. They were Ada's filthy papers. He would ultimately have to confront Ada with them later. Ada. Squirreling away her blackmail material for a bad winter when the seasons changed abruptly and it grew too cold. God. How had she planned to use these?

The day had been long and arduous and he felt suddenly exhausted. He longed for a shower and a cool, soft bed to sleep in. He wanted only to remember the cabin up north and that wonderful night he spent with Nicole. He wanted more than anything to forget the fight ahead.

The telephone rang and he was startled. It was almost two in the morning and it was the private line. With great trepidation, he reached for it and said hello.

"Mike?" The voice was throaty and hoarse, almost the sound of a whisper.

"Who is this?" Michael demanded. There was silence, then Michael shouted. "Hank? Is that you?"

"Yes," Hank whispered. "It's me."

"Thank God you're okay." Michael breathed a sigh of

relief. All day long he'd been praying for this and now he was grateful.

"I called earlier," Hank whispered, "but you were out I guess. I wanted to apologize . . . for checking out on you like that."

"It's all right," Michael told him. "I understand. I'm the one who should apologize. For leaving you. Just promise you won't do it again."

Hank was silent and Michael persisted. "Promise me, Hank. I mean it. I want to help you but you've got to help too."

"I don't know if it matters anymore, Mike. My career's gonna go in the toilet. Everything I am, or ever hope to be is finished once Jason spills everything to the press." He began to weep.

"Jason!" Michael exploded. "What's Jason got to do with this?"

Michael listened as Hank described how Jason had called him and how despondent he'd felt that morning. How Jason had successfully killed any hope he had harbored for recovery. So he took the pills and booze, hoping to die quietly, thus solving everybody's problem.

Hank's voice waivered like some wounded bird that had forgotten the tune to his song. Michael insisted he stop talking and rest. For ten minutes Michael tried to reassure him that Jason Stone would never again hurt him. Hank said he believed him and Michael placed the receiver on the cradle wondering first how Jason knew, then, more importantly, how he would deal with him. Perhaps, if Jason thought he had a real stake in Hank's career, that would do it. Then, Jason would have to think twice about killing his own golden goose.

The only other action he could take was to cut out Jason's tongue and that idea really tempted him.

Chapter 13

NICOLE DROVE THE VENTURA FREEWAY east towards Universal City. The loud rock music on her radio obliterated any thoughts she might have had of Michael, or Jason, or her own state of mind which had been precarious since returning from San Francisco. She wanted only to consider the interview and the words of her agent.

"Nicole? Allen Greene. You've got a meeting at Universal for three this afternoon."

Nicole was ecstatic when the call came. Michael had planted the seeds a few days before and now they were sprouting.

"It's a good part. Comedy. Some independent producer named Lars Homas. He may want you to sing something, dance, so be prepared. Look pretty and let me know what happens."

The interview was all that mattered. She wanted a job more than anything. She needed it. It was necessary for her survival. All week long she'd contemplated the past weekend with Michael. All her thoughts had converged on what he'd said about her, her future—their future. It was true. She was very unhappy and she was unwilling to spend the rest of her life this way. There were changes that had to be made and they were obvious. Leave Jason. Give her career a real try. Find a way to face her irrational fears. To make the plan was easy. To carry it out was something else. She could see what had to be done. Doing it was another story.

Nicole loved Hollywood and she hated it. It was a wonderful schitzy town filled with people she understood. Optimists at one end of the spectrum still hoping for that big break, cynics at the other, despairing it would ever come.

In between were those living in limbo. Those whose lives were spent in protracted pauses and endless intermissions, waiting—always waiting for the phone to ring so their real lives could begin.

The lives they lived were only temporary; the apartments they rented or shared were only provisional; relationships were transitory. What they said were promises, regurgitated from their agent's mouths. Only their hearts and souls were pure. And their hearts would be broken eventually, their souls spent to ransom a down payment on a dream.

She left the freeway at Universal City, curved around the exit ramp and swung left on Lankershim. She turned right, rolled down her window, parked at the glass island. She was ready to enter fairyland. A red-haired guard smiled and checked his clipboard for her name.

"Okay, Miss Stone," he said writing her name on a pass and placing it on her dashboard inside. "Go straight on past the production building, beyond the sound stages, then hang a left and a sharp right. You can park under the big willow tree. Mr. Homas' office is opposite."

She drove through the gates and felt the excitement tingling in her toes and fingertips. No matter how many times she'd entered this lot it was still thrilling.

She approached Building 50 and stopped as workmen carried full-sized room walls across her path. Behind them were uniformed spacemen heading for a rehearsal of the "Buck Rogers" show.

Near the sound stages a wig-wag was spinning its red light while a uniformed flagman blew his whistle and waved his red banner to stop all noise and traffic in the vicinity. Jack Klugman was filming "Quincy" inside and absolute quiet was essential or the tape would be ruined.

When the taping had ceased, the flagman blew his whistle, waving everyone on. She drove half a block then paused as a wrangler led three snorting horses down the street. A young girl on a bicycle pedaled past toward the commissary.

There were carpenters hammering, creating mythical kingdoms to an art director's specifications. White-gloved editors racked film back and forth on Moviolas trying to find that magical frame at which to stop and start a scene. Stuntmen calculated again and again the distance between here and there so the jump they'd planned to execute wouldn't execute them. All this and somewhere in the distance, a piano echoed its tune across the breeze. Then, all at once, the noises ceased and the air was very still. She was far out on the back lot.

She parked the car under the weeping willow tree and exited. All around her were green country lawns and rolling hills except for several quaint white offices, one of which she knew belonged to Homas. Several bees buzzed by her head flying toward a white colonial mansion which was surrounded by magnolia trees. The sweet scent of honeysuckle and jasmine filled the air.

She loved the back lot and she loved the movies. The movies had made her young life bearable. They'd helped her cope and survive. They'd opened her up to new ideas, new vistas. They'd given her hope for the future and designed her dreams. There in the darkened theatres her sadness would always disappear. For two or three hours she'd forget, be transported. They were her passage to other times, other worlds. She'd always loved the movies and now she needed to be a part of them again.

Her cotton gauze bandana dress of peach and white fluttered in the soft breeze. She carried a brown ballet bag with rehearsal clothes, makeup, her resumes and photographs while her lips hummed the melody to some Marvin Hamlisch tune. She wondered how she looked.

Inside the waiting room, two secretaries criss-crossed each others paths, moving from file cabinet to typewriter to the ringing of ever-present telephones. Three other actresses were seated reading scripts for the same part. Occasionally, they'd look up, glance at one another with slightly bowed heads, smile, size up and psych out the competition, then return to their scripts.

Nicole's excitement turned to anxiety. It was going to be a cold reading and she dreaded those. For some reason she always seemed to freeze. To hell with them, she thought, turning, ready to run, but the secretary called her name. She smiled weakly, and reluctantly followed the young woman inside.

Two men were seated on plush white wicker couches in the midst of sunny bay windows, yellow ginger jar lamps and carpeting the color of mud.

"How are you, Miss Stone?" Lars Homas said taking her hand. "This is John Giles, our choreographer." John Giles smiled.

They were a study in contrasts. Mr. Homas was blond, tall, with a diabolical grin and matching beard. Giles was black with silky ebony skin, a strong muscular body and fine facial features.

Mr. Homas pointed to an upright chair opposite his and she sat down as he studied her resume. "Your pictures don't do you justice," he said looking up at her. She blushed. "And, I can see you've had lots of good training. Very important. Too many young women these days don't seem to have the training necessary for comedy and musicals."

She nodded and wondered where the hell her tongue had gone.

"Are you related to *the* Stones, Ada Stone, by any chance?" he asked.

She hesitated, then blurted it out. "Yes. She's my mother-in-law."

Mr. Homas glanced quickly at Giles then back at Nicole. "Why don't you tell us about yourself."

"I'm twenty-four," she lied. But they all did. Youth translated itself into longevity which then translated itself to more money. "I've had extensive training in jazz and tap and a good ballet foundation, as you can see. I spent a terrific summer with Stella Adler in L.A. Now I'm with David Sellers." Giles liked that and nodded his approval.

"I've heard of him," Mr. Homas said. "Very impressive."

"I've danced with the Bolshoi on tour in Los Angeles and the New York City Ballet for one summer. I've done some local theatre, a little summer stock: *Chorus Line*, *Oklahoma*,

Carousel.'' She was feeling better, sensing new energy creeping into her voice. ''I sing, play guitar, swim, roller skate, play good bridge,'' she added then thought for a moment. ''And I make great tunafish sandwiches.''

Giles burst out laughing. ''Give her the script, Lars,'' he said and stretched his muscular legs across the coffee table.

Mr. Homas handed it to her. ''Study pages 20 to 25, the part of Cynthia. Let's see what you can do with it.''

Outside, she drank some water from a cooler then sat down to study the dialogue. One by one she watched the competition file in then out of Homas' office as she contemplated Cynthia's plight. Twenty minutes later the secretary called her name. She stood, carried her gear back inside and waited for Mr. Homas to direct her.

The scene went well and she felt wonderful. John Giles had her sing a cappella from *A Chorus Line*, then followed that with an intricate dance combination. Here was her strong suit. She dazzled them with her retentive memory for combinations, she staggered them with her long extensions and fleet footedness. Giles nodded his affirmation.

''Okay,'' Homas said smiling. ''Tell Greene to call me this afternoon. If we can work out the money, you've got yourself a part.''

Her face lit up. She spun around and clapped her hands together. ''Thank you both,'' she said grabbing one set of man's hands, then the other. ''I'll be wonderful. You'll see. You won't be sorry.'' She stumbled, bumped the couch and left sailing on a cloud.

She wanted to call Michael, her agent, her maid, somebody, anybody to tell them how happy she was. She suppressed an urge to shout out loud in the streets. She wondered briefly if her connection to Ada had something to do with her getting the job, then decided to hell with it. She didn't really care. The tour bus passed again. This time she smiled and did a time step on the pavement. Everyone waved and clapped. Somebody snapped her photograph.

She drove through the lot and found a phone booth. Inside, she called her agent and told him the news. After much deliberation she called Michael. Within half an hour they were sharing a cocktail at her favorite place, the Polo Lounge.

She was there, sipping a strawberry daiquiri when he entered. Afternoon sunshine streamed through the patio windows of the famous Beverly Hills watering hole.

"Hi," he whispered, pressing his lips against her ear, inhaling the scent of lemons. He sat down opposite her in the booth and ordered himself a drink.

There was a fiery glow to her eyes, a flush on her cheeks as she leaned across the table and took his hand. "I know we promised not to see each other," she said, "but I just couldn't stand it any longer. Oh, Michael, I'm so excited." She squeezed his fingertips. "The most wonderful thing has happened. I've got this terrific part in the most fabulous movie. It's a comedy, it's a musical. God. It's a dream come true." She was halfway out of her chair with excitement.

He wanted to tell her he knew. That Lars Homas had called him right after she'd left his office at Universal but instead he smiled and watched her colors fly.

"Hey, that sounds great! And I'm glad you called," he said. "I've missed you so damn much." Her glowing smile radiated warmth throughout his body. "Tell me all about it."

"You should have seen me, Mike. I was really wonderful. No. I was terrific." He laughed out loud. "Really." She was indignant. "I mean it." She threw her hands in the air. "Maybe I'm nuts then. That's what's so crazy about this business. You begin to believe things about yourself . . . and other people, too. You're nobody one minute, then all of a sudden you think you're somebody special. They made me feel so important. Oh, Michael," she sighed, "they weave dreams. Beautiful, wonderful dreams."

He bit his bottom lip. Is that what they were? he thought. In the last few weeks he'd encountered only nightmares. The waiter set down his drink then gracefully disappeared. Michael lifted the glass to his lips and drank.

"Don't you see?" she continued. "I've always believed what Jason told me about myself. That I'm a nothing; less than nothing. Now I can prove that he's wrong. I can taste it Michael. I can feel something wonderful happening, really happening, to me. This is my chance. My chance to prove that I'm talented and creative. That I'm someone. That I can really do it."

She'd driven her speech to a light crescendo and heads were turning in her direction. She pressed her fingers across her lips and she lowered her voice. "It all sounds so crazy when I say it but I believe this part could change everything for me. It could actually change my whole life."

He smiled. He'd seen this Nicole before. Spirited, animated, alive. Like when Jason had first married her and brought her home to meet the family. But what she was saying frightened him a little. She was so damn vulnerable. Especially now. She could be devastated, pinning all her hopes on one film. It took more than talent and creativity to make it in Hollywood. It took strength and stamina. Staying power. The ability to bleed day after day, building scar tissue to survive the long run. And she didn't have it. Not yet, anyway.

And they weren't dreamweavers, they were dreambrokers. Hollywood didn't weave dreams; they manufactured them. For her to live with those illusions would be costly. Buying them outright, he knew might break her.

She crumpled her cocktail napkin in the palm of her moist hand, clutching it like a child with a security blanket. "And I've been thinking, Mike. About the two of us," she said. "I want to be with you so much. More than I realized. But I need to realize something before that happens. I want to feel a sense of myself. I want to leave Jason now. Move out on my own. This job can help me do it. Honestly, I'm tired of hiding inside some shell. It's like I'm living someone else's life and I'm sick of it."

He hated to rain on her parade but he felt the need to explore what she was saying. "What about the nightmares?" he asked. "You're so frightened when you're all alone at night. You'll need someone there with you."

"I've thought about that, of course," she said sipping her drink. "A lot. During summer stock, I always had a roommate. I could do that again. Only this time have Tiu Phong come and stay with me; sort of like a babysitter."

Her amber eyes were wide and filled with hope but her hand was still clutching that crumpled napkin. "And, I want to start seeing someone," she continued. "Like a psychiatrist, I mean. Someone who can help me exorcise Joe from my head once and for all. God. I'm so tired of it. I don't want to spend the rest of my life being afraid. I have to do something. With this job, everything can change for me."

He felt relieved. Proud for her. This was her victory. Whatever else she was, no matter what she'd choose to do, she was a survivor and that instinct for self-preservation would prevail.

She gazed nervously at his face. "Okay," she said, "tell me what you think about the whole idea."

He smiled. "I think it's great," he said without hesitation. "I think you're beautiful and wonderful and I'll do everything I can to help you if you need me to."

He could hear her audible sigh. "I knew you would, Michael. I counted on it." She raised her glass to his. "To changes, Michael. To grand and fabulous changes."

"To life and to love," he said joining her.

"And hope, Michael. Don't forget hope," she said. And they drank.

She parked in the carport then pushed her key into the side door latch. The telephone jangled persistently and she ran to catch it.

"Nicole, honey? Allen Greene. Congratulations. It's all settled. You got the part. I don't know what you did but they really loved you."

She began screaming questions into the telephone, jumping up and down.

"Hey. Calm down a minute," he shouted. She listened while he explained the deal he'd made for her. "We got three weeks rehearsal at $1,500 a week and two weeks filming at $2,500 a week."

"Tell me about my credit," she said.

"Fifty percent of the card. It's a real break for you Nicole. Congratulations again."

She hung up whirled around, and hugged a nearby foam pillow. She searched the house for Tiu Phong then remembered she was still staying with sick relatives. She dialed the answering service and took her messages.

"Your agent, Mr. Greene called."

"I have that," Nicole told her. "Go on, please."

"Mr. Stone called. He'll be out of town for the next two nights. Something about Las Vegas."

Nicole felt a quick surge of panic. It was awful when Jason was home but much worse when she was alone.

"Also, a Mr. Del Gado has been calling you all day. He wouldn't leave a message. Just said he'd get back to you later."

She slammed down the telephone and felt her blood run icy cold, her skin, tight and crawling. She shuddered. God. What did he want? Why was he calling? Terrifying images. Flashes of him standing in her bedroom passed before her eyes like horrible living phantoms. She could smell his stinking breath, see his fierce black eyes examining her, piercing her body like sharp steel knives, feel his bold angry hands as he searched and grabbed at her shoulders, experience the force and power of his arms as he lifted her from the floor and carried her to the bed.

Her terror intensified, gaining on all her senses like a hound pack closing in on a doomed rabbit. She checked the time. Within two hours it would be dark and she would begin to walk the house alone, wringing her hands, weeping like a helpless baby. She needed help. She needed someone. Only Michael understood.

She dialed his number and Elaine Shagan answered. Michael wasn't there. She left an urgent message for him then swallowed some Valium.

She passed the hall mirror and caught her reflection. It was the face of a stranger and she shrank from it. Her pretty pink rosebud mouth had wilted, shriveling to a dark ugly brown smear. Her hair lay tangled around her face and neck damp with perspiration. Her eyes were wide, the pupils dialated. She had the look of a startled night animal paralyzed by the glare of speeding headlights, unable to move.

She rinsed her face in the bathroom sink, and brushed her teeth. She combed her hair pinning it on top of her head. She turned on the television, swallowed more Valium and swooned onto the couch. She prayed for Michael to call then waited for the darkness to cover her like the lid of a coffin.

When she woke it was dim and shadowy inside the house and Armando Del Gado was standing by her side looking down at her.

"You left your keys in the side door," he said tossing them on the coffee table. "You should be more careful."

Nicole's mouth opened wide to force a scream but she only whimpered.

"Hey, c'mon," Armando said. "I'm not drunk this time. I won't even touch you." He stepped back to demonstrate sincerity and held his arms out away from his sides. "I really want to apologize to you . . . for that time in San Francisco. That's really not my style, you know."

She heard nothing he said. Just covered up her bare thighs, stood and backed away from him.

He shot her an angry look. "Shit lady! I mean it. C'mon, don't be afraid. Just say you accept my apology and I'll leave." He thrust out his hand for a handshake.

Her voice suddenly broke through her gripping paralysis. "Noooo! Hellllpppp! Somebody help meeeee!" She ran for the marble steps.

He clenched his fists and ran after, grabbing her by the shoulders, spinning her around. She felt her adrenalin pumping, her heartbeat thrusting inside her rib cage, the room reeling around her.

He was holding her arms, cursing her, begging her, pleading with her just to listen. She struggled, sobbing, resisting the strength and power of his arms. She kicked his ankles and scratched at his face. He grabbed her wrists to protect himself.

And it happened again. Michael whipped Del Gado's body around and struck a powerful right cross toward Del Gado's face snapping his head back.

The surprise caught Del Gado off guard and he staggered backwards down the staircase, somewhat dazed falling against a table in the darkened hallway. He wiped blood from his mouth with his hand then spit a mouthful at the floor. He flared his nostrils, baring his teeth like a wildcat, pulling something from his trouser pocket. Michael leaped down after him, heard the familiar click of a switchblade knife and jumped sideways. Nicole stood horrified, perched on the staircase as the two men circled each other in slow motion in the eerie shadows. Canned laughter and applause burst forth from the television set as Del Gado poised his knife in the air.

"Hijo de su chingada madre," Del Gado snarled and threw a wild roundhouse swipe at Michael's arms. *"Bastido,"* he shouted as he missed. His feet moved quietly, soundlessly along the carpeting.

Michael fixed his gaze on the blade, groping his way around the darkened living room searching for something with which to defend himself. He grabbed a heavy crystal vase and hurled it. It missed Del Gado's head, splattering against the wall, like a fistful of crushed ice. Nicole's body leaped at the sound of it.

He could see Del Gado's face sneering hatefully in the moonlight, the wild savage expression on his face as he spoke. "You think your *chocha* is better than anyone else?" Del Gado snarled and then lunged, impaling air.

Michael jumped back. Del Gado lunged again and Michael felt the rim of a low table snap against the back of his knees. He faltered and Del Gado sprang swinging the knife in a wide arc, thrusting it up and across Michael's chest. Michael flinched and bounded sideways. He felt the unmistakable sensation of warm blood sliding down his ribcage. Nicole covered her eyes at the sight and whimpered.

Suddenly Del Gado stumbled and Michael lunged, kicking his groin. Del Gado's body bent forward twisting in pain but he held the knife fast.

Michael grabbed Del Gado's arms, jerking his wrist again and again toppling him onto the floor and covering him with his body. They grunted and groaned, straining against each other with equal force, rolling around, struggling for possession of the sharp knife.

Michael dug his nails and fingers deeply into Del Gado's wrists, wrapping them, squeezing, pinching the veins and muscles, eventually finding and gouging the sensitive nerves. Their heads were inches apart as Del Gado pulled his knees up toward Michael's belly pushing hard against the soft, vulnerable flesh.

"*Puto! Órale cabrón!*" Del Gado shouted with one last breath then spit at him. A viscous bloody mass hit Michael's face, slipping down his cheek. "*A mí me la pelan!*" he yelled defiantly as Michael finally forced the knife from his hands. Then Michael pinned Del Gado's chest. Del Gado lay defeated under Michael's weight, moaning on the floor, out of breath.

"You've made a costly mistake," Del Gado whispered. "Before this is over I'll have you . . . your family . . . all of you in jail. Your names will be mud. You'll begin to know the meaning of sorrow." His words had the hiss and promise of a lit fuse snaking its way towards an explosion.

Michael breathed heavily. "No," he said. "You're dead wrong. The sorrow's all yours, Armando. And your baby sister's."

Del Gado's eyes flashed lightning bolts. He looked dumbstruck then struggled heroically to get Michael's hands away from him but collapsed from exhaustion, his eyes wide with terror.

"I'd think twice about sacking the agency," Michael continued. "I'd think twice about destroying everything my mother's worked for. I know all about you. How you snuck into the country in the middle of the night carrying your sick baby sister. How a U.S. border patrol almost found you. How you tried to keep her from crying out loud so they wouldn't discover you and you accidentally suffocated her. I have your own words on tape in my office." He was out of breath.

Del Gado cried out like a banshee, covering up his ears, rolling his head from side to side on the floor. "Stop! No more! God forgive me. It was an accident," he cried.

Michael hated himself. At this moment, he was no better than Ada. Guilty of everything he loathed. He felt an intense compassion for Del Gado. He wanted to extend his hand, tell him he was sorry. But he didn't. He had no choice. Del Gado had brought this moment upon himself. Michael gripped the table pulling himself up from the floor.

"You," Del Gado shouted. "You're not fit to talk

about my sister, about me. You and your easy life, your fine education. You and all the others like you. You don't know anything. *Nada*!'' Del Gado lifted himself up on his elbows, then his knees. ''You know *mierda*!'' He stood, walked a little then turned and stared. ''Well, you have me, don't you? We're even, aren't we? I don't make trouble for you and you don't make trouble for me. Okay. All right. But don't push me too far, Stone. I have important friends.'' He moved to the front door and opened it wide. *''A mí me la pelan,''* he yelled once again then slammed it.

When he had gone Nicole ran into Michael's arms. They embraced, clinging to one another for a moment, then she stepped back and examined the blood oozing from his side.

''Oh, my God. You're hurt,'' she cried and began to shiver uncontrollably.

''It's okay,'' he said calming her. ''It's just a scratch.''

''But you're bleeding, Michael,'' she said and dragged him into the small bathroom where she tended him with alcohol and bandages.

''How about you?'' Michael asked lifting her chin. ''Did he hurt you?''

Her voice was strident and she kept repeating the phrases over and over like some crazy prayer. ''No. Oh, no. I'm just fine. Really, I am. He didn't hurt me at all.''

But Michael knew better. She had been hurt. Much more than she realized. Unlike his wounds which were exposed, hers lay buried, hidden deep inside her psyche and it would now take a miracle to treat them.

Chapter 14

THE WHIRLWIND TOUR HAD GONE WELL. Roxanne's movie, in release only two weeks, was big office. Distribution deals and contractural offers were coming in from all over the world. The famous, highly regarded English producer, Lord Wade had made numerous transatlantic phone calls. Sidney Gross was a happy man. His clever stunt had garnered sympathy and publicity, which had then translated itself into box office millions. Publicity regarding "the incident" was still paying off. And Luis was doing well, almost fully recovered from his knife wound. That was good. Sidney hated hurting him. But a little blood-letting was always healthy for business.

He leaned one plump elbow on his desk and snatched the persistent buzzer. "Yes?"

Tony Meredith's voice boomed back at him from the small box. "It's Fred Kaye. He wants to know if you've read the script."

"What did you tell him?"

"I know better than that, Sidney." Tony's voice had a snap to it.

"Touchy, touchy," Sidney said. "Are we on the rag today?" Tony was silent. "Okay." Sidney continued, "put the son of a bitch on."

"Sid baby, Fred Kaye." The voice was deep, distinctive.

"Hey, Freddie. How the hell are you?" Sidney leaned

back in his chair, resting his arm behind his head, cradling the phone between his ear and shoulder.

"Did you read the script I sent you?" Fred Kaye asked.

"Not yet," Sidney lied. "I've been very busy. I'll give it a look-see sometime today. Later on perhaps when I have more time." He grinned and chewed on a hangnail.

"C'mon," Fred Kaye said. "Give me a break, will you? Don't you read the papers? There's going to be an actor's strike any day now. I've got to sign all my people before they start picketing. I could lose the whole goddamn deal."

"Tomorrow, Fred. As God is my witness," Sidney said and hung up.

Of course he had read Fred Kaye's script. It was pretty good. A decent story with a good part for Roxanne. And he'd let her do it. But only if his own plans fell through. Plans for a package deal that included Hank Mason and Roxanne. If he could only convince Mike Stone to let him have Hank on a loanout he could sew up the deal in less than two days.

Together, Hank and Roxanne would break box office records all over the world. And he wanted that. He wanted that more than anything. All he needed was Stone's cooperation. All Stone had to do was say "yes" and *The Cowboy and The Lady* could go ahead. He dialed Hugh Parker's office and waited.

"Hugh?"

"Hello, Sidney. Congratulations on the tour," Parker said. "I'm glad it went so well for Roxanne, especially after what happened to Luis."

Sidney grinned. "Yeah. Wasn't that awful?"

"What's up?" Parker asked.

"Have you talked to Mike Stone about the Hank Mason loanout?"

Parker hesitated. "Uh, yes. I spoke to him. He's still not very keen on it, Sid."

"Why, for shit's sake?" Sidney snorted. "Is he dumb or something? Everybody in the industry is laughing at him. Here's his chance to really do something."

"It has nothing to do with Michael. He likes the idea.

It's Hank he's worried about. The boy needs a rest," Parker said.

"He needs a *schtup* up his ass, is what he needs."

Parker laughed. "You're impossible, Sidney. But seriously, besides the suicide, there's Alma. She's filed for divorce. The kid's fighting too many uphill battles."

"Is this a stall? Cause if it is, tell Stone he's got a new custom Corniche, gross points, a yacht, girls, boys, whatever the hell he wants. Only give me Hank Mason for one fuckin' movie."

"It won't work, Sidney," Parker said. "He's already given a final *No*."

Million dollar bills flew past Sidney's eyes and out the window. He had to try harder. There was far too much at stake. "What about Ada?" he demanded. "Does she know about my offer? You stick that contract in front of her eyes—she'll come in bed."

"Will you forget it, Sidney," Parker said. "Ada's left everything to Michael. There are strict orders for her not to get involved in the business for a while."

"Try him again for me, will you?" Sidney said, unwilling to surrender and hung up the telephone.

There must be something he wants, Sidney thought, staring at Roxanne's photograph. Every man can be bought. *Even* Mike Stone.

Hugh Parker placed the receiver on the cradle and rubbed his right shoulder. His hand, wrist and forearm hurt from writing briefs and a headache was beginning to scream behind his eye sockets.

His secretary knocked softly and slowly opened the door. He looked up, straining, felt the pain above his eyelids and promptly shaded his eyes. "I'm sorry," she said. "I know you're busy, but Mr. Steele is on the line. Something about Christopher."

A shock wave passed through him. "What line?"

"Two," she answered softly and closed the door.

He picked up the receiver and touched the flashing button.

"What's wrong, Sam?" he asked.

Steele's voice was tense, low, filled with strained pauses. "He's gone. Run away, Mr. Parker. Just run away."

Parker's fist clenched involuntarily, his nails digging hard at the soft skin inside his palm.

"When? What happened?"

"Half an hour ago," Steele said. "We drove to the market like always. He wanted something at the cheese counter. I swear to God I watched him, Mr. Parker, honest. But he must have slipped out the side door and disappeared into thin air."

"Nobody disappears into thin air, Steele," Parker snarled. "Did you check around?"

"Sure I did. I asked everybody. Nobody saw him. It's like the earth swallowed him up or something. Why? Why would he do a thing like that to me? To you? To himself, for Christ's sake! He was going good, Mr. Parker. He was practically clean."

Steele's voice resounded, pummeling, vibrating inside Parker's skull. He wanted him to stop. He wanted to shut his ears and eyes, suspend his awareness, dive into a dark tank somewhere and experience nothing. "Find him," Parker shouted. "Call Shauna, his buddies, Terry, Eugene, that bar he liked to drink in . . . but find him." His fingers nervously pulled at his earlobe.

"I'll do my best," Steele said and clicked off.

Hugh Parker stared into space. The headache was now a full-blown migraine. Why? he thought. Why *did* he do it? To show me he could? To get loaded? He stood up and began to pace. And where did he go? The beach? Some local bar? To jam with his old rock group? Where?

The pain in his head made him feel as though his brain would explode. Every sound jarred his nerves, every movement he made brought shock waves to his equilibrium. He downed two aspirin with half a cup of cold, bitter coffee and sat down again staring at Annie's picture. He was afraid. This time, he was really afraid. Chris was all he had left. Since Annie's death they'd become close, he thought. So very close. Maybe that was a mistake.

Maybe they hadn't been as close as he thought.

Hugh Parker was ambitious, had always been ambitious.

He was brilliant, tenacious, a man endowed with excellent reasoning powers, a man who could sit down, extract, isolate and define a primary problem from any point of view, then successfully design, plot and counterplot some concrete, highly functional and advantageous solution. He had the ability to capitalize, to seize and exploit, to trade, even in the vernacular. Some called him shrewd, cunning, wily, even sly. It made him laugh. Whatever they thought didn't really matter in the long run. He simply didn't care. He wanted only to be where the action was. And he found it. After graduation, in Chicago working for a synidcate. He even married a synidcate daughter.

Annie Morello was beautiful, vulnerable, the youngest daughter of the oldest Mafia chieftain and Parker fell madly in love with her. She had strawberry blond hair and soft brown eyes. She was intelligent, delicate, shy and winsome. They courted with Papa's full blessing. Their marriage was exciting, thrilling. They were deeply in love.

Then Annie told Parker she wanted him to leave her father's organization. She was expecting a baby. She didn't want their child growing up in the bosom of corruption. He was stunned, bewildered, caught in the middle of familial crossfire and he didn't know what to do.

''It's your job to control her,'' Papa Morello said, sucking on his thick Havana cigar. ''Women are like children. They must have Gods to worship, to teach them right from wrong. She must be disciplined. You must beat those notions out of her. It's your duty as a man; your moral obligation as her husband to convince her . . . anyway you can. But, she must never leave the bosom of her family.''

At home, Annie's pleadings were tearful. She literally fell to her knees begging him, imploring. But it was useless.

''Be sensible, Annie. Our place is here with your family,'' Hugh told her. Parker had firmly delivered Papa Morello's message.

After Christopher's birth, Annie grew heartsick and despondent. She drank more cocktails, swallowed more tranquilizers, to steady her nerves she told everyone. Then a strong and lingering paranoia overcame her. On every streetcorner there lurked an enemy, some unknown assassin ready to kill her son. As her paranoia grew, her need for peace grew. And finally she reached for heroin, seeking it, locating it on the streets of Chicago's southside, squeezing it inside her veins to escape the awful plots and counterplots against her and her baby. The same heroin Papa's organization brought into the city.

Parker's work kept him busy. Las Vegas, New York, Miami, Washington, Los Angeles. He didn't notice the changes taking place. To him, she seemed to adjust, even sharing some weekends with him on two of his trips. Yet now, whenever he'd look back, in retrospect, he'd remember the long-sleeved dresses she always wore, the ever-present trousers, the way she'd never trust herself to hold the baby, leaving his care and feeding to a nurse. How she'd never permit him to see her naked or make love to him with the lights on. The signs were all there, bold as black graffiti sprayed on a white wall.

Only he didn't see them.

When he looked at her, he saw the tiny China doll he had married: the loving mother, the obedient daughter while she slowly dispatched herself into hell.

When she died of an overdose, Parker was stricken, plunged into grief. She had been everything to him. Everything he did or had ever done, he'd done for her, for Christopher. Everything he'd ever wanted, he wanted for them. He was, of course, only fooling himself. He'd been selfish, aspiring, pretending it was for them when it was all for his own sake, his own self-aggrandizement.

Papa Morello blamed him, of course, and Parker blamed Morello. They fought constantly, bitterly. Threats and counter-threats were hurled. Claims were made on Christopher. Morello demanded custody of the child. Parker laughed in his face. Against Morello's expressed wishes, he resigned, packed their bags and left Chicago.

They moved to Beverly Hills where Chris attended the best schools, wore the finest clothes, was given everything his heart desired. He grew and flourished. Parker had provided a rich life for the two of them. Morello did not interfere; then four years later he died, leaving Christopher a rich young man.

Christopher's teenage years were happy. He formed a rock group called "Jitters," found a small speaking part in a feature film movie about unhappy teenagers. He developed a strong, independent streak with plans for a future. Then, they found him one night, lying in an alleyway, incontinent, choking to death on his own vomit, strung out on drugs.

Once again Parker was dumbfounded. *Why*? he asked. Why Christopher? It was Annie, all over again.

Parker pledged his help. He dismissed half of his workload to be with Chris. Whatever problems there were could be solved. He believed that. They found a psychiatrist and shared the hour together. None of this "I'm well, you're sick" shit. And there were vacations, holidays together in Spain and London. On the advice of the psychiatrist, he hired Steele. Chris had to change his life. Steele was to dry him out, live with him, supervise his life twenty-four hours a day. All of Chris's friends were forbidden to visit for six weeks, including Shauna. Chris agreed to all that. Agreed to it of his own accord. And Chris was doing so well. At least that's what Parker had thought.

At last they were beginning to communicate, to discover each other as friends, as father and son, as individuals. It was all going so well and now this.

Parker swallowed two more aspirin and closed all the blinds. He poured more coffee into his cup, sat down and watched the phone buttons flash chaotically. For a very clever man who had always prided himself on solving other men's problems, when it came down to himself he could not see the trees for the forest.

* * *

Shauna Stone Candelli parked her gleaming white Porsche Targa in Sally Quinn's cement driveway. The Malibu sun was high and the air, cool for July, smelled clean and refreshing. Plan "B" had worked beautifully, just as Sally said it would. But still Shauna wondered if they were really doing the right thing.

"Chris needs some fun, for Christ's sake," Sally had said. "He needs to surf, to sun himself at the beach. Just a few hours of freedom. Jeeze, whose side are you on anyway?"

Shauna was hesitant at first but then Sally had a way of

making everything sound so righteous. In the end Shauna had agreed.

In so many ways Shauna understood Chris. Hell, she loved him. They'd practically shared a childhood together. Each had lost a parent and somehow found it easy to confide in one another. He knew how she felt about Viva. How sick she was of hearing everyone say, "God, your mom's terrific. She's so young, so beautiful." Ha! If they only knew. She was sick of all that. She wanted, needed a mother. Not some oddball celebrity with mammoth tits that men catered to, who called everyone on earth "Darling." And she missed her father. More than anything she missed Maurice. Missed his warmth. She felt empty without him.

And she knew how Chris felt. About his father, his background, his mother. How he hated the way his father kept trying to force him to do things together, like take vacations or go fishing. How he hated being locked up with Sam Steele, unable to take a dump on his own. "I'm not my mother," he told her one afternoon when they were alone. "Just because I like to get loaded once in a while, he thinks I'm sick or something. He's obsessed—on a guilt trip and I have to pay for it." She understood.

Except for Chris and her talks with Elaine Shagan, Shauna had no one. She didn't know Ada at all. And from what her friend Elaine Shagan had told her, Ada and Viva were pretty much alike. There was always Uncle Jason. He was fun. She could always call him and talk to him occasionally but mostly he was busy. Grandpa Max was impossible and Uncle Mike was always away.

So there was Sally. Good old Sally. But lately, she was getting sick and tired of her, too. Sick of catering to her kinky desires day after day, doting on her, fulfilling her every demand. And, Jesus, there were so many demands lately. They were even the same size, wore practically the same clothes like the white jacket she was wearing right now and her red canvas bag.

But, she loved Sally too. Sally made her laugh. She was good company. She was always there. But most of all, Sally always had great dope.

Shauna saw the garage door open and started the motor.

Inside the garage, Sally tossed her blond mane and swung her arms onto her hips. "And where the hell have you been all this time?" she said.

"Hey," Shauna retorted, sliding out. "The traffic got heavy around the Marina." She pulled her red canvas purse from off the white leather seat and slammed the car door. "Why? Is anything wrong?"

"Nothing yet. But you know Chris. He's bound to get nervous all alone. The last thing I need is for him to get frantic and call me from the damn motel. Have my fucking telephone number on the bill. His old man would skin me alive, not to mention screwing up my career if he found out."

Inside the French provincial living room, furnished in colors of pale blue and sea green, Shauna found a pecan-framed wall mirror and combed her silky brown hair.

"Where's the stuff?" Sally asked.

"In there," Shauna said pointing to her purse.

Sally dived onto the pale blue rug and opened the red canvas bag. She pulled out a neatly folded brown paper bag and examined the contents. "Any problems?"

"No. I paid him and left like you told me."

"Good," Sally said and slipped on a lightweight, white jacket identical to Shauna's. She tucked the brown paper bag inside her jacket pocket and joined Shauna at the mirror. "Look," she said poking Shauna's arm. We're twins."

Shauna bridled at the words but managed to smile. Sally was right, of course. Except for the color of their hair and eyes, at this moment in these clothes they were very much alike.

Outside, on the beach, they were just two more, swallowed by hordes; sun worshippers sloshing oils, joggers running the distance, children building sandcastles shouting challenges, grunting volleyball champions, preening lifeguards, surfers, laughing voices all served on a platter of sand, sky, crashing surf and calling gulls.

They jogged the half mile to the Fiesta Motel and slipped unnoticed up the private white wooden staircase into Chris's suite which overlooked the beach. Inside, all the oceanside windows were opened wide, a steady breeze struggling against the heavy velvet curtains. Chris was lying on the kingsize waterbed in his shorts grinning, a bottle of brandy in his hand. "Where the hell did you find this place?" he asked laughing. He was handsome, with brown eyes made for soft light and bedrooms, his dark hair thick and straight.

Sally giggled. "Wouldn't you like to know?"

Shauna stood amused, her eyes wide and searching the room.

The suite was large with a small kitchen and a large bathroom. The kingsize bed was covered with fake leopardskins made of heavy velvet. The drapes and floor coverings matched. A headboard behind the bed was built onto the wall and had mirrored shelves. The fireplace, real at one time, housed several plastic logs with bright red cellophane paper. One flip of a switch started a red cellophane fire which sounded like a sack of sick crickets. There were plastic ferns, plastic flowers, and fake parrots, all covering every open area of the room. It was screaming, tawdry and garishly grand. On a rattan desk there was stationery with flowered Fiesta letterhead and large glass ashtrays marked similarly.

"Well we did it kiddies," Sally squealed hugging Shauna. "We freed the prisoner. Power to the people," she yelled and thrust her fist into the air.

"Right on," Chris chimed in. "Attica, Attica, Attica!"

"Now," Sally said, "Quiet down and let's have some fun." She pulled the brown paper bag from her pocket, draped her jacket across a flowered rattan chair and sat on the bed. Shauna threw her jacket over Sally's and joined them.

"Look what Momma has for all her little babies," Sally said and dumped the contents of the bag onto the leopardskin covered bed. Shauna's face lit up like a television screen. Chris placed his half-empty brandy bottle behind him on a shelf and ran his fingers through the treasure. "Take your pick my children," Sally said and sat back watching them bounce.

There were Quaaludes, mini-bennies, mushrooms, Placidyls and one vial of cocaine.

"Placidyls," Shauna said looking up at Sally. "My

favorite little red cocktail. How'd you get him to give you those?''

Sally cocked her head to the side glancing at Shauna from the corner of her dark blue eyes. ''A good Momma knows,'' she told her, sounding like Mae West. ''She knows how to get them and she knows how to keep her babies happy.''

Shauna scooped up two red capsules and swallowed them with water from a kitchen glass. Chris blew some coke and followed that with two ludes he washed down with brandy. Sally only observed.

There was ice, then fire soaring inside Shauna. The red jelly capsules were pure happiness. She felt weightless floating on air within five minutes. If she had any doubts about Plan ''B'' before, she had none now.

Chris removed his shorts then turned and slowly undressed Shauna. He threw her shorts and t-shirt on the floor beside his, then observed her body which was slim and tan, her breasts round and full like Viva's. Suddenly their faces were close and he kissed her cheek, her lips, the crook of her neck, her pink nipples which were growing hard. She searched his thin, firm body with eager hands, kneading his wiry, well-muscled arms and shoulders.

Chris straddled himself across Shauna's thighs, bent over, touched his full, sensitive lips onto her smooth tight belly, licking, biting a pathway down and around to her vagina. When he found her pink clitoris, he flicked his tongue and pulled it between his teeth sucking her, stroking the soft flesh of her thighs with his fingers.

Transfixed, Shauna reached up for him, murmuring, ''I am the sea, the naked sea.'' Christopher shut his eyes, held his penis in both his hands, stroking, rubbing it, pulling it back and forth till it was almost hard, the tip glistening with drops of his own milky juices.

Sally licked her lips at the sight and size of him. She ripped off her clothes, kneeled closely behind him, reached between his hairy legs, kneading, massaging his balls and cock with both hands.

He moaned at the heat, the friction, the pleasure of her expert hands and fingers teasing him, pulling all over him. He rotated his buttocks around and around, thrusting his pelvis into her hands until he was hard and ready to burst.

Then she stopped, lay back on her side, positioning her head between Christopher's thighs and Shauna's cunt. She breathed in the musky smells then jerked the head of his cock and took it between her lips. Chris arched his back at the sensation of her warm wet mouth and shoved himself deeply into her throat.

"I'm gonna come, mother fucker," he whispered. She withdrew him quickly, clamped her fingers tightly around the head of his penis and forbid him to.

"Not yet baby," she said slapping his ass hard. "I'll tell you when." She pushed Shauna's legs apart, inserted her fingers and gently separated the moist folds of flesh teasing and pinching her way inside. She opened her mouth, wet her lips then ran her pointed tongue slowly around Shauna's vagina. Shauna tensed, grinding her pelvis.

Sally licked Chris's cock, then Shauna's cunt, back and forth, then raised up suddenly and guided Chris into Shauna's vagina. "Now baby. Now you can fuck her," Sally said and watched as Chris plunged his body, working back and forth until he came in one deep, long spasm.

Spent, Christopher rolled off Shauna and lay there exhausted, his dark straight hair rumpled, falling over his eyes. Then, he sat up, sniffed some coke and fell back on the bed laughing at Shauna. She was dead asleep, dreaming, her mouth wide open.

He sat up, crawled over Sally, stood, wobbling in place. "I got to piss," he said and weaved his way toward the toilet. Inside the bathroom, he giggled like a lunatic then bumped against something and fell. Sally ran after him.

"Shit," he said looking at the mess and splatter of urine on the wall and floor. "This bathroom's crooked."

Sally laughed. "It's not crooked, stupid. Your brain's fucked." She helped him to his feet.

"Is that what it is?" Chris said trying to flush the toilet. He quickly showered, found his way back to the bed, blew more coke, swallowed more ludes with brandy and collapsed on the bed.

Sally checked her watch. Everything was happening as planned. In a little while, she'd wake Shauna, convince her to leave Chris here to sleep it off, then later anonymously telephone the hotel and tell them to wake Chris up. They'd find him smashed, asleep and call the cops. Parker would force Chris to dry out again and Shauna would be forbidden to see him for at least six weeks.

That's what Jason wanted. To separate them. That would make Jason happy. And that's what Sally wanted. That's what this whole thing was about after all, wasn't it?

Shauna wakened and glanced at Christopher. He was sound asleep snoring, sucking air, hissing and whistling. She glanced around the room, rose and stumbled from the bed to where Sally was sitting, joining her on the carpet. "What happened to him?" she asked yawning, pointing at Chris.

"He thought the bathroom was crooked and pissed on himself," Sally said. "I guess it was too much for him so he passed out."

Shauna smiled then turned on the television set. They watched four commercials in a row and Sally grimmaced.

"Shit I'm sick of commercials," Sally said.

"Me too," Shauna chimed in and began to change the channels.

"No. Stupid. I mean for myself. I want to do some movies, a television show, a soap opera. Something where I'm challenged. I'm so damn bored shooting stupid commercials. I want something I can sink my teeth into."

"How about a turkey leg," Shauna said and fell giggling on the floor.

"Very funny," Sally said, folding her arms across her bare chest. "But I mean it."

Shauna sat up, her brow furrowing into deep lines. "Why don't you do something on your own? You're pretty creative. Like reporting. Like reporting the Olympics or sporting competitions. You could even travel again."

"I don't know," Sally said. Then her face brightened. "But I could do something like it." She leaped up and began to pace. "I know." She grabbed the motel stationery and a pencil then jotted down her concept for a brand-new television format. "You know those television shows that are like magazines?"

Shauna nodded. "You mean like *Real People* or *Two on the Town*?"

"Exactly. Only this one would be strictly a sports magazine. Like a television *Sports Illustrated*. I'd do a weekly report on sports all over the country, the world even. *Sally Quinn Reports From London*." She wrote the concept and title down on the paper and shoved it quickly inside her jacket pocket. She checked her watch. "We'd better leave," she said. "It's almost four."

Shauna had a puzzled look on her face. "But Sally. How will Chris get home? We were supposed to drop him off near the market."

"He and I worked that out before you arrived," Sally said. "He wants to swim a little. Be by himself. And he has enough cash in his wallet for the bill plus a taxi." Sally glanced quickly away from Shauna's puzzled gaze and began wiping the television set, the doorknobs, packing all the loose articles they had touched, tossing them into her canvas bag.

"What the hell are you doing?" Shauna asked.

"Look kid," Sally said. "Let's face it. Chris is not very reliable. He might just talk. He might tell his father where he spent the day when he gets home."

"Don't be ridiculous," Shauna said. "Chris would never say we helped him. Never."

"I know that. But just in case he slips with the name of the motel or something. Parker's a very clever man. He could come here and have the place dusted. If he finds our fingerprints, you and Chris are finished. Do you want that? Do you really want that to happen?"

Shauna shook her head. "No. I guess you're right."

"Good," Sally said breathing a sigh of relief. "Let's get dressed and get out of here."

* * *

Everyone thought he was in Vegas. That was good. He'd need an alibi. Jason climbed the hospital steps one by one, inching his way, wondering all the time if he really had the courage. He reached the second floor and was beginning to sweat. The smell always got to him first. The sickening odor of alcohol and disinfectant. He looked up. The hall was illuminated by a hazy white glow from overhead bulbs that were laced with wire. The bannister felt cold. A breeze seemed to whirl around the staircase, yet he was drenched in sweat.

All he had to do was take one pillow and stuff it over her goddamn face, hold it there until she stopped breathing. That was all. That would end his pain, the humiliation, the disappointment he'd suffered all his life because of her. Then Max would no longer make demands for the return of the stock.

He shivered. There was an acid taste in his mouth. He heard a door slam somewhere above him and stood very still against a wall. Someone ran down one flight of stairs and slammed another door. Now he was shaking. He wiped his forehead and eyes, the top of his lip. He was going to vomit, just like he did when Michael was born.

Nothing had changed.

Nothing had changed. He gripped his stomach, almost began to wretch, and then he ran back down the stairs and out.

* * *

It was almost eight when the office telephone rang. Hugh Parker sprang from his chair and grabbed it.

"It's Steele, Mr. Parker. Christ I'm sorry." He started to weep.

"God, what is it? Tell me what happened?" Parker cried.

"They found him. In a motel on the beach. God forgive me. He's dead."

Chapter 15

THE TRAGIC DEATH OF Christopher Parker provoked no front-page headlines. As reported in the local press, he was one more sad statistic, one more lost and troubled child; a bewildered youth who had delivered himself from loneliness the only way he knew how. In so doing he paid the ultimate price.

One investigator interviewed by the press put the scenario this way. "He was fed up with his routine, saw a chance to get away, hitched a ride, maybe took a bus to the beach where he bought a bottle of brandy. There, he scored some local dope, checked into a motel, drank too much, popped too many pills and collapsed."

When questioned about a missing water glass and a reported telephone call to the room, he said this. "We are satisfied that the kid died of an accidental overdose. The maid isn't sure she put a glass in the room in the first place and the switchboard operator claims she took three calls at precisely the same time that evening. She cannot swear that one of those calls was meant for his room. At this time, we have no reason to suspect foul play."

Off the record, he repeated his theory to colleagues, only couched in different terms. "He was one more indulged Hollywood brat who just couldn't hack it."

Parker finally fell asleep. It was his first rest in almost five days. He looked rumpled and shabby, still wearing yesterday's clothes. Viva studied his face in repose. It was pale, drained, his breathing labored and uneven. And why not? He'd been through hell. He had just buried his son.

And she was worried about him. Worried about the endless hours he was spending on the telephone, asking outrageous questions, demanding explanations, reading and rereading the coroner's report, the police report, searching, looking for the overlooked. She was disturbed by his drinking, his self-imposed neglect, his prowling about the sprawling Brentwood ranch house talking to himself, formulating theory after theory about Christopher's last hours, possessed, obsessed, ranting and raving. He was convinced that someone had somehow contributed to the death of his son.

"Chris may have died of accidental poisoning," he told her, "I'll grant you that. But somebody helped him get away from Steele and somebody gave him that goddamn shit. That somebody's going to pay."

Viva didn't try to reason with him. She sensed his deep-seated need to mourn, to grieve in his own way, to be absolutely crazy just as she had been when Maurice died.

She poured herself another drink and swallowed it quickly, grimacing as the strong liquid burned its way down her throat. She felt an ache for him deep inside her chest and pressed her fist between her breasts rubbing to relieve the anguish.

He grumbled in his sleep, blinked open his swollen eyelids and sat upright. Disoriented, he scanned the dimly lit room, recognized Viva and slumped back against the den couch. He pulled bits of sand from his eyelashes with his fingertips, rolling the pieces back and forth between his fingers.

"I must have dozed off," he said scratching a two-day old stubble.

"Thank God for that," she said. "Lord knows you need it." She poured Coca-Cola into a large glass of crushed ice and sat down beside him. "Here, drink this."

He arranged his features into a thoughtful smile. "Thanks," he said, swallowing it all at once. "What time is it?"

"About one."

"Any phone calls?"

"No," she answered. "Only one wrong number half an hour ago."

His half-dead eyes came suddenly alive only to hide again, retreating somewhere inside him.

"Why don't you take a shower?" Viva said. "I'll fix you something to eat." She took the empty glass from his trembling hand and started for the kitchen.

"No. Don't," he called after. "I'm not hungry." He reached for the telephone. Viva moved quickly and took the receiver from his hand.

"Please, darling," she said, placing it back down. "You must stop. Get hold of yourself. You're going to wind up very sick if you continue like this. Believe me. I know what I'm talking about."

He began to say something, then seemed to change his mind. "There are things I still have to find out, Viva," he said after a while. "I just can't sit here and do nothing."

"You can and you must. Give yourself time, Hugh. Time to mend, to heal."

The look in his eyes seemed hard and calculating. "Before I can heal, someone will have to pay for my son's death."

She stared at him helplessly. "Listen to me," she said softly. "I've read the coroner's report *and* the police report. They all say the same thing, Hugh. There is no 'someone.' Chris swallowed that poison himself." She felt his body stiffen at the words. "Oh God, I know how painful this is for you, but you must face and accept the facts. Chris's death was nothing more than a tragic accident."

Parker's body shook violently. "No way," he shouted. "Somebody helped him. Somebody gave him that stuff."

"Yes, of course," she said. "Some goddamn pusher. Some bastard you're never going to find." She was suddenly sorry those words had escaped her lips but he was no longer listening.

"Somebody gave him that stuff," he repeated over and over staring at the floor. "Somebody helped him get away."

Viva knelt on the carpet and grasped both his hands. She wanted desperately to help him; to make him realize and accept what she felt was the truth. "Hugh. There was an autopsy. You've petitioned an inquest—brought in your own forensic pathologist. You've asked for and received a decent court date. You're a good lawyer. If there's anything wrong, anything at all suspicious, the truth's going to come out there."

His cynical laughter filled the room. "You really believe that shit don't you? Well I know better. I've listened to forensic men dig holes for one another. Autopsies aren't always reliable. Inquests aren't always reliable." He turned away. "As for the truth, I don't know what the hell that is anymore."

It was all useless. He was not ready to respond—to listen to reason. She would have to first open a door before a light could penetrate the dark place in his heart. She cupped his unshaven chin in her hands and tilted his head. Her heart sank at the expression of pain in his eyes. She really wanted to sweep him into her arms; keep him there pressed tightly against her, soothe him. She wanted to tell him she understood, that like her, he would grieve, never forget, but in time, good time, he'd be able to go on with a part of his life.

"Can you be without me for a little while?" she whispered. He nodded and reached for a cigarette. She watched as the match hovered about in his hand.

She stood, gathered up her things, straightened her skirt and blouse. "There's coffee on the kitchen counter if you like," she said, "and some sweet rolls warming in the oven. I'll be at Shauna's if you need me." She bent to kiss him, felt his agony pull something deep inside her and fell to her knees clutching him tightly.

"Dearest Hugh," she cried. "Please, help me, help you." His eyes shut tightly and a single tear slipped down the side of his nose. He turned his head away from her and she sensed his private need. "Take care darling," she said rising quickly. "I'll be back in a few hours."

He watched her walk away, heard the door slam, then listened as the motor of her Excalibur rumbled away. He sat back and wiped his face, thinking of how much he had to do. How much he had to think about. Little odds and ends in this case that made no sense to him. Like that missing water glass and the telephone call. Everyone else had those real easy answers. He was not prepared to accept any of them.

And how could he talk to Viva? And his crazy notions about Shauna or Sally Quinn or even Jason Stone. And were they crazy, for that matter? Was it so crazy to imagine that Shauna had something to do with Chris's escape? Yes, of course it was. Shauna loved Chris. Loved him almost as much as he did.

Then what was it about her that bothered him so much? Was it Sally? Sally Quinn and that strange visit she had paid Christopher at the apartment? Was it Shauna's relationship to Sally? He dragged on the last of his cigarette and ground out the stub.

He thought of Jason Stone and the crack he had made in his office. The one about Chris. One about Annie. He had never mentioned the cause of Annie's death to anyone. How had Jason found that out? Why did he mention it? And more importantly what the hell did it all prove? Nothing. Absolutely nothing.

He stood, removed his jacket. The strong odor from his sweaty armpits sickened him. Viva was right. He was going crazy, lying in filth, thinking filthy, crazy thoughts.

Well, he'd do as she asked. He'd shower and shave and have something to eat. He started for the bedroom, but the ring of the telephone startled him. He answered it.

"It's Gypsy," a man's voice said, "checking in."

"You're late," Parker said looking at the hall clock.

"I called before," Gypsy said, "but some dame answered so I hung up. There's nothing anyway."

"Okay," Parker said. "Just stick with it."

"Your dust," Gypsy said and clicked off.

Parker hung up, drummed his fingers on the cluttered desk and sat down. There was a photograph of Chris taken last summer. He lifted it, studied the dark handsome features and suddenly recalled the awful moment of Steele's call, felt the pain that gripped at his heart, the ice that froze in his veins at the sight of his son lying there on a slab. He could see the mortuary, hear the click of the elevator as he rode it down to select a coffin. He felt his vision blur, a terrible hammering in his brain. His head fell to the desk, buried itself in the crook of his sleeve.

"Oh God, help me," he screamed.

He recalled choosing Chris's burial clothes, his anger at the mortuary man because he had pushed his boy's dark hair over to the wrong side. He could see the gravesite; everyone standing there, the multitude of flowers stinking all around him. He could see Shauna's face as she wept and swooned, clinging onto Viva and Sally Quinn.

Then he felt it all coming. The thunder crashing around him, the frantic beating of his heart, the sickening anger and rage bursting, spilling out. "Oh God, no," he wailed. "Help me," he cried, as all the pain of the last four days smothered him. He gasped for air as the tears rolled down his cheeks in a deluge. He was dazed, dizzy and reached for something to wipe his nose and dry his eyes.

He opened the desk drawer for a tissue and felt the hardness of his revolver lying there inside. He reached for it, held it tightly, studied the four-inch dark, steel barrel and examined the cylinder. It was empty. He pushed the muzzle against his cheek, felt the hard steel lay cool against his hot skin. For a moment it relieved the awful ache in his head. He found the bullets, inserted one in an empty chamber, spun the cylinder, aimed it at nothing and pulled the trigger. There was a sharp hollow click, which he didn't even hear. He spun it again, placed the barrel deep inside his throat and squeezed the trigger slowly. There was an instant when his heart stopped beating then the sound of the hollow click again.

He looked down at the gun, realized at once what he had tried to do and collapsed.

"You'd better clean up your damn face before your mother gets here," Sally said. She pulled Shauna into the bathroom and turned her face towards the mirror. "Look at you. You're a wreck. Do you want her to see you like that?"

Sally turned on the hot water and wiped Shauna's face with a warm, wet cloth. She brushed Shauna's tangled brown hair and pushed it behind her ears.

"And change your nightgown too," Sally ordered then searched Shauna's bedroom drawers for a fresh gown.

"Here, put this on," she commanded, tossing Shauna a mint green cotton gown with pink satin ribbons.

Like a robot, Shauna obeyed, dressing mechanically, then settling back in her bed.

"Now what's wrong?" Sally asked. Shauna was quivering, sitting on her knees.

"We killed him, Sally," Shauna whispered in a small squeaky voice which bordered on hysteria. "We killed him."

Sally grasped at her shoulders then thought better of scolding her and hugged her tightly to her chest. God, it was awful. She was just as scared as Shauna. Maybe more. And so was Jason. He was in a terrible state. But she and Shauna were in deeper shit. They had been in the room with Chris. As careful as she had been, things could be traced to them. But so far so good, she thought. As long as she continued to stay strong, keep Shauna calm, everything would be okay. And everything depended upon her ability to keep Shauna calm, absolutely everything.

"No baby, no," Sally crooned rocking Shauna back and forth caressing her shoulders. "There, there. It's going to be alright. I know how you feel. You miss him. He was your beau, your best friend."

She pushed Shauna gently away and tenderly brushed wisps of hair from her cheek and brow. "But, it was an accident. You and I, we had nothing to do with what Chris did to himself after we left him." She carefully monitored Shauna's face, the brown eyes, which were staring vacantly from swollen slits. She had to fill up the blanks in Shauna's crazy mind—anticipate and answer the questions Shauna had kicking around but couldn't seem to articulate. "You do believe that? Don't you?" Shauna's head wobbled a tentative yes. "He must have taken stuff even before we got there, for heaven's sake. Remember all that brandy he was drinking?" Shauna nodded again.

Sally lowered her voice and leaned close to Shauna's ear hugging her. "Can you honestly believe for one minute we'd have left him like that if we knew what would happen to him?" she said so earnestly. "You know me and I know you. We love one another—like sisters. We're not criminals.'' She had used the collective ''we'' effectively and it was working.

Shauna's blood-shot eyes peered up at Sally's face. ''But what if they find out?'' she said. ''What if they find out we were in there with him?''

''I told you. They're not going to. How can they? Remember? We cleaned up the room before we left him. And we were careful. Nobody saw us go in and nobody saw us leave. And my mother's vouching for both of us. Swearing we were in her apartment in Century City all afternoon. We have a perfect alibi: There's no way anybody's going to put us in that room. Unless you tell them.'' She grasped Shauna's elbows and focused her blue eyes on her.

''And you won't do that will you? Promise me you won't tell anyone.'' She felt her fingers tighten about Shauna's arms, and relaxed them. ''You don't want to go to prison do you, baby?'' She felt Shauna shiver. ''Locked up in some jail cell with a bunch of criminals? They could rape you, beat you up, even kill you. I mean God, if it would bring Chris back or something, I'd be the first one to say something, tell them everything we know. But honey, what would that solve? Nothing. It wouldn't bring Chris back. Just put the two of us in some roach infested cell for the rest of our lives. And for no good reason. Besides Chris wouldn't want that, would he?'' Shauna's eyes were glazed. Beads of perspiration covered her top lip. Sally dabbed at her tender skin with a pink tissue wondering how much of what she was saying was actually getting through.

Was she somehow succeeding? God, she hoped so. She had to.

She needed Shauna frightened enough to shut her mouth but calm enough not to crack. Just a few more days of brainwashing should do it.

As long as Shauna kept it together, everything would be alright.

The doorbell rang and like a fragile souffle baking in the oven, Shauna collapsed. She clawed at Sally's arms quivering, gasping for air, hyper-ventilating. Sally had to do something fast and there was only one way to deal with Shauna.

"Just a minute," Sally yelled at the door. She took two Placidyls from her pillbox and placed them in Shauna's hand. "Here baby," she said pouring her a large glass of water. "Take these and go to sleep. I'll tell whoever's there to go away."

Shauna greedily swallowed the red capsules and lay back against the pillows drawing the blankets tightly around, her body curling into a fetal position.

"That's my girl," Sally said. "Now go to sleep." She watched Shauna's eyes flicker. "Coming," she yelled again and walked slowly to the hall mirror. She brushed her damp blonde hair back, toward the nape of her neck and pinned it. She pinched her cheeks for color took a deep breath and moved to the door. She opened it and smiled. It was Elaine Shagan. She was carrying a large bouquet of white daisies her eyes searching the living room for Shauna.

"How is she?" Elaine asked.

"Shhh," Sally said placing her fingers on her lips. "She's just falling asleep."

Chapter 16

ADA WAS FINALLY HOME. And she should have been happy. She was feeling well, improving daily, her prognosis excellent and she had been shown respect, devotion and attention by her family.

But she wasn't happy. She was depressed, filled with alternating feelings of rage, despondency and bitter disappointment. As her awareness grew, her ability to comprehend what had happened grew. The realization that bits and pieces of her life had been stolen from her mind, whole chunks lifted by some night-thief. What had been left was difficult for her to assimilate, to gather together, to recognize as belonging to her.

It was as though her memory had gone haywire and her clotted brain with centrifugal force had wantonly whirled, discharging selected installments of her life into thin air. She wondered, despaired mostly, if she'd ever again recover them.

''We're mighty lucky,'' her day nurse, Sara Brady, told her. ''President Eisenhower, God rest his soul, and that Mr. Churchill, both had strokes like ours and they each recovered completely. With hard work, we'll be walking and talking in no time at all.''

All day long her nurses and family fed her platitudes and medicine, doting on her every move, explaining things to her as though she were some helpless infant. Sometimes, she'd get so outraged she wanted to scream out loud, to remind them she was only sick, not stupid. It was her speech, her faulty memory, a temporary incumbrance she would soon overcome—not some mental deficiency—they seemed to be treating her for. Well, no matter. Like everything else in her life, she'd overcome this and win in spite of everything and everyone.

"Push. Release. C'mon Ada baby, we can do better than that. Relax. Good girl. Now rest."

Ada grimaced in pain and observed her therapist through homicidal eyes as she worked over her arms and legs. Who in the hell did that woman think she was, talking to her like that. Next, she'd be tossing her a bone or sugar cube.

"Push. Release. Relax. *Very* good." Sara Brady poured water from a pitcher into a crystal goblet and handed one tiny white pill to Ada. "Time for our medicine," she said with authority and waited until Ada had swallowed it. "Good girl," she said taking the glass from Ada's hand. "Now we can watch some television."

Max Stone poked his white-haired, round head into the room. Sara Brady dismissed him quickly with a wave of her hand.

"When?" he asked smiling at Ada.

Sara Brady held up four fingers then pointed to her watch.

"Four o'clock?" Max asked. Sara Brady nodded.

Ada lay back breathing heavily, exhausted from the workout.

Sara Brady adjusted her short orange curls then searched the pages of the *TV Guide*, moving it back and forth in front of her until the words were in focus.

"Lord, Lord," she said flipping on the television set, watching as some fire and brimstone preacher explained the rapture of heaven. "Don't hardly understand it," she said shaking her head. "All that yelling and hollering about can't wait to get to heaven, then come to all those healing services so's they can live longer. No sir. Don't hardly make no sense to me."

Ada wanted to laugh out loud. It was the first time in weeks she had felt that particular urge.

"Well Ada, baby, what'll it be? 'I Love Lucy'? 'Bob Newhart'? or 'Mary Tyler Moore'?"

"News," Ada said with some difficulty.

Sara Brady's lips pursed like a prune, her shoulders hunched then slumped. "Told you before. No news and no sad stories. Those are the rules. We got Lucy, Mary, Newhart or Mickey Mouse. For reading, we got movie magazines, romances or comic books. And that's it Ada, baby. Can't have too much thinking. We need to laugh. Cures everything, from piles to pimples."

Sara flipped the channel to 'I Love Lucy,' watched as Lucy frantically hand wrapped chocolates which were racing along a conveyor belt, then howled with laughter when Lucy stuffed some into her mouth as the belt went bezerk. "Yes sir Ada baby. Lucy's our best friend. Best medicine in the world." She glanced at her watch. "Time for our lunch, then our nap." She smiled, tucked Ada's blanket around her legs and left the room.

Ada was glad she was gone. She wanted to think, to try and piece together whatever she could of her life. To remember. To visualize her husband, her children, her work.

She thought of Viva. *Viva*. She had been here every day like clockwork reading *Variety* and the *Hollywood Reporter* to her. Telling her about a Paul Kiley. Who in the hell was Paul Kiley?

And Michael. Her son Michael. For some reason she remembered him. He was the last one, the lost one, the baby she hadn't wanted for so many reasons. He had never inspired confidence in her and here he was, taking care of business, handling Stone Management like a Hollywood veteran. God, she could hardly believe it.

And Jason. She could barely remember Jason at all. It was all too difficult.

The pill Sara Brady had given her made her feel calm and drowsy. She pressed the button on her mechanical bed, lowered it to a more comfortable position and closed her eyes. Despite everything she was very glad to be alive.

* * *

Nicole signed the register at the Beverly Hills Hotel and took the key. She forced a smile for the room clerk, turned and walked away. She wore Ralph Lauren's pumpkin-colored cavalry shirt and white cotton twill jeans. There was a thick 18-karat gold braid around her throat and perfect one-karat diamonds glittering in each ear lobe. Every eye in the hotel lobby rested on her. With her wide-rimmed sunglassed and beige straw hat, she looked like a movie star.

"There's Faye Dunaway," one patron whispered to another.

"Don't be ridiculous. That's Cheryl Tiegs you idiot."

Nicole disappeared out the back way through a hedge of dark-green split-leaf philodendrons then up a green carpeted staircase. Inside the modern vanilla-colored $280 a day private bungalow, she threw herself down on the neatly made bed and sobbed.

Michael was anxious. Nicole's phone call had him deeply concerned. She had sounded desperate to him before, but this time there was utter chaos and confusion in her voice.

He turned the Jaguar left on Sunset Boulevard then drove along the curved hotel driveway lined with coconut and date palms and thickly clustered birds of paradise. He passed a familiar looking white Rolls Royce, couldn't seem to place it and continued on stopping at the tidy carport.

He had not seen Nicole since the night Del Gado had broken into her house, except for Christopher's funeral the week before where she had been quiet and withdrawn. And he wondered what made her rent a bungalow here.

Inside the hotel lobby, he had the clerk phone her room then headed out back to the Spanish-style pink bungalow. He had the strangest feeling there were eyes following him, then decided the notion was ridiculous and dismissed it.

He knocked softly at the door. Instantly she opened it and was in his arms sobbing. He held her for a moment then guided her back into the living room and closed the door.

"I'm so glad you're here," she said clinging to him. "So glad."

"It's all right," he said hugging her tightly. "You're okay. I'm here."

"That's just it," she said moving away from him. "It's only when you're with me that I feel safe and protected. Oh Michael," she pleaded, "how long? How long can I go on like this? How long can I keep living in limbo? Tell me it's going to end, to change. Tell me there'll come a time when I won't be afraid—when I'll be able to handle my own life."

"Hey! Don't be so hard on yourself. It will come," he comforted her. "In time. Everything takes time. Everything worthwhile. Nothing changes overnight. You're doing all the right things and the right changes will follow. That's a promise."

He took her in his arms and kissed her salty cheeks, her tear-filled eyes, found the corner of her mouth and gently pressed his lips to hers. If he thought it would have helped, he'd have given her his right arm and leg to ease her pain. He guided her to the couch.

"I'll order up some drinks and sandwiches," he said, "then you can tell me everything, okay?" She nodded, reached for a tissue, while he telephoned room service. "There," he said, hanging up the telephone. "Now, talk to me, tell me what happened. What brought you here?"

She began slowly, gasping for small breaths of air. "I had to get away. I had to." She sighed, made a false start and began again. "It's Jason. Something's very strange. He's been home alot lately. Ever since Chris died. He's so different, acting very weird. He's up all night long talking on the telephone . . . to someone. Whispering. I don't know who it is, and I don't care. Then, all of sudden he's nice to me after the conversations. Sweet in fact. Then, out of nowhere he flies into a rage and accuses me of sneaking about, eavesdropping on the phone. Of course I haven't. And there's Max. He's been at the house a dozen times asking for Jason—demanding to see him. And I have to lie, say Jason isn't home, when he is. And Max gets so angry at me." She began to cry. "Oh why? Why is Max so angry? Why doesn't Jason want to see him?"

Michael took her hand, kissed the tips of her fingers. "He's not angry at you, honey. He's mad at Jason. Jason pulled a fast one on some of Ada's stock transfers. Max just wants them back, that's all. Don't worry. I'll talk to Max."

There was a soft rap at the door and Nicole jumped. "It's probably our drinks," Michael said and opened the door. A waiter in dark trousers and a white jacket wheeled in a neatly covered table with a set-up of red roses and crystal glasses. There was a tray of fresh sandwiches, an ice bucket with a chilled bottle of Dom Perignon and a large pitcher of fresh orange juice.

"Thanks," Michael said to the waiter and signed the bill. The waiter held up the champagne bottle for Michael's inspection then uncorked it and poured champagne into one glass. Michael tasted it and nodded approval.

"Will there be anything else, sir?" the waiter asked.

"Thank you," Michael said and closed the door. Michael mixed champagne and orange juice in two glasses. "Here," he said to Nicole. "Drink up. It's good for you. Vitamins A to Z."

She smiled, swallowed one full drink quickly and extended her glass for another. "You're good for me, Michael," she told him and patted the spot next to her on the couch. He filled her glass once more and joined her there.

"How are the sessions coming along?" he asked.

"Okay, I guess," she said. "I've never been to a psychiatrist before so I can't really tell if I'm improving or he's good. And he's not really a psychiatrist he's a psychologist. A Gestaltist."

"What's that?" Michael asked.

"I'm not sure, but he's a nice man. He's warm. He's kind, but he's also strange. Once I was depressed and he let me sit on his lap. No, don't look worried. I didn't have to. I asked. I wanted to. To see what it felt like, not being afraid. He rocked me back and forth like I was a baby and it felt so good. I felt like he was my father or something."

She paused, sipped some more of Michael's concoction then relaxed against the soft couch. "Then," she continued, "sometimes he seems almost cruel. But later, when I have a chance to think about it, the point he makes is so important that the end justifies the means . . . or is it the other way around? I don't know. Yesterday, I was upset about Christopher and I noticed a sick goldfish floating on top of his fishtank. All the other big goldfish were swimming around peeking at him, while he struggled to breathe . . . to live. I couldn't stand it, Michael, so I asked the doctor to take the fish out of the tank and isolate it until it got well. He wouldn't. He looked at me and his eyes were cold and he said, 'Absolutely not—that fish will have to make up its own mind to live or die.' I thought he was cruel and started to cry. But later, when I thought about it, I realized he was trying to teach me something. I was like the fish—trying to breathe, to live, but allowing others to peck at my body." She stopped, took a deep breath and began again. "When I went there to see him today, that fish was better; he was swimming with the others. I felt good. I knew that Dr. Simms had been right."

She finished her glass of champagne and Michael lit his Dunhill, waving his hand through the smoke to scatter it away from her face.

"Today," she began again, "I was upset about Jason and about us. I feel so guilty. God, I'm so in love with you." She reached for his hand and placed it on her cheek. "I began to cry terribly in his office. I talked about Joe, about trust, about how I hated being lied to. I told Dr. Simms how sick I was of putting all my trust in people and having them pull the rug out from under me and all of a sudden he went into a closet and took out a large piece of rug and put it down on the floor and told me to get up from my chair and stand on it. I walked right over to the rug—you know me, eager to please—and I stepped on it and he pulled the rug out from under me and I fell on the floor right on my ass." She rubbed the spot on her backside.

"What the hell kind of nut is he?" Michael said, his face contorted in questions and anger.

"No. Listen to me," she said. "I was shocked. Just like you are now. And while I was on the floor I got angry, but instead of yelling at him I just cried. I asked him how he could do something like that to me? How could he fool me like that when I trusted him? And he said, 'Because I love you and you have to learn.' He told me that I did it to myself. That it takes two people. One to put the rug out and the other to step on it. The choice was mine. I didn't have to get on the rug. His rug or anybody elses. Don't you see? Don't you understand what he was trying to teach me?"

Michael nodded. "Sounds to me like you've found the right man."

"But, he's gone, Michael. He'll be gone for a month. Something about an emergency in New York. And it's the new doctor who's taking over for him that I don't like. He's cold and he frightens me. I can handle Dr. Simms and the crazy things he does because I know he likes me. He wouldn't really hurt me. I just don't think I can handle someone I don't like throwing me on the floor or whatever it is he'll do."

"Is that what this is all about? Is that why you're so upset?"

"No . . . yes . . . no. It's a big part of it." She hesitated then let it out. "It's Jason! He's been so crazy lately. Pawing me all the time. Forcing me to sleep with him, to constantly make love to him. I can't stand it anymore. It makes my skin crawl."

Michael felt sick. The thought of Jason even touching her filled him with loathing and disgust. She was so delicate, so lovely and loving. Jason might as well be pulling the brightly colored feathers from a beautiful songbird he had trapped in a cage.

"Not only that," she continued. "He's put the house up for collateral again on one of his big deals. I had to sign the paper. Oh Mike, I'm so frightened. That home's the only one," she choked on the words, "the only one . . . I've ever . . . had. He could lose it. And I'm so afraid. I don't want to be afraid. I want to be strong and independent. Oh Mike, I'm so tired of it all."

Those words spoke some unknown terror inside him. He felt his skin peel away from his bones. "No. No. Listen to me," Michael said caressing her hair. "All of this will change. I promise. We have a future together. You have a future for yourself. I—"

She interrupted him with a ferocity he had never seen before. "No. You listen to me. I told you before. This is my fight and I've made my decision. It's the only thing for me to do. Before he left, Dr. Simms recommended I spend some time at a kind of hospital, a rest home, where I'll have therapy every day. I'll be away from Jason, from all the guilt and the pressures. It's a chance to help myself. Be away from everything. Sort things out. There's time now before I start the movie. No one has to know. I've thought about it for days and I want to try it for one week. I would just talk to a hospital therapist, sit in the sun, read, talk to other people who are in the same boat—like in group therapy. But I need to know that you'll be here when I return. That you'll still love me. Because as much as I need to be independent, I also need your love."

"God," he said, taking her in his arms. He was overcome with so much emotion, with so much desire for her. He wanted to soothe and calm her, to eliminate all her pain and fear and desperation. He thought he would die with all he wanted to give her. His love, his support, his compassion. He knew only one thing for sure: that if he ever found the courage, he could kill his brother.

He massaged her spine, her shoulders, his arms encircling her body, her head resting on his shoulder.

"We'll do what you think is best," he told her. "We'll do whatever it takes to make you better, happy, whatever it takes. I love you and I'll be with you, no matter what."

He felt the tremors moving through her body like the aftershocks of an earthquake and he listened as she sobbed softly at his words. As though the saying of them had brought her a measure of relief. And the feel of her close to him was exquisite pleasure. He kissed her lips, her chin, her neck, buried his head in her breasts. Was this a time, he thought, to take her? To make love to her? He pulled away but she drew him back. She pressed his head close to her breasts, arching her neck and back, her mouth open, ready to receive.

"Make love to me, Michael," she whispered. "It quiets me. It makes the shaking go away. I feel safe and calm and quiet." She moved her body against him, her fingers and hands searching—roaming and caressing the soft hairs on the back of his neck, moving up and under his shirt. His mouth closed passionately on her lips, swallowing her words, searching and probing the warm sweetness of her mouth.

"I want you," he said, when her fingers squeezed at the corded muscles on his back. "I want you so much." He lifted her from the couch, their garments rustling together like two sparks ready to ignite into flames and carried her into the bedroom.

Sidney Gross observed the bungalow at the rear of the Beverly Hills Hotel, watched the lights go out in the bedroom, smiled as he thought about his movie deal and the Hank Mason loanout. All this time he'd wondered what a Michael Stone would want in exchange for the services of Hank Mason and now he knew. Like the purloined letter, it was sitting right under his nose.

In the Polo Lounge, he sipped his drink, listened to some industry gossip at the next booth, then called the head waiter for a telephone. He dialed slowly and in two hours Michael Stone was sitting in Sidney Gross's home office.

Sidney Gross offered Michael Stone his hand. Michael refused it, sat stoically in a corner chair with crossed legs, folded arms, his body language eloquently expressing his feelings. He watched Sidney Gross move about the room and made a conscious effort to quiet his breathing.

"Well Michael. It's so good to see you. Good of you to come. I hope I didn't interrupt anything important." Gross's smile flashed like quicksilver, his eyes coldly sizing Michael up.

Michael felt uneasy, tense—like quarry in the presence

of a big game hunter. *Well so be it*, he thought. Gross would find out that like big game, he had his own defense mechanisms: He was beginning to understand the laws of the jungle. "Don't screw around, Gross," he said. "Just tell me what the hell you want and get it over with."

Gross rose and walked to an antique liquor cabinet. "Can't do that. It's my first chance to talk to you. Got too much on my mind."

"Can't be too much," Michael said, "considering your mind." Gross ignored the remark, poured himself a drink and offered Michael one.

"Bourbon and ice, double," Michael said with rancor and waited as Gross finished pouring. Michael took his drink and watched as Sidney sat down behind the massive desk.

They were an odd combination. Like oil and water; perhaps even dynamite and matches.

"Would you prefer something else?" Gross asked noting Michael's drink still setting in his hand, untouched.

"As a matter of fact, yes. I'd prefer the truth, thank you. If you could manage it."

"You want to get right down to it, don't you?" Gross said smiling. "Right to the core."

"Don't make me laugh. There is no core. Only facade. That's what I've come to know about people like you."

Gross's smile evaporated. "Don't kid yourself. You know nothing about me. Nothing at all."

Michael glared at him, banged his glass down on the table, spilling half the contents. "I know all I need to know," he exploded. "You ripped my mother off you son of a bitch and you're trying to do it again. You think I don't know what the hell you're up to?"

"Your mother?" Gross's voice was filled with anger. "That's a laugh. That's a big joke. What I did was an act of survival. Your mother was burying me . . . eating me up alive! Paying me shit! Using me! Using my talent!"

"You really believe that, don't you?" Michael said. "That's what's wrong with people like you, Gross. Up front you pretend. You're sweet as honey but to people who know, you're slime. Behind their backs you step on people like my mother. You use them! And when you're not invading their minds, you're ripping off their brains, their hearts, their guts. Then you sit back and look at the carcass, screaming about how you had to do it to survive. Gross, how many times did you say, 'Sue me, baby' today?"

Michael paused. "Well maybe you chewed off a few of my mother's fingers, but you didn't get the whole hand—and you won't! Not as long as I'm around to keep you from doing it. You're all wrapped up in yourself, Gross, and I must say it makes a very small package."

Gross looked as though he would explode, his eyes darting back and forth blazing with fury. "Some people's voices carry more than sound, Stone, and yours just did. But I have a few things you ought to hear before you polish that phoney halo on top of your bloated head."

Michael swallowed his drink and placed his empty glass down on the table. He sensed the tension of Gross moving in for the kill.

"Suppose I tell you I don't even need you," Gross snarled. "Suppose I tell you that I already have a deal for a merger with Jason. That you're out on your ass."

Michael burst out laughing. "I'd say that was your tough luck, Gross. Your mistake. But save the paper it's written on. You can always wipe your ass with it."

Gross pretended to ignore him. "When the merger goes through, I won't need your approval for the Hank Mason loanout. We'll go on without you and we'll see whose luck is tough."

"Don't hold your breath. Ada's practically on her feet again," he lied. "And Jason's out. He doesn't even figure here. In fact, he'll be lucky if Ada doesn't sue him. Along with you, of course."

"Oh but he does figure here," Gross said, looking confident again, lighting a cigarette. "We can consider another alternative." The gray smoke from his cigarette covered his face like a curtain. Dramatically he waited until the smoke drifted away. "I want Hank and you say I can't have him. So we'll have to make a different deal. One where you oblige me and I don't tell your hot-headed brother about your afternoon affairs with his charming wife. I'm sure he'll be pleased to discuss it with the both of you."

Michael bridled at Gross's words. This was what he had been waiting for. Now he knew for sure that the Rolls Royce he saw parked at the hotel belonged to Sidney Gross and that the eyes he felt stabbing at his back, following him to Nicole's bungalow were also his. "What is this Sidney, blackmail?"

Gross chuckled. "Ada used to call it influence. I learned alot from her you know. Mothers are wonderful people. Especially yours, Stone."

Under other circumstances, Michael would have jumped him knocked his teeth down his throat, but he sat instead and continued the verbal sparring. "Then it must be a threat," Michael said.

"No. Of course not. I'm merely making some suggestions. Setting the perimeters for a business deal. Negotiations would be a better word."

There was a brilliant light shining behind Michael's eyes as he prepared to ask Sidney the next question. He stood, ambled to the liquor cabinet and poured himself another drink. "Have one yourself Sidney," he said holding up the bottle. "I'm beginning to enjoy these 'negotiations'." He clinked several ice cubes into his glass, poured the bourbon and spun it all around. "Now I have a deal for you."

Sidney drew as close to Michael Stone as his desk would allow, leaning his fat elbows across the desk, his round eyes wide in rapt attention. This moment was electric.

"You can have Hank," Michael said. Sidney's face lit up like a new pinball machine. "We'll do a gross deal. I'll take script and cast approval. You make the arrangements." He paused and said the next words with great relish. "There's one condition." Michael felt like a ripe red apple concealing a nice fat worm inside. He could hardly wait for Sidney to take the first big bite.

"You got it," Sidney said all too quickly. "Name it." He sucked securely on his cigarette and listened.

Michael said it slowly and clearly. "I want the rights to 'The Roxanne Caulder Story.' "

Sidney choked on the smoke. His eyes said *tilt*. Beads of perspiration popped out on his face like toast from a toaster. "What the hell do you mean?"

"Sidney, baby. Don't play games with me. It'll be the story of the century." Michael took Sidney's view-finder from his desk and began to block the story—visualizing everything for Sidney. "Let's see." He swept a hand. We'll start in the hospital, 1963. No. No." He shook his head. "Maybe when the twins were born in 1962. Now that would be interesting." He spun around on his heels. "No. No. Best place to start is always at the beginning. Isn't that what all writers say?"

"Listen, you punk," Sidney exploded. Get the hell out of here because I don't know what you're talking about."

"I'm talking about your big star, Sid. The one who earns you millions. The one you stole from Ada, whose hospital reports are lying in my safe deposit box. The one who is not the natural mother of her children, but the father. I'm talking about Roxanne Caulder, or should I say Robert Webber. Whose wife died in childbirth, who then hired caretakers for the kids until she—or is it *he*—could care for them when his sex change was complete. It would be the story of the century. Don't you agree?"

The look on Gross's face was one Michael would always remember.

"You wouldn't do that to her, Stone. You wouldn't hurt her kids like that," Sidney pleaded.

"Wouldn't I? Well, I've been learning, Gross—from bastards like you. You taught me all about victims and casualties, and I don't intend to be a victim. My choice is clear, just as yours was when you screwed my mother. I'd do it, I'll love doing it. And I'll consider it an act of survival."

"It's not fair, Stone," Gross sputtered.

"Fair is for children."

"All right. All right." Sidney was frantic. "Tell me what you want. What would it take to keep you from telling that story to anyone? Money? Deals? Drugs? You name it."

"It would take something simple," Michael said. "Something so damn simple it would never occur to you to think of it." He pointed his finger at Sidney. "Get the hell off my back, mister. Get the hell off my family's back. And stay the hell off for good."

He threw the view finder down on the chair and headed for the door, opened it and slammed it shut without a backward glance. He stood there for a minute in the hall and felt a warm flush racing through his body. Unlike the time he had squared off with Del Gado and felt sick at heart, this time he was triumphant, accomplished, like slipping between small raindrops or maybe parting the Red Sea.

Chapter 17

SHAUNA FELT ALONE IN HER BED. For too long she had been numb, semi-conscious, one step away from oblivion. And no one had been able to reach her. Not Viva, not Michael, no one. Had it not been for the diligence of Elaine Shagan, Shauna Candelli might have died.

Every day, Elaine visited, remained steadfast, succeeded finally by tossing Shauna into a cold shower, flushing all her pills down the toilet and unplugging the doorbell and telephone. For three days and nights Shauna ranted and raved, heaved, soiled her bed clothes, rattled her body against a locked door. For three days and nights Elaine stalked her, feeding her black coffee and cigarettes.

"I won't let you do this to yourself," Elaine had told her. "Sure you miss, Chris. We all do. But enough is enough." Elaine rolled up the hem of her dress, exposing track scars on the inside of her thighs. "Dope is never the answer to anything." The sight of Elaine's scars was sobering and by the end of the fifth day, Shauna could bear the intrusion of sunlight into her bedroom without heaving up her insides.

"I want you to think about something," Elaine had said. "A friend of mine and I are starting a talent agency. It's time for me to make changes, now, while Ada's sick and the actor's strike is on. Come in with us. Don't answer me now. Just think about it."

Shauna had thought about it. Though about it alot. But

there were so many other things she had thought about too. Like Chris and Sally. For the first time, since Chris's death, she thought clearly about that awful day in Malibu.

It had taken her a while to piece it all together and when she finally did, it seemed odd. Like Sally's visit to Chris's apartment. The evolution of Plan B. Sneaking up staircases, cleaning off fingerprints, taking that dumb water glass. She wondered about that phone call too, and why Sally had provided her with enough dope to kill herself. She was beginning to believe that there was more to what had happened that day than Sally had led her to believe. She had the awful feeling that somehow she had been used, had been a patsy, but for what reason?

Why? Why would Sally want to hurt Chris.

And worst of all, she was a damn devout coward. How could she possibly point a finger at Sally, without pointing one at herself?

She wanted to run, to empty her mind of everything, to bury her thoughts, submerge them in some kind of hard-driving sweat. She would jog, stomp her feet on the city sidewalks, feel nothing but the sweet ache and pain of strenuous exercise, forget about everything for now.

She washed her face and pinned back her hair. She slipped on her white sweat pants, a yellow t-shirt, her Nikes and her white jogging jacket.

She drove her Porsche along San Vincente Boulevard to Gorham, parked near Westward Ho Market and began to stretch her catlike body on the wide, grassy lawn that divided the boulevard. She did some deep breathing, deep knee-bends then took off with long, easy strides.

The traffic was light in both east- and west-bound lanes, cars spewing their usual dose of foul-smelling fumes into the moist, morning air. She kept on accelerating, running as though she were being chased.

She could hear Elaine's voice booming out at her from distorted traffic sounds, felt Sally tugging at her legs and ankles, saw Christopher's sad face staring down at her from the clouds.

At Kentor there was a red light. Stop. Caution. Go. Like a good girl she obeyed, running in place, then dashed across when the light changed.

She shot out like the wind, running, tearing, light of heel, dry ice growing in her lungs, sweat falling in huge drops around her face and head. Every thump of her foot punished her legs, back, her head. *Oh Chris, Chris, Chris.*

She stumbled, fell, hugging her cramped belly, gasping for fresh air. She threw off her jacket, rolled it into a bundle to use as a headrest.

She watched a small piece of paper tumble from her pocket, almost let it go then reached out and snatched at it. When she opened it, she was overcome. It was the piece of paper Sally had written her program notes on that day in Malibu.

She crumbled it angrily and hurled it into the breeze. Through tear-filled eyes she watched as it tumbled along the grass rolling over and over, propelled by traffic gusts until it stopped dead in the gutter where a fast-moving Cadillac crushed it.

She buried her head in her hands and sobbed. "Chris, Chris. I'm so sorry. If only I could change things, bring you back, do *something* to make it all up to you."

And then she thought of something and her mood brightened. She stood up quickly, tears still streaming down her face and fled into the busy intersection.

She didn't see the black Mercedes, speeding, barreling down upon her—she just heard the awful screech of brakes as she bent to fetch the small piece of paper in the dirty gutter. When the car impacted her body, there was a thud. Tossed sideways up into the air, she fell onto the grass. She was a terrifying sight.

Somebody screamed. The driver leaped from his car and cradled her head in his hands. "Get an ambulance," he yelled at the gathering crowd.

"It's on the way," someone shouted back.

There were traces of blood on Shauna's face and legs, her brown hair a tangled mess, but the paper she had sought was still clutched tightly in her gnarled fingers.

She stared at the paper then up at the frightened driver. "I'm fine," she said smiling. "I'm going to be just fine." And she meant it.

* * *

Sally reached for the telephone. It was Jason's third call that night. She was sleepy and irritated.

"It's four A.M. for Christ's sake," she whined.

"I know," he whispered. "I'm just nervous that's all. Is everything alright? Is Shauna keeping her mouth shut? Did you convince her?"

Sally's patience was wearing thin. "Jesus—I've already told you she's under control. Now hang up and go back to sleep."

"Dinner tomorrow," he said. "Pirate's at eight."

"That's not exactly smart, Jason."

"I don't give a shit. Just meet me!"

"Okay. If that's what it's going to take to keep you from waking me up the rest of the night." She heard him grunt, then the telephone click. She didn't bother to put the receiver down; she just pulled the telephone plug from the wall. Then she wondered what she'd do if he talked.

* * *

One hour had given Nicole so little time, but she would be ready. The new therapist in whose care Dr. Simms had left her had finally agreed to admit her to the hospital.

"I don't understand why you're insisting upon this," Dr. Conroy said. "In my opinion, you're not crazy."

"I'm not going because I'm crazy. I have to get away. Besides, Dr. Simms and I agreed on this last week."

The remark had clearly annoyed him. "Why don't you try a nice Palm Springs hotel, my dear, or some quiet ranch in Santa Barbara."

She tried to explain her paralyzing fears, but he simply shook his head, then reluctantly dialed the hospital.

She threw her things into a nightcase. Some nightgowns, makeup, Valium for sleeping, Empirin Codeine for her ever-increasing headaches, some extra designer jeans and t-shirts.

She drove her Mercedes the twenty minutes to the hospital then paused in front, considering the hospital exterior. It was totally disarming, nestled in an expensive Westside residential neighborhood, surrounded by well-tended shrubs and evergreen trees. She parked her car in the lot, locked it then entered the reception room, a forced smile on her face.

A white-suited intern shook her clammy hand and relieved her of her nightcase. She trembled as she spoke. "Hi, I'm Nicole Stone."

"Ah, yes," he said. "We've been expecting you. Follow me."

Inside a small office they filled out forms. "You understand you must stay here seventy-two hours," the intern explained. "You can't leave without your doctor's consent."

Her heart skipped a beat. "Oh, I see," she said.

"It's routine actually," he assured her. "Everyone's required to stay that long. Otherwise you can't get in." The expression on her face made him touch her shoulder. "Hey, it's okay. Don't be frightened. We're very capable here." She tried to smile. "That's better," he said. "Now c'mon, let's get you settled. Once you make some friends, you'll feel a lot better."

At the nurse's station the intern introduced her to Mrs. Hilburn the head nurse. "Good luck," the intern whispered, and left.

The head nurse looked austere and clinically efficient. She had laser blue eyes and short hair as white as her uniform. She took Nicole's nightcase and led her into a small dormitory containing six beds. Across the way, a young girl sat on a bed watching them. She had thick bandages on both her wrists and hideous red and black scratch marks up and down her arms.

Mrs. Hilburn emptied Nicole's nightcase onto the bed and snatched up her pill bottles.

Nicole panicked. "What are you doing?" she protested.

The nurse was stern. "You are not permitted medication of any kind unless authorized by your doctor. Empty your purse please."

Nicole was obedient. She had learned from cruel experience how vital it was never to make enemies of people in charge. A voice from the past jostled her memory. *"You're going to a new foster home today. Stand up straight. Smile. Do whatever it is they tell you to. Otherwise no one will want to keep you."*

Mrs. Hilburn removed Nicole's belts, scarves, her shaving razor from the nightcase. "You can have these back when you leave," she told Nicole and left the room.

"Hey," called the girl, "What's your problem?"

"I'm not sure," Nicole said. "Anxiety I guess."

The girl seemed disappointed. "Is that all? No battle scars? No attempts?" she said holding up her arms with obvious pride. "You do coke? Smack? Acid?"

"No. I . . . ."

The girl approached Nicole's bedside. "Then you must be one of those Beverly Hills alkies or script druggies come to dry out."

"No. I hardly take medicine," Nicole said protesting— "only to sleep or for a migraine headache."

"Hah," the girl burst out laughing. "I saw the shit Burnsey took from your purse. Don't kid me."

There was a call for lunch on the intercom. The girl shrugged her shoulders and left. Nicole lay down on her bed, wondering if she had done the right thing. Only time would tell, she thought. And she had plenty of that . . . .

She spent a restless and terrified night. In the morning she was nervous, distraught, nameless terrors lurking at every turn.

After a tasteless breakfast, she was compelled by the staff to join other patients in a volleyball game. Her nerves were still jumping, her body rigid as though rigor mortis had set in.

She was led outdoors onto the volleyball court where a heated game was already in progress. She watched the white ball fly back and forth across the net, listened to the sound of hollow thuds as the ball slapped at wrists and palms, heard the loud shouts of victory, the groans and grunts of defeat. Behind the tall chain link fence, she could see her tan Mercedes and she wished with all her heart that she were in it, flying down some nameless freeway.

There was an out-of-bounds hit, which stopped the game cold and Nicole was introduced to the group. There was moaning and groaning by everyone.

"Whose side's she going to play on?" a boy with pimples asked.

"Where are you the weakest?" an aide asked.

"Give her to Marcy's group," the boy said smiling. "We already have Schmucko." There were shouts of laughter and a self-conscious attempt by Schmucko to laugh, too, then Nicole took her position.

The game was under way immediately and the ball fell into Nicole's hands. She missed and ran after it.

"Move, lady, move. This isn't ping pong," Marcy yelled.

"I'm sorry," Nicole said.

"We have a real winner here," Marcy shouted, referring to the newest team member.

At lunch she sat alone, picking her food, watching as the others ate heartily, laughing. She wanted desperately to join them, to become a part of the group. There was a loud shout from the doorway for someone to play bridge and Nicole eagerly volunteered. Here was her chance.

She found a group in the parlor where a middle-aged woman with frizzy brown hair pointed a silent, nicotine finger at the empty chair opposite her. Nicole sat down, her hands wet and trembling with anticipation.

The woman's voice had the sound of an angry animal. "I hope you don't play bridge like you play volleyball," she snarled. A large gallery of onlookers tittered at her remark.

"No," Nicole said. "I have some Master Points."

"Well, well. We have a live one," she told the gallery and lit the first of an endless chain of cigarettes. "Goren or Culbertson?"

"Goren," Nicole answered.

"Blackwood?" The smoke from her cigarette filtered out through her pointed yellow teeth and floated up Nicole's nose.

"Yes. Blackwood," Nicole replied clearing her throat.

"Let's cut for deal," the woman said and shuffled the cards. Nicole drew high and the game was on. The cards flew around the table from hand to hand then Nicole collected and sorted hers, counting twelve points with strength in spades.

"One Spade," Nicole said.

"Pass," said the next player.

"Two Hearts," responded the frizzy-haired woman as she raised her eyebrows.

"Pass," said the next player.

Nicole felt a migraine beginning. Playing the hand was

the last thing she wanted, but there was no choice. "Two No Trump," she said with trepidation.

"Pass."

"Three No," said the woman smiling wickedly. "Looks like it's your hand."

The first card was led and the dummy hand came down. Nicole perused the dummy. If the clubs held, it would be a piece of cake. She began to play, pulling the tricks in one by one with an air of certitude. But when the weakness in clubs revealed itself, she could hardly hold onto the rest of her hand.

She stared first at the cards then at her frizzy-haired partner, felt an anvil pounding away at her skull. She heard the buzz and light laughter of Monday-morning quarterbacks as it became obvious to everyone she had lost control of the hand and when the last card fell they were down one.

Nicole stood up. She was shaking all over, her eyes unable to focus on anything. "I have an awful headache," she said excusing herself, running from the room.

A trail of derisive laughter followed after her and at the top of her lungs the frizzy-haired woman screamed, "Anymore Master Players here?"

Nicole made it to the nurse's station and begged for her medicine. "Please," she said. "I need something. My tranquilizers, my headache pills, something please."

"Lie down," ordered the nurse. "I'll call your doctor."

In her bed Nicole twisted and turned, terrified she would lose control and they would lock her up or even worse, tie her hands inside a straight jacket. She thought of Dr. Simms, saw visions of goldfish tanks lying on top of huge ugly rugs beckoning her, waiting, just waiting. She lay there feeling ice cold, her teeth chattering.

"Your doctor has forbidden all use of medications for you," the nurse said entering the room. "He's still on the telephone, if you want to talk to him."

Nicole felt her veins pulsating against her head. She began to run from the room, caught herself. No, she thought. She would not run. Running would bring an aide, another nurse, a straight jacket. She would be the picture of control, walking slowly to the telephone.

"Please," she told the doctor when she reached the telephone. "I'm frightened. I need something to calm me, something to stop the awful pain in my head."

"It's against my policy," he said. His voice was stark and severe. "My patients work through their fear and pain—and so will you when I see you tomorrow."

She clenched her teeth and spoke as softly as she could, but her voice was distorted, squeaky, almost crazy. "Then I must leave this place right now. You were right after all. I don't belong here." There was a pause as she waited for him to speak. "Sign me out, will you?"

"No, I'm sorry. I can't. I don't think it's wise at this time."

"Why not?" she shouted then forced the calm exterior again. "You said so yourself! I didn't need to be here."

"That was yesterday. Today you sound as though you need some kind of restraint. I can't take the responsibility of your harming yourself. Only your husband can sign you out now."

"God, you can't mean that," she said crying. "Please let me go home."

"I'm sorry," he said again and hung up.

* * *

At Casa Piedra they watched Paul Kiley's screen test. Michael enjoyed Ada's blossoming excitement as she sat gripped, enthralled, thoroughly immersed in the image of Paul. How she loved to play God. To find and nurture new talent, develop it, conceal it like some top-secret A-bomb, then detonate it and bask in the powerful fallout. With Paul Kiley to look forward to, Ada would recover that much faster.

They had agreed not to discuss some of the more unpleasant events of the last weeks, such as Hank's attempt at suicide or Chris Parker's death. There would be plenty of time to hit her with news like that. Nor would they mention Elaine Shagan's two-week notice. Ada would find out soon enough. She laughed when they told her about the current actor's strike.

"Good," she said. "It's only fair that when I have a stroke they should have a strike."

Viva sat closest to the telephone and when it rang she

answered it. One second later her brow furrowed and she gestured for Michael to take the call on the hall telephone.

"Hello," he said.

"Thank God, I've found you," Nicole squeaked. "I've got to get out of here. I've made a terrible mistake. Oh my God. I'm scared to death." Her voice waivered. "It's awful, absolutely awful. The doctor won't release me unless Jason accepts full responsibility." She sounded desperate, her words tumbling out, one sentence stumbling over the other. "I've called Jason," she continued, "but he won't do it. You've got to do something, Michael. Something. Dear God, if I don't get out of here right now, I don't know what will happen to me. I'll freak out. They'll tie me up. My hands. They'll put me in isolation, a straight jacket. God, Michael, help me."

"I'll call Jason," he said. "You hold on. Think about us. Think about how much I love you, but just hold on." He hung up and noticed Viva standing in the hall doorway. He took a deep breath and held it.

"It's all right, darling," she said. "I've known about it ever since you left for New York. She was and always has been written all over you."

Michael was dumbfounded. "You're not upset?"

"I've always been a little jealous, darling, but upset? No."

He sighed with relief, blew her a kiss then dialed Jason's number. "She's checked into some psychiatric hospital," he told Viva, "and she's scared. I've got to get her out."

"It's Mike," he said into the phone when Jason answered. "I've just talked to Nicole. She needs to get out of that nuthouse and you're the only one who can legally release her."

Jason's voice ripped at his eardrum. "I didn't want her in there in the first place," he screamed. "And you've got a hell of a nerve calling me. You've been screwing her, haven't you?"

He didn't want to discuss it now, but he wasn't about to lie. "It's not . . ."

"It's not what?"

"Jason," Michael pleaded. "We can talk about it later. Just sign her out of there."

"We'll talk about it now, or she'll rot in there," Jason yelled. "Meet me in Santa Monica—under the pier."

Michael heard the telephone *click*, then turned to Viva. "I don't know what he's got up his sleeve this time, or what it is he wants. But I'm probably going to have to give it to him." He hung up, slipped on a white windbreaker and grabbed her car keys.

"Wait," Viva called after him. "Where are you going?"

"The Beach—at the Santa Monica Pier, what's left of it. He says he might sign her out if we talk about it."

"For God's sake, be careful," she called after. "He's crazy!"

* * *

Hugh Parker felt old and tired. He wanted to die, to disappear into thin air. Like heavy smoke, he drifted about the malodorous room, his dark thoughts sticking to him like hi-grade epoxy. *Jason. Sally. Shauna. Christopher.* The glass. The telephone call. His clenched fist struck the desk with a terrible force. Where were the links? the clues he needed to tie the pieces together?

He had been drinking heavily, the beautiful ranch house littered with empty bottles, overflowing ashtrays, the smell of rotting food in the kitchen. It was almost nine in the evening when he heard Viva's Excalibur pull into the driveway. Just what he needed. Lectures, discussions, reason and logic; even nagging. Well not tonight! No. He was not in the mood.

"For God's sake, Hugh," she said when she entered. "Look at you. Look at this place. All this drinking, this self-abuse. It won't change anything. You might as well be holding a gun to your head."

"I've considered it," he said, watching her empty ashtrays and collect whiskey bottles.

"Don't say that," she told him. "I have enough on my mind worrying that Jason will do something awful to Michael tonight."

His curiosity was piqued. "What do you mean?"

"I'm not sure. But Jason's practically challenged Mike to a duel under the pier in Santa Monica. He's probably planning to drown him after he shoots him."

"Mike can take care of himself," Parker said lighting a cigarette. "I wouldn't worry if I were you."

Viva stopped what she was doing and glared at him. "How the hell do you know what I should worry about? Look at you. You're a mess. This place is a mess. Please, Hugh, you've got to try and snap out of this."

His veneer-thin patience had grown even thinner. He reeled about and stepped in front of her. "Snap out of this? How? Like you did? With drugs or a steady stream of sex partners? Maybe you didn't love Maurice as much as I loved Chris. Maybe you didn't give a damn . . . ."

He felt the sting of her palm as it slammed across his face. He grabbed her wrists and held them tightly. She struggled and when the tears spilled down her cheeks he pulled her close against him. "God forgive me," he said. "I didn't mean all that. I swear it. I love you, Viva. My God, I've always loved you."

"Let me go, Hugh," she demanded. "I want to leave. I don't want to talk about this anymore." She grabbed her shoulder bag off the table.

"But I do." He clutched her even tighter. "I do. God, I need to hold you, to be held. I have to tell somebody what's going on in my brain—a million crazy thoughts, whirling around and around." He finally released her and walked away. She followed after.

"What kind of thoughts?" she asked softly.

He stopped and spun around. "There's no doubt in my mind that Jason had something to do with Chris's death."

"That's absurd," she said. "You're not thinking clearly. Jason is a bastard, but he had no reason to harm Chris. He didn't even know him for God's sake. Besides, he was in Vegas."

"He knew a lot more than you think," Parker said, then fell into a heap onto the couch.

She bent over and lightly touched his shoulder, kissing him good-bye. She felt him flinch. "There's no evidence, Hugh. You can't indict someone based on anguish. You can't prosecute someone based on sorrow. And you can't convict Jason because you hate him."

That was her exit line. He heard the door slam and felt as though a knife had been plunged in his heart. Before he could do anything, the telephone rang and he stumbled to the desk to answer it. It was Gypsy.

"You were right," Gypsy told him. Parker felt the hackles rise on the back of his neck. "They had dinner together at Pirate's . . . ."

There was a fire igniting the inside of Hugh Parker's body as Gypsy went on about Jason and Sally Quinn. Flames were licking at his fingertips, raising his temperature. His face twitched and his vision blurred. "You've got to tell this to the authorities, Gypsy. Swear to everything you heard them say tonight, in open court."

"Wait a minute, Jack. I told you when I took this gig. No authorities. No courts. No, sir! I gather the dirt—you clean it up. I never heard of you, mister. You're on your own."

There was a sudden click of the telephone, then an explosion in Hugh Parker's brain.

* * *

It came to her like a flash while she lay there in the hospital waiting for someone to rescue her. She was still cold, yet sweating, shaking like a leaf, wishing she were dead. Ten times, the rugs had been put down on the floor in the last few days and ten times she'd happily leaped out onto them all. Ten times they'd been pulled out from under her and ten times she had fallen. God, when would she learn?

And those goldfish. She was tired of floating to the top of the tank: tired of having to call for help, wait for help, always hoping someone would remove her, isolate her from the bigger fish. A coward dies a thousand times, someone once said. This would be the last time for her.

She pulled her car keys from her purse, tucked them in absorbent cotton so they wouldn't jingle, then placed them under her pajamas inside her panties. She walked slowly from the darkened room, peered down the hallway and waited for the nurse's station to clear.

Suddenly, the girl with the bandages on her wrists sat bolt upright in her bed, the whites of her eyes gleaming in the antiseptic darkness. Nicole panicked, but the girl only smiled and whispered "Good luck."

When the way was clear, Nicole tip-toed down the hall

heading for the side door, gently pushing it open. Her heart flew into her mouth as she sucked in the cool night air. Her knees and legs went rigid. But it was now or never and she flew across the volleyball court like a caged bird finally set free.

She climbed the chain-link fence, fingers clutching cold, twisted steel, her bare toes cut and bleeding. But she was doing it.

From a window, an aide spotted her and shouted for someone to stop her. She reached the top, dropped down, over the other side and heard her keys spill out from her panties falling to the ground. She spotted them, scooped them up, opened her car door and tried to start the motor. It was cold, choking and stalling. From the corner of her eye, she saw three aides enter the parking lot and rush towards her. She locked the windows and doors, turned the ignition key once again and pressed down on the gas pedal.

They were there pounding on her windows when the car finally started. She gunned the motor and released the brake. The aides scattered as the Mercedes lunged toward the street and she smiled, feeling free and alive as she never had before.

Chapter 18

THE THOUGHT OF DAVEY'S COCK, the tan, well-muscled body lying next to his, filled Sidney with lurid excitement. He was eager, frenzied, piggishly aroused. He felt his cock throb and grow hard in wild anticipation as he conjured up lascivious images of the two of them together. He quickly reached for a tube of Nupercainal ointment.

Quickly, he uncapped the pain-killing substance and lightly dabbed some on the sides and tip of his small, quivering penis. It would prolong his erection for hours and keep him from coming too quickly. Davey was a dear sweet virgin. It just wouldn't do to take his cherry too quickly. That meant he had to spend time. Time to prepare Davey; to see that he was properly, sensually debauched. The ointment would work to that end.

He lit a joint, dragged deeply then exhaled. Instantly, he felt calm, more mellow. He put the joint down, leaned back on his Louis XV bed and reached beside him for a large, green velvet jewel box that lay on a white marble table. He rubbed the top of the box and smiled. Green. His favorite color. The color of money.

Dear, dear child, he thought as he opened the top drawer of the jewel box and stared down at his tray of sexual accessories. Tonight, dear Davey would have his consciousness raised, as well as his lovely prick.

He fingered the tray of toys and wondered what special thing he would use tonight. Dildo? Cock rings? Butt plug?

Tit clamp? No. None of these specialties tonight. That would really freak the kid out and Sidney didn't want that. He wanted Davey calm and receptive.

From the tray he lifted a long, thin string which had, at one-inch intervals, tiny plastic balls attached to it. Yes, he thought, smiling—this was it. He would use these, along with some artistic rimming, and of course his "amies." These plus his other surprise would do the trick.

Sidney brushed his hair, lightly dabbed his neck and chest with cologne. He looked into the antique mirror and flashed a smile. He was not beautiful, not even remotely good looking, but this evening he would be a King and Davey Sullivan would have a night to remember.

Davey had resigned himself. If he really wanted to get ahead in this business, he would have to do as strangers in Rome had always done; imitate the Romans. All he had to do now was simply relax, grin and bear it. But that was precisely the problem. He just couldn't. He was frightened, shaking all over, as his fantasies grew more disgustingly weird by the minute.

What exactly was Sidney Gross going to do to him? Whip him? Chain him? Maybe give him one of those Golden Showers he'd heard so much about in Newport Beach? Perhaps a scat shit, maybe? Oh, God, no, he thought. Not that, please!

The rich and famous Sidney Gross, a shit freak, fingerpainting feces all over his body. He began to gag, then quickly recovered, reminding himself of that nice, juicy co-starring part Sidney had just arranged for him. He grinned. Fuck it all, he thought.

If Sidney Gross wants to shit on Davey Sullivan's pretty face—so be it.

If he wants to use his sweet asshole for a vacuum cleaner, Davey would learn to shit through his ears.

But in the end, because of his end, he'd be a star.

And that's what really counted.

There was a soft knock at Davey's bedroom door and it startled him. He walked to and opened it very slowly. The young Filipino houseboy, Franco, bowed his head. "Mr. Gross has asked that you join him now, Mr. Sullivan."

Davey swallowed the lump in his throat, tied his red silk

robe more tightly around his naked body and followed Franco down the hall. Silently they rode the ornate slow-moving elevator down three floors. When the doors finally opened Davey stood there frozen, transfixed, unable to speak. His eyes fastened on a scene out of the Arabian Nights. He waited till his eyes grew accustomed to the dark.

It was beautiful. An explosion of color in dim twinkling lights. Large, lush fur rugs were strewn across the finest Persian carpets draping themselves like soft and inviting animals across the floor. Pillows covered everything.

Overhead, the sheerest silk and chiffon canopies hung in grand and colorful profusion, gracefully rippling down from above while tiny lights set deeply into the ceiling twinkled like faraway stars providing the only light source in the room.

In a corner, water lillies floated in a bubbling pond which sat smothered in a cascading forest of lush green leaves and small trees. Burning incense sent off waves of sweet, pungent aromas and exotic harem music throbbed softly in the background.

In the midst of it all Sidney lay wrapped in his green silk robe languishing on a soft pile of pink and plum satin pillows. Wide-eyed, Davey moved toward him. "My God, it's like a fairy tale," he said, then blushed and wished he hadn't used quite those exact words.

Sidney laughed. "Welcome to tonight's fantasy, Davey," he said gesturing with his arms. "Sit down. Enjoy."

Davey sat across the pillows somewhere near Sidney's velvet-slippered feet.

"What's your pleasure?" Sidney asked. "Caviar? Champagne? Paté, brie, or fruit?" He paused and grinned. "A little recreational medicine perhaps?"

From the corner of his eye, Davey noticed Franco undressing. Dope, Davey thought. He definitely needed dope. "What have you got?" he asked, hoping for some first-class downers.

Sidney reached behind and opened the lower drawer of his green velvet jewel box, offering Davey the variety of contents: cocaine, Quaaludes, rainbows, reds and several joints, which were rolled neatly in gold paper. Davey took two ludes, swallowed them quickly with champagne, then lit one of the joints. He sucked in deeply, held his breath, then exhaled. He choked, looked down at the cigarette and passed it back to Sidney. "What the hell is this shit?" he said coughing. "I feel like my ass is on fire."

There was a secret smile on Sidney Gross's face as he smoked, then passed the joint back to Davey.

"Jesus H. Christ," Davey went on. "This stuff is wild; shit man." He stretched, rolled over nonchalantly on his stomach, reached his head toward some food, then felt Sidney's fingers cover his. Their eyes met for an instant and Davey felt butterflies playing hopscotch inside him.

"No," Sidney told him. "You're my guest. The servants will feed you." He clapped his hands twice and Franco approached. He was naked now except for a pair of black satin briefs.

"Got any nuts?" Davey asked him then realized what he had said and burst out laughing. "My God, I didn't mean that. Honest. It's this shit I'm smoking." His fears had practically vanished. Those terrible fantasies, the horrible torture images he'd spent the day conjuring up drifted away, disappearing with the smoke. He was high; he was happy; he was enjoying himself with Sidney Gross—Class A queer—and everything was all right.

Sidney laughed at the joke. "It's okay," he said. "Lie down now. Over here and Franco will feed you." Sidney patted a satin pillow next to him. Davey slid closer, unaware that his robe had slipped open revealing his tan, naked thighs and part of his dark scrotum.

"Peel me a grape," Davey said playing the game, "and feed it to me." He closed his eyes, lay on his back drifting, unaware of Sidney's gaze— experiencing only the taste of peeled purple grapes exploding their sweet juices across his tongue and lips, then sliding down his throat. Hell, he thought, if this is what being queer is all about: *Hello*!

After a while, Sidney clapped his hands again and Franco turned up the harem music. Davey sat up and blinked his eyes in surprise. From behind a sheer pink curtain, a voluptuous, dark-haired beauty appeared. Her body was wrapped in red chiffon scarves, while strands of glittering gold coins and shimmering red rubies were draped provocatively across her ample breasts.

Her dark eyes flashed first at Sidney then at Davey and she began to slowly twist her arms and rhythmically clash the tiny brass cymbals that were fastened to her fingertips. She danced to the beat of the Dabuka drum, bouncing her ample hips, jiggling her large jelly breasts, jerking her round, succulent buttocks under Davey's delighted nose. He sat there hypnotized, finishing his second joint, his eyes fastened to her body like glue while she swayed provocatively to the music. She covered and uncovered her attractive face and dark eyes with the red chiffon, whirling her body around and around till suddenly, she froze and fell breathlessly, as the music ceased, across Davey's thighs.

The sight of her had given him an erection. Now the feel of her moist skin against his burning groin was more than he could handle. He stared down at her, then up at Sidney.

"She's all yours," Sidney said. "Yours for the evening. She'll do anything you ask her to."

Davey blinked his heavy eyelids. So that's what Sidney was into, he thought. Voyeurism. Sidney got his rocks off watching. Davey grinned. If that's what Sidney wanted, then that's what Sidney would get. Davey Sullivan would show Sidney the best fucking time of his life.

He felt the stirrings of a real power trip brewing. He was an actor after all and here was a captive audience. As the lead performer, he would now give Sidney one hell of a show.

"Get up," he told the girl. "And take off my robe, slowly." She did exactly as she was told then Davey reached across and viciously ripped the few scarves from her body. She stood there perfectly still, naked, ripe and round, her large coppery pointed breasts covered only by the thick, long black hair that fell loosely around her shoulders.

His erection was burgeoning hot between his thighs, his buttocks quivering with excitement. He reached down for another quick toke and Sidney grabbed at his leg.

"She likes it up the ass," Sidney whispered to Davey. His voice was trembling as he spoke.

Davey smiled. He wants me to fuck her ass, he thought. Okay. We'll do it. We'll give Sidney what he wants; probably get an Academy Award for the performance.

"On your knees," he commanded and the girl obeyed. She knelt before him and the sight of her exposed anus excited and exhilarated him even further. He fell to his knees close behind her. He pushed her head to the floor and grabbed at her shiny buttocks, kneading them, spreading apart the round, plump cheeks. He reached under, between her soft plump thighs and with his thumb and forefinger slowly massaged her clitoris. She was wet, slippery, moaning and rocking with his every gesture.

He played it all at first, to the wild-eyed Sidney who sat hypnotized, quivering, watching Davey's every move. Then he forgot about Sidney and played it all for himself.

He massaged her cunt, then with her own juices, he lubricated her rectum. He mounted her slowly and began to slip his hard distended cock into the small tight opening. She rotated her ass around and around until Davey was deeply inside her. His own excitement flared and he bent, sinking his teeth into the soft flesh on her back.

From behind, Davey felt the unmistakable senation of a moist tongue suddenly licking the rim of his asshole. The heat it generated inside him could have lit up New York City. He knew it was Sidney but it somehow didn't matter. He was sailing high up into the stratosphere and there was plenty of room for one more.

He reached forward for the girl's large breasts and pulled at her hardened nipples. He wanted to roll her over and suck on them. But, behind him, Sidney was expertly squeezing and kneading his buns, opening and closing the cheeks, licking, sucking and nipping the sensitive flesh around his asshole. Her nipples would have to wait.

He was fully conscious of Sidney's tongue sliding its way around his anus, but then he felt Sidney's fingers suddenly slipping inside him. He quickened at first, then breathed deeply and relaxed his body into the sensations. It was all too fantastic for words. Without even thinking, he sought the pleasure of Sidney's mouth against his ass and perched up on his knees, reaching behind to pull Sidney's head more deeply between his buttocks. Below him, the girl shifted her position and his cock slipped away.

Sidney's head seemed to disappear from behind him and dreamily, Davey pulled on his own penis. Then the girl settled down under him again and someone's expert hands guided him back inside her ass with ease. He sucked in his breath as she jerked more rapidly, violently, opening herself to him. He thrust himself inside her harder and harder, sweating profusely, his breath rapidly ascending. Then suddenly he stiffened, grimaced, gripped the cheeks of her ass and howled as he began a frenzied climax. Someone shoved a cap of amyl nitrite under his nose while someone else pulled something slowly out of his asshole.

For five full minutes Davey Sullivan was out of control, flying off somewhere into space, screaming his lungs out, writhing and ramming his cock into the girl's ass.

When he finished he fell like dead weight on top of her and reached forward to caress her cunt. He jumped when his fingers held a sticky, shriveled penis instead and he pulled quickly out. He turned her over to face him. There, in the dim light he saw Sidney Gross in her place, naked—lying in deep and breathless satisfaction.

"Sorry I had to sort of 'butt' in like that," Sidney said still out of breath. "It's my own version of the shell game. Now you see her, now you don't."

Davey's eyes scanned the dimly lit room. Franco was masturbating, holding onto some crazy string of plastic balls while the girl sat dreaming in a corner, sniffing a cap of amyl nitrite.

Later, they moved upstairs to Sidney's huge bedroom where Sidney took command from his mammoth rosewood bed.

"I feel wonderful," Sidney said, purring like a fat cat.

Davey Sullivan pulled the silk red robe more tightly about him and walked to the bar. He poured himself a stiff drink, finished it in one gulp and started fixing another.

"Are you okay?" Sidney asked.

"Sure. Why shouldn't I be?"

"Just checking," Sidney said stretching, sliding out of bed. He waddled naked across the vast room and opened the door to a Louis XV armoire. "Here," he said tossing Davey a small wrapped package. "For you."

Davey grasped at the small box as it flew toward him. He glanced once at Sidney, then quickly opened it. Sidney watched as Davey's face came alive with excitement. "Oh God. You're kidding," he sang. "Is it for me? Is it all mine?"

Sidney nodded then sauntered lazily back to bed. "All yours baby. Lock, shift and white walls."

Davey Sullivan flipped the 14-karat gold keys to his new Mercedes, provocatively untied his robe, then dressed.

"Where are you going?" Sidney asked.

"For a ride."

* * *

Michael flipped the signal on the Jaguar then turned west off Pacific Coast Highway heading toward the beach parking lot. The air in the car felt oppressive and he rolled down the window to breathe in the ocean. He was glad for the darkness of night and everything it would hide about his apprehension.

He was nervous, tense, teetering on a ragged edge. He was finally feeling the strain of the last few weeks. The confrontation with Jason was inevitable, but he had no notion at all that he would feel this unnerved. More than anything in the world he loved and wanted Nicole, wanted what was best for her and he was prepared to promise Jason anything to convince him to sign her out. He did not know, however, what he was prepared to do if Jason refused.

He parked beneath the Santa Monica Pier and extinguished his headlights. Outside, he leaned against the Jag waiting anxiously in the cool, salty ocean air for Jason's red Ferrari to skid in beside him.

Above him, along the pier, footsteps, as young couples walked arm in arm. Children with laughing bodies hung onto pier railings munching hot dogs. The gaily lit arcade was alive with clanging bells, rifle shots and happy laughter. Hawkers barked the joys of pink cotton candy and popcorn while dark-skinned Gypsies whispered tall, dark and handsome tales.

Across the beach, against the crash of waves, a group

sat huddled about a small campfire. Someone strummed a soft blues guitar.

He was finding it difficult to wait and began a slow walk in the sand alongside the creaking pier columns. He glanced up at the sky. It was pitch-dark and littered with a thousand tiny stars. He zipped up his white windbreaker and walked toward the water.

A gust of wind whipped across his face and a peripheral glance caught Jason's menacing form as he stepped out suddenly from under the pier shadows. It was then Michael realized he'd been there all along scrutinizing him. Beads of sweat lined his forehead as Jason approached. Three feet away from Michael, Jason stopped and launched a swift attack.

"How long have you been screwing her?" he said.

Michael flinched but said nothing.

"How long?" Jason demanded.

Michael turned away. "It isn't like that, Jason."

"It never is." Jason's tone was profane and combative. He lit a cigarette shielding the lighter flame from the hearty sea breeze. His stare lay constant seige to Michael's face as he inhaled, exhaled, then quickly dragged again. "Was that the first time? In San Francisco?" he asked. "Or have you always been sniffing around her?"

Michael felt ashamed. Part of him wanted to slink away and hide—another, to strike out. "You want to act out a dramatic scenario, don't you?" Michael said bending, running a handful of dry, cool sand through his fingers. "You want me to say we've been running around behind your back for years. But you know me better, don't you?" He was silent, then closed his eyes. "It happened in the Carmel Valley, and so help me God, neither of us went looking for it."

Jason laughed derisively. "I'm not so sure about that," he said. "Before she left, I told her to. I just didn't think she'd take me quite so seriously."

Michael stood up, smiled. "I don't believe you."

"Ask her, damnit."

"Sign her out and I will."

"Not so fast," Jason said. "Let's take a walk first and talk a little." Michael watched him go and followed after.

Jason's voice sounded almost playful now, like a large hungry cat playing with a juicy mouse. "It's been a long time since we talked. We're family and I hardly know anything about you."

Michael grasped at his arm and swung him around, saw the mean look on his face and quickly dropped his hand. "Let's not get off the track, Jason. We're here to talk about Nicole, not reminisce.

Jason leaned his shoulder against the damp wooden pilings. "But that's my point, Mike. I want to reminisce. For as long as I can remember, you've been taking things from me. Ever since you were born. My family, my mother's business. Now you want the only thing in the world I have left. That's not exactly brotherly, now is it?"

Particles of wind-blown sand stung Michael's cheeks. "You're a little mixed up about who took things from who, Jason but let's not turn this into *Playhouse 90*, for Christ's sake. No one set out to hurt you. Believe it or not, I'm sick at heart about the whole damn thing."

Jason's voice was cold and bitter. "And I'm sick to death of you and all your piousness. You want my wife, but you can't have her. I'm not going to let you walk right in and take the only thing I love, the only thing I have left."

"Love!" Michael shouted. He heard the sound of his voice echoing across the beach and consciously lowered it. "You really expect me to believe you love her?"

Jason inhaled once, twice, then tossed his glowing cigarette into the wet sand just beyond. It made a wide arc like a shooting star. "I know you won't believe this, but I've always loved her, Mike. From the moment I first saw her, I loved her and wanted to marry her."

Michael hesitated for a moment, then when he finally spoke his voice sounded sharp and impatient. "You're full of shit Jason. You married her to humiliate Ada. You thought if you sucked up to Sidney, he might do something for you. But even Sidney was too smart for that so he fired Nicole instead.

Jason's breath came in short gasps, one agitated hand rubbing across the left side of his jacket. "You're dead wrong, Mike. I love her, all right. I've always loved her.

He paused. "And so help me God . . ." He bit at both his lips, "I love her now." He began to speak more rapidly—to plead. "She's all I have. The only thing I could ever count on in this fuckin' world. If you take her away, I won't have anything. You've got it all, Mike. Don't take her, too." He made no effort to conceal the tears that were glistening in his eyes.

Michael was taken by surprise. Jason Stone had never shed a tear in his life. He began to feel sick. How did this all happen? Why hadn't he stayed where he was, in Cambodia? There at least, he had been doing the world some good.

Someone doused the small beach campfire and the teenagers drifted across the darkened sand, heading for their cars in the parking lot. Michael waited for them to go by. He felt sorry for Jason now, was confused by his own sympathies, then suddenly he remembered poor Hank.

"Some crazy part of me wants to believe what you say Jason," he said, "but I just can't. I'm finding it hard to buy those sentiments from the same man who pushed Hank Mason to the brink of suicide, for whatever reason you had."

"That was an accident," Jason said sounding frightened. "I swear it. I never meant to harm him." A sudden noise from behind, made Jason swing nervously around. A small dog barked at his legs then bounded away.

"But that's always been your problem," Michael told him. "You never mean to cause harm but somehow, somebody always gets hurt. Do you realize you almost killed him with that trick you pulled?" Michael grew solemn. "There was a time when I worshipped you, Jason. A time when I thought you were something really special. Then, that day I caught you rifling through Ada's purse? It made me sick. After you threw me up against that wall, I never felt the same about you again."

"All of that was her fault," Jason said in disgust. "She always tried to humiliate me. Always tried to make me beg for everything. She wouldn't lift a finger to help me, always wanting things her own way. Well, shit on that. I had to help myself, and I did."

"You're wrong about her. She wanted you to start out

right—learn things, from the bottom up. You don't have to tell me how rough she could be, but you have to take some blame for the way things are between you. You were lazy, always hanging around with the wrong kind of people like Meyer Wolfson—"

"You!" Jason interrupted, jabbing Michael's chest with his finger. "You're not fit to talk about Meyer—or pass judgment on him. He's a damn better man than your own father."

"Don't compare Meyer with Max," Michael said dismissing the remark.

"It's not Max I'm talking about," Jason shouted. There was dead silence and a faint smile beginning on Jason's lips. Michael's brow furrowed deeply as Jason's voice softly lulled. "I'm talking about *your* father . . . Julie Stone."

Michael felt sick to his stomach. For a split-second he almost lost his balance, but then he lunged for Jason's throat and pinned him to the damp wood column. "What the hell are you saying?"

The smile on Jason's face lingered through Michael's fury, continuing to taunt him. "I'm telling you that Max is not your father. You, dear brother, are Uncle Julie Stone's little bastard."

Michael's senses were reeling. He could hardly catch his breath. He wanted to punch Jason's face—to see it bleed—to feel Jason's bones disintegrate under his bare knuckles. He refused to accept what Jason had told him as truth. Perhaps Jason was testing, seeing how far he could push. "I won't listen to this shit," Michael said letting him go. "I just won't listen."

Jason smelled blood and moved in for the kill. "Tough news, squirt," he said adjusting his collar, "to find out your old lady's a whore. But don't let it get you down. She had to do it—to get those cushy jobs Uncle Julie kept handing her. How else would she have made it so far in this business?"

A young couple had turned around to watch them.

"And just how do you know all this?" Michael asked.

"I found a letter she wrote to him about you, inside her purse," Jason said.

"I've had enough of this," Michael shouted. "I came here to help Nicole get out of that hospital, not listen to lies. I'm asking you to sign her out, Jason, before she does something to hurt herself."

Jason shrugged. "That's all up to you, Mike; in your hands. You have to promise not to see her again. Promise to leave her alone. Then I'll do it. She's my wife. She belongs to me. I'll never let her go."

Michael had had enough. Like the roaring tide that finishes a long and tiring journey against the rocks, he bellowed. "She doesn't belong to you. She doesn't belong to anyone, dammit. She doesn't even know who the hell she is anymore because of you. I can't promise what you're asking. I love her and if she'll have me I want to marry her."

Jason grabbed onto a pier column to support himself. The look in his eyes was wild, rabid, demented. He turned his back for a moment into the darkness and his whole body shuddered. Then an unintelligible scream emerged from inside him, echoing under the pier. When he turned back around, Michael faced the steel-hard muzzle of a .38. "Don't move," Jason said. "Don't make one move."

The few people who had been attracted by their shouting quickly scattered. Someone screamed out for the police. Michael stepped back, then remembered that other time. "You can't scare me with a gun again," Michael said. "We've been through this before." He moved slowly toward Jason.

Jason stepped backwards. "I mean it, Mike. It's not a trick this time."

"No you don't," Michael said confidently then remembered Viva's last words to him. *Be careful, he's crazy.*

The gun muzzle gleamed in the fractured moonlight and Michael held out his hand. "I want the gun," Michael said again, then made a sudden lunge for it.

They fell to the ground rolling around and around in the sand near the water's edge. Then, with a free hand Jason brought the gun butt firmly down on the side of Michael's head. He lay there dizzy for a moment, stunned, staring up at Jason's menacing form.

"I'll teach you," Jason shouted.

Michael leaped back up at him. The sudden sharp report of two lonely shots pierced the night, reverberating across the darkened beach.

Screaming accompanied the wail of distant sirens. Random flashlights eagerly poured over the sight, illuminating the grotesque faces of two bloody bodies lying close to the encroaching ocean waters.

"Mother of God," a woman cried softly. "They're both dead."

There was an eerie stillness, then the rush and roar of the ocean as it continued on its endless journey. It swelled and carried its sweet gentle waves across the damp sands, cleansing the bodies of the dead, covering the cries of the living.

Chapter 19

SIRENS SCREAMED AS SPEEDING POLICE cars topped by flashing amber bars careened into the parking lot. Behind them, the paramedics. There were the sounds of screeching brakes, doors quickly opening then slamming shut as half-a-dozen uniformed men, silhouetted by glaring headlights, raced to the scene. Some pulled back the crowd, while others sailed under the pier.

When the paramedics found Michael Stone he was slumped against the pier pilings cradling Jason's bloody head in his lap. Someone gently unraveled his fingers as he sat there dazed, his head bobbing about on his neck as though it were not a part of him.

"This one's in shock," a paramedic shouted. "Call the base station for instructions."

Police dispersed the crowd and cordoned off the area with barricades. They notified Homicide and the Coroner's office, then the newspapers.

Paramedics soothed Michael with soft speech, then followed instructions and fortified him with a saline I.V. They lifted him onto a stretcher and carried him past the curious crowd towards the waiting ambulance.

"When can we question him?" an officer asked.

The paramedic looked down at Michael. "Couple hours or so, maybe."

* * *

Nicole quickly opened the door to her home. She was

exhausted, exhilarated, enveloped in feelings she had never before known. Accomplishment, self-worth and independence.

She locked the door behind, stared about into her darkened living room and experienced the pleasure of what she had done. It was good to be home; wonderful to be among the possessions that were so familiar.

As she moved across the room, she reached out, her hands lightly grazing everything she passed. The beautiful crystal she treasured, the warm woods she loved, the sculptured glass, the soft, woven fabrics—even a two-day-old bouquet of flowers felt sweet to her touch. She had done it. She had finally taken her own life into her own hands. She had finally done what she had dreamed of doing all her life. The feeling was incredibly delicious.

She switched on the hall lights and walked up the marble staircase to her bedroom. There was a moment of panic when she reached the top and realized she was alone, but a few deep breaths seemed to calm her and she relaxed again. She would not give in to the fear. She would not set the house ablaze with lights. She would not turn on the television set for comfort. She would call no one for help. Instead, she would experience the aloneness, ride the terror as it mounted and subsided.

She would throw away her torn clothes, take a long hot shower, wash her matted hair, cover her body in a cream satin gown, open the windows wide to life—then go to sleep.

* * *

It was midnight and Shauna was clearly nervous. She sat waiting in her Porsche, drumming her fingers along the dashboard and flipped the radio stations back and forth to soft rock. She had worked the details out in her head; now she needed the courage to pull it off. It wasn't much, but she had to do it to make things right again. There was no doubt in her mind she was somehow unwittingly responsible for Christopher's death and she was determined to get to the bottom of it.

The idea of prison terrified her, even for one day and the thought of facing Hugh Parker, telling him the truth, terrified her even more. Yet if she could do this one, small thing, her heart might just be still again. All she had to do was convince Sally Quinn she meant business and that's what frightened her. Sally Quinn was a ruthless young woman.

Her white Porsche gleamed in the darkness as the headlights to Sally's Cord blinded her, bounded off the white paint and continued their glare into the garage. Shauna left her car and scrambled under the automatic garage door before it closed behind her.

Sally turned, startled, then breathed easier. "You scared the shit out of me," she said locking her car door. "Don't ever do that again."

Shauna's voice was cold. "I've been waiting for you all night," she said. "Where have you been?"

Sally tossed a pink lace jacket over her bare shoulders and gestured with her hips. "I had a hot date," she said with gay abandon, then opened the side door, turned on the lights and entered the large pale-blue kitchen. Shauna followed behind. "I'm really not surprised you're here," Sally said. "I didn't think Elaine Shagan could give you what you really needed."

Shauna ignored her nasty remarks and sat down on a blue leather stool beside the kitchen counter. "I have to talk to you," she said peering across the counter at Sally.

Sally eyed her suspiciously for a moment then picked up the coffee pot and filled it with spring water from a cooler. "You must want something real bad, baby, to wait outside my door all night long like that. Now what could it be? Uppers? Downers? A little lovin' perhaps?"

Shauna's nervousness was replaced by feelings of disgust. "It must have been some hot date," she said with a bite to her voice. "Your clothes are all covered with dirt, or is that shit you're wallowing in these days?"

Sally stopped measuring the coffee grounds and stared defiantly at Shauna. "Well, well. Listen to the little bitch. You've grown big fat claws in my absence, haven't you?" she said then finished the last coffee measure and plugged the pot into the wall. "It's not dirt, baby, not shit or shinola, though you wouldn't know the difference. It's chocolate. And you ought to try some. Might sweeten your newly acquired sour disposition."

"It hasn't done a hell of a lot for you, Sally, so I'll skip it if it's okay with you."

"Suit yourself," Sally said and relaxed on a stool in the kitchen. She stared across the counter at Shauna, her electric blue eyes glowing with hostility. "Well then, let's have it. To what do I owe the honor of this late visit?"

Shauna's nervousness returned. "I want the truth," she said in a low voice.

Sally cocked her ear toward Shauna. "Can't hear you baby, speak up."

"I said I want the truth," Shauna repeated.

Sally crossed one leg over the other and swung her foot back and forth. "About what?"

Shauna blurted it out. "The truth about Chris."

Sally stopped swinging her leg, then tossed back her head, laughing. "You were there, sweetie. You know as well as I do what happened."

Shauna shook her head. "No, I don't think so. I may have been there, but things happened that day that don't make any sense to me."

Sally rose, checked the cofeeemaker and opened a cupboard door. "Coffee?" she asked, glancing at Shauna.

Shauna nodded affirmatively and listened as the china cups and saucers clattered in Sally's hands. "I'm not sure what you're trying to say," Sally said, "but if memory serves we were together in that room the whole time. There isn't one thing you don't know about it, except of course," Sally grinned, "you did pass out for awhile."

"Don't hand me that," Shauna snapped. "I bought that story last week when I *was* whacked out on dope, but it won't work now. My brain's clean. I'm not stoned anymore."

Sally filled their cups with steaming hot coffee and passed one to Shauna. "Now, that's what's wrong with you, baby. That's why you're talking such nonsense."

"Don't *baby* me," Shauna cried, rising to her feet. "Everything that happened that day was weird. You didn't like Chris, you never did. He came between you and me and you were always jealous of him." She pointed a finger. "I should have figured you had something up your sleeve when you started planning his escape to so-called freedom."

Sally sipped her coffee. Her pretty, tan face assumed a sly, smug countenance. "Sit down," she commanded, "and drink some coffee. Your nerves are shot."

Shauna exploded. "I don't want your damn coffee, Sally. I want the truth. Why the hell did you persist with Chris? Why was it so important to wipe fingerprints off doorknobs and bedposts when we left the hotel, unless you had something up your sleeve? Why in hell did we leave him alone when he passed out for God's sake? Tell me damn it, tell me."

Sally was the picture of poise. She reached for her cigarette box, removed a fat joint and lit it. "Let me refresh your memory," she said dragging deeply. "You planned it with me, baby. And, as I recall, we did it so Chris could have some freedom, some fun. He just got carried away, that's all." She passed the joint to Shauna. Shauna's hand swiped across the counter at Sally. "Good shot," Sally said watching the cigarette fly across the kitchen and land in the sink.

"Stop it," Shauna cried. "Stop being so goddamn flip about the whole thing." She blinked her brown eyes shut and fought back the tears. If there was one thing Shauna Candelli would not do, it was cry. "Chris is dead. He's dead. And I know you're not telling me the whole truth."

Sally smiled. "My God, Shauna. You should have been an actress. You're very good, you know. I'm convinced you're serious about all this nonsense."

"I am serious. And by God, I am good." She felt her courage returning, swelling inside her now. "I'm so damn good, I'm going to convince you to come with me to the police and explain things to them."

Sally tilted her head. "Now why on earth would I do something as stupid as that? His case was officially closed. Christopher Parker died of an accidental overdose. Besides, I wasn't anywhere near the scene."

"Then I'll just have to go myself, Sally. I'll have to tell them what I know and let them question you."

"I'll deny I was there, baby. No one's going to believe

the word of a grief-stricken girl who's half whacked out on drugs, against that of a gold medal champion." Her mammoth chest swelled with confidence. "I skated for the U.S. of A., baby. I brought home the gold."

Shauna smiled at that. "You are smart, Sally. But I'm smart too. They may not take my word for it, but I have something they will take. A pretty piece of stationery with Fiesta Motel stamped on top." The smile on Sally's face faded and she began to fidget. "Ah," Shauna continued, "I see you do remember. A little slip of paper with your handwriting. Something about a Sally Quinn program. You accidentally slipped it into my jacket pocket.

The smile on Sally's face was completely gone now and a fearful expression took its place. Shauna sensed she was almost home and began to relax.

Sally's eyes narrowed to slits. "And just what **are** you trying to do to me?" she asked.

Shauna lifted her coffee cup. "Nothing. I'm only giving you a last chance to tell me the truth."

"I honestly don't know what—"

Shauna stood, banged her cup on the counter. "Okay. That's it!" She grabbed her purse and headed for the door. "You leave me no choice but to take the note to the cops."

"I don't believe you. You're just trying to scare me," Sally said. "You wouldn't do that because we'd both rot in jail and you're afraid of that."

Shauna swung around to face her. "Well that's where you're wrong." She was shivering inside, hoping Sally wouldn't see her trembling hands. "I won't have to rot in jail. I'll turn state's evidence or something, in exchange for information. But unlike you, I have nothing to lose. No million dollar career; no jet-set future. When I get through with you, baby, every commercial house in America will dump you so fast you won't know what hit you. This scandal will kill every dream you've ever had." Shauna started for the door again.

Sally's face contorted and her eyes were filled with terror. "Okay, okay, damnit. Stop! I'll tell you." Shauna breathed a sigh of relief and turned slowly around. Sally explained it all to her. Her meeting with Jason and what he had asked of her that night. "Believe me, Shauna," she said with sincerity. "I didn't want to hurt Chris. Jason didn't either. He's a basketcase now, calling me every night, scared out of his head. He said he was doing it for you and I believed him. It was an accident. I was as shocked as you, when Chris died. I swear it." By the time she had finished, her head lay resting on the countertop and there were tears in her eyes. "Honest to God, I wish it had never happened. I wish there was some way I could convince you of that."

Shauna fought back the tears again and took a deep breath. "You can," she said with surprising authority, "and so help me you will." Sally raised up her head. "Tomorrow morning, you'll call your agency," Shauna barked. "Tell them you're leaving. You can invoke the ninety-day clause or whatever it takes." Sally's face crinkled in bewilderment. "I'm joining a new talent agency as an agent and you're signing on with me. You're going to be my first client Sally. Together, we'll earn a lot of money—enough to start a foundation to help young addicts like Chris. There'll be speaking engagements for you around the country, in high schools and youth centers. Television spots to announce. You, Sally *baby*, are going on a crusade for the Chris Parker Foundation, just as soon as you can." She swung her purse across her shoulder, smiled at Sally's amazed expression, then glanced at the joint still lying in the sink. "And get rid of that. It's bad for your new image," she said and slammed the door behind her.

Outside, Shauna wept in the front seat of her car. Chris, she thought. Forgive me. It's not like I've joined the enemy. It's more like the enemy's going to work for us.

Michael dragged his heels along the dark and empty streets of Bristol Circle agonizing, wondering how he would tell his family about Jason. His own well was almost dry and he could not imagine the source from which he would dredge up the strength and courage he now needed.

He thought of Max and Ada, wondering how they would react to the news. And he thought of his Uncle Julie and whether or not what Jason had told him was the truth. Was

Julie Stone his father, or was it all one of Jason's sick jokes?

He leaned against the wrought-iron gates surrounding Casa Piedra and listened to morning birds perched in the pepper trees, chatter around him. Automatic sprinklers whirled a fine spray across the lawn and the sun slipped its first dim rays through the early morning darkness. It was his favorite time—dawn: heralding an end to sad yesterdays, and a chance for new beginnings.

He wanted to lie down in the wet grass, let the mist settle over him and wash away the ugly images still etched in his brain. Jason. *Why*? he thought. The birds soothed him, lulled him with their simple songs. He wished they would carry him off, lift him high into the air, fly him to another corner of the world where he could be alone, where he could rest his head, his tired bones, his weary soul.

Why had it all happened? For what reason? To what end? He thought of Nicole. Sweet Nicole. How would he tell her? What would he say? He shuddered. It had all been a horrible nightmare.

He reached inside a pocket for his pipe, felt the familiarity of the smooth wooden bowl, caressed it, filled it with tobacco and lit it. It was the first sweet taste he'd had in his mouth for the last ten hours and he relished it.

He was filthy, rubbed his palm against his day-old beard, noticed his dirty hands, his filthy clothes. There was blood on his white windbreaker and he touched his fingers to the dull, rusty red stains. It was all he had left of his brother and he swallowed a lump in his throat. No matter what had happened between them in the past, no matter how many times Jason had behaved badly—they had been brothers and Michael felt the loss deeply.

And, he was overwhelmed with guilt. Terrible gnawing guilt. Had he not given vent to his selfish feelings for Nicole, they would never have met at the beach and Jason would still be alive.

He walked quickly, tears brimming in his eyes, vaulted the gate and crunched his shoes along the gravel driveway. When he reached the front steps, Viva was waiting.

"Where have you been? I've been up all night long."

She was frantic and searched his face for answers. Then she noticed the dried bloodstains on his jacket. The color drained from her face. "Dear God, what's happened?"

He took her shoulders, then pressed her head tightly against his chest. "I have terrible news," he said. She struggled to see his face. "No," he said, "don't. Just hold me. Hold me tight. Tell me I'm not going mad." He began to falter.

She helped him over to the steps. "Sit down, darling. Sit down and tell me what you can," she said. Her voice was surprisingly calm, soothing and he was grateful for it.

Tears burned behind his eye sockets as he began. "The cops will be here soon and everything will be up to us." He fought against the deluge, but then the dam finally broke. "Jason's dead," he blurted out. "Hugh Parker killed him, then shot himself."

Viva's hand flew to her mouth. Then, she sat still, no sound coming from her, like a chunk of marble, unwilling to invest her emotions. "No," she finally said. "I don't believe that. I—"

He shook her shoulders. "It's true," he cried. "It's true." His head fell into her lap. "It was awful. The whole thing, awful. We argued. Jason said some terrible things. We were both angry. He pulled a gun." Viva stared out into space. He twisted the hem of her skirt. "Jason threatened to kill me, Viva. He told me to leave Nicole alone. He said he would kill me if I didn't. I went for his gun. I couldn't believe he'd really load it. Then, I heard a shot and Jason just fell into my arms."

He swallowed hard. "A second later, another shot and I saw Hugh fall." Viva's skirt was drenched in sweat and she wiped his face with her hem. She cried softly, rocking him, rocking herself. "It happened so fast," he continued, "I didn't have time to think." He looked up at her. "Viva, the cops will be here soon. They want to know why Hugh did it and for the life of me I can't answer that."

She closed her eyes and the tears slipped down her cheeks as she spoke. "Hugh, darling. It's all right. I'll talk to them. I think I know why." He didn't hear her speak, just felt her, as she helped him up from the ground and moved his body toward the house.

"Wait," he said before they entered. "One more thing. I have to tell Nicole. I don't want the cops to do it. And I need your help. I just can't face her alone."

It was 8:00 A.M. when they telephoned the hospital for permission to see Nicole. It was 8:30 A.M. when they arrived at her doorstep in Holmby Hills.

Chapter 20

THE FUNERAL PROCESSION WOUND its way around the early morning streets like a deadly black snake: Its solemn quietude was disturbed only by the powerful rumble of police motorcycles riding out front and behind to keep the cortege from splintering.

Along the dusty route the curious lined the streets. Some opened blinds and drapes peering out of second-story windows pointing fingers, straining chicken necks to observe the slow-moving caravan.

"Who died Mamma?" a young girl asked.

"Must be someone rich and famous," said the mother.

"Oh," the young girl sighed. She closed her eyes and repeated her mother's words. "Rich and famous."

At the chapel, a frenzied mob surged forward, eager for a glimpse of their favorite movie star. Overhead, a helicopter circled, its occupants reporting the tragic events to a stunned Hollywood community and a spellbound nation.

The news had made the front pages and reporters and foreign paparazzi jockeyed for photographs of Hollywood's most famous while crowds of the morbidly curious shoved each other for position.

The murder/suicide had all the ingredients of a great Hollywood melodrama and no less than three producers sought immediately to buy the television and/or cable rights.

Those attending the funeral, those who had known the two men, buzzed with only one question. Why? Why had it happened? What thing had driven the gentle, erudite Hugh Parker to kill Jason Stone, then turn the gun on himself? There were no easy, no obvious, answers. It was all a puzzle.

Though the police had investigated thoroughly, they refused to speculate on a rumored Mafia connection between the two men. The media, however, wove a fascinating tale around Hugh Parker's dark Chicago past and Jason Stone's Las Vegas connections. It made grand headlines and sold lots of newspapers. Those who had known Hugh Parker, however, dismissed that possibility entirely. Those who had not, considered the words.

At the gravesite Nicole sat near Michael and wept. Jason Stone had been the only family she had ever known. All at once she'd lost a father, a mother, a husband. Like Michael, she felt a profound sense of guilt and shame.

Max braced himself against the back of Ada's chair clutching at her shoulders, whisking a faded handkerchief across his baggy, tear-filled eyes. Ada sat straight as an arrow, tightly gripping the arm rests on her wheelchair. From the corner of his eye, Dr.Morgenstern studied her closely and watched for signs of a relapse.

Viva clung tightly to Michael's arm. Every terrible memory of her dead husband Maurice came flooding back, invading her mind. She openly wept for her dead brother, her friend Hugh, for herself.

Shauna did not attend. She stayed at home huddled in bed knowing it had all happened because of her stupidity. She wished she could find the courage to come forward and put all the rumors to rest. She knew, however, she never would.

Meyer Wolfson stood hunched over in a far off corner. He wore dark sunglasses and his boney fingers were occasionally drawn to the corners of his eyes. He had lost a dear friend. Five years ago Jason had put his house up to make Meyer's bail when no one else would. Had he gone to jail instead, his ulcer might have perforated and killed him.

And everyone held his own secret thoughts. If only Viva had stayed with Hugh that night. If only Michael had not given vent selfishly to his feelings for Nicole. If only Ada had helped Jason when he was a young man. If only Nicole had understood Jason's feelings of desperation. If only they had each known the truth.

And what was the truth? Like beauty it lay in the eye of the beholder, changing as the eye shifted or the human heart fluttered. Like a fistful of dry sand it can never be revealed. When the grains are held tightly, they cannot be examined; exposed to scrutiny they slip quickly through the fingers.

There were prayers and eulogies, tears and recriminations. Then it was all over. As in all great battles they buried their dead. It was time now to tend to the wounded.

In the days and weeks that followed, the Stone family stayed in seclusion. Somehow they managed. Except for a few friends and close business associates, they saw no one. Max spent his days and nights clutching Ada's hands, staring into space. To satisfy his sense of history, he said Kaddish for Jason at the synagogue and lit a memorial candle which burned for three consecutive days and nights.

Nicole, hounded by the media at her Holmby Hills home, sought refuge at Casa Piedra.

Viva spent her time reflecting, contemplating Hugh Parker's last words to her. They had been spoken in anger, in the height of his insanity and depression, but they held an awful and terrifying truth. She had successfully, deliberately avoided all meaningful relationships since the death of her husband, Maurice, and she never had the slightest notion that Hugh Parker had cared.

Because Jason's gun held no bullets, Michael continued to blame himself for everything. Had he not gone to the pier, had he not loved Nicole, Jason would still be alive.

Mourning is a dirty business but in the days and weeks that followed, the healing finally began to set in.

* * *

Sidney Gross sat poolside at a glass table, dressed in his green velour robe. He was reading *Variety* and visibly fuming. It hadn't been sufficient humiliation that his secretary Tony Meredith had left him after all these years, he had also stolen one of Sidney's up-and-coming young starlets in the bargain.

"Look at this," he yelled across at Davey who had just emerged dripping wet from the swimming pool. "That son of a bitch Tony really screwed me. So that's why she left the same time he did." He mouthed a full strip of crisp bacon. "How do you like that," he shouted still chewing. "Give a guy a finger, he takes off your fucking arm."

Davey dried his wet nude body with a green terry towel and moved near Sidney's shoulder. He stooped over and studied the article in the newspaper. "Far fuckin' out," he said laughing. "Shauna, Elaine and Tony opening up a talent agency."

"Don't get any bright ideas, sweetheart," Sidney warned slapping his rump with the pages.

"Don't worry, I won't," Davey told him. "They'll probably wind up killing each other before they ever get started." He reached for his robe.

Sidney glanced behind at Davey's well-muscled thighs his smooth dimpled buttocks then quickly turned and buried his nose back in *Variety*. "Hank Mason's up for another Grammy," he said, "and the great Armando's doing a two-hour Movie-Of-The-Week." Then he began to chuckle

"What's so funny?" Davey asked drying the inside of his ears.

"It says here that Bobbi Sands has left Stone Management Associates and signed with Elaine and Tony's new agency. Serves Ada right." He studied Army Archerd's column for a moment then his eyes drifted across to the opposite page. There was a photograph of Paul Kiley smiling. "Well, well, would you look at this. Ada's found some gorgeous new meat." He held the picture up for Davey's inspection. "Cute, isn't he?"

"I wouldn't know," Davey said wrapping himself tightly in a green robe and sitting down.

Sidney smiled an all-knowing smile. "You will, darling. You will. I have a theory that all men are really gay. Some just take a little longer than others to figure it out."

The butler emerged from inside the living room carrying a green telephone. "It's Syble Kane," he said and connected it into the wall.

Sidney grasped the receiver. "Syble, darling," he sang and lifted his feet up on a chair. "What's doing?"

"Have a heart, Sid," the woman said. "Don't make me write this stuff. It's lousy. It'll never sell."

Sidney stiffened. "What are you, a critic?" he snarled. "Do you know how many writers like you are kicking around this town? It's a buyers' market baby and I bought you." There was total silence, then Sidney spoke again. "Why don't we talk about it at lunch tomorrow, darling, okay?"

"No thanks," the woman snapped. "It's not my habit to dine with royalty."

Sidney caught her sarcastic drift and the remark angered him. "You're making a big mistake biting the hand that feeds you, my dear."

"I've never bitten a hand that feeds me, Sidney, just a hand that bites me."

"Listen, bitch," he said. "I'll give you some good advice about this town just in case you don't know. Here, you live by the golden rule—remember that."

"I don't follow," Syble said.

"It's simple. The man with the gold *always* rules," he said and slammed the phone down on the hook. He looked across at Davey then lifted his coffee cup. "This industry," he snarled, "it's going straight to the dogs. Completely overrun these days with cunts."

"What's the difference," Davey laughed. "It's always been overrun with pricks."

* * *

The horse racing season had drifted south to Del Mar, but Max didn't have the heart to follow it. Instead, he stayed in the gardens of Casa Piedra tossing bird seed at the finches and sparrows. An hibiscus tree bloomed on the patio and in the mornings when the sun's rays brushed against the dark green leaves, he'd sit there and watch the humming-birds flutter their wings, sipping nectar from the brilliant red blooms.

Ada's health steadily improved. Except for her kneecaps which had been bruised on the night of her stroke, she was almost back to normal. Her memory and speech had gradually returned, and she had begun the arduous task of finding a replacement for Elaine Shagan.

Though they had never before been close, Viva tried

desperately to communicate with Shauna. The loss of her brother and Hugh had stunned her, brought back memories of Maurice. But it was to no avail. Shauna had immersed herself in the Christopher Parker Foundation with tremendous zeal, leaving little time for them to try and recapture lost years. Viva found solace instead in the arms of her new young chauffeur.

And they spoke of Michael's plans for the future. He briefly considered returning to his government post, but he couldn't see his way clear to leaving just yet. Maybe he had been kidding himself. Maybe he had made the decision to stay in Hollywood a long time ago.

He felt a sense of accomplishment at having kept Stone Management together. Although he had made no great impact on the agency, he hadn't lost it either. Like Rocky Balboa, he had gone the distance and for him that was more than satisfying.

He'd lost the few pounds he'd gained when he had arrived and his hair had grown long once again. And there were so many things he'd discovored about himself that amazed him. He loved his mother—actually cared about her. The feelings had always been there, submerged, hiding beneath layers of old childish hurts and misunderstandings. It had taken this string of tragedies to bring them to the surface.

And he thought about Jason. He thought also about the things that were said that night under the pier. Then he decided none of it really mattered. Whether or not Julie Stone was his father wasn't important. Max Stone had always been there for him, no matter what. If those things were not the measure of a father, then what was?

He dismissed completely the notion that Nicole had slept with him because Jason had asked her to. He had decided it was simply not within her nature to do so.

Michael and Nicole began taking early morning strolls along the beach. They were acutely tuned to each other, sharing deep unspoken levels of comprehension and understanding. That kind of thing had always been between them. A certain look, a touch, a smile, some expression hidden deep within the eyes. There were times when they could actually read each other's minds.

"Forgive me," he told her one day.

She was taken by surprise. They had chosen not to speak of Jason's death for a while. "We agreed not to talk about it anymore, Michael. Especially about placing blame."

"I know," he said. "I know. But I can't help thinking about it, feeling as if Jason, everything was my fault."

She took his hand and the tone of her voice was soothing. "I know how you feel, Mike, but you're wrong. I've thought about it alot and I *know* Jason did this to himself. He was his own worst enemy. Somehow, some way, he managed to set this all up, then bring it all down around him. You can't imagine all the time he spent plotting things, planning things, all at someone else's expense. Even from his grave, he's the typical victimizer, turning things around in your mind, confusing you, making *you* feel responsible."

This time, she was consoling him and the feelings he felt were warm and wonderful. He kissed her cheek and they continued silently along the beach. A tiny wave tossed a seashell at her feet and she stopped to examine it. "It's pretty isn't it?" she said holding it up to him.

Michael nodded then helped her to her feet. "Do you still think about him?" he said after awhile.

She kicked at the sand and stared ahead of her. "Sometimes," she said. "He was the only family I've ever had. I even miss him a little. I can remember a time when he used to make me laugh. It's funny sometimes, when people close to you suddenly die, you seem to recall all the good things about them and tend to forget all the ways that they had of hurting you."

"I know what you mean," he said. "I keep remembering when we were kids. I used to think he was some kind of hero." They were silent again walking, then an awful feeling came over him. He wondered now if Jason's death had driven some permanent wedge between them; one that might never be removed. . . .

One morning they sat on the crest of a sand dune, watching a lone surfer ride his board out against the waves.

"They're going to make it, aren't they?" Nicole asked.

"Who?"

"Ada and Max."

"Sure," he said, brushing sand from her arm. "She's one tough old bird. And so is he."

"It's funny being here with her now," Nicole said. "She still scares the hell out of me."

"I know exactly what you mean," he laughed. "She rolls those big gray eyes, and you feel like you've been in a war." Nicole smiled. "You just give her some time, babe," he said. "Just give her some time."

He noticed a lone seagull circling overhead and the cries that it made unnerved him. They were sad and plaintive, recalling memories of that time in Paradise Cove long ago. That seagull was still alone and searching for its mate.

"Have you decided what you're going to do?" she asked. "I mean about your job."

He stood and tossed a piece of driftwood across the sand into the waves. "Not really. My leave of absence has been extended a little while longer, courtesy of the U.S. Government. I'll stick around until Ada can really take over again. And," he paused, "there's always the possibility I might just stay for good—resign my post. Become some kind of mogul or something." She smiled.

They were quiet again and Michael wanted desperately to reach out and hold her. He needed to feel her arms around him, her lips close to his. "What about your own plans?" he finally asked.

"When the strike's over, I'll start on my movie," she said. "I'm looking forward to that. It'll help me forget the last few weeks and I need that more than anything."

He understood that. He needed to forget too. "Are you still seeing Dr. Simms?"

She giggled and her dimples dented her cheeks. "No. He threw me out last week. Told me to get lost. He said I didn't need him any longer. He actually slammed the door in my face."

Michael shook his head. "The man is crazy."

"All doctors should be as crazy as he is. He did more for me than anyone in the world. Except for you, Michael."

He gazed lovingly at her. "Except for yourself, you mean."

"Yes," she whispered and crossed her arms around her knees. "Except for myself."

In mid-September Nicole put the Holmby Hills house up for sale. Michael was with her the day she signed the papers and it frightened him.

"I love you, Nicole," he blurted out. "Marry me now, right away."

She touched his cheek. "I love you too, Mike. But I just don't know." She moved toward the window which overlooked the pool. "All my life, I've always done the easy thing. Looked for some easy way out. To run right into your arms now would defeat everything I'm trying to accomplish myself. I do love you and I do want to be with you, but I've got to try living on my own." She turned to face him. "You understand that, don't you?"

"Yes," he said, but his face had already gone ashen and he felt as though the life had been kicked out of him. He deliberately lowered the sound of his voice and tried desperately to follow her train of thought. "What's your next move then?"

"I'll pay off Jason's gambling debts, his bank loans, which are considerable, then just rent an apartment and see what happens."

"You sound as though you've got it all together," he said in a hushed voice, then turned away.

* * *

Duggan pushed Ada's wheelchair down the rose pathway toward her office.

"Goddamnit," she yelled in anger and disgust, "how long do I have to sit in this—this thing." She was getting better, growing more and more cantankerous by the day.

"Don't you be shoutin' at me now," Duggan admonished. "It's the doctor's orders and he knows what's best."

He leaned, then lifted the chair up and over the steps through the open front door and into the outer room. She turned her head, glanced behind at him and smiled. "It's good to be back, Duggan," she said patting his hand. "Thanks for putting up with my nonsense."

"Call me now, when you're wantin' to come back," he told her. "And don't you forget."

She stood up, waited for him to close the door, then slowly walked inside her office.

It was the first time she'd been inside the room since her stroke and she was fairly overwhelmed at the sight. Everything in the room was just as she'd left it.

Conscious now of how dry her medications had made her mouth feel, she walked to the cooler, drank some water then threw the cup in the wastebasket.

God, how she'd missed it all. Missed the excitement, the network battles. Missed the industry dirt, the crazy interplay of things and people; the game of chess and chance wrapped up in one vital package. No matter what she'd been through, no matter what anyone had said, she missed and loved it all.

She heard a key in the front latch and called out. "Is that you, Lois?"

The door closed and a pretty young woman in a white suit and red silk blouse perched her head in and smiled. "Good morning, Mrs. Stone. It's good to see you up and around," she said. She had vibrant green eyes and dark brown hair. "Will you take your calls today?"

Ada thought for a moment. "Yes," she said. "We'll go full tilt." She paused. "For a few hours at least."

Lois entered the room carrying a steno pad and yesterday's phone messages. She spread them out on Ada's desk. "Six inquires on Paul Kiley," she told Ada excitedly. "Three of them for features—the others are television."

Ada felt the saliva trickle back into her dry mouth. The games were about to begin. The money games, the ego games, the games of strategy; everything she'd looked forward to participating in again.

She studied the notes. "Call him and also him," she said to Lois, pointing at the pages. "Make appointments for this week. They can come here for lunch. Tell Cranston to set up the menus for me tonight so I can choose."

The young woman wrote on her steno pad. "What about that Mr. Markley?" she said. "He's a very important filmmaker, I've been told."

Ada smiled up at the woman. "That's precisely why we

won't return his call . . . not just yet, anyway,'' she said. ''It's the beginning of my kind of strategy. Stick around Lois—you've got a lot to learn.''

Lois arched her eyebrows. ''I see,'' she said. ''I see.''

Ada watched her leave the room. She recognized the excitement in the young woman, the eagerness. Those were the same qualities she, herself, had possessed so many years ago when she, too, had first started out. The very same eagerness she had seen develop and grow in Elaine Shagan.

She shook her head and laughed lightly. Welcome, my dear, she thought. Welcome to the fold. Then, with her own eagerness and excitement turned her attention to the ringing telephones.

* * *

By the end of the month Michael's loneliness had driven him to distraction but he did as Nicole had asked. He didn't press her. He didn't phone her every day. He just waited. He thought about her though. And he ate. He slept. He did all the things that normal people are supposed to do. He even prayed.

At night he'd stare into the fireplace, watch the flames leaping up the chimney walls, then wonder why he'd lit one in the first place. And then, one night she just called him. Her voice was so low he could hardly hear her.

''This hasn't been an easy time, Mike,'' she told him. ''For either of us. I've made a decision and I want to talk to you.''

He swallowed hard, couldn't help thinking it was all over between them. ''Shall I come over now?'' he asked.

''No, it can wait,'' she said. ''Sometime tomorrow; late afternoon is good. We can have dinner.''

He started late, telling himself he was trying to avoid the heavy beach traffic then realized he was really trying to avoid the meeting. He drove quickly pushing the Jaguar to sixty, seventy then eighty miles an hour. Maybe he'd get lucky and crash, he thought. Maybe the cops would pick him up in some radar trap and arrest him. Then he wouldn't have to face her decision at all.

He parked on Highway 101 and waited a while. His

mind was in a turmoil: He was experiencing the worst state of apprehension he had ever before known. He brushed back his long, dark hair with his palm, wiped the back of his damp neck with a handkerchief. He brought out his pipe, started to fill it with tobacco then changed his mind. He finally opened the car door.

Inside her apartment he gauged her greeting as somewhat warm. One for my side, he thought and gratefully accepted the glass of sherry she was offering.

"Something smells good in here," he told her.

"Veal scallopine," she answered. "Specialty of the house."

More like my last meal, he thought.

On the balcony they stood side by side sipping sherry watching the blazing ball of orange sun slip down into the ocean. Overhead, the gulls screamed. Then, she touched his shoulder and his heart leaped into his mouth.

"Look," she said softly, tilting her head up towards the vivid purple and red sky. "Lovebirds, two o'clock."

It hadn't struck him at first—he'd been prepared for the worst and he followed her gaze up toward the birds. But then suddenly he realized what she was trying to tell him and he breathed one long sigh of relief. He turned to face her and smiling, offered his glass for a toast. "Yes," he whispered. "Lovebirds, indeed."